Cold Steel or

by

Rick Brindle

Rick Brindle was born in Dorset, England to an Army family. He was educated in Germany, then returned to the UK, working mainly in pubs before joining the RAF Regiment for three years. Afterwards, he trained as a nurse. He is currently working on his next novel.

Also by Rick Brindle:

Cold Steel on the Rocks

We Are Cold Steel

Cold Steel and the Underground Boneyard

It's Not For Everyone

For Linda,
I am made of you

"The keeper looked me up and down, then he grinned.
Come inside, he said, I don't care that you've sinned.
This house shelters sinners, and all of the lost,
A chance to think on what you've done, to reckon the cost."
Sinners Sanctuary – Cold Steel

Prologue

1715

Flames danced as palm thatch collapsed into the burning ruins of the house, swirling the air high above the forest. Sparks and hot ash flew outwards, while the men, filthy from trudging through rain-slicked forest paths, strained to lift the large chest that was lashed between two wooden poles. All of them sailors, their lives ruled by timber, and ended by gunpowder and flames, they kept a wary distance from the fire as they cleared the bare plateau that sat above the trees like a monk's bald spot, watched over by a man with a thick black beard.

'So this is what a Captain's share feels like?' one of the men, gap-toothed, grinned as he walked past.

'It's what any man's share would be like if he didn't waste it on shine and good company.'

The crewman grunted and the men shuffled along an uneven path through the trees. The bearded man looked at the remains of his house, now little more than a ruin of burning spars. His reputation had become too dangerous for him here. This close to the Main too many people knew him, knew his movements. It was time to leave. His home's torched remains would speak of abandonment, and he took care to remove any sign of where he was going. He smiled, then followed his men, knowing they'd soon be tiring and demanding a share of the rum goatskins he carried instead of pistols. It was the only time he'd been seen ashore without them, although he still wore a cutlass and hand-knife with easy familiarity. The only man he truly trusted was back aboard *Salome*.

Barely into the tree line, the men had already sat down. They massaged aches in their muscles, real and imagined, and stared at their Captain as he approached.

'Are you dockside whores tired already?' he growled. 'Maybe I need to throw you overboard and get some real men.'

'We're the ones doing the hot work, Captain,' replied one of the seamen, his stubbled jowl plastered with mud and sweat.

3

'Hot work,' sneered the captain. He unslung a goatskin and flung it at the man's feet. 'And who dug up that chest in the first place? Who lit the flames to my own home? And who's going to lead every last one of you whoreson bastards to fame and riches?' His long coat swung around him as he turned and kicked a large stone. 'Hot work,' he muttered. 'You poxers stand with me on the burning deck of a Spaniard's ship, and I'll show you what hot work is.'

He turned once more to see the men gulping the rum and passing around the rapidly emptying goatskin. One of them belched and looked up with a sullen, enquiring stare.

The Captain's hands blurred, there was a rush of air and a sharp *chunk* as his hand-knife thudded into the tree trunk an inch above the crewman's head. They all looked at the knife, then heard a rasp, a grunt, and a solid thump as a cutlass buried itself into another tree-trunk, equally close to a second crewman. The living wood shuddered to the blow; trees rustled overhead and birds shot into the sky.

'On your feet. Now, you idle bastards.' The Captain yanked free his cutlass and faced them. 'Maybe you've forgotten who I am. Maybe I need to kill one of you so's you remember me.'

One of the men moved towards the knife blade buried in the tree-trunk. 'Stand fast, Drummond,' the Captain growled. 'Step clear of that knife or I swear I'll have your insides feeding the birds.' He stepped towards Drummond, cutlass pointing at his chest. Drummond backed away, glaring at the Captain.

'Are you impugning my authority, man?' The Captain spoke quietly, but the other men cowered away, leaving Drummond isolated. Finally he lowered his gaze, while the Captain trembled and fought to control his voice. 'Don't any of you buggers forget who I am; don't *any* of you forget who's in charge. Now pick up that chest and step lively.'

Slowly, the men shouldered the wooden poles. The chest swung between them and they shambled along the narrow path. Above them, the birds sang a constant cacophony, while they kept a wary eye on their feet for tree roots that might trip them, or worse, snakes. A bite would condemn them to hours of torment before an abandoned death on the island. Inside the forest, the heat built like a dockside baker's oven, and the Captain sweated inside his coat.

He finally pulled it off, but there was no wind, and his shirt, once white, now clung to him, transmitting its dirt and sea salt onto his skin.

The men toiled in silence, none of them daring to ask for rum. Thin leather sandals rubbed blisters on their feet, and the wooden poles dug into their shoulders, despite headscarves rolled up and being placed between raw wood and skin.

No one knew how long they had trudged through the forest. Only the Captain had a watch, and that was aboard ship. The sun still pierced the leaf canopy in places and the heat still beat down on them as one tormented footstep followed another. The men grunted and moaned, while the Captain muttered murderously to himself and glared at the green infinity all around him, with its strange sounds and unfamiliar hostility. At least they were going downhill; at least they were getting nearer to *Salome* with each snagged step.

Approaching as slowly as a ship on a calm sea, a faint light appeared at the end of the path. The men felt a freshening wind, smelt the salt air, and knew they were close to the beach. A few smiles and laughs now punctuated their misery, and even the Captain looked less likely to commit murder. Then, as though in a dream, another crewman walked towards them, far off but getting nearer, waving an arm over his head.

'The end's in sight, boys,' gruffed the Captain. 'What better welcome than Mister Hands? Still tired, Drummond?'

'Yes, Sir, and you would be too if you'd done what we had.'

'Damn you for an insolent bastard, Drummond. You can take tonight's watch and reflect on your fatigue while your shipmates sleep below. And as you'll need to be alert, you can give up your share of the rum as well. You wish to complain some more?'

Drummond shook his head and looked away as the first mate greeted them. 'You made good time, Captain.'

'It's a wonder we got back at all, Mister Hands, with these mermaids trying to be seamen. They'd rather drink rum than do honest work. Here.' He gave Hands the goatskin. 'They've done just enough to get some grog and be the last boatload aboard, but they've had an easy morning of it and I want them worked hard as soon as we set sail. Especially Drummond.'

5

Israel Hands' blond hair had been bleached by a lifetime of sea and wind, and white strands escaped his headscarf as he nodded and carried out his Captain's orders. Clear blue eyes set in a tanned, lined face glared at the shore party.

'Drummond, Axtell, Pope, Parkes. Get some shade, get some grog. The boat will come for you last and make the most of it; you're the deck party when we get aboard. And Drummond, you stupid bastard, if you ever defy the Captain again, he won't need to kill you, I'll do it myself. Now hand that chest over to some real men.'

*

Standing on *Salome*'s holystoned deck, Captain Edward Teach looked ashore. Two weeks of cloud and no fix on either sun or stars had left them blind anchored off a deserted, uncharted island. He traversed his telescope and saw no movement, no signs of settlement. It was the fifth island he'd looked at after he'd burned and abandoned his home, but he knew even he couldn't hold the men forever. Israel Hands stood at his side.

'This one will do.'

'You said that about the last four, Mister Hands.'

'And I meant it. If you mean to leave that damn chest on an island in these waters then any one of them is as good as the next. The men can't navigate, these islands have no name, and God knows they all look the same. Your crew don't want to see you bury your riches, they want some of their own.'

'Oh, they'll get them, Mister Hands, I promise you.'

'How, then?'

'We sail north, to New Providence. Plenty of enterprising gentlemen based there, all with the sole purpose of disabusing the Spaniards of their desire for gold. Easily enough room for another crew, I feel.'

'Aye,' nodded Hands. 'The men will have that.'

'Then we have an accord. And while I'm ashore I'll thank you to sail around the island and make a chart as accurate as any you've ever made. If my plans in the north swing to starboard, I'll need to come back here, and I rely on you to give me the means to do it.'

*

6

For another week, *Salome*'s crew baked beneath the dry season sun and sailed around the island. Shore parties rowed back and forth, filling water barrels, collecting fruit and smoking meat from any animals they could catch. Aboard ship, Israel Hands stared hard at the island, looked through his telescope and drew pictures from each changing angle. Like finely distilled rum, the chart strengthened and matured under his skilled eye, although he knew the map itself would prove worthless without the internal details his Captain was committing to memory ashore, along with readings from the Davis Quadrant to tell him where the island was. And that information, Hands knew, would be written down just the once.

*

Ashore, the forest soaked up the gentle sea breezes, and the men sweated and cursed, carrying the chest to a spot picked by Teach, before digging out the cave's floor. Rum flowed more freely this time, and the work took longer than Teach would have liked. He felt the outlaw's natural aversion to staying anywhere for too long, but the rum and the time seemed a good bargain for the men's silence.

The regular crunch of picks and shovels through the loose earth lulled him, and he watched the men. Soon, only their heads were visible above the rim of the hole, while dirt flew in all directions the deeper the men dug. He placed torches in the small campfire, then thrust them into damp cracks in the cave's wall.

'Deep enough, lads. Well done.'

He held out a hand and pulled the first man out, then walked away, leaving Drummond to turn and help his mates out of the hole. Thick ropes snaked around the chest and Teach joined in. Together, they lowered it into the pit. He then reached amongst the stores for the stone bottles of rum. He passed a bottle to each man and they drank easily.

'Your health, Captain,' they roared.

'And yours, lads,' he replied. 'You're my best men, and you know I wouldn't trust anyone else with knowing where my treasure's buried.'

'Your best men also do the most work,' grumbled Drummond, as he rubbed his blistered hands.

'Aye,' said Teach. 'But riches come from hard work, and that chest proves it. Maybe one day you'll be burying one of your own.'

'Or maybe digging that one up for myself, hey?'

'Have a care, Mister Drummond, the rum will do the talking for you only this once.'

'Your pardon, Captain. A jest, no more.'

Teach filled the men with another bottle apiece, but drank little himself. 'Rest easy tonight, lads,' he smiled at them. 'You've earned it. I'll take the first watch, and come the morning, we'll fill that hole in together.'

Strong drink and exertion quickly brought slumber to the men, and within an hour all four were laying around the campfire and snoring rum fumes. Teach sat calmly on a fallen tree trunk and slowly unloaded, then re-loaded his pistols. This time he'd come ashore with his usual triple-brace, six pistols hanging like grapes from leather holsters. The island's dry heat had preserved the powder and it poured easily into the barrels and priming pans. He caressed the handles and lay them down next to him. Queen Anne pistols. He smiled, knowing he couldn't have picked a better name for them himself. How he had served her, suffered for her, in a place half a world away from her, and she didn't even know he existed.

'Such is the price of service, my lady,' he muttered, then picked up a pistol in each hand and pointed them at his sleeping men.

*

Abraham Giddens drifted awake as the dawn sun climbed over the island treescape. He blinked last night's rum from his mind and slowly sat up, fidgeting. The sun-warmed sand worked through his clothes, and he stood and brushed himself down, then put more wood on the campfire and looked to the smoking racks. The shore party had done well, filling the longboat with bananas and pineapples, and barrels of fresh water; they had even shot five squirrel-like animals that were now skinned, filleted and smoking over low fires. At first, he'd felt as though he was doing the menial work, wishing instead that he'd been one of the chosen men, selected to help the Captain bury his treasure chest. All of the crew agreed it must have contained immense wealth if he'd decided to take it to this unknown wilderness. But then old Billy Thackary,

8

veteran crewman with a dozen other pirates, warned Giddens that burial parties only ever returned with one man, no matter what assurances were given.

Giddens hadn't believed the old, one-eyed pirate. To be sure, the Captain was strange, sometimes putting brimstone over a stove in his cabin when he consulted his officers. And his discipline, while harsh, was no worse than most other privateer Captains, or so the older crewmembers said. Giddens expected the Captain and his four crewmen to emerge from the island's inner forest, all alive with tales of a hidden interior unseen by any man until now.

But just one man emerged from the dense vegetation that grew right up to the beach like a thick, natural wall. One man, with a long coat, a wickedly sharp cutlass, six pistols that hung with easy familiarity from worn leather holsters, and a thick black beard that circled a fierce face.

'Captain,' stammered Giddens. 'Where are the others?'

'They're gone, lad.' Teach stared past Giddens and looked out to sea. 'They're gone.'

'But – but how?'

'A snake longer than a man did for Pope. Axtell slept too far from the fire one night and by morning ants the size of your finger had crawled all over him and he was half-eaten. The rest of us never heard a thing. Parkes slipped on a stone as we crossed a stream, was knocked senseless and drowned before we could get to him. And Drummond...'

'Captain, what about Drummond?'

Teach pulled out a pistol and looked at Giddens for the first time. A cold smile curled his lips. 'Drummond? Drummond forgot who I was, lad. So I reminded him.'

9

Chapter 1

Sullen disappointment settled over the audience like a wet blanket as Cold Steel lumbered onto Tokyo's Budokan stage. Once dubbed the last metal band standing, media stories about their decline fixed onto them like herpes, then followed them on their world tour like bird flu. Drink, drugs and egos had exploded around them like a surface-to-air missile near an airliner, and the damage seemed equally terminal.

Maxwell Diabolo, the band's singer, had seen the news reports. He'd read them online and heard his manager's constant complaints. *It's no problem,* he thought, *the album's selling well, we're just having a few low gigs, that's all.* The hangover from the previous night's party was only partly held back by the half-bottle of tequila he'd just had, and he strode onstage, his large nose hooked over a crooked-teeth smile in the face of the crowd's roar. He looked at guitarist, Vince Fire. Was he staggering? The slug of sake he'd downed right before the gig might not have been the first, and now that he thought about it, Vince had been drinking a lot lately. He had no time to think about it anymore as Mike Vesuvius smashed out the drum intro to Sinners Sanctuary. Maxwell almost missed his cue, raised a fist to the roaring crowd, then grabbed the microphone and screamed out the first verse.

*

The band's manager, Andreas P, had also heard the stories. In fact, he was so concerned he was actually staying to watch them play. Normally, he'd see the band safely to the venue and consider his responsibilities done. Normally, before the support act had even finished their slot, he'd be back at the hotel, either cooking up some horse and spiking a vein, or getting it on with groupies anxious to do anything, even anything with overweight, odorous Andreas, as long as it meant seeing the band on a personal basis. Lately though, he'd been doing more and more smack.

He squeezed his wobbling gut through the small gateway that set the mixing desk apart from the ocean of fans, and realised he wasn't built for sex anymore. It wasn't just his pendulous abdomen. His legs wobbled, his chin, his arms, even the back of his head quivered like whole-body bingo-wings. So even when the bright-eyed nymphettes offered to go on top, he could rarely be bothered, unless of course they brought some skag with them, which always made his eyes widen like a camera lens on maximum exposure.

Not that he needed to use other people's gear. Ever since Spacey appeared at the album release party, Andreas had on-tap access to more opiates than a trauma ward in an inner-city hospital. But he loved to experiment, and what better way to test some new oblivion-trip than with a sometimes good-looking girl who offered to share her wrap of whatever, along with twenty minutes of anything goes in exchange for a backstage meet with the band?

The band. The band. Focus on the band, he reminded himself. That was the reason he'd turned his back on a Jacuzzi, five lines of weirdly-named Yokohama flameball, and two former models who, it seemed, were prepared to do anything to feature in the band's next music video. The band. The god damned motherfucking band, who weren't sticking to the script.

Whatever magic ingredient it was that transformed merely good bands into stratospheric legendary ones, Cold Steel had it. Or, Andreas reflected, they used to have it, nearly had it, could so easily have had it. Having sold enough albums and made enough money to be able to each buy their own small island nation, their collective hunger had dried up and flaked away. Their self-induced and widely predicted implosion seemed more likely with every passing concert, each one tracking a decline like an unravelling scarf caught in a wind tunnel.

Onstage, Vince was pissed again, and as he staggered around the mike stands, Andreas nudged the sound engineer, who turned down the feed from his guitar, so the audience could only see his parody of himself, and not hear his failed notes. Andreas didn't need the huge screens either side of the stage to see the anger of the other guitarist, Andy Stains, who covered for Vince, while at the same time trying to keep his own performance level.

Vince stumbled across the stage, bounced against Maxwell, then recoiled and nearly fell over. He looked at the stage floor and his head jerked forward. Then his mouth opened and a stream of green and brown vomit exploded over guitar, clothes and the stage, while diced food matter stuck to guitar strings and fingers.

11

Maxwell glanced to his left, saw what was going on and gamely carried on singing. He stepped in front of Vince, hoping to shield him from view, but the combination of singing, posing with the mike stand and looking in disbelief at his drunk guitarist was too much, and he slipped on the spreading pool of vomit. His feet flew out from underneath him, and for a second he seemed suspended in midair before crashing down and performing a barebacked splashdown into a caustic mixture of sushi, sake and gastric acid.

The music instantly changed as Maxwell's voice disappeared from the equation. Andy looked at Mike, who nodded and launched into his solo, while Andy and the bass player Joe Dimitri ran to help Maxwell. The singer's face was crumpled in agony, and he held his left arm to his body and rolled around near the monitor speakers at stage front. The rancid puke was now ingrained into his trousers, smeared all over his bare torso, and matting his long black hair, although he didn't seem to notice as he writhed in pain.

'No,' said Andreas, but no one heard him over the concert's noise. 'Not towards the switches.'

It was as though Maxwell had heard Andreas and was mocking him. He rolled over a foot pedal controlling the pyrotechnics, and seconds later a wall of flame erupted all along the stage, obscuring the band from view, and when it cleared Andreas saw Joe and Andy on their knees, while between them Maxwell lay with his head resembling a huge candle. Joe and Andy swatted Maxwell's rapidly disappearing hair in a vain attempt to put out the flames, and seconds later a skinny roadie stormed onto the stage with a fire extinguisher and sent choking white clouds over the whole area.

'Oh, God, no,' moaned Andreas. He nudged the sound engineer next to him. 'Kill it,' he shouted. 'Kill it.'

The engineer, unable to hear, looked at Andreas with no understanding. Andreas ran a finger across his throat and the engineer understood. The drums' sounds were doused and Andreas picked up a microphone.

'Ladies and gentlemen.' Andreas hated the sound of his voice through the speakers, hated any public experience. 'We've had a few technical problems tonight. Sorry to say we've got to end the show early. Cold Steel thank you for coming to see them this evening, and we hope to see you again soon.'

He felt anger build like a summer thunderbolt as his words were translated into Japanese. Boos erupted all around him, but the crowd's anger was directed at the stage. Andreas had seen it before. People in the front row pelted the now empty stage with half-used drinks, empty bottles and food waste, and Andreas knew enough to sit tight until the place was empty. With any luck, by the time he got backstage someone else would have sorted out Maxwell's injuries and got the rest of the band back to the hotel. Goddamn, he needed a hit, fast.

*

Maxwell's left arm was numb from the elbow down, but that was nothing to being blinded and half choked to death by the fire extinguisher, then getting friction burns on his back as a roadie dragged him offstage by his feet. His head banged on every step and he was pulled down a set of stairs to the dressing room, while the drum solo drowned out any sounds of protest he may have made.

Suddenly the drums stopped, and Maxwell knew the plug had been pulled. 'For fuck's sake, Dixie,' he shouted at the roadie, his staged Devon accent now gone. 'I can walk, just get the doc.'

Dixie let go of Maxwell's feet and they thudded to the linoleum floor. He bobbed his head, face half obscured by a straggly mass of unwashed brown hair, then scampered off to search for the strangely effeminate, permanently stoned tour doctor, who Maxwell doubted had any medical training at all. He stood up, his left hand numb and his elbow now twice its normal size. What had gone wrong with the band? They had been so close to having it all, and now they were just caught in a shit-storm that got worse by the day. He ran his right hand over his head and dried stalks of charred hair came away, along with chunks of cooked vomit. He needed to find someone normal and get help. He staggered out of the band area and up to one of the marshals.

'Hey, hey,' he shouted. 'You speak English?'

The young man looked dumbly at Maxwell.

'Help,' he said, pointing to his elbow. 'Arm knackered. Doctor, now!'

The marshal looked at Maxwell and gaped at his injured arm. He nodded and ran off. Maxwell stood alone in the dimly lit area, with deserted tour trucks and buses around him. He heard the

13

crowd, and their boos and whistles slammed into him like a hammer. He looked around again, and the marshal had returned with two ambulance-men wheeling a stretcher. One of them smiled at Maxwell.

'You taking me to hospital?' he asked.

Without a word, they pulled out an elasticated sling and secured Maxwell's left arm to his body, then flung him onto the stretcher and strapped him in, before turning around and clattering out of the arena.

*

With half of the audience now outside, Andreas decided it was safe to leave the mixing desk and go backstage. Flashing his pass at the ground staff, he squeezed along narrow corridors to the band's dressing room where he found Dixie bundling up clothes and damp towels, and throwing empty booze bottles into a nearby bin. 'Dixie,' he said. 'Where the hell are the band?'

'Well, I put most of them on the bus, they're probably back at the hotel by now.'

'Most of them? What do you mean, most of them? Were they broken into little bits and pieces and you left their legs behind?'

Dixie guffawed. 'No, man. Maxwell's disappeared.'

'What? Oh, Christ, this night's getting worse and worse. Well, when did you last see him?'

'I got him off the stage after we put the fire out. He asked me to get the doc.'

'The doc?'

'Yeah, man. You know, the tour doctor.'

'Dixie, we haven't got a tour doctor. The band plays in modern cities with hospitals.' Andreas split the last word into three syllables to emphasise the point. 'If anyone gets ill, we take them to a local hospital. And just who the hell have we got playing at being a doctor?'

'Calls himself Florence.'

'Himself? Florence? Oh, fucking hell, it's that mad fuck transgender nurse who latched onto us in Thailand. He's not on the team, Dixie, so the next time you see him, her, whatever, make sure he gets the point. So what about Maxwell?'

'He was holding his arm when I got him offstage. Looked pretty painful. Well anyway, I came back with Florence, and Maxwell was gone.'

'Gone?'

'What can I say, Andreas? He wasn't there.'

'Well, where the fuck is he?'

'Maybe he went to a hos, pit, al.'

Chapter 2

1866

His horse limping on a loose shoe, Tobias Finter rode through
Bath, North Carolina. The sun sank beneath the trees surrounding a
small collection of houses. Scars from the war still ravaged the
small settlement. Fire-blackened ruins sent a silent accusation to
the world, and their inhabitants stared suspiciously at Finter. He
could see both ends of Bath from his saddle, and he quickly
reached the seaward end, then settled beneath two pine trees and
set up his camp for the night, conveniently close to a burned-out
ruin. He looked at the dead house, a corpsed building that once
might have sheltered a whole family, but now clearly belonged to
no one. *Which means I'm not robbing anyone,* he thought as he lit
a small fire, boiled his coffee and munched on a strip of peppered
jerky. He then rolled himself into his thin blanket, edged close to
the fire and slept.

Early the next morning, the incoming tide woke Finter, the
waves thrown ashore with a rolling crash. In the grey light he
slipped free of his blanket, packed his saddlebags and left his horse
hobbled in the trees while he searched the wrecked house. Since
the war's end he'd made a decent, if unsteady living rifling
abandoned houses for anything he could sell on. Some things he
kept, but most he sold. His small house on the edge of Charlotte
was more like a curiosity shop than a family home, or so his wife
kept telling him whenever he returned from his foraging trips.

Finter had learned during the war, as well as afterwards, where
to look for hidden keepsakes. He crept through the ruined house,
imagining it built, and then worked out where the fireplace would
have been. Amazing that no matter how big or small the houses
were, some things occupied the same relative positions. Brushing
aside fallen leaves, pine needles and a small layer of earth, he
found the hearthstone almost exactly where he thought it would be.
No new ashes here, he thought, *no one's lived here since way
before the war.*

He smiled to himself, anticipating an unclaimed find. He scraped the soil away from the stone and heaved it upwards. Ants and cockroaches scurried away from their onetime home, and he heaved the stone to one side. Underneath, in a hollowed-out space, sat a small wooden box, timeworn but still intact, half a foot square. Finter pulled it free from the ground, and with a suck of air it slid out. No lock, just a catch. He forced open the corroded latch and pulled up the lid. In the growing light he pulled out a sheaf of papers, the old script barely readable. He leafed through the roughly cut notes, and nearly left them where they were until he came across a diagram. Finter looked more closely at it and his eyes widened, suddenly remembering the stories of pirates who had been killed near Ocracoke Island, close to the fort he'd once served inside. He was looking at a map. A map with no bearing, no name. He turned it over, and squinted at the barely readable script on the other side. Then, looking around to make sure he was still alone, he stuffed the papers into his pocket and quickly moved back to his horse.

*

Andreas ran a hand through his spiked yellow hair and knew he had no choice. He had to ring the record company. They had to know, but he dreaded telling them. Picking up his phone, he flicked through the numbers and dialled.

'Randall Spitz.' The gravelly New York accent terrified Andreas, who felt as though he were talking to a gangland executioner.

'Randall, hey, it's Andreas P.'

'I can read the incoming, asshole. What the hell do you want? It's five a.m. for Christ's sake.'

'Yeah, sorry about that, Randall. I didn't realise the time difference, but we've had a few issues here in Japan.'

'Issues that can't wait until later in the day? Issues that can't be dealt with by our Japan office? Issues that can't be dealt with by *you?*'

'Well, yes and no.' Andreas started sweating. 'The band had an accident onstage, Maxwell's been hurt.'

'What do you mean, hurt?' Randall chuckled. 'Some groupie's father punch him out?'

'He fell over onstage.'

'Is that it? You're making me listen to the goddam dawn chorus tweetie birds in LA to tell me that?'

'He broke his elbow.'

'Can he still sing?'

'I guess so.'

'You guess so? You're the goddam manager, you'd better be telling me you know so.'

'Yes, yes, he can sing.'

'So okay,' said Randall. 'He wears a plaster cast and carries on singing. What's the goddam drama?'

'He can't fly for two weeks. Something about the anaesthetic he had at the hospital while they set his arm, and cabin pressure affecting the surgery site. I didn't understand all of it, but the hospital has already been onto the border department, and we're grounded.'

'Jesus Christ, Cold Steel are set to open in Europe in a week. The flights are all booked to get you assholes over there. And the venues, oh God, the venues. The promoters will want blood for this. That mofo is gonna cost this company a goddam fortune.'

'What do you suggest?'

'What do *I* suggest? What the hell do *you* suggest, dickhead?'

Andreas forced his sludged mind into action. 'I'll try and reschedule the dates.'

'Reschedule? With a week to go? Bullshit, my friend. Maybe cancel and reschedule for next year. You know how far in advance these things get arranged. What's your grid for week one?'

'Spain and Portugal, six dates.'

'Right, well, they'll have to be shitcanned. I'll talk with insurance to cover the venue fees. What's their newest album called?'

'Beer Doctor.'

'Yeah, that's right. Goddamn stupid name for an album. I hear sales are holding up well, so you tell your boys they'll take the hit for ticket refunds. Maybe that'll focus their minds the next time they want to jerk around onstage.'

'It was an accident, Randall.'

'Don't Randall me, you bastard. I don't believe in accidents. Right, week one is scrubbed. Week two?'

'Two more dates in Spain, then two days clear to get to the UK.'

'Okay,' said Randall. 'Here's what's going to happen. Forget Spain and Portugal. Cold Steel will play there at the start of their next tour without fail, same venues. All bought tickets remain valid, and you jerkoffs will spit the dough for anyone who wants a refund. I want the whole shooting match in England for the first show there, and I want you all leaving together. I don't need Cold Steel shit-showers in two goddamn places at the same time. So I hope you like eating seaweed or whatever the hell else they eat in Japan, because you're there for a little while longer. Anything else I need to know, now that you've woken me up and pissed me off?'

'There might be a bit of bad press about last night.'

'No shit. The singer breaks his arm onstage, it can't get worse than that, can it?' There was a pause on the line. 'Talk to me, Andreas.'

Andreas opened and closed his mouth, then forced himself to speak. 'Vince threw up onstage, Maxwell slipped on the puke, broke his arm, touched off the pyros and set his hair on fire, so we ended the show early.'

'How early?'

'An hour.'

'Freaking hell, you bastards. This tour started on a low and it's just getting worse. Listen up, a-hole, here is the news. You sons of bitches are now reading empty and you're running on fumes. Your album sales are the only thing stopping me pulling the plug on you right now. Get your goddam acts together as of ten minutes ago, because if you screw-ups cause me another early morning call, we'll take direct control, and you know what that means.'

'Hey, Randall, don't worry. I'm on it.'

'You'd better be, motherfucker. 'Cos if you're not and we have to have another conversation like this one, your ass'll be feeding the goddam sharks in the bay. You get me?'

*

The next day, Andreas' runny nose and aching limbs told him his withdrawal had arrived. Without even thinking he reached for his phone and speed-dialled Spacey.

'Andreas,' Spacey crooned as he picked up. 'That was some wild shit at the show, man. How was the flameball?'

19

'I wish I knew, Spacey. By the time I got back to the hotel, the girls had gone, *with* my stash, the bitches. And now I'm starting to rattle.'

'Well, it's a good job you've got your uncle Spacey to keep you supplied. Sit tight, my friend, I'm there in ten.'

*

As good as his word, Spacey knocked on Andreas' hotel door and breezed into the suite with a crammed man-bag under one arm. His dyed-bronze Afro, one foot thick, squeezed through the doorway and he smiled, his teeth like strip-lights. Andreas grabbed for the bag.

'Hey, not so fast. We need to talk.'

'Talk about what? Give me the stuff, Spacey; I've had a shit twenty-four hours. We'll talk afterwards.'

'We talk now.'

Andreas collapsed onto the sofa. 'What, then, Spacey? What, what, what?'

'Last night was a disaster, man. The word is the band's thrown a rod and there ain't no mechanic in sight. It all makes me wonder how you'll be able to pay for my services.'

'What do you mean?' spluttered Andreas. 'I'm on top of my bills. You want more? You want me to prove it?'

Spacey chuckled and shook his head. 'Look, man, the kings are off their thrones. Cold Steel are looking like yesterday's men, and that'll give us all less toys to play with. You've developed quite a habit, how will you pay for it if the band goes down the tubes?'

'Shit, Spacey, you're right. I hadn't thought of it before. Christ. And Randall warned me too. One more fuck-up like last night and the band are history. Oh, shit.'

'Don't worry,' smiled Spacey. 'It's sorted.'

*

Exactly two weeks after Maxwell's left elbow shattered on the Budokan's stage, the band loitered in the VIP lounge at Tokyo's Narita airport. Andreas had managed a total news blackout on the band after the accident. 'Melted metal' headlines, pictures and phone movies of the Budokan fiasco had gone viral, and after cancelling the Spanish and Portuguese shows he decided that no more publicity meant no more bad publicity. The forced rest had been good for everyone. Maxwell's injury had time to heal, although he wasn't there yet, and the rest of the band had grabbed at the unexpected break. The tour up until that point had been punishingly intense, and maybe, Andreas reflected, he could have put his foot down with the schedule and spread the dates out a bit more than they had been. He looked at the band. Maxwell, his burned hair replaced with expensive extensions, still nursing his left arm, but grinning like one of the pirates he spent all his spare time reading about. Vince Fire, still contrite, and rearranging his hand luggage for the hundredth time. Andy Stains, always angry, and glaring slow death at Vince. Joe Dimitri, permanently reeking of cannabis; and Mike Vesuvius, quite possibly taking steroids, but now content to dismember the metal wrist exercisers he always carried around with him.

Andreas dragged himself out of the deep sofa. 'We'll be out of here soon, boys,' he said. 'I'll find out how much longer before boarding.'

He stood up and walked towards the uniformed attendant. He tried to appear calm, as Spacey had told him to. 'Look cool,' he'd said. 'And you'll be cool.' Andreas hoped he did, but then again, he thought, if he'd been made, they wouldn't have got this far. He was just about to speak to the attendant when he felt a hand on his shoulder. He turned around and saw a short Japanese man in a suit, flanked by two uniformed police officers.

'Are you Andreas P?' he asked.

'Yes,' he stammered, feeling his guts slide.

'Police. We've checked your luggage, checked equipment. Drugs are everywhere. You're under arrest.'

'What? But I'm not carrying anything. Honest. It's nothing to do with me. It's Spacey. Talk to Spacey. He's the one you want, not me.'

'We've seen Spacey, he's talked. You will come with us, now.'

Chapter 3

Five years earlier

Ray Grimes loved poker, but as he sat around the table in a crumbling Lauderhill house, a world away from his Miami hotel, he cursed his obsession. Crickets buzzed around the single low-watt bulb that barely illuminated the cards, and Ray's fear grew as he kept on winning.

More than anything, Ray wished he was back home in Essex, playing safe pub matches for a free meal. Anywhere, in fact, other than this flaky house on a seedy estate, from where, if the taxi driver didn't come to get him, he'd have no idea how to get back to his hotel.

At the start of each of the last six hands, Ray promised himself he'd quit, but now he really meant it. The haphazard pile of dollar bills, euros and traveller's cheques in front of him turned him into one almighty target all the way to the tourist district. And in Miami, a lot of people had guns.

The two tourists from other hotels and the two locals who'd organised the game had backed out and now just watched, leaving Ray, and Doug, an unwashed, longhaired greybeard with a southern accent. His Cold Steel T-shirt sparked sympathy from Ray, a fellow fan, but not his aggressive game play, and despite his fear, Ray had become obsessed with clearing him out. If he won this hand he'd do it, and he resolved to be more careful what he wished for in future.

He looked at his hand. Four kings. He placed the cards face down and looked across the table. 'I'll see you.' He pushed his entire pot into the centre. 'All in.'

Doug made a show of counting his dwindling banknotes. 'I can't match it,' he whispered.

'You want to see what I've got?' asked Ray.

'Dammit, yes.'

'What else can you add?'

Ray was being a bastard. He'd brought a hundred dollars to the table, expected to lose it, and now he had a thousand in front of him. Doug reached into his biker jacket and pulled out a pile of uneven, yellowing pieces of paper. 'Here.' He added the papers to his money and slid them to the centre of the table. 'They're historic documents, hundreds of years old, been in my family for generations. They're worth your stake, now show me your goddamn cards.'

The madness of winning consumed Ray. He didn't care about the danger of how much he won; it was all about that unquenchable thirst to be the last man standing. Without even looking at the papers he nodded.

Doug smiled and slowly turned over his cards. Ten of hearts. Queen of hearts. Ray tensed, wanting to lose to a royal flush and have a safe trip home, but also wanting to win, to win and be the man. A second queen, then a third, then a fourth. Four queens, an amazing hand. Ray made no show of triumph but kept his gaze fixed on Doug as he turned his own cards over. Doug didn't look down until he heard the buzz of comments from the other players, then his eyes dropped, and his mouth sagged.

'Damn it, damn it, damn it,' he whispered. 'Y'all just cleaned me out, boy, but you played a better game than me.'

Ray felt empty: he always did after winning. The prize, the jackpot was nothing. Knowing he'd won was everything, it was all that mattered. 'Here, mate.' He passed two hundred dollars back to Doug. 'Start your next game on me.' He then turned to the other two tourists, painfully conspicuous in shorts and flowered shirts, just as he was. 'Share a taxi back to the hotel? I'm buying the drinks when we get there.'

Five years later

Randall Spitz opened the balcony doors, stepped onto the wooden veranda and sat down with a large bourbon. A blood-orange sunset washed over the empty beach and shone off the calm sea. It was Randall's favourite time of day, away from the office and lost in the calm solitude of his vast, empty beachfront house. It was a whole world removed from the slums of Queens, where he'd been the only member of his family – hell, the only guy in the entire street – to go legit. But his greased black hair, permanent sunglasses and black suits always alluded to a dangerous past, and

23

Randall used the image to great effect in Ozone Records' corporate world, a world that had almost the same rewards for the same type of personality.

The bourbon fused through his body, slowly loosening the tension of the day, and as he felt his nerves start to smooth out, he was jarred back from his reverie by the phone.

'Randall Spitz,' he growled.

'Randall, hi. It's Lucy Penhalligan, from Ozone UK.'

Randall's mind clicked back to the office. His CCTV memory scouring the personnel files. Lucy Penhalligan, he had her. Slim, maybe too slim for his taste, short dark hair, and probably used her aristocratic background to get ahead in the company as much as he'd played on his own lesser beginnings. In a world where image was everything, it made sense. He smiled and realised the accent she assumed during interviews and conference calls was a lot more cultured than the one she was using on him. 'Hey, Lucy. What's happening in the foggy city?'

'We've got a situation with Cold Steel.'

'Aww, Jesus Christ, not again. I chewed out their fat fuck manager after Tokyo. Told him if they stepped out of line again they were all history. What the hell have they done now?'

'*They* haven't done anything,' said Lucy. 'Well, nothing since then. It's him.'

'*Him?* Three hundred pounds of jerkoff? That guy couldn't do himself in a cathouse. What the hell happened?'

'He got himself arrested at the airport. It seems he and a drug dealer tried smuggling heroin, hidden in the band's equipment.'

'Are you sure it was him and not some asshole band member?'

'Quite sure. The police interviewed everyone. The dealer struck a bargain and spilled the juice. It was all down to him and Andreas. Some sort of fallback plan in case the band went pear-shaped.'

'Lucy,' said Randall. 'I need to know, did the band have anything to do with this?'

'Nothing at all. The Japanese cops scared the shit out of all of them. Even Andy Stains kept his gob shut and behaved himself. They were put on polygraphs, the works. They're clear.'

'Alright then. So Andreas has shot his last chance and Cold Steel have got it instead. He can whistle for corporate legal. He can rot in Japan for all I care.'

24

'What about the band? They touch down here in a few hours with all their equipment impounded in Japan and no manager. Their first British show is tomorrow night. They're in trouble and for once it's not their fault. I think we should throw them a line.'

'Getting soft, Lucy?'

'I said throw them a line, not wipe their arses.'

Randall smiled. He loved the way high-rise limey women, even skinny, high-rise limey women, said ass.

'So okay,' he said. 'Instruments shouldn't be a problem. The manufacturers always fall over themselves to supply. Any band playing their gear is the best goddam advertisement going. Not much notice though.'

'I've got an equipment manifest, and I've faxed suppliers. There shouldn't be a problem getting off-shelf instruments to the O2 by tomorrow. The sound system might be a bit more tricky.'

'How so?'

'Kids at concerts don't buy banks of speakers like they buy guitars,' said Lucy. 'Product placement doesn't mean as much to the sound people. Plus we had to cancel Spain and Portugal. Worldsound say they've already supplied once and want to renegotiate for a duplicate rig.'

'Bastards. They can sing patty-cake. Anything else?'

'The shows will be a little bare, Cold Steel go big into stage props, the ruined pirate ship's been part of their show since day one.'

'Really? Well, those wonder boys need a new world reality check. They're lucky we're letting their limey asses perform at all. Let 'em rock it out on a bare stage and if they're that good, their music is all they'll need. If the Japs release their goddamn ship, it's theirs. Until then, they either live without it or build a goddamn new one. As for their sound system, we need someone to take care of it. Suggestions?'

'What Cold Steel need is a decent manager, someone who's centred on the music and cares about the band. Then we can leave all of this to him.'

'Yeah,' said Randall. 'But I don't want another asshole like Andreas taking his eye off the ball and lining his own goddamn crib. You got any ideas?'

'We've got one guy on the radar who's ticking a lot of the right boxes. I think we can use him.'

'Okay, Lucy, it's yours. Take care of it.'

*

Midnight plugged into the sound system and started their set in front of a painfully empty Islington Academy. Their manager, Johnny Faslane, stood at the monitor station, just out of sight at the edge of the stage. His scuffed cowboy boots poked out from beneath leather trousers, and he ran a hand through his prematurely thinning hair, the remnants of which were tied back in an untidy light-brown ponytail. He looked past the band at the tiny audience space and grimaced. He could practically spit at the double-door entrance from where he was standing.

Midnight's opening riff electrified the thin audience, and Johnny felt for the band. Their demo album had done the company circuit, attracting polite interest but nothing else, and Johnny shared their stabbing disappointment. Midnight's music was fresh and tight and they deserved a break. Infinitely more so than Sunset Dawn, the headline act, and still together after thirty years – although for the last twenty, all they'd done was relive the glory days, and songs, of the first ten. *No wonder they're losing their audience,* thought Johnny. *If I'd been running the show, they'd have still been up there.*

Midnight powered through their short set, and standing to one side of the brightly lit stage, Johnny sensed the blacked-out audience pit filling up, heard the loudening cheers as they worked the crowd. After forty minutes the guitarists slammed the last power chord into the darkness and the house lights revealed a packed crowd barrier at stage front. Johnny clapped his hands and smiled at the band, walking past him, sweat-soaked and grinning. For three hard years they'd developed, their music was sharp and addictive, and Johnny matched their onstage tirelessness in his attempts to get them signed, only to face an unbreakable wall of indifference.

He moved to follow the band back to the dressing room, then stopped short. A zero-sized woman with an all-areas pass walked up to him.

'Johnny Faslane?' she asked.

26

'That's me,' he smiled, trying to gauge her. Groupie? No, she seemed far too together. Reporter? Not supercilious enough. What then? 'What can I do for you?'

'Lucy Penhalligan, Ozone Records.' She held out her hand.

Johnny shook her hand and hope fired through his body like a pulsing bass-line. *A company worker! Holy shit, they never come to us. It's a deal, it's a deal!*

'Is there somewhere we can talk?' she asked.

'Sure there is,' he replied, wondering if there was anywhere at all in the tiny venue to have a meeting with a suddenly announced record company A and R? Trouble-shooter? Exec? He'd never even seen the Islington Academy before: he knew how to get to the stage, the dressing room, and out. Christ, he didn't even know where the bogs were. 'Do you want to talk to the band as well?' If it were a sign-up deal, surely she'd say yes.

'I need to speak to you first.'

Johnny took in her casual clothes: jeans, T-shirt and combat jacket mixed uncomfortably with a Knightsbridge accent and her direct level stare beneath a short brown fringe. He'd always imagined, even sometimes seen, record company execs. In his mind he expected that magic deal-offering moment would happen with a suited archangel from another world. 'Okay, then,' he stammered. 'Let's find a spot at the bar.'

'The pub down the road will be better.'

'What? No way. I can't leave the band after a gig.'

She smiled. 'That's a habit we approve of. Don't worry, my colleague's with them right now.'

'Talking to them right now? Then there's even more reason for me to be there. That's my job, for Christ's sake.'

'Johnny, it's okay. Just hear me out, all right? We've got something for everyone.'

*

A two-minute walk from the Academy, The Nag's Head on Upper Street was squeezed between a bank and a clothes shop. Outside the pub, three longhaired drinkers sitting at a rickety table had their beers gently seasoned by exhaust fumes from the busy London traffic that thundered past just feet away. Inside, the tall, three-storey frontage gave an impression of narrowness, and despite lacking bodily broadness himself, Johnny unconsciously held his arms by his sides as he stepped through the doorway and onto untreated wooden flooring. His curiosity at Lucy's actions competed with irritation, with himself as much as her for not even looking in on the band before coming away. He ordered two bottles of beer without even asking her what she wanted and placed one in front of her on the small table at the back of the pub.

'So,' he said. 'What's so important that you can't tell me in front of the band?'

'Interesting name, Johnny Faslane.'

'Don't change the subject.'

'No, I'm curious. How did you come by it?'

Johnny sweated inside his trousers. Far from ideal summer wear, they were almost trademark clothing for him. He sighed and drank his beer. 'Okay. I tell, then you tell. Faslane is a submarine base in Scotland.'

'I've heard of it. Is that where you're from?'

'Never even been there. So, you know it's a sub base, right?'

'Yes.'

'So you know they're nuclear powered?' said Johnny. 'And they can dive really deep, right? Some say they can even reach the ocean floor.'

'And what's that got to do with you?'

'That's how low my luck rides with most of the bands I manage.'

Lucy chuckled and put down her beer. 'A little harsh.'

'Really? Rolling Thunder: split up, unsigned. Aztec Cyanide: one support tour, split up, unsigned. Lycanthrope: offered a deal, then arrested and deported.'

'No different to most bands. Come on, Johnny, as many managers as musicians don't make it in this game.'

'Which makes me pretty average. So why this conversation? And incidentally, who exactly from Ozone *am* I talking to?'

'Head of Artists and Relations, Ozone UK, if you want the official line.'

'So shouldn't you be talking to the artists?'

Lucy smiled. 'I've got other people to do that.'

'And what exactly are they saying to my band, if you don't mind me asking?'

'We're going to sign them.'

Johnny's eyes shot open and he twitched as though he'd been electrocuted. 'You're signing Midnight?' he shouted.

'Yes, but you might not want to scream it out for the whole pub to hear.'

'But that's amazing,' he said. 'That's unbelievable. I've got to tell them. This is fantastic. I knew it. I knew they had it. You've made a smart move there, Lucy. That band is really going places.'

'They are, Johnny. But not with you.'

'What?' His earlier elation suddenly fragmented. 'What do you mean, not with me? I'm their manager.'

'Johnny. Midnight are getting this deal because of you. You believed in them, you kept the support slots coming in, you made sure they arrived in town on time, kept them writing songs, and kept them out of trouble.'

'Of course I did, that's my job.'

'That's right, and that's what we want.'

'I don't understand. If that's what you want, why are you cutting me loose?'

'What we want is a manager who knows the road, knows how to keep a band focussed, keep them creative.'

'That's what all managers do.'

'You'd be surprised. Some are worse than the bands, some get the fame-trip and can't see past the next party once their band hits it big.'

'But I've been with Midnight since the beginning. Please, Lucy, I can take them to the top, I know it.'

She shook her head. 'They're going straight into the studio, and we'll find someone else who can take them from there. Whatever happens, they'll still have you to thank. You got them to this point.'

'So why break up a winning team? They need me.'

'They need a good producer and a business advisor, not a road manager. We want you for something else, someone else.'

Johnny looked at her. 'Sunset Dawn. That's it, isn't it? You want me to manage Sunset Dawn.'

'No. We came here tonight to shut down Sunset Dawn.'

'What?'

'They haven't played ball for years. We've told them time and again to get into the studio and do another album, but all they want

29

to do is crank out the same old songs to smaller and smaller audiences. None of their fans are new, and the ones they've got…' Lucy shrugged. 'Let's face it, they aren't getting any younger, they aren't as keen to go to concerts.' She shrugged again. 'And they're now starting to die off. We're getting no juice from their old albums, and now that their tours have stopped making money as well, that's it. Tonight they'll play their last gig.'

'Jesus, Lucy, that's cold. And I suppose you've got *people* to do that for you?'

'If I wanted, but that's not my style. Once we've got Midnight sorted out I'll tell Sunset Dawn myself.'

'So what do you want me to do?'

'We want you to manage Cold Steel.'

Chapter 4

Four years earlier

Ray Grimes, still deaf from being front-row at the Cold Steel
Concert, clutched at his fan club membership card and stood
outside Wembley Arena's backstage door. Driving rain made him
pull his jacket closer round him, and he joined the rest of the fans
in moaning about how long it was taking. Next to Ray, a teenager
pulled up his jeans as they slid past his arse. *And I thought mullets
were embarrassing,* he thought.

The door scraped open and a tattooed bouncer filled the space,
making it no less accessible. 'Membership cards,' he growled.

One by one, they were let in. Ray, the youth with low-rise
jeans, plus two girls who looked nervously at the bouncer and had
to be pushed inside by an irate old rocker who reminded Ray of
Doug. They followed the bouncer along narrow, breezeblock
corridors and into a tiny plasterboard room where the band waited,
still sweating from the concert.

Ray stood still for a moment, not knowing what to say or do.
He'd seen Cold Steel three times, but had never met them, or in
fact any musician before. Maxwell Diabolo walked over to him.
'Easy, mate,' he said. 'Have a beer.' He handed Ray an opened
bottle. 'You liked the show?'

Ray took the bottle with numb acceptance and nodded, his
entire thought process fudged. 'Have you travelled far to get here
tonight?' asked Maxwell. Ray nodded once more.

Still smiling easily, Maxwell tried again. 'What did you think of
our latest album? Is our third one as good as the other two?'

Ray's thoughts finally kicked into gear. *If you don't say
something soon, he'll either think you're a retard, or you want to
shag him.* 'I've got a map!' he blurted.

Maxwell's grin disappeared for a second before returning. 'Is
that how you got here tonight?'

'No. No.' Ray shook his head and his mind slowly cleared.
'I've got a map to show you.'

'To me?'

'Yes. It's an old one, a really old one. I read on the internet that you like all that old seafaring stuff, nautical history. Well, I got this map last year, I'm not sure about its history or anything, but it's old, it's a map of an island. Maybe you'd autograph it for me?'

'Let's have a look.'

Ray pulled out the creased paper and gave it to Maxwell, who put down his beer and stared intently at the map. He turned it over and looked at the numbers on the other side. 'Definitely looks old,' he muttered. 'Especially if this date's right: twenty-first September, seventeen-fifteen. Where'd you get it?'

'I won it in a poker game.'

'Interesting. Where?'

'Where what?'

'Where was the game?'

'In Florida, last year, when I was on holiday.'

'The Caribbean, eh?' Maxwell's eyebrows rose. 'So what about the bloke who had the map before you? What did he say about it?'

'Not much, just that it had been in his family for years.'

'And him, mate? Was he from Florida too?'

'He had a southern accent, could have been from anywhere in that area.'

'Yeah.' Maxwell paused, then looked at Ray. 'Mate, I'll tell you what. This here map looks like it's hundreds of years old, and it don't seem right for me to be scribbling my name across it. But you're right about me and my hobbies, so how about I buy it off you, give you a CD signed by the whole band, and mention you by name on our next album?'

'You want to buy it off me?' asked Ray.

'Sure,' grinned Maxwell. 'You good with a thousand?'

'Jesus.'

'Alright then, two?'

'Holy shit.'

'Okay, mate, let's sort this out once and for all. Five thousand?'

Ray's speech left him again, and he nodded dumbly.

'Andreas,' roared Maxwell. 'Get me some cash!'

Four years later

32

After leaving Lucy at the pub, Johnny returned to the crumbling B and B where he was staying with Midnight. He nodded at the Ozone reps who were already there and paying the bills, before collecting his gear and getting a taxi to the hotel where Cold Steel had been installed after their flight from Tokyo. He looked around at the plush fittings and his sense of unreality smothered him. He'd heard all about Cold Steel since the start of their fourth tour, and knew he'd been given what seemed like an impossible set of problems to solve. They had new instruments arriving just hours before the gig, no sound gear and no stage props, and Lucy had left him with no illusions that it was his job to sort it out.

As instructed, he gave Lucy's card to the immaculately suited receptionist. 'Johnny Faslane,' he said. 'I believe you've been told to expect me.' He still thought the whole thing must be some kind of elaborate joke and he half-expected to be thrown out. But the receptionist smiled and handed him a room card.

'Welcome to the Imperial, Mister Faslane.' He smiled, then looked curiously at Johnny's battered holdall. 'Is that your only item of luggage?'

Johnny nodded, self-conscious about his possessions for the first time. He sheepishly followed the porter towards the marble-floored lift, his cowboy boots tapping loudly on the solid stone tiles.

Inside his room, which seemed the same size as the entire B and B he had just left, Johnny's phone rang as he was tipping the porter.

'Are you at the hotel yet?' It was Lucy.

'Just got here.'

'I've got the band together in Maxwell's suite. Room six-fifteen, can you be here in five?'

'On my way.'

Johnny shoved his key card into his pocket and walked along the corridor towards the lift, still not fully believing that not only was he just about to meet Cold Steel but that he would do so as their manager. Things were happening fast, too fast.

The lift whispered up to the sixth floor. The doors hushed open and he nervously looked at the door numbers. He stopped outside six-fifteen and knocked on the oak-panelled door. Lucy answered and ushered him inside.

The sixth-floor suite was even bigger than Johnny's room, and he walked into an open living area and saw the band members sprawled on easy chairs and sofas, looking him with open curiosity. Maxwell Diabolo's left arm was still splinted and he held a half-drunk beer bottle with his right hand. The black hair extensions blended seamlessly with what was left of his real hair, and if Johnny hadn't read about the Budokan show he'd never have known the difference. Sitting next to him, Vince Fire fiddled with a set of guitar strings, constantly looping them up and then unravelling them, his face a mask of determined concentration beneath slicked back hair. Andy Stains sat on a chair and glared malevolently at Johnny, his filthy clothes belying his status as one of the world's premier guitarists. Joe Dimitri sprawled as though his spine had been ripped out, smiling at Johnny with a stoned grin, while Mike Vesuvius sat like a stone Buddha, arms like tree-trunks folded over an oil-drum chest.

'Okay,' said Lucy. 'You all know what happened to Andreas. He's history and that's not negotiable. In fact, you're all bloody lucky the dealer squealed, otherwise you'd be in a Japanese jail alongside him. Now, you've had some time off so let's get back to work.' She nodded towards Johnny. 'This is Johnny Faslane, your new manager. He's just clinched a deal for Midnight, and he knows all there is about managing a band on the road.'

'Does he know how to get our equipment flown in from Japan?' asked Maxwell.

'That's out of our hands and you know it,' snapped Lucy. 'Now, this tour has been toxic from the start. The only reason you're still on the road at all after your last fuck-up is down to album sales and nothing else. Album sales, I might add, that are good, but not as good as before, and that's a worrying sign. We need to know that this is as low as it gets, and you need to impress with sales *and* what's left of this tour, or you're all history.'

'Bollocks,' growled Andy. 'You haven't got the juice for that.'

Lucy spun round and faced Johnny. 'What happened at the Academy tonight, after Midnight got their deal?'

'Ozone ditched Sunset Dawn.'

'And who did it?'

'You did.'

'And *who* are Sunset Dawn?' asked Andy.

34

'Oh, they're an *old* band, man,' said Joe. 'Are they still going?'

'Until tonight they were,' said Lucy. 'But they stopped listening to the record company and their manager had no control over them. Sound familiar?'

'Yeah, man, but they're hardly in the same league as us.'

'Joe?' asked Lucy. 'Do you know what happens to bands who don't make money?'

'No new albums, just touring the smaller venues.'

'No. No new albums, and no more music at all. Their contract gave Ozone the rights to all of their music, live and recorded. So, no live performance goes ahead without our say so. Sunset Dawn won't play another concert again, not a pub, club, not even their neighbour's garden, unless we decide otherwise.' Joe squirmed under Lucy's direct stare.

'So?' said Maxwell. 'What's that got to do with us?'

'You haven't looked very closely at your contracts, have you? Any of you?'

Silence.

'Well, that was what we paid Andreas for,' mumbled Andy. 'He took care of all that.'

'Oh, shit.' Maxwell's jaw dropped.

Lucy smiled. 'Care to discuss the fine print of *your* contract?'

'Did Andreas know about it?'

She nodded. 'He didn't take much convincing, either.'

'That's crap,' sneered Andy. 'If you were going to ice us, you'd have done it already, and you wouldn't have bothered doing us the *favour* of getting a new manager.'

'Don't believe me?'

'No. You're just a company lightweight trying to scare us.'

Lucy picked up her phone and set it on loudspeaker.

'Randall Spitz.' A gravel-track voice permeated the hotel room.

'Randall, it's Lucy. I'm here with Cold Steel and Johnny.'

'Did you give those jerkoffs the word?'

'They seem to think we're not serious.'

'They what? The dumb fucks. Put me on loudspeaker.'

'Listening to you now.'

'Good, now listen here, you longhaired limey cocksuckers. This is Randall Spitz, and for those of you who don't know, I'm the ass-kicker of this whole organisation. You mofos have been shooting

35

the shit for too long and it ends right now. We're through with hearing stories about your tour going down the tubes. You screwed up in Tokyo, your manager's ass is grass, and we had to cancel Spain and Portugal. You think we won't shitcan you? Hell, I'll dig your holes right now, you bastards. Lucy speaks with my voice, and you *will* do as she says. If I hear from her or your manager that you're not playing ball, it's over, you get me?'

Johnny looked from one band member to the next and felt the hostility building. The silence stretched out, and none of them questioned Randall.

'Thanks, Randall,' said Lucy. 'I think they're in the picture.'

'It's their asses in a goddamn cement mixer if they're not.'

Randall hung up and Lucy faced the band. 'You've got just one chance to pull your arses out of the fire and that's on these UK dates. If you fuck up, fuck around or fail to deliver live, it's over. We know the equipment issues weren't your fault, and that's why we've brought Johnny in. He's the best road manager we could find, he'll get you the gear you need, *and* he'll stop you acting like idiots. As far as Ozone is concerned, he's your boss and you do as he says. If I have to see you guys again, it'll be to tell you that Cold Steel are officially over. Understand?'

'What?' said Maxwell. 'You mean this one bloke'll get us the live props, the pirate ship, and all the instruments we lost in Japan?'

'I said he'll get you what you need, not what you want. Brand new instruments straight from the crate will be waiting for you tomorrow morning. You'll have enough lights to be seen and enough sound to be heard. Here in the UK it'll be your music talking, nothing else. Prove that you can still do that, and we should have a bit more for you to play with on mainland Europe. But it's up to you. There are no second chances, and don't think we won't cut you loose if you give us reason to.'

Andy smirked. 'That's a match made in heaven. Which one of us gets to kill him?'

'Save your bullshit for the groupies,' said Lucy. 'If any turn up. Tomorrow night, we expect a proper concert. No puking onstage, no broken bones and no early finish, understand? Johnny, a word.'

Johnny followed Lucy out of the suite into the corridor and she turned to face him. 'It's a tough brief,' she said, 'but you knew that already. Can you do it?'

'Maybe.' He ran a hand over his thinning scalp and sparse ponytail. 'I don't know, Lucy. I'll give it my best shot.'

'We're relying on you, Johnny. The band needs to be back on form for continental Europe. Their album's selling well, but it could do better. And between you and me, it *should* be doing better.'

'Will the tour really make that much difference to album sales?' asked Johnny.

'More than you'd think,' replied Lucy. 'Bad publicity won't help, nor will cancelled shows, and they didn't make many friends in Spain or Portugal. It's a shame, because musically this album is their best work yet, but they need to ditch their eighties mentality. We're fed up with picking up the pieces after them.'

'I think they got that message loud and clear.'

'You think? I think they're a bunch of arseholes who believe the good times can last for ever, and convincing them otherwise will be harder than anything else we're asking you to do.'

'I guess my future's dependant on theirs as well?'

'Get them through the UK leg in one piece, and we'll see where we are.'

He nodded. 'Right. Well, I'd better get to know my new mates.'

'Mates? You're optimistic.' Lucy walked down the corridor and Johnny went back inside. Iced enmity froze the air, the band glared at him, and Johnny didn't blame them. Andreas simply hadn't been there, and the reality they were left with was hard for Cold Steel to face.

'Look,' said Johnny. 'I know this can't be easy for you, but I'm on your side, and I'm here to try and get the best out of you guys.'

'Leave it, mate,' said Maxwell. 'We know what's best for us.'

Johnny held up his hands. 'Whatever. Anyway, I'm downstairs in three-twenty if you need me. I'll be back at ten o'clock tomorrow.'

'Ten o'clock? What for?'

'So that you can show the crew how you want the stage put together, so that you can sort out your new instruments when they arrive, which right now you haven't got, and so that you can do sound check, alright?'

'Look, mate. We're Cold Steel. We *don't* do sound checks.'

'You'll stand up, wear a suit and sing like a fucking choirboy if I tell you to,' snapped Johnny. 'Ten o'clock tomorrow. Be ready.'

Chapter 5

'Pull harder.'

'Fucking hell, Max.' Mike sweated with the strain. 'Maybe we should leave it where it is.'

'Bollocks.' Maxwell heaved at the television, but the wall mounting resisted all five band members. 'We've never done this before, this could be our last chance.'

'Yeah,' puffed Andy. 'And maybe there's a *reason* why we've never done this before.'

'This is so seventies, man,' said Joe.

'Too right,' said Vince. 'Even the bands we looked up to when we were nothing hadn't done this.'

'Shut up and pull,' grunted Maxwell.

The metal brackets behind the television creaked and bent, slowly giving way. With a sudden jolt it came free. The band collapsed on the floor with the fifty-inch television lying on top of them. Loose cables with bare wires hung like exposed tendons.

'Bloody heavy,' said Andy.

'Good job there's five of us here to lift it then,' said Maxwell. 'Come on, lads, let's get it to the window.'

'Are you sure, Max?' asked Vince. 'We've been told to keep a lid on it. I can't even remember the last band that actually did this.'

'Stop being a pussy, Vince. Joe, get the window open. And make sure there's no one down below.'

Joe slid open the suite window while the rest of the band grappled with the television. They heaved it to the window, rested it on the sill, and then slowly slipped it out. For a second the television balanced on the window ledge, then it tipped over and out of sight.

As it plummeted groundward, one of the severed cables looped around Joe's ankle. It tightened and threw him onto his back, pulling him feet first towards the open window.

'Oh no,' he wailed, kicking ineffectually at the windowsill. 'Oh, heavy heavy. Help me, guys.'

The rest of the band grabbed the taut wire and tried to stop the television dragging Joe out of the window.

'Mike,' bellowed Maxwell. 'Untangle Joe.'

Mike pulled on the cable and secured some slack, then grappled with the snarled wire that looped around Joe's dirty flares. 'He's clear, Max,' he shouted. 'Let go.'

The rest of the band released the cable and it shot out of the window. Seconds later they heard a muffled crash as the television slammed into the pavement six floors below.

'Quick,' said Maxwell. 'Everybody grab a beer, sit back and look innocent.'

*

Johnny flicked through equipment suppliers' websites and punched their numbers into his phone. A plan slowly formulated in his mind, and with his eyes fixed on the laptop he was oblivious to the sight of a television shooting past his window, while the thick glazing muffled the sound of it landing.

An hour later, his room phone rang. 'Johnny Faslane.'

'Mister Faslane, this is the duty manager. Could you please come to room six-one-five immediately.'

*

Johnny stood next to the duty manager inside Maxwell's suite. His eyes took in the gaping hole on the wall, the severed wires that hung like dead snakes and the rawlplugs littering the beige carpet. Then he looked at the band members, all of whom looked back at him with wide-eyed, counterfeit innocence.

'None of us know anything about it,' said Maxwell.

'About what?'

'About whatever it is you want to ask us about.'

'Oh, for Christ's sake.'

'Mister Faslane,' said the duty manager. Immaculate appearance, mirror-shined shoes and clipped hair told Johnny he was ex-forces and not easily intimidated. 'We've examined the remains of the television that landed on the hotel forecourt, and the serial number, combined with the vacant space in this room, leads us to the obvious conclusion.'

'We were in the shower,' said Maxwell. 'Never saw a thing.'

'What?' asked Johnny. 'All five of you?'

'That is immaterial,' said the duty manager. 'Mister Faslane. These actions are unsustainable at this hotel, and I must ask you, and your colleagues, to make immediate reparation for losses incurred, and thereafter you will be escorted from the premises.'

Chapter 6

The Sunshine Bed and Breakfast was as far removed from the
Imperial Hotel as the Islington Academy was from the Tokyo
Budokan. But at one o'clock in the morning, Johnny just wanted to
sleep. He was tired of trawling around London, crammed inside a
taxi while Cold Steel collectively rejected one alternative after
another.

'I didn't stay in a place like this even before we made it big,'
said Vince.

'I'd have been happier where we were as well,' replied Johnny.

'Yeah, right,' sneered Vince. 'I bet you're loving this, a chance
to show us where you came from.'

'It wasn't me that got you lot thrown out of the hotel.'

'It wasn't you who stuck up for us either.'

'Right.' Sarcasm coated Johnny's reply. 'Because chucking a
television out of the window is so acceptable, isn't it? Show me a
band right now who still do that. Christ, show me a band in the last
twenty years who did that.'

'You won't break us,' growled Andy. 'Better than you have
tried.'

'I'm not trying to break you, idiot. I'm trying to stop you
getting canned, which you don't seem to realise is closer than you
think.'

'Hey, man,' said Joe. 'We didn't hurt anyone, and the hotel gear
is insured, right?'

'I don't want to hear about it,' snapped Johnny. 'There are *no*
reasons to excuse what you did. Outside, now. Maxwell, pay the
driver.'

'Jesus, mate, have a heart. We settled up at the hotel, didn't
we?'

'Too bloody right you did. You *caused* it. And unless you want
Randall to know about what happened tonight, you're paying for
the B and B as well.'

Maxwell scowled and passed his credit card to the driver while
Johnny led the rest of the band inside. Worn carpets and smoke-
stained walls reminded him of where he'd been staying with

42

Midnight. *It didn't take long to go full-circle,* he thought. The receptionist stared at the band through thick-rimmed glasses and rearranged his comb-over. 'How many rooms have you got?' asked Johnny.

'Three,' replied the receptionist.

'Fine. You lot can have three in one, two in another, and don't disturb me till breakfast. And if any fixtures and fittings even get touched, Randall will know about it, understand?'

'Who's paying?' asked the receptionist.

'Him.' Johnny pointed at Maxwell, who had just squeezed through the small doorway.

*

Johnny sat in the Sunshine's small dining room and scooped up the last of his breakfast with a thick slice of buttered bread. His bedroom had been sandwiched between the two used by the band, and while they squabbled the rest of the night away in stereo, he'd drifted off to sleep, knowing he'd be the only one to turn up for breakfast.

'Any more tea?' he asked the East European waitress, who looked at him nervously. She nodded and disappeared into the kitchen, returning minutes later with a pot of hot tea.

'Your friends,' she said. 'They eat?'

Johnny looked at his watch; it was nine-thirty. 'No, but I'll have one of theirs if that's okay?'

'Is not normal. Usually one breakfast, one guest.'

'Charge one extra to Mister Diabolo, he won't mind.'

A second breakfast arrived and Johnny filled up before wiping his mouth and climbing the stairs. Five to ten and he knew the band weren't getting up. He beat loudly on each door until a bleary-eyed band member opened it and cursed him.

'Up and out,' he barked. 'I want you downstairs and ready to go in ten minutes.'

'What about breakfast?' asked Maxwell.

'You're too late. It's just finished. Get your arses into gear and maybe I'll feed you at the O2.'

*

The O2 sat like a huge white abscess by the side of the Thames, and under its shadow the crowded taxi disgorged its contents. Johnny ushered the band through the gates and led them towards

43

'Here,' said Maxwell. 'Look what Mossy showed us.' He grabbed a sheaf of thin wires that disappeared into the arena's ceiling.

Bushfire suspicion flared in Johnny's mind at the mention of Silas. 'What are they, fishing lines?'

'Suspension cables.'

'Suspension for what?'

'Not what, who. We can hook up to them and fly around the stage.'

Johnny's mind dredged up images of cheesy music videos from more than twenty years before. 'That's a bit eighties, isn't it?'

'With a blank stage and borrowed speakers, it's all we've got. What do you say?'

'How safe is it for you to be flying around? Your arm's still not fixed properly, you don't want to add a fractured skull to your CV.'

'Are you my mother now?'

'It feels like it sometimes. It's too chancy, you're not doing it.'

'Is that an order?'

'Yes. What's your set list?'

'Same as we had in Asia.'

'Right, run through it, start to finish.'

'What?'

'You heard me,' said Johnny. 'Your instruments got here this morning; it'll take days to get them adjusted properly. If something doesn't work, find out now without an audience or a reporter noticing. There's going to be a lot of attention out there tonight and you need to be perfect.'

'Leave it out, mate. We know what we're doing.'

'Maybe with your old instruments and effects, but not now. The whole set, start to finish.'

Johnny folded his arms and stared at Maxwell, who shrugged and turned to the band. 'He wants to hear some real music, lads.'

Sinners Sanctuary surged through the speakers and Johnny nodded, then walked backstage. With them going through their whole set, he had two hours to do his job without worrying about anything happening to the band. And he had plenty to do. Replacement instruments were a good start, but at Cold Steel's level, things had to be exact, right down to the colour of plectrums and tolerance of guitar strings. And there was still the sound system to sort out. He pulled out his phone and went to work.

Chapter 7

Jack Sarin sat back in his office chair. He crossed his combat booted feet on his desktop, then lit a cigarette, daring anyone to tell him it was illegal inside *his* building. *Not if they value their jobs.* He laughed at the sense of power he possessed within his own world.

Jack was expecting a call. He knew it was coming, knew what it would be about, he just didn't know who it would be from. Didn't matter though, it was a call that would put him in the driving seat, give him power over others, and also make him another huge wedge of cash. All the things he liked.

His scalpel-sharp perception cut right, and he answered his phone on the first ring. 'Sarin Sound, Jack Sarin speaking.'

'Jack, hi. It's Johnny Faslane, Cold Steel's manager.'

'Cold Steel's *new* manager, right?'

'Sure. I suppose you dealt with Andreas in the past?'

'If you can call an email followed by a bank transfer dealing, then yes. Are you just a temporary stand-in?'

Jack prided himself on being able to goad anyone to anger, then taking advantage of their skewed judgement to fleece them. It was so easy when he had what they wanted. He wondered how long it would take to push Johnny's buttons.

'No one's on a permanent deal in this game,' replied Johnny.

'Except me,' replied Jack. 'I've been doing this for twenty years and the big boys always come to my house. Just like you, right? So what do you need?'

'Cold Steel need a complete sound suite for the rest of the UK dates.'

'And the Continent?'

'Just the UK for now.'

'That's a lot of work for not much, new boy.'

'I'm sure your numbers will keep you comfortable.'

'You'd better believe it. Send me the dates and venues. When's your next gig?'

'Tonight's more or less covered with the O2's back room kit. Tomorrow we're in Manchester for two nights.'

'The MEN?'

'Yes.'

'You won't want borrowed sound there. If I had another six hours notice I could have helped you in London.'

'If you can kit us out from tomorrow and it's good, we've got a deal.'

'And the price?'

Johnny's laugh annoyed Jack, knocked his confidence. 'I think we can discuss that as we go along, Jack. I haven't seen the goods yet, never mind heard them.'

'You'll get what you want, new boy. I know what I'm doing.'

'So do I, Jack, and I don't want you doing to Cold Steel what you did to Tigershark with your upfront fees and no gear on time. I don't *want* you to come through for us, I *need* you to.'

'Hey, none of that was my fault. You've got my word, what more do you need?'

'A wall of sound tomorrow night.'

'You'll get it.'

'Hopefully better than Soundsphere.'

'What? Don't even mention those losers to me.'

'Why not? They'll be showing us their goods for the second Manchester night. Whichever outfit gives us the best gets Cold Steel.'

Jack choked as he inhaled and felt his face flush. 'You bastard,' he wheezed.

'No one gets a prize for being nice, Jack. Not in this business. I'll speak to you tomorrow once we've seen the gear.'

*

Silas paced back and forth inside Chainsaw's dressing room. 'This is your chance, lads,' he said. 'Play a blinder tonight and you'll upstage Cold Steel. It'll be you the press are talking about, not them.'

Zip Fly, the band's singer, looked at Silas. His long hair was split down the middle, black on one side, pure white on the other. Although Silas was in no position to cast opinions, he thought Zip's hair looked fucking ridiculous. Thank God his voice sounded a lot better than he looked.

'You reckon?' Zip's accent was fifth-generation London, reeking of fume-blackened, brick-built slums, chip shops and rain.

'Their tour's had bad press since the start. All they need to do is make one wrong move and it'll keep on sticking. That'll make you lot look even better.'

'I don't know, Silas, their new album's pretty damn good, and they're on home ground now.'

'Yeah, right. They've also got Johnny Faslane hanging round their necks.'

'So?'

'So he's the unluckiest manager in the business. He could put Cold Steel on the rocks even if they weren't in trouble. All it needs is a little help, and that's where I come in.'

*

Chainsaw's set speared through the arena, its thudding beat vibrating the small dressing room as Johnny spoke to Cold Steel.

'Your warm-up sounded pretty good today,' he said. 'Any surprises?'

'Five song changes,' grumbled Maxwell.

'These instruments just don't sound the same,' said Andy.

'Then it's a good job you found out,' replied Johnny. 'Anyway, we've got two different sound systems to test in Manchester, a different one on each night, and you get to pick the best. But what's important right now is that you focus on tonight. Keep it tight and basic, and finish in one piece, okay?'

'What about the ship?' asked Maxwell.

'It's still in Japan.'

'It'll feel strange without it being there.'

'You've still got the music. Prove you can cut it without anything else and that'll silence the critics.' Johnny forced a smile that was frozen by iceberg stares from the band. 'Okay,' he said. 'I'll let you get ready. You're on half an hour after Chainsaw come off. I'll come and get you.'

*

Joe waited till Johnny was out of sight, then sparked up a joint and passed it around. 'Wow, man,' he drawled. 'He's a bit hands-on, isn't he?'

'Bleeding babysitter,' grumbled Maxwell.

'Andreas would be back at the hotel by now,' said Andy. 'Up to his nuts in drugs and groupies.'

'Yeah,' said Vince. 'And letting *us* get on with the show.'

50

'At least he gave us some good advice about the set-list,' said Mike.

'Oh, bollocks,' said Maxwell. 'We'd have worked it out for ourselves. We don't need him. He's just protecting his meal ticket.'

'It's helping us too,' replied Mike, stubbornly.

'How?' steamed Maxwell. 'By telling us what to do? Pay the taxi driver, play the full set, do this, don't do that. *I'll come and get you.* Fucking arse-wipe was managing no-hope bands two days ago, and now he's telling us what to do? *Us?* Well, he needs to learn we don't always play by the rules.'

'Careful, Max,' said Mike. 'You heard what that company rep said last night.'

'Hey,' growled Maxwell. 'The company makes a bloody fortune out of us. They won't chuck us just for a few off-centre gigs. Jesus, there wouldn't be a band left with a contract if that was the case. We need to show the new boy here that he can only order us around so much.'

'What's on your mind, man?' asked Joe.

'Already sorted,' grinned Maxwell. 'Are you with me, lads?'

*

Johnny stood at the monitor desk by the side of the stage. Chainsaw powered to the end of their set and the house lights came on to an expectant audience that had heard the stories about Cold Steel, but still believed. He felt the rising tension, saw the congestion build in the unseated area near the stage. Onstage preparation was minimal, but the roadies did a good job of creating illusions by building a drum riser out of speaker cases and placing the squadron of brand new guitars on display. How would the fans react to not seeing the ship there? The band had to make up for the visual deficits with a newly reviewed set played on new but minimally adjusted instruments, with a singer who had one arm in a splint. It wouldn't be easy.

The arena filled like a slow dawn lighting an empty beach, and Johnny could taste the expectation. He'd been there himself, the single-minded metal fan who believed in nothing but the band: not the reviews, not what his friends or the music press said. He knew that if he could just give the bands he followed his complete support and appreciation, then they couldn't possibly fail, which

51

was how he applied himself as a manager. He knew that the fans in the O2 that night felt the same. They believed in Cold Steel, wanted them, willed them to triumph against the whole world. When that trust was proved, it was the best thing ever; when it was broken, the worst.

Johnny looked at his watch and threaded along narrow corridors back to the dressing room. 'Okay, lads,' he said. 'It's show time. Knock 'em dead.'

Chapter 8

Maxwell led the band out of the dressing room and followed Johnny towards the stage. His arm still ached and there was no hiding the splint. He walked along bare-chested, his black hair, fake and real, snaking down his back and the familiar fear and madness settled in his stomach and sent sparks through his whole body. He fed off the feeling. He was Maxwell Diabolo, and this was Cold Steel, the best metal band on the fucking planet. To hell with the reporters, news crews, hangers-on, anyone who doubted him, doubted them. Cold Steel were unbeatable, untouchable, and they'd show everyone, especially this balding, ponytailed stooge who'd been forced on them by the company.

Johnny froze just short of the monitor desk and Maxwell nearly walked into him. The lights suddenly dimmed and the crowd roared. Johnny tapped Maxwell on the shoulder and he strode onto the stage, right fist in the air. The lights snared him in a tunnel of illuminating heat and the audience screamed recognition. Maxwell grinned like a returning hero and the music started.

*

Close enough to almost touch the band from his invisible, cramped recess backstage, Johnny watched them fire off their opening riffs at the audience. Maxwell strode to the front of the massive stage and bellowed a greeting to the crowd. They roared back approval and Sinners Sanctuary returned to British ears.

Cold Steel owned the pared-back stage and Johnny's eagerness built. He felt the music reach into him, while a boiling sea of fans at the front of the stage swirled and churned against the barrier. The band hurled one song after another outwards, and with nothing but themselves and their music, they were in constant motion, brushing against each other with sparks of musical energy. The new instruments gave an added vibrancy to the music, and Vince, Joe and Andy added their backing vocals to Maxwell's voice, creating a concert that was as different as it was unexpected.

*

Onstage, Maxwell felt the hot adrenaline run like lava through his veins, felt the spiritual connection with the fans, felt as though he could carry on all night. Even his aching arm had stopped bothering him. The music's driving force fed him like a drug, and the roaring crowd fuelled his desire to give them more. He canon-fired the final verse from Whipped Up a Storm, and heard twenty thousand voices scream the lyrics back at him. This was it, this was life, this was what it was all about. To hell with the bean counters and their rules and threats. And as for Johnny, he needed to know when to back off.

'London!' he screamed as the song ended, and the crowd roared back at him. 'We've had a bad time lately, but are you having a good time?'

A wall of cheers crashed over the band, almost as loud as the music they'd kettled outwards.

'That's good,' shouted Maxwell. 'That's real good. There's too many people out there telling you what to do.' Cheers erupted. 'There's too many people out there telling *us* what to do.' More cheers. 'And here's Cold Steel's answer for all of them!'

Maxwell hooked his microphone to the stand, turned around with drillmaster precision, and ignoring the pain in his left arm, fumbled with his sweat-damp tight jeans and dropped them to the floor, displaying a chalk-white arse. Cameras flashed like spotlights, and after half a minute, he yanked up his trousers, grabbed the microphone and the band launched into Chasing the Sunset.

*

Johnny's fledgling confidence shuddered at Maxwell's onstage moon. He couldn't rush out there and stop it, and he groaned, unheard, at the thought of more confrontation after the show. But Maxwell had connected with the audience, and the band pushed the concert on. Soon, Johnny's concerns flaked away, and he found himself enjoying the show more and more.

The main set crashed to a halt and the band lined up onstage, grinning and waving at the crowd before walking off. Johnny cheered with them, and clapped the band members on their shoulders as they walked past him, then followed them through to the dressing room.

'You still think Ozone are going to ditch us?' exulted Maxwell, shaking his head and flicking sweat over Johnny.

'Keep playing like that and you'll be fine.'

'A bit more trust from *you* and we'll be fine.'

'Yeah,' said Andy. Johnny could practically taste the testosterone sweating from every band member's pore.

'Hey,' he said. 'You did a great show. Well done. Now, how about the encore, or is that me telling you what to do?'

'So we're agreeing on that,' smiled Maxwell. 'Let's give them some more, lads.'

*

The band reappeared, and an incoming tide of cheers energised them. Maxwell threw his arms above his head, jumped up and down and grabbed the microphone. As he did so, Joe, Andy and Vince walked to the far end of the stage, furthest from Johnny. *Boss, my arse,* thought Maxwell. A single spotlight caught him as he sung the first haunting lines from Chief Smoke, then Mike followed with a soft but steadily building drum line. As the guitars joined in, the stage was lit up once more, and Maxwell grinned as he saw Joe, Vince and Andy floating across the stage, suspended by the cables Johnny had forbidden them to use.

*

Standing at the monitor station, Johnny felt his burning fury like an impotent volcano inside him. He'd said no to the wires for good reason. The band had never used them before, they'd not prepared and for all he knew, they weren't even safe. His mind performed a horror preview of what could go wrong, but there was nothing he could do except watch and hope the band would realise it was harder than it looked before disaster swallowed them up.

*

The band's last song of the night, No Nation, erupted, and Maxwell forgot his aching arm, worked through the vocal, and felt the crowd's emotion. The cables had worked seamlessly and the audience loved it. He'd had enough of Johnny's caution; he was going to insist they added the cables to the tour programme from now on. Vince and Andy fired broadside chords and solos, drifting across the stage at a height of ten feet, while Joe, somersaulting above Mike's drum riser, was having more fun than ganja.

It was time for the finale. Vince, Joe and Andy slowly floated back to the stage. Vince and Andy stood at extreme left and right, while Joe planted himself in front of Mike's drums. Maxwell screamed out the final lyric, Mike smashed the terminal drum line,

55

and Vince, Joe and Andy ran towards each other and slowly rose into the air.

*

No Nation built to a climax. Silas stood at the opposite side of the stage to Johnny and nodded at the roadie controlling the suspension wires. He'd sent prayers of thanks when Maxwell approached him for assistance after Johnny had forbidden Cold Steel to use them. It was just the insurance he needed if they actually did their jobs that night, and, he had to admit, they had. He felt no remorse at ruining their perfect comeback, this was the business, baby, and he ran it. The roadie looked back at Silas and his hands moved away from the controls. Silas clenched his fist and glared at the roadie once more.

*

Johnny's fear built as the encore progressed. He forced himself to watch, and the band's building triumph made him feel even worse, knowing they'd simply fall from a greater height. Once again his nickname came back to haunt him. No Nation flared out from the speakers and Johnny's heart trip-hammered, his eyes fixed on the band's aeronautical guitar section. The song ended and their feet touched the ground. Johnny's relief was almost like arousal. Then they ran towards each other and took off once more.

*

The plan had been to come together and miss each other by inches, just like the Red Arrows. Vince and Andy took off, picking up speed, moving faster than they had at the start of the encore. They shot up, straight towards each other, remaining focussed on their playing until they both looked up at the same time, then crashed into each other a second later. Two heads smacked together, their guitars dropped to the ground while they hung senseless above the stage like a pair of gibbeted pirates. They swung slightly apart and Joe rocketed between them. His wire pulled him towards the front of the stage before it suddenly snapped and catapulted him headfirst into the seething mass of fans.

56

Chapter 9

'I'm sorry, Mister Faslane, they've both suffered head injuries, they need to have scans.'

In the middle of a teeming night-time Casualty department, Johnny could barely hear the doctor, even though he was standing next to him. Jostled by nurses wheeling patients, drunks rubbing bloodied noses and carrying vomit bowls, and a besieging army of photographers, he asked the doctor again, 'How long will that take?'

'An hour, maybe two. We have a lot of other ill people in here tonight.'

Johnny sighed and the timetable shot through his mind. A press conference had been booked for the following morning in Manchester. It was tight, but if they'd left on time they could have got there, grabbed some sleep and managed it. Now it looked increasingly unlikely. 'What about Joe?'

'Ah, Mister Dimitri. Thankfully the audience cushioned his fall somewhat. He's got several cuts and bruises, but they're superficial. He was severely traumatised by the experience though, and according to his account very nearly trampled to death.'

'He tends to dramatise.'

'Being thrown headfirst into a crowd of people from thirty feet was no dramatic invention.'

'No, but it was probably his fault.'

The doctor looked at the floor and Johnny felt himself being judged. 'Look, doc,' he said. 'Would it help if I got these damn reporters out of here?'

'I rather thought they were here at your invitation.'

'Jesus, no.'

'Then it would help the department immensely if they were asked to leave.'

'I'm already there.' Johnny marched towards the phalanx of reporters that surrounded the end cubicles in the packed treatment area. He pushed them back from the trolleys occupied by Vince, Joe and Andy, pulled the curtains around them and glared once more at the reporters. 'You've seen all you need to see. And those of you who were at the concert know how it happened. So unless you're applying for medical school, I've got three band members who need to get better. They won't do that with you around, so please leave. I won't ask so nicely a second time.'

'How prepared were the band for this stunt?' asked one reporter.

'Will there be any cancelled dates as a result?'

'How long do you think you'll last as the band's manager?'

Johnny held up his hands. 'That's it. Dixie, I want them out, now.'

Dixie shouldered through the reporters and stood next to Johnny, dwarfing him and shoving him to one side as he folded his arms and formed an impenetrable barrier. At the back, hospital security arrived and started ushering the reporters out. Johnny walked behind the curtains. Vince and Andy lay on trolleys, while Joe was sprawled in a wheelchair between them, and on either side of him, drinking beer, stood Maxwell and Mike. Johnny snatched the cans away and threw them in a nearby bin.

'Hey,' said Maxwell.

'This is a hospital,' snarled Johnny. 'You know, the same type of building you ended up in after Tokyo. Is this going to become a habit for you lot?'

'This place ain't so bad.'

'There's the small matter of needing to be in Manchester tonight. We've got a press conference in the morning and two concerts, in case you'd forgotten.'

'Hey, man.' Joe spoke from his chair. 'We didn't think there'd be any problems with the wires.'

'You mean you didn't think, period,' snapped Johnny. 'I *told* you not to do it. Maybe next time you'll listen.'

'It was an accident,' said Vince.

'Accident my arse,' said Johnny. 'An accident waiting to happen. No training, no rehearsal, no checks. Jesus.'

'Mossy said there wouldn't be a problem,' said Maxwell.

'What?' Johnny shouted. '*Mossy* said it would be okay? Let me get this right. I, me, your manager, tell you not fly around the stage like a bunch of fairies on heat, so you talk to Silas Moss, *Chainsaw*'s manager, about it instead?'

'Pretty much,' shrugged Maxwell. 'He said he'd take care of it, not to worry you about it.'

'Fucking hell,' hissed Johnny. 'I don't know who's the biggest wanker, him for kissing your arses or you lot for going behind my back. And now we're delayed in London for God knows how long.'

'Oh, chill out,' said Andy. 'You're always finding problems with everything. Andreas wouldn't have been on our case about any of this.'

'Yes, and look where he's ended up.'

'Boys. Oh, boys.' A husky, feminine voice drifted towards Johnny and the curtains opened. He turned around and looked at a tall Asian girl in jeans, stilt-like heels and dark glasses that covered most of her face. She walked up to the band and Johnny wondered where the all-areas pass nestled between her barely covered breasts had come from. 'It's okay,' she purred. 'They'll be doing the scans soon.'

'Who the hell are you?' asked Johnny.

'I'm Florence,' she said.

'Florence?'

'Yes,' she giggled. 'I'm the tour medic. Who are you?'

'Who am I? Who am I?' Johnny felt his face flushing and he knew that within seconds his mostly visible head would be redder than a match-top. 'I'm Johnny Faslane, the band's manager, and we *don't* have a tour medic.'

'Oh, sure you do, sweetie. I've been with the band since Bangkok. Andreas took care of everything.'

'Really? Well, darling, Andreas isn't around anymore and we don't have a tour medic. As you can see, we're in a hospital, so we don't need you.'

'But Andreas —'

'I don't give a shit what Andreas said. We don't have a tour medic.' He grabbed her pass and pulled it away from her, snapping the string that held it around her neck. 'Now, unless you've got some other function around here, go home.'

'You bastard!'

Florence slapped him hard and Johnny's face exploded with pain. His head flew to one side, his vision starshelled, and she spun around, her heels clicking into the distance, while at the far end of the department, cameras flashed as the few remaining reporters photographed her departure.

Chapter 10

Crammed into a people-carrier, with Dixie sitting next to the driver, Johnny glared at the band.

'What?' asked Maxwell. 'No damage done at the hospital. All the scans were clear, and we're headed to Manchester.'

'We're four hours late,' snapped Johnny. 'And we're not there yet.'

'So we're a few hours late, big deal. It's not like we're going to miss the gig.'

'No,' said Johnny. 'But the press conference will have to be put back, which will piss them off no end. They're already smelling blood after the way the concert ended.'

'But it was the encore, the *end* of the encore.'

'Bloody lucky for you. Any earlier and Ozone would have classed it as an early finish, and you know what would have happened then.'

'Bollocks, mate. We couldn't have asked for a better homecoming gig.'

'What? Vince and Andy using each other's heads as blunt instruments, and Joe doing a kamikaze into the crowd?'

'We did a great show until then.'

'Yes, Maxwell, *until* then. And that's the big factor that'll have you lot bent over and your arses used as bike stands. Jesus, what is it with bands? You work your butts off to get success, and once it lands in your lap, all you want to do is have it taken away from you.'

'It's a short life, mate, but a merry one.'

'What?'

'Didn't take him long, did it?' asked Mike.

'I don't follow,' said Johnny.

'Apparently that was the main recruiting line for pirates,' said Mike. 'Maxwell's obsession when he's not singing and giving you a hard time.'

'I'd heard that about you lot. So it's true, then?'

'Well, true about Maxwell, maybe. The rest of us just have it rammed down our throats twenty-four seven.'

Johnny looked at Maxwell, who pointedly stared out of the window as the night-time landscape shot past. 'I guess that onstage ship had to come from somewhere,' he said.

*

Overnight road works, diversions and single-lane delays behind slow-moving trucks ate even further into Johnny's projected timeline. Low cloud and fine, spraying rain occluded the rising sun and a grey dawn welcomed the band into Manchester. Squeezed next to each other like a loft full of roosting pigeons, the band snoozed until bumps in he road woke them up and they knocked into each other. By the time the car whispered to a halt outside the hotel's red-carpeted entrance at nine o'clock in the morning, tempers were filed down to nothing.

Johnny rubbed his eyes clear while the black-and-grey-clad porter slid open the car door. He climbed out and loosened up, then waited for the band to come awake. 'Right, then,' he said. 'Notice how nice this hotel is. I don't expect to be evicted from it because you lot want to act like pricks, understand? You're all going straight to bed. Don't even *touch* the televisions. No room service, no shower parties, and no music either. There'll be plenty of time to wild it up after the gig, not before. The press conference this morning isn't going to happen until this afternoon, by which time you lot will have slept and showered – in *that* order.'

'What if the press won't wait?' asked Maxwell.

'They don't have a choice. The first thing I'm doing is rescheduling. Now, I don't need to tell you what a bunch of tossers the press are. They're going to be pissed off enough at having the conference postponed, so *try* and keep them friendly, all right? Now get some sleep, you'll need it.'

Johnny escorted the band to reception, where porters silently ushered them to the waiting lifts and their suites. Johnny followed, half-wishing he could put a guard outside each of their doors. After being shown his own room, he switched on his phone.

'Lucy Penhalligan.'

'Lucy, hi. It's Johnny Faslane.' He ran a hand over his unwashed stubble.

'Johnny. You've had a busy time. What do you think of London hospitals?'

'Jesus, how did you know?'

62

'Twenty thousand people saw it at the concert, we're in a world of instant news via social media, and it's my job. Luckily it happened too late to hit the tabloids, but it's all over the news sites.'

'The band will be keeping their feet firmly on the stage for the rest of the tour, believe me.'

'At least you're not making excuses. Good job it happened at the end of the show.'

'That's exactly what I told them.'

'Then I hope they listen to you more than they did Andreas. So why are you calling, other than to have told me about last night?'

'Vince and Andy's scans were clear, but it's delayed us; we need to reschedule the press conference.'

'Where are you now?'

'We've just arrived at Manchester.'

'What about re-equipping the band?'

'Sarin Sound have a sample setup for tonight's show, Soundsphere the same tomorrow. The band will pick the best package.'

'That's good. We'll authorise costs if they can supply for the rest of the tour. The Japanese are kicking their heels with the release of the gear.' Slight pause. 'We can put back the conference till one o'clock, but I don't want any more delays, understand?'

'Got it.'

'And you'd better stay out of the news as well.'

'*Me?*'

'Check the sites before the conference.'

*

Johnny's irritating mobile phone alarm dragged him awake and he stared at the room's ornate ceiling. There was an hour to go before the press conference and he was nervous. He'd never done one before, but he knew how irate reporters became when they had to hang around for people whom *they* thought were less important than them.

He emerged from the steaming, multi-jet shower and almost wept with joy at the huge cooked breakfast that arrived from room service. He pulled on his clothes, freshly laundered – another perk from his sudden rise in status – then wolfed down his meal. After filling and emptying his impossibly small teacup four times, he

63

walked towards the band's suites, the hard heels of his off-white boots making no sound on the deep pile carpet.

He flickered from one comatose rock star's room to the next, his hopes of finding any of them awake fading. He couldn't even *find* Maxwell in the suite's echoing emptiness, and he realised he'd have to face the media on his own. Leaving a hastily scribbled note stuck to the wide-screen television that thankfully was still in place, he headed for the ground floor like a condemned man off to face the firing party.

His apprehension grew as he reached the large meeting room. Rows of cheap plastic chairs sat incongruously on brand new red carpeting. On a raised platform at the far end, another six empty chairs stood behind a table covered with a simple white cloth. He climbed onto the platform, his footsteps loud in the empty room. He sat down, poured himself a glass of water and sipped his drink. The clock on the wall behind him approached the hour, and one reporter after another silently filed in, sat down, and looked up at him with disillusioned eyes. Johnny's trousers stuck uncomfortably to his legs, and a stocky journalist stuck up his hand and pointedly asked him where the bleeding hell Cold Steel were.

'We didn't come here to talk to *you*,' he said. 'We want to hear what Cold Steel have to say.'

'I'm Johnny Faslane, the band's manager.'

'Ozone's panic measure, you mean.'

'Meaning?'

The reporter smirked. 'You're hardly top drawer, mate. Who were you with previously?'

'We're here to talk about Cold Steel, not *my* résumé. Now, the band have just completed a very long journey from London. They've got a sell-out concert tonight, and right now their priority is to make sure they're ready for it. So if that means they've got to spend more time in bed than talking to you lot, that's what they'll do.'

'Look.' The reporter stabbed his pen in Johnny's direction. 'We came here for a press conference with Cold Steel, and they'd better bloody well be here. One word from us and they'll end up with zero publicity. Don't forget, *we* made this band.'

'The hell you did,' snapped Johnny. 'Cold Steel got where they are through hard work, talent and loyal fans. And anyway, your

64

paper *never* gives them a good press. If you're not happy with what's on offer here, then bugger off and cover some bloody boy band instead. Go on, piss off and leave the real reporting to the music press.'

Without realising, Johnny was standing up, his clenched fists braced on the table as he leant over it and glared at the reporter. An electric anticipation crackled around the hall, and he forced himself to sit back down, while above his gleaming forehead, which still glowed angry and red beneath its thin covering of hair, the clock struck one. He took a deep breath.

'Right then. Welcome to Cold Steel's press conference, and thank you for turning up. First of all, let me apologise for having to postpone the proceedings. I'm sure you all know about the mishap at the end of last night's concert. As a result of our delay in getting here, the band got very little sleep, and with a concert tonight I'm sure you all understand how important it is that they're fully rested.'

A trouser-suited woman stood up. 'Rachel Shaw, entertainment desk, World News. After Spain and Portugal were cancelled, last night wasn't a good start to the European leg of the tour, with three of the five band members being taken to hospital after their midair collision.'

'A precaution, that's all.'

'A precaution? Vince Fire and Andy Stains hanging unconscious above the stage, and Joe Dimitri catapulted into the audience. I'd say they were lucky to be alive.'

Muted chuckles percolated around the large room. 'They're tougher than they look,' countered Johnny.

'They would have to be. How's Maxwell's arm?'

'It'll heal twice as quickly after your concern.' Johnny's quip drew more laughs.

'And the cancelled shows?'

'They'll be Cold Steel's first concerts after their next album. Same venues, all tickets valid.'

Straight black hair framed Rachel's heart-shaped face and she fired a tiny smile at Johnny. 'Who knows what will happen before then?'

'Before then, Cold Steel's European tour will continue. Then they'll take some time off before making another album.'

'You hope.'

'I know. I've got the band's back, Rachel, and I believe in them one hundred per cent.'

'Of course do you, Johnny, you're dependent on them.'

'Meaning?'

'We all know about Andreas P's problems in Japan. Then you suddenly turn up running a press conference for the band. That's a lucky break for someone no one's ever heard of before.'

'You think they should manage themselves?'

'I think they'd be in an even worse state than they are now if that happened.'

'Then it's a good job I happened to be around, isn't it?'

'I don't think Florence would agree with you.'

'Florence?' Johnny noticed some other reporters grinning.

'I take it you haven't been online today?'

'No, I've been a little busy making sure the band got here.'

'Of course you have. Maybe it would have been easier if you hadn't tried to blackmail the tour doctor?'

'What?'

'Florence? You know her, Johnny. Tall elegant Thai girl.'

'We don't have a tour doctor, we never have. If you mean that hanger-on who claimed to be a tour *medic,* sure, I showed her the door last night. But I didn't blackmail her. I didn't need to.'

'Not what she says.'

'And of course you're never going to believe me, are you?'

'She claims you offered to keep her on, but only if she slept with you.'

Johnny's whole body jerked as though he'd been plugged into the mains, and Lucy's words from that morning scythed through his mind. 'That's unbelievable,' he spluttered. 'What else has she said? It's bloody slander. I said no such thing.'

'She's gone to a lot of trouble to say otherwise to the news networks.'

'And I'm sure the thought of getting paid for a juicy story meant nothing to her.'

'She's got to finance her gender reassignment somehow.'

'Her what?'

'Come on, Johnny. You didn't know? She says it's what drew you to her.'

'Oh, Jesus.' Johnny ran a shaking hand through the remains of his hair. 'Look, Rachel, all I saw last night was a Thai girl claiming a free trip with the band. I told her to sling her hook, and that's it. The truth can be pretty boring, can't it? Now, can we get back to Cold Steel?'

He looked around the hall and pointed at a longhaired, denim-clad reporter.

'After the disappointment at the Tokyo concert, and having to cancel some of the European dates, Cold Steel came out fighting last night. Can we expect more of the same for the rest of the UK shows?'

'We ain't even started yet!'

Johnny looked to the back of the hall, and relief washed through him as he saw the band. 'Get ready for salvation,' Maxwell boomed. '''Cos we're here to unlock your souls.'

Everyone in the now-packed room turned to follow Johnny's gaze. Maxwell stood at the hall's double-door entranceway, flanked by the rest of the band. At the sides of the hall, a scattering of die-hard metal fans cheered. The band strode towards the speaking platform and sat down. Johnny leant towards Maxwell. 'Where the hell have you been?'

'Fashionably late.' He grinned at Johnny, cracked open a two-litre bottle of whiskey and took a large gulp before passing it round. 'Brides do it all the time. I'm told it builds suspense.' He turned towards the reporters. 'Right then. What are we gonna talk about?'

The press conference defibrillated into life. Johnny pushed back his chair and sat in silence as, like a battleship's broadside, questions were fired at the band. They ranged far beyond the musical aspects of Cold Steel's lives, and for the next hour all five musicians were interrogated. Banked along the hall's sides, cameras recorded everything, and Johnny resolved to get a copy. A shortened, more concentrated version would make a stunning introduction to a film of the tour.

'I don't know what he was getting so shirty about, I only wanted to shag his daughter.' Vince Fire.

'Playing the drums feels like punching a reporter.' Mike Vesuvius.

67

'Scared? Hey man, I shat my pants and screamed like a woman.' Joe Dimitri.

'What's my favourite chat-up line? "Bite the pillow, baby, I'm coming in dry."' Andy Stains.

'If you've never been to a Cold Steel concert, then you might just as well be a virgin.' Maxwell.

The press conference tanked onwards, and at two o'clock Johnny intervened. The hall reluctantly released its occupants, and Johnny watched the handful of fans at the back move forward. Poignant memories of himself as a teenager shot through his mind, and he made no objection as they produced cameras. Photographs were taken as tour programmes, CD covers, T-shirts and even underwear changed hands, returned minutes later with musicians' names scrawled all over them, before the fans dispersed like sea mist.

Chapter 11

Sarin's sound system climbed above both sides of the MEN's stage like silent black watchtowers, and Johnny looked at the band's approving stares. *Finally got something right,* he thought. 'Same as before, lads,' he said. 'Sound check before anything else.'

'Again?' whined Maxwell.

'Yes, Maxwell, again. We're trying out the speakers, and it's your opinion we want. Tomorrow night it's Soundsphere's turn, and I need your input on both sets, unless of course you want to run on borrowed gear for the rest of your lives.'

The band shambled towards the stage while Johnny stalked towards the dressing room in search of Silas Moss.

*

'Johnny, you're getting this way out of perspective.'

Johnny grabbed Silas' jacket and threw him against the dressing room wall. 'I don't think so,' he growled. 'I specifically told them not to use those cables, and *you* encouraged them.'

'I wanted them to do a good show, that's all. That's what any *decent* manager would want.'

'That doesn't include you then, does it?'

'And what about you, new boy? You can't have that much control over your band if you let another manager help them out with effects.'

'Yes,' snarled Johnny. Their noses were almost touching as he stared into Silas' eyes. 'And if you try anything like that again, I'll use what's left of your hair as a bog brush!'

*

Johnny walked back into the arena and watched the band. A full, rich sound flowed through the Sarin speakers, and Cold Steel's growing confidence was palpable. They stalked around the stage, got used to the dimensions and played off each other's talent. Johnny's emotions always came alive when he watched live heavy metal, and soon he was tapping his feet and nodding his head to the sound of Cold Steel.

The sound check firecrackered to a halt and the band vanished backstage to the large takeaway Johnny had ordered, while the road crew swarmed over the abandoned stage and prepared it for Chainsaw.

With the returning hush, Johnny walked over to the mid-arena mixing desk and its tangle of cables and control switches, and he felt the road crew's rising excitement. They might not have been the ones onstage, but they were still part of the magic. The doors opened and the cavernous arena began to fill up with fans, and Johnny felt a mounting sense of pride at his own involvement. He had no idea how many concerts he'd been to over the years, but he never lost the feeling, the delicious, addictive anticipation every time the lights dimmed and the crowd roared.

He could taste the tension all around him. A metal playlist poured from the sound system, the human congestion built and the expectation became a physical thing. He changed from his normal backstage spot, deciding to stay at the mixing desk and get a fan's view of Chainsaw. The floodlights went out and he joined in the avalanche of cheers that greeted Chainsaw, who invaded the stage as though they owned it, cocksure and proud of themselves, their guitars slung across leather-clad shoulders. Zip Fly, skinny, almost anorexic, leant against the microphone stand, then grabbed it as though it was a penis substitute, and put on a display of simulated masturbation that was guaranteed to have the tabloids baying for his public execution. Inside the arena, it was all part of the show, and along with everyone else, Johnny threw a clenched fist into the air and yelled himself hoarse. Seconds later, his eardrums compressed inside his head and a titanic burst of sound hit him. Chainsaw had begun.

*

Joe meandered outside for a smoke once Chainsaw's set started, and he sparked up with shaking hands. The night before had been a bad scene, man. He'd feared for his life when the cable snapped and the crowd stomped him, although he appreciated Johnny's presence at the hospital. *Andreas wouldn't have been there like Johnny was, even if he did bollock us sideways.*

Maybe Johnny was right; maybe they were blowing their ride. Either way, things needed to chill. He just needed to get back to some regular smokes and his music. Why couldn't things be simple anymore?

'You okay, Joe?' Silas appeared at the doorway.

'Oh, hey Mossy.'

'Look, Joe, I had no idea how things would turn out last night.'

'That's okay, man. I guess these things happen.'

'No harm done?'

'Just to my nerves. I wish I had a bit more weed to get me through the gig.' Joe shuddered. 'I'd rather we had a night off.'

'What's your normal take?'

'Black Moroccan,' Joe grinned. 'Don't get any on your clothes, man. This is my last one, though. You haven't got any, have you? There's no way I'm asking Johnny.'

'Ever tried Nederhash?'

'Nederhash? What's that?'

'Fresh from Holland. Good stuff.'

'You got some?'

Silas pulled out two joints and handed one to Joe. 'I've got plenty. We'll smoke some together.'

*

For over an hour, Johnny stood intoxicated by Chainsaw's power, watching them surge through one riff-fuelled song after another. Then, just before the end of their last song, he made his way to the mosh-pit, the vibrant, boiling mass of fans closest to the stage, where they jumped around like demons for the entire concert. He skirted around its edge, wistfully remembering his youth. Clothing and hairstyle had changed over the years, but little else had, and Johnny longed to cast aside his responsibilities and mosh the night away. He flashed his all-area pass to a security guard, then walked through the narrow corridors that led to Cold Steel's cramped dressing room. Once again he faced false virtue from the band sitting before the dregs of their takeaway.

'Don't give me that,' he said. 'You must have done something.'

'What it is to be trusted,' sighed Maxwell.

'What it is to earn it.' Johnny looked at Joe, who appeared asleep in his chair. 'Is he alright?'

'Went outside for a smoke,' said Vince, rolling his eyes. 'Know what I mean?'

'How much did he smoke?' Johnny looked closer. 'Christ, he's never this stoned.' He slapped Joe's face, who groaned and made vague waving motions with his hands. 'Shit. Joe. Joe!'

Johnny shook Joe and threw a cup of water in his face.

'Hey, man,' he mumbled. 'Is the show over yet?'

Johnny dragged him to his feet. Joe swayed but managed to stand.

'Joe!' Johnny shouted. 'What have you been smoking?'

'Nederhash, man, mixed with Spice. Shared some with Mossy.'

'That bastard!'

'What's he talking about?' asked Maxwell.

'Nederhash is Dutch weed, strong as hell. Spice is a synthetic, also guaranteed to blow your head off. Shared it with Mossy, my arse. I bet he gave Joe the whole lot. Shit on a flagpole, he could be out of it for hours. What does Joe normally spark up with?'

Maxwell shrugged. 'Just weed. I thought that shit was all the same.'

'Yeah, and I bet Joe did too. Mossy knew otherwise though, I'm sure.'

'What are we going to do? We're on in half an hour.'

'Get him under a shower and ram as much coffee down his neck as you can without choking him.'

'What about Mossy?'

'Leave him to me.'

*

Johnny stalked through the backstage area, looking for Silas. He found him in Chainsaw's dressing room, standing with his back to him. Johnny spun him round and sent a fist crashing into his jaw. Silas sprawled on the ground and Chainsaw backed away from Johnny's white-hot fury.

'Stay away from Cold Steel, you interfering bastard! And the rest of you…' He glared molten granite at Chainsaw. 'Keep your manager out of my sight for a bloody long time. He's tried fucking us over twice now, so you'd better not give me a single reason to kick the whole lot of you off the tour.'

*

'Cold Steel! Cold Steel! Cold Steel!'

The audience chant filtered down to the dressing room as Johnny returned. 'What's happening with Joe?'

'See for yourself,' said Maxwell.

Joe sat jellied on a chair, soaked through from being showered with his clothes still on. Dirty coffee stains ran down the corners of his mouth and dotted the high colour pattern of his shirt.

72

'Is he talking?' asked Johnny.

'Just barely.'

'Shit.'

'We can always go on late,' said Maxwell. 'How long does that stuff last?'

'Spice and Nederhash mix? Christ, he could be like this for hours.'

'Isn't there an antidote?'

'Sure there is. Not taking it in the first place.'

'So what do we do?'

'Well, you're not going on late. There's an eleven o'clock curfew at the MEN and that doesn't change for anyone. You start late, you do a short set, and that will piss everyone off. Somebody get this stoner a bass and see if he can even hold it.'

*

'It's not looking good,' said Johnny.

'It's not sounding good either,' replied Maxwell.

Joe plucked at the bass strings with little attention to timing.

'At least he knows to hold it right,' said Mike.

'Yeah,' said Andy. 'And not much else.'

'It's your call, Johnny,' said Vince.

'Well, first of all, you're going on. On time.'

'But –'

'But nothing. If you go on late, you'll play a short-change show and Ozone will skin you alive.'

'How can we play with Joe like this?'

'You can't, this is what we'll do. Vince, Andy, which one of your guitars has the lowest range?'

'I've got an SG that'll hit rock bottom,' said Andy.

'Right, here's what's going to happen. Vince, you're playing lead guitar, Andy, set up the SG, thickest strings, lowest octave going, play rhythm only. That'll cover for the bass.'

'What about Joe?'

'He's going out as well, with his volume on mute. When he starts coming round enough to play, we'll turn him up and swap Andy's SG for a regular guitar.'

'That's not bad,' said Maxwell. 'Not ideal, but not bad.'

*

73

Maxwell followed Johnny to the monitor station and then stopped. The house lights dipped and the crowd roared. He felt the band's presence behind him. He'd sung at hundreds, thousands of concerts, but his insides still churned as he faced the fans. *They've put it there for you by being here tonight. Don't let them down.* He could hear 'Cold Steel! Cold Steel!' being chanted over and over again. No time to delay. He took a deep breath and strode onto the stage. His senses danced with adrenaline, and the wall of screams swept over him like the sea. He saluted the audience with a raised fist, and from the peripheries of his vision he saw Vince and Andy pick up their guitars.

Sinners Sanctuary opened up without its distinctive bass line. At the monitor station, Johnny shoved Joe out onto the stage. He sprawled flat on his arse, and looked imploringly at Johnny who stared granite-faced back at him. Joe struggled to his feet and stared intently at the strings.

Mike's drum-thud exploded from the speakers, Andy's low-pitched riffs gave a passable bass cover and the audience exulted. Maxwell, bare-chested but already sweating under the spotlights' harsh glare, felt a rushing excitation fuse through him. Ignoring the residual pain in his left arm, he stepped forward and grasped the mike stand, temporarily blinded as the spotlights flared.

The band lashed through Sinners Sanctuary, and despite Andy's cover, it sounded limp and weak without Joe's thudding bass lines. He was barely pulling the strings in time and Maxwell's frustration bit chunks out of his insides. They'd survived Tokyo, they had shown in London that they *could* still play, and now Joe was shrivelling away onstage, dragging the rest down with him. He took the band straight into Women Wanted for Cash, but still Joe blundered around like a fifty-year-old boxer after his last fight. Andy's reworked guitar filled some of the void while Vince struggled with two solos. It was four band members doing the work of five, and thanks to Johnny's idea it was workable, but still noticeable. *He saved our butts this time and no mistake,* thought Maxwell.

*

At the monitor station, the sound engineer's hands flew over the dials and screens and Johnny concentrated on the band. For the last half hour, Joe had come round enough to have his lines played

74

through the speakers. Dixie scuttled onstage with Andy's regular Fender, and fresh life breathed into the band's performance. Johnny wondered what the audience reaction would be, if they would notice. The rest of the band – he had to admit – had done an inspired job in covering for Joe, and the sound system provided by Jack Sarin was sharp and clear. But the changed roles had left a slick of fatigue around the band, and the concert churned to a finish, followed by an encore that trickled energy instead of flame-throwing it. He followed the band back to the dressing room.

'Are you awake yet?' he asked Joe.

'Kind of,' he mumbled. 'What happened, man?'

'Mossy fed you as many super-joints as you wanted. You've been off your face for most of the concert.'

'He didn't say anything about that.'

'Of course he didn't. And if he offers you any more, what are you going to say?'

'Er, no?'

'Bloody right, no.'

Joe nodded off at the back of the dressing room.

'Right,' said Johnny. 'For the four of you who can still see straight, tonight was your chance to test the Sarin system. What did you think?'

'We'd welcome your thoughts, mate,' murmured Maxwell.

'It's not up to me, for Christ's sake. You're the musicians; you're the ones using the stuff. It's my job to get what you want; it's your job to use it. So what did you think?'

Vince turned to Maxwell. 'I think this might be a bad time to ask him, Max.'

'A bad time to ask me what?' said Johnny.

'Well,' said Maxwell. 'We've had a bit of a rough time lately.'

'Yes,' said Johnny. 'And you can thank yourselves for that. You've also had a two-week holiday in Japan, and any problems in the UK have all been your fault, or maybe someone held a gun to your heads and told you to chuck a telly out of the hotel window? Or perhaps you were forced to go skydiving at the end of the London gig, and maybe Joe's life depended on him having zero sense when it comes to smoking weed? Stop me any time if you think I'm wrong.'

'You're not wrong, mate. You're not wrong.'

75

'Bloody right I'm not. So what were you going to ask me?'

'Maybe this isn't the time.'

'Maxwell, is there *ever* going to be a good time?'

'Oh, ask him,' said Vince. 'He's going to say no anyway.'

'Say no to what?'

'I can't wait to watch this.' Vince sat back, smiled and opened a beer.

'Well, mate…' Maxwell looked back at the rest of the band as he spoke. 'It's like this. Piracy's not just a hobby of mine, it's kind of an obsession.'

'Yeah,' said Andy. 'Don't we know it. Your house is decked out like an admiral's bridge, and as for going to bleeding museums when the rest of us are on the piss, say hello to Mister Middle-aged over there.'

'Really?' asked Johnny, intrigued.

'They're exaggerating,' said Maxwell. 'I went to two museums once on a previous tour.'

'For a week at a time,' said Andy. 'Flown there especially and ten grand added to the costs.'

'Sounds like an obsession to me,' said Johnny.

'It's better than some bands who go mooning after comic book characters, or starting their own commune, or collecting guns,' replied Maxwell.

'All right,' said Johnny. 'You've got my attention. So what do you want to ask me?'

'Well,' said Maxwell. 'So now you know I've got an interest in the subject, and it just happens that I've got a lead.'

'So you're a detective now?'

'Call me an anorak with long hair. You heard of Blackbeard?'

'He was a pirate, wasn't he?'

'Yes, and he died without anyone knowing where he'd buried his loot.'

'Assuming he buried it at all,' sniped Vince.

'Had to have done,' persisted Maxwell. 'Everyone's heard of him. He fleeced Charlestown, went legit, became a gentleman, made a fortune. So what happened to his treasure?'

'Spent it, drank it, shagged it,' said Andy. 'Without visiting any museums.'

'Yeah,' said Mike. 'This short life and a merry one you're always on about, that's what he did. No wonder he was skint when he died. All of these pirates you've gone on about for years either died without a penny or got strung up.'

Maxwell looked at Johnny. 'They've heard all this before, mate. But four years ago, on our last tour, I had a new lead, a *real* lead.'

'A lead for what?' asked Johnny.

'Blackbeard's treasure.' The rest of the band groaned at Maxwell's words, but he stared at Johnny with a zealot's intensity. 'I met a fan backstage who showed me a map he'd won in a card game over in the States.'

'And?'

'And it's the real deal. I knew it straight away. Bought it off him for five grand.'

'*Five grand* for a map?'

'I'd have paid twenty and called it a bargain.'

'What the hell is this map of?'

'An island with no name and some writing on the back. A date.'

'That's it?'

'Dated seventeen-fifteen.'

'So this map's actually that old?'

'Seems to be.'

'And what's the significance of the date?' asked Johnny.

'I checked it out,' said Maxwell. 'And it corresponds to a dated entry in Blackbeard's log. His complete log survived his last battle. I read it myself on a trip to Carolina. On the same date written on the back of the map, Blackbeard took a navigational reading and plotted it in the log.'

'And this point is where, exactly?'

'That's the interesting part. On that date, the log states they were in open sea, no landmarks. So why put an empty bit of sea as a signpost for a missing island?'

'I don't understand.'

'Join the bloody club, mate,' said Andy.

'Don't you see?' Maxwell persisted. 'That navigation heading isn't a blank spot of sea; it's where this island is. The log is *calling* it a blank bit of sea, but the map is telling us that it's a reference for the island. I'm guessing this map wasn't meant for anyone to see, it was a secret, and only Blackbeard knew about it. The map

77

on its own, the log on its own, meant nothing. Put them together and you've got some buried treasure, and it was a secret that died with him.'

'Until now?' asked Johnny.

'Until now,' said Maxwell. 'So what do you say?'

'What do you mean, what do I say? What do I say to what?'

'After the tour's done, how about us looking for it?'

'What? You want to go looking for an island with no name, based on a reading in a three-hundred-year-old ship's log that says open sea?'

'One way of looking at it, I suppose.'

'And there's another way?'

'We'd be following some pretty strong leads and finding a long-dead pirate's buried treasure.'

'You *are* joking, Maxwell.'

'I've never been more serious.'

Johnny spluttered and waved his hands for five seconds while he struggled to find something to say. 'Jesus.' More hand-waving. 'Fuck.' Head-shaking. 'Fuck a duck.' He paced around the dressing room.

'Is that a yes?' asked Maxwell.

'Is it bollocks. Where are all these clues leading you, anyway?'

'The Caribbean, mate. Where else?'

'Well, I'm not one to piss on your fire, but at the end of this tour you're all headed straight for the studio. And even if everything runs immaculately from now on, which I seriously doubt, you bastards have got a lot of lost ground to make up with Ozone, *and* your fans. You won't do that by swanning off on a treasure hunt.'

'Hey, Johnny. Lots of bands take a break after their tour.'

'Yeah, and lots of bands earn it as well. That doesn't describe Cold Steel.'

'And suppose we do turn things around?'

'Oh, Christ, Maxwell. Listen, if you five don't get a grip, you won't even see mainland Europe, and you sure as hell won't get back to the studio to make your next album, which incidentally had better be good. I don't think you realise just how much shit you're in with Ozone, or how nasty they really are.'

'Come on, we're not *that* unpopular.'

78

'He's coming round now. Wake up, Sir. It's the police. You're safe now.'

Johnny groaned and stirred. His nose throbbed and he coughed snot and dried blood on the deep pile carpet, then rolled over. He felt like his brain had been scooped out and replaced with a million hammers and gongs that kept up a deafening, throbbing mass of noise that took him to the brink of insanity. He looked up at a kneeling policeman who surely should have been at school. *So it really is a sign of getting old,* he thought. 'Can you remember what happened, Sir?' asked the policeman.

'Fight,' mumbled Johnny. 'A fight.'

'We know that,' chuckled the policeman. 'That's why we were called. Can you remember who started it?'

'He's their manager,' said another voice, further away. Johnny sat up, groaned and held his head as the movement sent lances of pain down his spine.

'Tequila,' stuttered Johnny. 'Tequila. Tried to stop them.'

'Never come between a drunk and his tequila,' smiled the policeman. 'Unless you've got pava spray and handcuffs.'

'What?' asked Johnny.

'That's pretty much what we had to do here. Eleven arrested and you on the floor, senseless.'

'Arrested?'

'All eleven. There were more fists flying in here than a Manchester derby. They're probably still being booked in at the station.'

*

Johnny sat in a taxi being driven to the police station, wondering if the band would be released before the concert. His phone rang and he glanced at the screen: it was the Ozone switchboard and he prayed he wasn't being patched through to Randall.

'Johnny Faslane.'

'I've got a Rachel Shaw for you.' A click, and Johnny repeated his name.

'I hear your boys were in trouble last night.'

'Good news travels fast. What did you think of the concert?'

'Unusual bass line.'

'Yeah, well, the band like to experiment.' Johnny heard her chuckle. He imagined her tightly curved figure, remembered her cheeky grin and found himself smiling.

'So where are you headed now?' she asked.

'Sounds like you're about to tell me.'

'Oh, I heard about a few accommodation issues last night.'

'Funny you should say that.' Johnny knew he'd be crucified for lying, but he wasn't about to tell a reporter, even a good-looking one, the *whole* truth. And he was damned if he was going to mention their potato-brained plans to go looking for buried treasure.

'There's all sorts of rumours flying around,' she said. 'Maybe we should meet, and you can tell me exactly what happened.'

'Christ. I get slapped by Florence, and you hammered me for it at the press conference. What the hell's going to happen if I *meet* you?'

'It's work, Johnny. We're not dating. Well, not yet.'

'So I'm your boyfriend now?'

'Interesting insight into your dreams.'

Johnny laughed and the taxi pulled up outside the police station. 'Look,' he said. 'I'm busy right now. Text me your number, I'll call you.'

*

'But I'm their manager,' said Johnny. 'Why can't I see them?'

The duty solicitor smiled and looked at Johnny over half-rimmed glasses. 'It's purely procedure, Mister Faslane.' He brushed non-existent dust from his pinstriped suit. 'You were involved in the disturbance, you're a potential witness, and if you see any of the detained gentlemen, there is a possibility, however slight, that they might try to influence you when it comes to your statement, should that be required.'

'So, what now?' Johnny sat in a small room at the Victorian custody suite. White-painted brick walls and a windowless metal door made the place look as much like a cell as the ones he imagined Cold Steel, Chainsaw and Silas were currently in.

The solicitor looked at his watch and smiled once more. 'They've been in custody for more than six hours, so the police will consider them sober, which means they can be interviewed.'

'And then?'

84

'It depends on the interview.' The solicitor looked at the papers in front of him. 'Affray, criminal damage, and additionally Misters Fly and Stains for resisting arrest.'

'And what does that mean in real terms? Are they going to jail?'

'Unlikely. However, the hotel manager has already made a statement, and they will be seeking recovery of costs.'

'That's not a problem. If they've got any sense, the bands will cough the cash. If they're feeling stupid, they'll get the record company to do it.'

'Stupid?'

'Cold Steel are one screw up away from getting booted by Ozone, and Chainsaw are in danger of not even being picked up in the first place.'

'I see. Well, Mister Faslane, it may favour a resolution if that were made apparent to your colleagues. As long as there is a broad agreement by the arrested persons to both admit their offences and agree to costs, we may look forward to cautions, fixed penalty fines and their release in a few hours.'

'As long as that's *all* it is. They're cutting it fine for sound check, *again*. One more thing.'

'Yes?'

'The word's already out about the arrests. There'll be a lot of press interest in this place once they come out. Can the Police release people in a discreet manner?'

'I'll ask them and see what can be done.'

*

Johnny looked at his watch for the hundredth time, and expecting little welcome from the hotel, he was taken by taxi back to the arena. With the Sarin system being dismantled and set aside for Soundsphere's setup, he sat in the empty dressing room, flipped open his laptop and checked the news sites. After everything that had happened, he doubted the coverage would focus on the music. As he started reading, his phone rang.

'Johnny Faslane.'

'Faslane, you dumbass limey fuck, this is Randall Spitz.'

Iced fear stabbed through Johnny's chest. 'Randall,' he stammered, 'good to hear you.'

'Don't give me that, you goddam liar, even my mistress hates the sound of my voice. What's this I've been hearing about your boys?'

Johnny was worried about what Randall knew, terrified about what Randall knew. 'What have you heard?'

'Too goddamn much is what I've heard. I've heard the dumb fucks did a midair collision after the London show, I've heard that Dimitri was so goddamn stoned last night he could barely stand, and then after the concert both bands have been frigging arrested. Tell me I'm wrong, you bastard.'

Johnny rested his forehead in his hands. 'You're not wrong, Randall.'

'A least you're goddamn honest. So what are you doing about it?'

'Well,' flustered Johnny, 'the London show was just one of those things. You might say the band were trying *too* hard.'

'Trying too hard to get their asses shitcanned, you mean.'

'No. They knew they were down to a basic stage, they just wanted to add to it.'

'You knew about it?'

A pause. 'No.'

'They had to have had help.'

'It's taken care of.'

'You gonna tell me who it is?'

'Not if you don't want me to.'

'If you're taking care of it, take care of it. So what the fuck happened at the hotel?'

'Some after-concert drinks, emotions were running high, things got a little out of hand.'

'A *little*? The damage reports from the hotel don't read little.'

'I've spoken to the band's solicitor about that. He's advising them they'd be better off paying for the damages themselves.'

'Goddamn right. If those mofos request a dime from us I'll come over there myself to shove it up their asses. What's the publicity doing over there?'

'Everything offstage is pure gold for the tabloids.'

'So what else is new? What about the shows?'

Johnny looked on his laptop. 'London was positive. The midair collision was close enough to the end to avoid any negative comments. Some of the reports thought it was part of the act.'

'Stupid bastards. What about last night?'

'Joe's coming in for some shit, he was clearly out of it, Andy played low-end guitar to cover until he came round.'

'Smart move. Now, you put Dimitri – in fact, you put all of those motherfuckers straight. We're watching them, and if they fuck up any more, they're history. Their asses depend on good reviews, *and* an expanded fan base leading to a clear increase in album sales. Was Dimitri holding his stash anywhere near the tour?'

'No.' Johnny blushed. 'It was given to him.'

'Who gave?'

Johnny hesitated.

'Don't wanna say?'

'I've got my eye on it, Randall.'

'And what about this cooze from Thailand? Florence? She's got a big goddamn mouth when it comes the press.'

'She's got her own agenda, she wants to make money any way she can. Cold Steel were just in the wrong place at the wrong time with her, she won't be in our hair for long.'

'Listen, pal. We think you've done pretty well so far. Lucy tells me good things about you. I know about your work on the sound system, and that's what we want. But you've been dragged up from the crapper to the penthouse with this job, and that's gonna piss some people off. Make no mistake, if Cold Steel cross the line, they're gone, and if they're gone, we don't have much need for you. But we don't want to do that if there's still some profit in it for all of us, right? So once, just this once, I can do you a favour. You don't need to tell me who it is that keeps pissing down your back, I goddamn know who it is. I hear things, I see things, and I've been doing this job since Jesus was cranking eight balls into his diaper. So this is what we're gonna do.'

*

Coal-dust Manchester rain sheeted down, and Johnny sat in one of the two cars waiting outside the police station. On release, the bands would have a fifty-yard walk to the cars. 'Security, Mister Faslane,' the solicitor had explained apologetically. 'You can't park any closer.' Johnny shrugged, knowing he had no clout to get it changed.

Not that the press minded. They were already banked three deep alongside the narrow footpath at the front of the station. Johnny smiled when he saw a small door at the back of the station open, allowing several figures to run out. They sprinted towards the cars.

'Drive,' said Johnny, and the cars wheeled towards the running men. The cars stopped and the doors flew open. Both bands raced inside, slammed the doors shut and the cars sped off, leaving the press looking bewildered and angry at missing their scoops.

'Nice one, mate,' grinned Maxwell. 'I knew you wouldn't let us down.'

'No,' seethed Johnny. 'I'll leave that to you. Another morning wasted, wiping your useless arses.'

'Come on, Johnny, we paid for the damages, again.'

'Because you caused them, *again.* Now, let's get this straight, *I'm* the manager for Cold Steel, not Silas, understand? If you don't like it, audition for Chainsaw. And as for *you.*' Johnny's finger stabbed towards Joe. 'Don't *ever* smoke that shit before a gig again. If you can't be relied on to play properly, it wouldn't take much to replace you.'

'Hey, man, you wouldn't do that, would you?'

'Yes I would. And don't look at the rest of the band for help; it was them who had to cover for you. If we hadn't chucked you onstage, if Andy hadn't reworked his guitar, if you'd gone on late, the whole band would have been shut down.' Johnny looked from one band member's face to another. Ragged defiance flared back at him. 'Don't believe me?' He picked up his phone and put it on loudspeaker.

'Randall Spitz.' As soon as the gravelly voice boomed around the car's inside, the band's eyes flew open and their faces went pale.

'Randall, it's Johnny Faslane.'

'Have they been bailed out yet?'

'I'm in the car with Cold Steel right now. Chainsaw are right behind us.'

'Can they hear me?'

'You're on loudspeaker.'

'Okay, listen in, dickheads. We've had just about enough of your fucking around. From here on in, you get onstage, you play your goddamn balls off, you go back to the goddamn hotels and you make less trouble than a bunch of frigging nuns. We've been covering your goddamn asses since this shitpiece tour started and we'd like some return for our goddamn love. If you bastards create one more headline, attend one more ER, if you even *think* about goddamn drugs, we'll cut you loose. No more tour, no new album and a legal goddamn straitjacket that'll stop you recording, or performing anywhere. Do you dickheads understand?'

Johnny looked at the band's stunned faces. 'I think they get the picture, Randall.'

'Well, it's about goddamn time. Is Chainsaw's bastard manager travelling with his boys?'

'Yes.'

'Alright, now that I've given you the good news, it's time I gave him the bad.'

Chapter 13

After ending the call with Randall, Johnny glared at the band, who
sat in uncomfortable silence on the short trip back to the arena. The
car jerked to a halt and the band members bumped into each other
like bowling pins.

'Get out,' he growled. 'And get inside. See what some of us
have been doing while you were relaxing in your cells.'

'There's no let-up with you, is there?' said Andy.

'Out.'

Johnny herded a reluctant band inside, where Soundsphere's
speakers had been set up and gleamed black and new.

'Took your time,' grumbled Vince.

'Yeah, right. Might be I'd have got this sorted out a bit quicker
if I hadn't had to babysit you in hospitals, police cells and
everywhere else.'

'We'd have managed. We always do.'

'Bollocks. You lot have got your heads so far up your arses
you're having your breakfast all over again. Now get onstage, do a
sound check and see how these speakers sound.'

*

Jack Sarin scowled at the security man who scrutinised his ID.
'Which band are you with, mate?' he asked.

'I'm with that big pile of speakers in there and they're good for
both bands, so let me in if you want to keep your job.'

The guard ran a hand over his sleeveless arm, which showed a
laurel-wreathed tattoo, a Latin motto and blood group underneath.
He stared with cold eyes at Jack. 'Wait here,' he said.

Jack shook his head and turned his back on the security man
who walked into the arena. Five minutes later he was back with a
balding man wearing a Cold Steel T-shirt, leather trousers and
cowboy boots. *Who is this prick?* he thought.

'Hello, Jack.' The man held out his hand. 'Johnny Faslane. We
spoke on the phone.'

'So *you're* the new boy. Not been canned yet?'

'Not yet,' Johnny smiled. 'Maybe I'll last long enough to
finalise the sound deal.'

'That's why I'm here.'

'A long way to come; we could have done it over the phone.'

'Well, I didn't come here for you, new boy, but your band are still big, even with *you* helping them out. And when a real band needs help, Jack Sarin comes calling.'

'Nothing to do with looking at the Soundsphere system?'

'I wouldn't waste my time on that shit. Is sound check happening?'

'Come on through.'

Jack followed Johnny through to the arena. Chainsaw were onstage. Zip's hips swayed to the music and his high voice pierced through the speakers. Jack knew the full, rich sound was good. As good as his stuff. Shit, he needed to stack the cards in his favour. He looked sideways at Johnny. *I thought he'd have gone before now, the guy's got no pedigree.* Johnny tapped his feet to the music, and as the song shuddered to a halt, he looked at Jack.

'Sounds as good as your stuff.'

'You only think that because you don't know anything.'

'Well, it's really not up to me, we'll see what Cold Steel think after the show.'

'They'll choose me, new boy. Soundsphere, they're unreliable, no reputation, haven't been around long, you'd be a fool to trust them. And where's their personal presence, eh? I'm here for my outfit, the top man. Where are they?'

'They were here an hour ago, said some good things about you as well.'

'They'd be right, too.'

Johnny smiled again. 'Well, Jack, like I said, it's up to the band. You want us to ring you tonight with the decision, or wait until morning?'

'You know what? I think I'll stay tonight and listen to this thin, tinny set of speakers. You can give me your decision in person.'

*

The house lights winked out, the audience roared, and Mike's pounding drum tattoo avalanched through the stacked speakers on either side of the stage, electrifying the rest of the band. Joe's precise playing was a world away from the shambles the night before. Watching the band from his usual place at the monitor

91

station, Johnny almost forgot his worries, his nagging suspicions about Jack Sarin. Almost.

*

Maxwell felt the adrenaline blaze and the cheers hit him like a hammer. The pain in his arm had now subsided to an occasional twinge, but Johnny insisted the splint stayed where it was until a doctor said otherwise, and musically at least, Maxwell was starting to heed his weirdly dressed manager's words. Vince and Andy's synchronised guitar riff buzz-sawed into the beginning of Sinners Sanctuary, and Maxwell's vision shrank down to the stage and the packed arena in front of him. He felt the euphoria take over, and his voice fast-bowled one verse after another into the night.

*

Jack stood next to Johnny. Then, seeing him absorbed by the show, he slowly moved backstage. A few turns left and right and he was alone. The spotlights' changing colours and the alternating light and dark hid obstacles and made walking difficult, and the loud music robbed him of more senses. But concerts were his life, his home, and sound systems were more familiar to him than his underwear. He knew what he was looking for. He edged underneath the stage, reached up and gripped an ordered sheaf of inch-thick cables. He felt their quality, knew their power and was impressed. *I need to poach their people if they're this good,* he thought, *it's almost a crime to end a system like this.*

A sudden bright light shone straight at Jack. He screwed his eyes shut and felt a wet impact, then smelled the opened can of warm lager that had been thrown at him. Beer frothed over his clothes and skin and he ducked out of the torch's beam. *Shit shit shit,* he thought, *if I'm recognised I'm screwed.* He rolled to one side, crashed into a collection of empty boxes, picked himself up and scurried away.

*

Dixie slithered through the maze of poles, cables and boxes that populated the space beneath the shuddering stage. His night vision gradually emerged and he saw Jack's shadow. His senses came alive and he felt a hunter's feral instinct take over his mind. He reached into his satchel, pulled out a beer can, cracked it open and then switched on his torch, stabbing the darkness with a spear of bright light.

92

The torch beam caught Jack on the point of pulling the wires. Dixie hurled the beer can and then climbed through the clutter beneath the stage, his drools and giggles unheard beneath the concert's noise and power. He sniffed like a terrier and followed the beer trail, occasionally switching on the torch, he hounded Jack through the mass of obstacles.

*

Jack stumbled, crawled and flailed along under the stage. He lost his sense of direction, just kept moving, knew he had to get away before he was trapped and identified. He tripped and rolled through cargo netting, tried to get up and scurry away, but felt his feet meshed in the nets. He reached down and tried to untangle himself, but the shiny metal toecaps and lace hooks snarled his feet even more tightly. He felt panic descend on his mind. He knew he didn't have much time before he was found. He unlaced his boots, slipped his feet free and fled.

He reached the edge of the under-stage area, grasped a tubular staircase and clambered up. His socks slipped on the first step, he felt the solid beam of torchlight, followed by another iceberg thump and a second beer whacked into him. He sagged against the light metal tubing, then slithered up the stairs, not knowing how far behind him his pursuer was.

*

Standing at the cramped monitor station, Johnny felt his attention diverted from the concert, and he saw shadowy glimpses of Dixie's lumbering form. Whenever Dixie vanished, Johnny's eyes returned to the stage and he couldn't help smiling. The band were finally coming together. They'd stopped taking risks, they kept it simple and straightforward and it was starting to work. The talent they'd proved they had in abundance on their first three albums and tours started to show once more. And the wraith-like movements of Dixie in Johnny's peripheral vision proved his suspicions about Jack had been right.

*

Sweat dripped down Jack's face. The finale was building, but he still hadn't managed to escape. Every time he neared a doorway that promised a getaway, an opened beer can exploded near or on him, a torch-beam stabbed through the darkness and he'd be forced to jink and swerve away from the teasing nearness of safety.

93

Whoever the hell was chasing him was more persistent than syphilis.

He reached for a rope ladder that disappeared into the arena's dark heights. He looked left and right, saw no one and started to climb. Christ, but he was taking a risk. If he dropped a goolie up there he was screwed, but he had to escape that relentless beer-chucking maniac. He gripped the swaying rungs and climbed, his feet leaving the ground. Suddenly he felt an iron grip on his trousers, yanking him back towards the floor. He held onto the ladder and felt as though he was being ripped in half as vicelike hands pulled him inexorably backwards. The rope ladder swung like a fishing line with a shark on the end, and Jack felt his grip loosening. He was seconds away from being caught, and with a sick slide in his guts he knew what he had to do. *Fuck me,* he thought, *it's the wrong day to go commando.* He unzipped his trousers and flicked the button through the hole, then tears of pain squirted as the opened zip scratched his balls and pulled free a handful of pubes. He shot upwards while his assailant's hand vanished, still holding on to his unexpectedly released trousers. Naked from the waist down, he slithered up the rope ladder like a squirrel on a mission.

He inched onto a narrow walkway high above the stage, then made the mistake of looking down. His vision blurred, his legs turned to microwaved mush and he gripped thin cable strands while the blackout rush slowly ebbed away. He could see the concert coming to a close. Cold Steel were standing at the front of the stage, arms around each other's shoulders and bowing to the crowd. Jack had to get away before the encore ended, before the house lights came on and there was no darkness to hide in, no shadows to escape into.

With his tackle flapping between his legs, he inched along the walkway. He concentrated on his footing and another opened beer can thudded into the back of his head. Starlight exploded in his eyes and his knees turned to rubber. He stumbled forward and didn't feel his ankles tangle with a lighting cable. All he was thinking about was escape and he blundered forward until the cable pulled tight and he fell down. His face smashed against the walkway and he felt the whole thing sway with the impact. Then came the juddering vibrations and he knew someone else was

94

running towards him. He turned around to see who it was, and rolled off the walkway. He screamed and plummeted downward, but the cable tightened around his ankle and he flew across the stage and swung sideways. His head smacked into the speakers and he hung senseless and upside-down in midair, still out of the spotlights' beams and invisible to everyone else.

Slowly, he came to and looked at the stage below. Blood oozed from his nose and he snorted it away, then tried to reach his ankles and prise himself loose. Bent over like a flashing gymnast, he gripped the cable and pulled at the knot. Without warning it came free and he shot ten feet to the ground, landing in a semi-clothed heap at the edge of the stage.

Stunned and terrified, he stood up on trembling legs. Was he still being chased? Christ, this was worse than a lynching. His nerves flew around his body and he didn't know what to do, where to go. Another beer can splattered against the Soundsphere speaker and Jack jumped, his judgement shredded. He turned and ran onto the stage, heard cheers from the mosh pit, then another can whacked into the back of his head and his body reserves finally abandoned him and he flopped facedown on the stage floor, illuminated by a strobe effect of thousands of flashbulbs.

*

Slumped in a chair in the band's dressing room, a damp towel covered Jack's lower half.

'Good work, Dixie,' said Johnny.

Dixie grinned and threw a bucket of water over Jack, who spluttered and opened his eyes, then looked around him.

'Right, lads,' said Johnny. 'Jack came up here in person to hear what we thought of the two sound systems. Let's not keep the big man waiting.'

Chapter 14

'Johnny Faslane.' He sat in the tour bus which droned through along an almost empty motorway towards Newcastle and the band's next venue, the Metro Radio Arena.

'How did the band escape jail yesterday?'

'Rachel,' smiled Johnny.

'Don't Rachel me, why didn't you call?'

'What, so now you're stalking me?'

'You'd know if I was.'

Johnny laughed. 'I'll be careful. Look, I'm sorry, things got a little crazy at the gig.'

'What happened?'

'It's complicated.'

'Let me be the judge of that.'

'Yesterday you were my girlfriend, now you're my therapist.'

'And you're just teasing me. That's not nice.'

'That's the business we're in.'

'But not always the people. I'm not the enemy, Johnny.'

'After the way you sliced me over Florence? What are you? Jealous?'

'Maybe.'

'Maybe,' smiled Johnny. 'I like that.'

'So what does a girl have to do?'

'For what? A story or a date?'

'You decide.'

Johnny's smile got bigger. 'I'll see what you write about the band first.'

'Then your future really is depending on Cold Steel.'

Rachel hung up and Johnny suddenly felt like a teenager. She was intriguing, interesting. *And out for the story as well,* his thoughts warned him. *Keep it in your pants, mate.* He dragged his mind back to his job. Jack Sarin's antics had secured the speakers for Soundsphere, and Silas Moss had also ceased to be a problem. Johnny didn't know what Randall had said to him, but it had worked, and the rumours that Chainsaw had spread about Silas having a new interest in his spare time would have made Johnny curious if he'd had the time to think about it.

The British dates began to wind up, and Johnny's authority was slowly asserting itself, but never fully controlling the band. At the end of the Newcastle gig, Johnny saw what had been occupying Silas' spare time. Florence stood next to him, holding his hand. *As long as they're busy with each other,* he thought. At Newcastle, Johnny had arranged for a printed backdrop of a wrecked pirate ship. It gave a welcome addition to the bare stage, as well as landing Johnny more headaches by fuelling the band's pleadings to go on a treasure hunt after the tour.

'No,' he growled. 'How many times do I have to tell you?'

'What's the problem?' whined Maxwell. 'The tour's picked up, we haven't been arrested or murdered. We're even getting good reviews in the tabloids.'

'And Ozone have got a long memory. Besides, Andreas' trial has just started.'

'Yeah,' said Vince. 'But that's nothing to do with us.'

'He used to be your manager, you're linked. Do you really need me to tell you how the press works? Look, you need to stay out of the news unless it's about the music. Ozone wants you to be seen as a band, not a bunch of delinquents, not a bunch of archaeologists, and *not* going on about pirates.'

'But we *know* where the treasure's hidden,' pleaded Maxwell.

'And Ozone have already got studio time booked. After the *next* album and tour, maybe. If you can get to that point without pissing anyone off.'

'So you'll put in a good word for us?'

'What?'

'Oh come on, mate. Ozone put you here; they obviously want you to look out for us. Stands to reason they'll listen to you.'

'They're listening to media reports and looking at album sales, and that puts things right back in your hands.'

*

The band's last UK shows were two concerts at Birmingham's LG Arena, and with Johnny's optimism slowly building, he watched the road crew bedding in the Soundsphere system and slotting the stage together. His phone rang.

'Johnny Faslane.'

'Johnny, it's Lucy. How's the tour going?'

'Good, Lucy. We've had positive reviews, the band are behaving themselves and, more importantly, playing well. Any news on the album sales?'

'Steady.'

'But could be better, right?'

'A lot better if they want their treasure hunt.'

'Oh, Jesus. You know about that?'

Lucy chuckled. '*Everyone* at Ozone knows about it. Cold Steel, and Maxwell in particular, have been going on about it for years.'

'So they've always wanted to go treasure hunting?'

'No, they usually just go on about pirates. But Maxwell thinks he's got a real lead with this map he bought off a fan a few years ago.'

'He told me about that, too.'

'We think he might be on to something?'

'Really?' Johnny's interest picked up.

'Yes.'

'But?'

'But it's still a long way from definite, and Cold Steel are a metal band, not historians.'

'So the answer's still no?' asked Johnny.

'As far as the band are concerned, the answer's still no. Between you and me, *if* they can keep focussed for the rest of the tour, *if* their album sales hit platinum in all the target markets, then we could be ready to authorise a two-month hold on their studio booking. But they can't know anything about it. If they do, they'll think they've already been given it, nobody will be able to control them and you can wave goodbye to the rest of the tour.'

'Any news about the impounded gear from Japan?'

'It'll be waiting for you in Paris.'

'That's fantastic.'

'Sure, but you still need to give your boys some bad news.'

*

'We're not flying?' spluttered Maxwell.

'It's not a big deal,' said Johnny. He sat in the tour bus and faced the rest of the band, who stood over him like a team of demonic surgeons.

'Not to you, maybe,' growled Maxwell. 'I bet you've never done an international concert in your life. We're Cold Steel, mate, and we *fly* abroad. Get it sorted.'

'No.'

'What?'

'You heard me. You're going to France by road, and that's it. This comes straight from the top.'

'But why?'

'Well, let's see. You chuck TVs out of windows, get booted out of two hotels, nearly commit group airborne suicide, get arrested for fighting, and you wonder why Ozone aren't buying you plane tickets? Jesus, even if they did, no insurance company in the world will cover you wonderboys at thirty thousand feet. You're crossing the channel on a ferry, you're being driven to Paris, and when we're there, we'll have two days to rehearse before the first show.'

'That's bollocks, mate.'

'That's reality, deal with it.'

Maxwell's shoulders slumped, and Johnny almost felt sorry for him. 'Look, lads,' he said. 'It's not that bad going by boat. At least there's no hanging around at the airport, no luggage checks, no getting papped at arrivals. And there *is* some good news.'

'What's that?'

'The stage props have been released from Japan. It'll all be waiting for us at Paris, including your bloody ship.'

'All right,' beamed Vince. 'We are *back!*'

'So put those two days to good use: make sure we're good with the new setup.'

Chapter 15

The convoy of trucks and tour bus streamed into Paris, adding to the mid-afternoon traffic that built up a smog-wrapped, citywide gridlock. The speed gently sped away to nothing, and the inside the bus, the tension slowly built.

'Screw this,' said Maxwell.

He stood up and barged past Johnny, then walked to the front of the bus, pulled open the door and disappeared into the directionless crowds. Johnny opened his mouth to speak, but events moved too quickly for his besieged thoughts. He sat catatonic, and the rest of the band followed Maxwell, while the driver looked back at Johnny.

'Anyone else getting off?'

Johnny shook his head in silence, and just managed to close his mouth before he started salivating.

*

Maxwell looked back at the tour bus. Eventually, Johnny shook his head, stood up and walked towards the doors, he turned back to the band.

'Right, lads. We've kissed his arse long enough. We've done as we were told and they put us on a fucking bus. We've got two days to show them that Cold Steel aren't ruled by anyone. Back here in time for the gig. Let's do it!'

By the time the bus doors hissed open and Johnny stepped out, Cold Steel had vanished.

*

Maxwell downed another glass of Chartreuse and looked around the Sorbonne bar he'd ended up in, close to the University. He'd spent the previous day trawling websites in an internet cafe, looking up anything about French naval history in the Caribbean at the time of Blackbeard. After pulling his hair back into a ponytail, and donning geeky thick-rimmed glasses and an army-surplus parka, he'd thrown off most of the curious eyes that might have recognised him. Now he could concentrate, think about what he'd found out. He signalled to the barman for another Chartreuse.

The barman brought his drink and then sat opposite him at the small, high table. He pulled off his bow tie and undid his top button. He was tall and thin, like the tables in the bar, like the chairs. Long dark hair dripped down beyond his collar. 'I didn't ask for a drinking partner,' said Maxwell.

'You are Maxwell Diabolo?' the young man asked softly, his English heavily accented.

'Who wants to know?'

'I am L'Ollonais.'

'Interesting name. Are you related to the cannibal pirate?'

'It is my *nom de guerre*.'

'Your what?'

'The name I use when I find things out.'

'Finding what out?'

'I know what you want.'

'And what's that?'

'Information.'

Maxwell's interest grew. He looked closer at the young man in the dark, cloudy bar. 'What kind of information can you get, and for how much?'

'You love the pirates. You love their history, yes?'

'You know me well, mate.'

'Knowing about people is my specialty. I am a student here, studying computer science.'

'A bit of hacking on the side?'

'Information acquisition, it pays my tuition alongside my job at the bar. If you want to know something, I can find out.'

'For a price, right?'

'For sure. But for you, Maxwell, I do this as a favour. Maybe a souvenir from you?'

'What did you have in mind?'

'I have your albums, Cold Steel albums. You sign them for me, take a picture with my friends?'

Maxwell knocked back his drink and smiled. 'Deal.'

*

Loud music thudded around L'Ollonais' flat and thin multi-coloured LEDs stabbed through the darkness. Maxwell felt like he was sitting in a nightclub, or better still, some weird concert. L'Ollonais seemed to have invited his entire faculty into his tiny flat, but the music was so loud, and the flashing lights so random, that Maxwell was able to wrap himself in anonymity. He sat on an uncomfortable sofa and opened one of the two Chartreuse bottles he'd brought with him.

The volume slowly increased and the alcohol inexorably lowered inhibitions. Maxwell could barely understand a word that was said. Occasionally someone would talk to him in broken English, then move on once the translation got too difficult. Everyone was getting more pissed, and Maxwell wondered if he was wasting his time. Was L'Ollonais really a hacker? Could he really add to what Maxwell already knew? Was there anything else he even *needed* to know? He stood up and walked over to L'Ollonais' computer desk.

'Info, mate?' he said. 'I did the autographs for you.'

L'Ollonais looked up at Maxwell. 'Watch this,' he smiled. His fingers blurred over the keyboard and password cookies appeared on the screen. 'French Navy,' he said. 'There's some dynamite information about the Caribbean.'

'And you've accessed it?'

'Some. I'm working on the rest.'

'You need to hope you don't get caught.'

L'Ollonais' finger hovered over the mouse. 'Ten minutes, my friend, then they start looking for us.'

'Will I understand any of it?'

'All of it. This report is a French military hack into the Royal Navy. It is written in English.' L'Ollonais clicked the mouse button and the page opened. 'Ten minutes. I can trust you to close down after then?'

'I promise, mate.'

L'Ollonais' eyes swivelled around his flat and he wandered away from the desk. Maxwell's finger clicked the mouse, and a mass of documents sprang up on the screen.

The minutes flickered past. Initially, Maxwell kept a watch on them, but once his attention was sucked into the data on the screen, he became oblivious to the time. The music got louder, the laughing and conversation rose in volume alongside it, and no one came to tell Maxwell his time was up. He was engrossed; he couldn't believe what he was reading, and all for the price of a few autographs. Memo after hacked memo appeared on the screen and

he pulled harder. The metal bent forward and one of the ropes slipped over the metalwork. He quickly untied himself and rolled off the bed, his limbs not doing exactly what he wanted. The booze slowed his brain and his anger blurred his judgement. He'd been robbed and embarrassed and he was going to get those damn bitches. He ran out of the room and along the narrow corridor. He heard their high-pitched voices ahead and roared as he ran after them. Squeals and the clack of high-heeled shoes on stone steps sounded ahead of him, and they fled down the stairs.

Vince crashed down the stairs, lost his footing and fell face down on a carpet that slid along with him on top of it. His head cracked against the solid wood reception desk and he struggled to his feet, the tricolour tied to his knob the only thing covering him.

The two nuns on duty at the reception desk stared in terror at Vince. 'I've been robbed!' he shouted. 'Fucking robbed! And I bet you're all in on it, you bastards. Where are they?' He marched up and down the small hotel lobby like a demented, nude fascist. 'The bitches, where are they?'

The nuns looked past Vince and he vaguely realised they weren't looking at him. He turned around, following their gaze, and saw three gendarmes standing in the hotel doorway, with Sophie and Veronique cowering behind them.

*

Three streets back from Marseille's marina, Andy Stains sat anonymously at a rickety table in L'Hermitage bar. He grinned over his beer glass, feeling at home despite the hostility that seeped towards him in an unbroken circle of malicious thought. He was a stranger and he wasn't welcome, and yet it was a place where he belonged. Maxwell, brash and larger than his onstage presence, would have been thrown out, while Vince wouldn't even lower himself to step inside. Joe would sit in a corner and nervously chain-smoke joints until he was told to buy a drink or leave, while Mike's sheer size would make him a target for everyone. But Andy had always been at home in such places. He sweated in the summer heat, which built like an oven inside the small bar and left condensation trails down the faded, light-green paintwork.

And how would Johnny Faslane survive? Andy still hadn't figured him out. Sure, he'd shown he could manage a band, and yes, he'd pulled their arses out of several potential disasters so far, but whose side was he really on? He seemed very keen to get the band to play to Ozone's rules. Maybe after they got back to Paris he'd realise that he needed to listen to the band a bit more.

He drained his beer and signalled for another. The handful of euros in his pocket was dwindling since his flight to the coast. *No phone, no plastic.* Maybe he should have planned things a bit better. He counted out how much he had left and cursed. *I might need to hitchhike back to Paris.*

His beer started to make demands on his bladder, and he stood up and headed for the toilets. A solid wall of humanity stood in his way, none of it seeming to understand.

'Come on, lads, let a fella through.'

Andy tried pushing, gently at first, then more insistently. Heads turned and looked at him, then turned back again. He felt his anger build. He slapped the nearest shoulder to him.

'Move out of the way.' He stared, eye to nipple with a broad-chested, dark-haired Frenchman. Resentment tsunami-waved over Andy, and he smiled at the challenge. The Frenchman shoved, and Andy staggered back into a table, knocking over two beers.

'That's what I'm talking about,' he said. 'What are you talking about?'

The Frenchman swung a clumsy roundhouse punch. Andy ducked and bounced upwards, kicking the man in the balls as he came up. The Frenchman bent over and groaned, clutching his groin, then slowly keeled over. Andy stepped over him and walked through a narrow doorway into a toilet with a single cracked urinal that reeked of mothballs and stale piss. When he came back out, a circle of locals barred his way. In the centre of them stood an enormous Frenchman with straggly black hair and stubble like rusty iron filings pasted to his face. In one hand he held a wad of crumpled euros.

'Je vous battre pour l'argent.'

Andy didn't understand the words, but he recognised the gesture. *Maybe I won't need to hitchhike after all.* And besides, Andy knew himself too well. He *didn't* want to hitchhike, but he *did* want to fight.

He pulled out his own remaining banknotes and looked around. *Who's the banker?* A short, spectacled man with a sweat-stained shirt and crumpled trousers smiled weakly at Andy and held out his hand. Andy handed him the cash, and the other man did the same. All around him he heard murmured conversations, and he knew that bets were being placed.

A small circle of space inside the gathered crowd gave the two men limited room to move, but Andy knew it wasn't about that. They wanted quick punches and a winning bet. Andy shuffled within range, feinted, head down, and shot a hammer-punch into the man's chest, then ran forward, pushing him back into a whitewashed brick pillar. The Frenchman groaned and Andy surged upwards, the back of his head catching his opponent's chin with a sharp crack that crashed both sets of teeth together. The Frenchman's head whipped backwards and hit the pillar with a thud that sent a cloud of white dust into Andy's eyes, and as he stepped back, the man he had just fought sank slowly to the floor. Muted cheers greeted Andy's win, and he smiled, looked around for the banker. He saw him staring nervously, and he held out his hand for the money. The banker smiled crooked teeth, shook a finger and pointed to his right. A bare-chested skinhead with a tattooed dragon running from bicep to bicep stood at the edge of the cleared space, holding a tight roll of euros.

*

Andy sweated through one fight after another, punching, kicking, kneeing and elbowing his way towards a flight back to Paris. His world shrivelled down to the small circle of dusty brick floor and whoever decided to take their chances against him. His movements were slowing and the sweat doubled the weight of his ripped combat trousers. His T-shirt had been torn from him in a fight he couldn't remember having, and although he kept saying each brawl would be his last, at least some of the crowd were now encouraging him on, and his own conceit kept him agreeing to just one more. The banker looked on him like a son returned, and Andy dimly realised he owed him some sort of percentage just for holding his cash.

*

Change came shockingly fast. Sweat in eyes, a second's slowness, a missed block and a scarred fist thudded into Andy's jaw. Starlight like a concert finale exploded in his mind and his legs turned into an iced slush drink left in the sun. He decked out, his back thudding into the floor and the air whooshed from his lungs.

107

Cheers as loud as the last night of the UK tour rang in his ears, his vision clouded over and the world skipped away from his awareness.

*

A hundred and forty miles further along the coast, Joe Dimitri basked in the Riviera sunshine. A day earlier, he'd flown into Nice, stumbled around the city for half a day before finding the local potheads, and from that point on everything developed a rose-tinged hue.

The local weed-gang of Nice were an ephemeral collection of backpackers, hippies and drifters held together by the usual vague mysticism brought about by their altered reality goggles. Joe was welcomed with hugs and smiles, and the handful of euros he eagerly handed over quickly translated into a huge block of resin. One of the group was a middle-aged Londoner called Misty, who'd been living on the Riviera for the last twenty years.

'An ideal time to come aboard, mate,' he said to Joe. 'We're off to Festival.'

'Festival?' asked Joe.

'Yeah, we gather here and then convoy up to La Turbie. Then, under the ruins, we have a midnight festival. It's amazing, mate, you've never seen anything like it.'

Joe smiled and toked his joint. A festival, a real hippy festival. He shuffled along with the rest of the group as they boarded a collection of battered buses, which drove eastwards out of the city, leaving a black cloud of exhaust fumes in their wake.

By the time they arrived at La Turbie, a small village on top of a hill overlooking the Mediterranean, Joe's eyes were watering from a caustic mix of dope smoke and diesel fumes from the leaking fuel and exhaust pipes. But that didn't matter, he'd been smoking resin non-stop, and he didn't need comfort to see the beauty.

Next to an old church, and still imposing despite its ruined state, La Turbie's Trophy of Augustus stood proud over the village. The buses pulled up on a grassed area next to the Roman ruin, where tents and campfires mushroomed over the green.

'Are we allowed here, man?' asked Joe.

'We come to this exact same spot every year,' said Misty. 'Then we move on in the morning. As long as we're gone before

108

they're awake, the locals are happy. No hassles. We leave the place clean, they let us back here next year. All good.'

*

Darkness softly shrouded the hilltop, and bottles of murky wine passed freely among the campfire gatherings. Joe restrung two ancient guitars into one acoustic bass and gave a sharp edge to the folky singalongs. He felt freer than he ever had before. No one even asked him about the band, it was like that side of his life didn't exist. *Maybe it's a sign,* he thought, *maybe I need to branch out, hang with these guys for a while. Cold Steel will manage without me.* He drank some more wine, felt a gurgling in his stomach.

'Hey, Misty. What's in this wine, man?'

'What, this?' Misty inspected Joe's bottle. 'Christ, man, that's some of the ten-year stuff. I didn't know we still had any left.'

'Ten years? You mean this wine is like ten years old?'

'No, it was ten years old when we labelled it.'

'And when was that, man?'

'Twenty years ago.'

'Heavy duty, man.' Joe upended the bottle. 'Medication for the nation. I'm drinking thirty-year-old wine at a festival.'

Misty snatched the bottle away from Joe. 'How much of this have you had?'

'Is this the same stuff?' Joe picked up an empty, unlabelled bottle. Misty looked at the glass bottom and squinted in the flickering firelight, then nodded.

'We scratch the bottles so we know what batch it is. It's the same.'

'Then I've had nearly two bottles of it, man.'

'Don't have any more.'

'Why not?'

'Because twenty years ago, everyone who drank it had the shits for a week. I don't suppose it's mellowed over that time. Here.' Misty placed a dirty tin bucket next to Joe. 'Keep that handy for the rest of the night, and if you need to use it, don't let any of the locals see you.'

'What?'

'Look, man. This is the best spot in our entire circuit, but the people who live here only just tolerate us. One night here on the green, and that's our lot for the year. If they think we're bringing an outbreak of diarrhoea with us, by morning they'll have blown it up into the goddam plague. They won't let us within ten clicks of the place ever again.'

'Hey, man, that's a bit –'

'You'll be shitting through a teabag in about ten minutes, Joe. Find a dark spot somewhere, stay there, and don't miss the bucket when you go. And *don't* fall asleep. A few people did that last time around; they woke up in the morning smothered in mister whippy, and I'm not talking about ice cream.'

'Oh, shit, man.'

'Exactly. We leave an hour after dawn, make sure you're aboard a bus by then.'

*

Misty's words sent more urgency pulsing through Joe than he'd ever felt in his life. Everyone was depending on him: not to be seen, not to fall asleep, not to miss the bucket. He crouched in the shadows of two low-growing bushes, away from the music and gentle laughter of everyone else, and he even tried to stifle his groans of pain once the cramps hit, followed by gunfire flatulence and hosing green shit that burned his arse like acid before it pebble-dashing the bucket. Again and again it flowed out of him like rancid lava. He thought it would never end, and he sweated, tensed and writhed in agony while the cramps and emissions continued without respite. At first he felt weary, then tired, then exhausted. Fatigue stalked him, ambushed him, possessed him. He fought hard to keep awake. It was easy to begin with, but once the music died away, and the voices quietened down, all he heard was an occasional snore to accompany the almost continual farting and spluttering as he shat the night away.

Squatting over the bucket, Joe's thighs burned agony. Waves of exhaustion smashed into him. His vision blurred and he felt his eyelids droop. His head sagged forward and he caught himself, sat up again with a jerking movement and a thunderclap of flatus shot out of him. After a few minutes he nodded off again. It was harder and harder to keep awake. All he wanted to do was curl up and go to sleep. This was hell, man. It wasn't his fault and he was suffering. No one was coming to help him and his last thought as he pitched forward and sleep claimed him, was that he hadn't told

110

anyone else where he was. How could they come and get him in the morning?

*

Joe woke up. The midday sun pierced the bush shadows and heated him up in blotches. The stench of a thousand crap houses burnt his nostrils and he stirred with a groan of residual stomach pain. His hands felt moist, as though he'd been covered in cream. He opened his eyes and lifted his hand, then wailed in despair as he realised what the brown and green slime covering him really was. He knelt up and looked around him. Surrounding the bushes were a dozen firemen with breathing masks, all pointing hoses at him.

'Hi, guys,' he warbled, and the hoses were switched on, high-pressure water hitting him from all sides.

*

Mike Vesuvius walked into the circular glass Porsche showroom in Grenoble, his bulk and clothing attracting more attention than the gleaming supercars that speckled the pristine white floor. He smiled easily at the city-suit salesman who walked towards him, disarming him with offered reassurance. Like most drummers, he was generally unrecognised in public, and people tended to assume he was trouble when they saw his ragged jeans, ripped T-shirt and hulking build. He couldn't blame them. He hoped they spoke English, or he knew he'd be escorted out. He looked at the blood-red Cayenne with covetous eyes, and the salesman, his eye on the chance, smiled back and offered a handshake.

'Bonjour, Monsieur.'

'You speak English?' asked Mike.

'But of course. Welcome to our establishment. I am Jean, and we welcome all nations. English, you say? I love watching your football.'

'You like our music?' The salesman faltered. Mike flicked his head towards the large four by four. 'I like this.'

Rich commission glazed Jean's grey eyes. 'We can draw up finance forms if you like?'

'How about a test drive?'

A slipped smile. 'This one? The Transsyberia, Monsieur? Why, it is a premium specification. We will need some insurance paperwork, I am sorry. And a small deposit, as a gesture of

111

goodwill. I must also ask for some confirmation of, shall we say, means? I do hope you understand.'

Mike smiled and flourished his credit card, then stabbed the screen on his phone, logged into his bank account and felt the near arousal he always did when he looked at the balance. Offshore investments, gilts and other disbursements reduced the real, accessible wealth, but there was still enough in the current account for half of the beautiful red car that stood gleaming next to him in the showroom. They'd know that Mike would be able to raise the rest. He was good for it. Not that he had any intention of buying it.

'Très bon, Monsieur.' Jean ushered Mike to a polished darkwood desk and dealt out a pile of documents like a casino croupier. 'First, the legal formalities.'

Mike had no idea what he was signing, but he didn't care. He felt the car calling to him, seducing him, and he had no resistance. He knew enough, though, to keep quiet about the prangs he'd had the year before. No point fogging the perspective for a test drive. And besides, he'd learned a lot since then.

Forced laughter and affability always surrounded Mike once his wealth was established, almost like a relieved reaction to his threatening looks, and he'd learned to manipulate it, to suggest that Jean only needed to look at his driving licence, not wait for any tedious checks on his current road status. Mike had done it before, he knew what he was doing.

Strapped into the driver's seat and feeling like a fighter pilot, Mike grappled to reach the ignition. The engine roared with a visceral claw-grip down his spine that he found more intoxicating than playing live. Better than Cold Steel, better than sex, better than *anything*. Jean looked at him from the passenger seat, casting a final look at the paperwork to make sure that Mike had signed everything.

Throbbing out of the showroom on virgin, knobbly display tyres, Mike frowned almost painfully, and concentrating on safe, legal driving, they dawdled through the narrow, cobblestoned streets that emptied out of the urban beard surrounding the Parc Naturel Regional de Chartreuse.

'Can you drive up that hill?' asked Mike.

'Indeed, Monsieur. You are driving most respectably, and the roads on hills such as these are what this car was designed for.'

Mike stepped on the gas and felt the bull roar and pull as the huge car sprang forward up the swing-back Saint-Pancrasse stretch of the D30. Extreme turns and a steep climb through pines that encroached on the roadside forced Mike's eyes wide open.

'A hundred metres further,' said Jean. 'Turn left, and there is a gentle forest track. You like to go off road?'

'Hell yes. Will we need the four wheel drive?'

'Not on a test drive, Monsieur,' Jean chuckled. 'That requires a purchase.'

'Maybe,' grinned Mike.

He guided the Cayenne onto the dry, tightly packed dirt track, barely less smooth than the road he'd just left. Frustrated, he slowly fed the power and they sped up on a downhill stretch. He looked sideways at Jean and saw no sign of concern. *He's not such a stiff-arse. Maybe we can really off-road.*

A sudden movement wrenched Mike's eyes to the front. A wild boar, the size of a fully grown Rottweiler, shot across the track just in front of them. He wrenched the wheel behind the boar's path. They slewed off the road, avoiding the fleeing animal, bumping across the shale edge of the track and ploughing into the forest.

Mike spun the wheel back towards the track. They rolled over a soft mattress of pine needles, a freshly chopped tree stump disappearing beneath their view and the car stumbled back onto the track. Underneath them, the newly sheared wood scraped along the virgin underseal, and the sound of buckling metal sent a flash-warning through Mike's mind. Instinctively, he stamped on the brakes. His foot slammed to the floor, met no resistance from the pedal, and there was absolutely no slowing in the car's speed.

Mike yanked on the handbrake and it flew upwards with the same lack of bite as the pedal. They picked up speed and he kept stamping on the brake pedal as though it would suddenly magically work, then changed his attention to the steering wheel and the life-depending need to keep on the track. They began going downhill faster and faster, with no way of stopping.

Twists and turns leapt at them with more speed and less warning. Mike dragged the wheel hard left and the car swooped round, dived onto a rutted track between a gap in the trees, then sliced through a wooden gate with a sickening crunch.

Even on the forest track, even with Mike driving, the Cayenne stuck to the ground like cold tree sap on a branch. But now they were out of control on a boggy, pitted grassed patch of forest, and Mike and Jean were thrown around against the seatbelts. Mike fought against the steering wheel, forced left and right by the harsh, wrenching movement. He started to lose coordination, his foot slipped and he stamped on the accelerator. The engine screamed in unison with Jean's fear-stained wailing and they cannoned over the uneven ground.

Mike slammed against the door and his head hit the roof. As he finally released the accelerator he felt the car roll. Metal screeched and bent and buckled, wood splintered all around them and glass shattered. Mike kept his eyes sealed shut, the Cayenne cartwheeled across a tiny clearing, while Jean screamed terror next to him.

The Cayenne stopped on its roof. Inside, Mike's view was zero as the airbag deployed in his face and pushed him back against the seat. He fought to release the seat belt and pushed the bag back far enough to speak.

'Are you alright, Jean? Sorry about the car, man.'

Mike heard a man weeping, and he guessed it was Jean. He heaved and pushed, struggled free of the airbag's enveloping hold. Finally he squeezed free and landed headfirst on the cab ceiling. The door had detached completely during the crash and he slithered out of the car.

Jean knelt by the car's corpse, tears streaming down his face. Mike's senses swam and he limped over to Jean.

'Jean,' he said. 'Are you okay? Are you hurt?'

'I am heartbroken,' he wept. 'This car, this beautiful, beautiful car.'

'Never mind the car, man. What about you?'

'I will survive, Monsieur.' He ran a hand over the Cayenne's crumpled panels.

Mike felt dizzy. He looked around at the destruction wrought by the crashing car. Small trees had been uprooted, and he saw what seemed like an inordinate amount of shredded bird nests. His directionless feet crunched over pale blue eggs. *Help,* he thought, *we need some help.* He rummaged for his phone and swept the screen. He wondered what the emergency number was in France. Maybe he could google it. He looked at the phone screen; saw the no signal sign and his vision starred. He was lost, alone on a hillside with a wrecked car and a heartbroken salesman, and no idea what to do next.

'*Ce qui se passe ici?*'

Mike looked around at the voice, French, but definitely not Jean. Approaching him through the shattered saplings and nests was a large, unshaven Frenchman, clad in blue dungarees with an enormous axe over his shoulder. He walked towards Mike, and two others appeared, similarly dressed, holding pitchforks.

Oh, fucking hell. Hillbillies! Disjointed thoughts steamtrained through Mike's over-extended mind. *Squeal like a hog, boy!*

Unreasoning terror seized Mike's decision-making process. He turned and ran blindly through the forest, heading downhill but not knowing where else he was heading. He heard shouts in French, didn't even bother to see if he was being chased, although in his mind he was. He thought about the films he'd seen. Shit, didn't these people have dogs as well? He chanced a backwards glance to see if there was a pursuit. He tripped, lost his footing, and crashed to the forest floor, picking up speed in an untidy roll. He smacked against unseen fallen branches, scraped the skin from his hands and face, then slowed, finding himself enmeshed in a tangled maze of nettle bushes. Within seconds of stopping, he felt the thousand sting-stabs from nettles that osmosed their poison onto his skin, and numbing pain started to blot through him. Then he heard the buzzing, and it was getting louder.

Chapter 16

Johnny forgot the luxury of his hotel room, and fury competed with pure panic as he received one police report after another. He picked up the charge sheets that had been faxed to him by the record company, and his hands trembled once he read the curt instruction to call Randall Spitz.

The second he picked up his phone, it rang.

'Hello.'

'Don't give me that limey bullshit, I told you to call!'

'Randall. Hi, I was just about to, I've only just read your faxes.'

'Frigging liar. What the hell is happening over there? We hired you because you had experience managing bands on the road.'

'Hey, Randall. The bus was stuck in traffic, and they just got up and walked off.'

'And I suppose you sat there like a stuffed pussy and let them?'

'Jesus Christ, what was I supposed to do? Stand in their way?'

'If you had to, then yes. If you had to stand there with a goddam twelve gauge and keep them in line, then yes.'

'I got out of the bus straight after them. By then they'd already disappeared. I think they might have planned it.'

'Bullshit. They haven't got the brains to think that far ahead. They were pissed at you for keeping them on a tight leash, wanted to show you they weren't completely buns up and kneeling. Well, they'd better offer you more than just their butts after the shit *they* pulled, *and* the strings *we* pulled to get their asses sprung from jail.'

'They're being *released?*'

'We called in favours at a level higher than Everest, you get me? Now, these sons of bitches are all coming back under police escort, and *you* will be signing a whole forest of French legal documents, placing Cold Steel in *your* care for as long as they're on French soil. How you keep them in line is up to you, but if they cross it, it'll be your ass in a sling.'

'Okay, Randall, you can trust me.'

'You'd better be right. And you tell those useless pricks that if they *do* fuck up like that again, while you're taking it up the joey

116

in a French prison, we'll be running them, corporate style, and you know what that means. Make sure they know as well.'

Randall hung up and Johnny heard a knock at his hotel room door. He answered to a small man in an immaculate suit.

'Bonjour, Monsieur Faslane. I am the duty manager, will you follow me, please?'

Johnny followed the manager to a lift, which whispered them both to the basement. The doors opened to utilitarian concrete and strip lighting, far removed from Johnny's opulent suite. He was led into a small, empty room. Empty apart from Cold Steel, handcuffed and surrounded by ten simmering gendarmes.

Johnny's anger rose, and he looked from one band member to the next. They were all dirty, they smelled terrible, Mike was covered with red sores that made him look even bigger than normal, and none of them could meet his increasingly hostile gaze.

'Welcome back, nice of you to get here. Remembered your jobs, did you?'

'Look, mate,' said Maxwell.

'Shut up.' Johnny slapped him with the faxed charge sheets. 'I've read everything. Hacking into French intelligence. Why, for God's sake? Is their government forming a band? Do they want to audition for Cold Steel?' He turned to Vince. 'Molesting an MP's two daughters?'

'Bollocks,' said Vince. 'They tied me up and robbed me.'

'So you flashed in front of a bunch of nuns?'

'It was an accident.'

'*You're* the bloody accident. Do you have any idea how many people Ozone leant on to keep those pictures off the internet? And as for you, Andy, bare-knuckle fighting in a Marseilles bar?'

'What?' asked Maxwell.

'Oh yes,' said Johnny. 'For money, apparently. Told the police he had to pay for his flight back here. Stupid bastard.'

'Hey, man,' burbled Joe. '*I* didn't do anything wrong.'

'You what? Spent the night with a bunch of squatters, introduced dysentery to the poshest community in France and you didn't do anything wrong? Are you still taking the antibiotics?' Joe nodded. 'For fuck's sake, how naive? I suppose they told you they were allowed to be there? You're almost as dumb as Mike and his car-crash eco-terrorism.'

117

'It wasn't my fault,' grumbled Mike.

'No? Have you looked in a mirror lately.'

'Yeah, I need a doctor.'

'You need a slap. Rolling a six-figure car on a test drive, straight through a bird sanctuary, then ripping up a forest garden of rare plants before disturbing a colony of protected bees.'

'*I* disturbed them? They stung me to buggery, man.'

'And tell me again why you took off down the hill on foot? I'm sure the band would love to know.' Mike fidgeted. It was hard to tell if he was blushing through the angry red stings that still covered his face and hands. 'He thought he was being chased by a bunch of everglades hillbillies, in France.'

'They looked like it,' said Mike.

'They were forest wardens, coming to see if you were okay.'

'*I* didn't know that.'

'No, none of you bastards knew anything, did you? And you wonder why you're always being treated like kids? Out of Britain for two minutes and you take off like a bunch of demented tourists. I suppose I could understand if you'd never been abroad before, but not when you've all been around the world God knows how many times.'

'Leave it out, mate.' Maxwell stared at the floor with bloodshot eyes. 'It's not as though we missed the gig. We're here, we're ready to go on.'

'Ready? You should have been at the Bercy hours ago. You haven't done sound check, you haven't tuned your instruments, and you haven't gone through your set list. We finally get your ship released from Japan, set it up on stage, and look at you.' He glared at his watch. 'Right. Chainsaw, who incidentally are now selling more albums than you, are due to finish any minute now. They will *not* be extending their set, and there will be *no* extra time in between acts. You've got just enough time to get there and get on stage, and if you end up getting shit reviews, it's your own fault.'

'We've had bad reviews before,' breezed Maxwell.

'Listen, dickhead, it's about more than that. First, it's an absolute given that you *need* good reviews, but you also need those reviews to translate into increased album sales. Ozone want bigger market coverage from this tour, and if that doesn't happen it's over. You remember the contract you signed, the one Andreas took care of? I've just got off the phone with Randall, and he and his office mates are just dying to impose direct control, which your contract allows them to do at any time. Direct control. Do you know what that means? It means you'll be churning out power ballads and nothing else, playing in car parks at corporate dinners, and forcing other metal bands to sign gagging orders. All it takes is for you lot to lose the plot just once more. And after the way they've bailed you out just to get you into this room, they so own you already.'

Silence soaked around the room and Maxwell's unwashed face circuited the police officers before settling on Johnny. 'I guess our treasure hunt isn't looking too good at the moment?'

'Maxwell, *nothing* is looking too good for you at the moment. And if by some miracle it does happen, it'll be on Ozone's terms, not yours. Believe it.'

'Look, mate. We cut loose; maybe we went a bit far, so we're sorry. But we've been pulled up for it.' Maxwell nodded towards the gendarmes behind him. 'These lads have made it pretty plain they're not fans. I think we know to stay off their radar from now on.'

Johnny snorted. 'Well, I suppose that's as close as I'll get to you admitting defeat.'

'So are we performing tonight in handcuffs?'

Johnny signed the band's release order. The gendarmes filed out of the room, leaving Johnny to stare at the French writing and wonder what he'd just put his name to. He picked up his phone and dialled for a hotel car.

'Right,' he said. 'Get in the car, get to the gig, get on stage.'

He watched over the band like a prison guard until the car drew up to the small door and they reluctantly filed out and took their seats. Johnny sat next to the driver, engaged the central locking, and glared in the mirror at the band during the short drive to the Bercy.

*

Cold Steel blundered onto the Bercy's vast open stage, and even the blindest fan could see they weren't prepared. Johnny's anger and frustration built, even though the wrecked ship moved and swayed like a living thing. The road crew had sweated for two

119

days to get it to work, while the band were unsure of the stage dimensions, had no feel for the hall's acoustics, and several times Maxwell even shouted out 'Nice' and 'Lyon' to the confused Paris crowd. Vocals and lines were mistimed, and the band's fatigue from the last two days showed.

The lumbering encore was more like a coup de grace than the explosive celebration of armour-piercing metal it was supposed to be. The fans cheered, but Johnny knew they always would. What they wouldn't do was tell their mates how good the gig was, and the press would be even less charitable.

'Fucking useless,' crowed Silas, standing next to Johnny at the monitor station. 'A band on the way down, a manager who was never anywhere else. Chainsaw will be headliners by the end of this tour, mate. That's guaranteed.'

Johnny stared shotgun barrels at Silas but said nothing. He went to join the band back in the dressing room, which was infinitely plusher than the British ones. Comfortable chairs and en suite showers, while photos of bands who had played there before hung from the walls. Cold Steel's picture wasn't there, even though that night's concert was their third one at the Bercy. They sat drinking beer from the well-stocked fridge, and Johnny walked in.

'Don't bother,' said Maxwell. 'We know what you're going to say.'

'I'm not going to say anything,' replied Johnny.

'What?'

Johnny took out his phone, held it above his head and pushed the screen. Silas' recent words to Johnny filled the room. 'Not much more to add really, is there?' he asked. 'In Britain, you were there, but nothing else was; now it's the other way round. You started this tour with it all. The biggest metal band on the planet, three multi-platinum albums, Beer Doctor was rated your best work yet, and for what it's worth, I agree. And now look at you. You've got instruments, sound, lights and your ship, but you'd rather fuck around than be where you could be, where you *should* be. Up to you, I guess.'

*

The next concert approached, but the audience at Rouen's Zenith basked in indifference. Johnny felt the steady work on the British dates being whittled away, with lacklustre reviews of the Paris

120

concert oozing among the music community. Gone was the anticipation, the *need* to see Cold Steel. People had bought their tickets months earlier, before the band's star had stumbled, and most were bound to turn up. But not all.

'Empty seats out there, lads,' said Johnny. 'Get used to it. Take Chainsaw's place as the opening act, or do something about it.'

'Seems like you're getting a big kick out of kicking us.' Maxwell's growl cut through the dressing room's cloying sense of defeat.

'I can only wipe your arses when you're not onstage. Out there, you're on your own. It's up to you if you want to come up with the goods.'

Johnny walked to the monitor station alone. He knew any words of encouragement he gave the band would be rejected. In their eyes he was in their way, spoiling their fun, like a teacher or a pushy parent making them do their homework. He could get them to the venue and back to their hotel rooms, he was learning who to call and who to lean on to get them out of their endless problems, but only they could get their hunger back. Nagging despair clawed at him, and he wondered if he'd ever be able steer any band to success. Silas' words clanged around inside his head. Arriving at the monitor station he nodded to the sound engineer who flicked a switch and the interval playlist stopped. Seconds later the house lights winked out and the arena was plunged into darkness. Applause boomed and Johnny tried to gauge the tone, then looked right at the low floor lights. Expecting the band to ignore him, he wasn't ready for the grim, tight-lipped determination on all of their faces.

*

Sinners Sanctuary usually started every Cold Steel concert, flash-firing a hailstorm of drums and guitars into the audience. That night Maxwell stood under a lone spotlight, the rest of the band obscured, and he sang the opening verse to No Nation, slower, more soulful than the recorded version. Unseen, Vince's and Andy's guitars, quietly at first and then louder and harsher, cut in and supported the haunting lyrics. Only when they traded solos did Mike and Joe join in, their timing making Johnny's chest squeeze with emotion. Then the lights flooded the stage and the wrecked

121

ship dipped and swayed behind the band, a tattered pirate flag fluttering from a splintered mast.

The band's timing was surgically precise, and while Maxwell still favoured his splinted arm, his movements were more fluid than Johnny had yet seen, and the rest of the band seemed to anticipate each other, their instruments almost alive. No Nation ghosted to an end, so different to how it had ever been played before, and the crowd's cheers engulfed the band. This was metal at its best, this was Cold Steel at their best, and it had taken until that point on the tour for it to be seen.

Pyrotechnics exploded at the front of the stage and Sinners Sanctuary lightning-surfed over the whole arena. Johnny felt a surge of triumph so powerful he could almost have been onstage himself. He didn't know if it was the indifferent reviews, personal humiliations or Silas' comments that had hit home. He didn't care; something had worked, and he just hoped it would carry on.

*

'I thought I was watching a different band.' Johnny threw beers around the dressing room after the concert, his confidence soaring into orbit.

'Never write Cold Steel off till you see the box going under,' grinned Maxwell. 'We're back on track, big time.'

'Yeah,' said Vince. 'It was only a matter of when.'

'Shame it took most of the tour,' said Johnny.

'Bollocks, Johnny, it was up and down, and you just happened to be around at the same time as we got it together.'

'Whatever, Vince. No credit at all to the road crew for keeping everything rolling while you found yourselves, or for setting up the ship prop while you were busy getting arrested.'

'They're good lads, but every band has them.'

'Hey.' Johnny held up his hands. 'You did a great concert. It was a pleasure to watch, and I'll be even more pleased to see it happen again tomorrow night.'

'Pleased enough to put in a good word for us about our treasure hunt?'

'Jesus, Maxwell, are you *still* going on about that?'

'We really want to do it, mate. If you spoke up for us, they'd listen to you.'

'And why should I speak up for the dumbest idea in the world?'

122

'You're not saying no,' grinned Maxwell. 'You know something.'

'I know you lot are certifiable.'

'You know more than that.'

'Well,' said Johnny. 'Ozone *have* got wind of it, and here's the deal. Tonight, you showed everyone what you can do, and if you can prove that every night for the rest of the tour, then maybe you'll get your little fantasy trip. But if you want Ozone to release you from your studio time, you need to rack up platinum album sales in every European country you play in. And the only way you'll manage that is to hit the spot every single night, like you did here. Happy fans make lots of comments on social media, and their friends read them, then they buy your album, *if* you're lucky.'

*

Events settled into a regular routine. Johnny stood silent but electrified at the monitor station, while the live shows blended together. Afterwards, the hours of darkness bristled with the band's hectic, dangerous and often illegal behaviour. Johnny kept up a text and email relationship with Rachel, also reading her blunt and often funny articles about developments in the music world. Cold Steel had dropped off the UK radar as the tour trundled on to the continent, and Rachel's work reflected that, but her messages told him she hadn't forgotten them, or him. She pestered him for news about the band's future, with perhaps more curiosity than Cold Steel warranted. Admitting it to no one but himself, he wondered at her ongoing interest, as well as his interest. In her.

Days drifted into weeks, and the European leg of the tour came to a close at St Petersburg's Ice Palace. Since Rouen, the band had performed with a Damascus-steel edge. Ecstatic fans blanketed social websites with their own spontaneous, unofficial reviews, and album sales slowly edged upwards. Johnny had taken to reading out the latest sales figures after each concert. They were easy enough for the band to find out for themselves, but the suspense and banter helped cement Johnny's relationship with the band. So far, they had achieved platinum sales just about everywhere, except in Russia.

'The tour's over,' said Johnny. The band relaxed in the dressing room and vodka mini-shots were being passed around. 'So what now?'

'You know what we want,' roared Maxwell. 'So how about it? Is it the studio or the Caribbean?'

'You all know the deal. Platinum sales everywhere, and in Russia that means fifty thousand albums shifted.'

'How have we done?' asked Andy.

'Okay, here's the numbers. Album sales of Beer Doctor, by Cold Steel…'

'Get on with it,' said Vince.

'As sold within Russia up to ten o'clock tonight…'

'*Tell* us,' said Maxwell.

'Fifty-two thousand, one –'

Johnny's words were drowned out by shouts from the band. Beer bottles were shaken and opened, spraying everyone with frothy liquor. Johnny held up his hands and slowly the band quietened down. 'You've got your trip,' he said. 'Ozone have put the studio on hold for two months, but I'm coming with you, and you bastards better behave.'

Chapter 17

Johnny's mind slowly climbed out of high altitude sleep, the plane's low engine drone now practically unheard after eight hours of level flight. He looked around the first class cabin and saw the rest of the band pose a spectrum between comatose, near-death sleep, and bleary-eyed barely-awake, like bears emerging from hibernation. Joe stared at Johnny with unfocussed eyes, his shaking hands pawing at the sponge earplugs that poked through his knotted hair like misplaced Frankenstein neck-screws.

Johnny cranked his pod-like bed back into a seat and looked out of the window. He'd never flown first class before, had never been to the Caribbean before, and had none of the band's jaded, all-seen-before attitude to the nine-hour flight. Outside, the sun poured bright warmth over the sea which flashed and glittered in the early morning, while tiny islands far below speckled the shiny blue with dark green palm forests, surrounded by strips of near-white beaches.

The pilot announced the plane's approach to Kingston and Johnny's excitement built. Even the band's blatant ignoring of the instructions to sit up and fasten their seat belts couldn't diminish his enthusiasm. *Let someone else nag them for a change,* he thought, *I'm sure I'll be doing it again soon enough.*

*

Johnny and the band breezed through passport control and then into the Club Kingston lounge. The last time Johnny had flown, he'd been on a package holiday, which felt as though he'd been squeezed into shrink-wrap and then fleeced for the three hours it took to reach the Canary Islands, where he was spewed out onto the demographic crush of a baggage collection resembling an industrial chicken farm. The air-conditioned luxury of Club Kingston made his last flying experience seem like an unreal dream, and he relaxed with an iced bottle of Royal Jamaican.

'I could get used to this.' He sank into a sumptuous easy chair.

'An hour for the connection,' smiled Maxwell. 'Don't get pissed and start a fight, or we'll grass you up to Randall.'

'Funny.'

'Talk about going one end to the other.' Johnny squeezed his spare frame along the DH-8's small cabin and sat down.

'St. Clements won't take long-haul.' Maxwell sat next to him and grinned. 'It's this way or the sea way to get there.'

The plane's engines fired up and Johnny looked out of the small window, watching Kingston disappear below. He fretted about whether their luggage had followed them from one aircraft to another and opened a beer, spraying froth over himself. He slowly sipped his drink and looked out at the dream scenery of multi-blue sea and palm-topped, beach fringed islands. At their now lower altitude, he saw fishing boats and the occasional cruise liner.

'We're not touring now,' grinned Maxwell. 'Kick back and enjoy it.'

An hour after leaving Jamaica in their slipstream, Johnny felt the plane begin a slow, controlled descent to St. Clements, a small island with no tourist infrastructure and no accompanying crowds of foreigners, some of whom at least would have been sure to recognise the band. Maintaining a low profile was the one thing Johnny and the band all agreed on.

'It's the perfect place,' Maxwell explained to Johnny on the flight across the Atlantic. 'Eight years ago, it was a French colony, but since then it's been run by an ex-pat called Henri Chevalier. He was in charge of a bar on the beach when the island got its independence, and he just decided to run for office. It was one hell of a shock when he actually got elected.'

'And how come you know all this?' asked Johnny.

'I've had this map for the last four years, I've researched the hell out of it. Everything I've read tells me that's where I need to be, so that's the place I've studied.'

'Okay, so the former barman became Prime Minister. What did he do next?'

'He kicked out all the foreign sugar companies, then nationalised the entire industry. America and Europe were pretty pissed off, and they tried an embargo on St. Clements' sugar products. So Henri sold cheap sugar to Africa and the Far East, and the profits stayed in St. Clements.' Maxwell picked up an in-flight magazine, flicked through to the map page and pointed to a tiny

Chapter 18

Henri Chevalier sat in his office and rested training-shoed feet on
his desk. Cool and relaxed inside the solid stone building of
Government House, he knew that his jeans and Hawaiian shirt
would be sticking uncomfortably to him within minutes of
stepping outside. He pulled his thinning hair back into its ponytail,
reflecting that some things had changed since his days as a
beachfront barman, but not everything. No one had been more
surprised than him when he'd actually been elected as Prime
Minister in the island's first post-independence election, but that
didn't mean he had to dress like one, right? And he didn't act like
one, either. At least, he didn't think so. With no experience at all in
politics, he simply ran the country like he ran the bar, trusting his
instincts and being grateful that the usual advisers and lobbyists
that metastasised around most modern politicians didn't surround
him in the same way.

With the sugar fields now owned and run by St. Clements, the
small island country had an income, but playing on the
international stage wasn't easy. There was no such thing as friends
among governments, and Henri struggled every day for his new
nation. The free trade deals that were being endoscoped down his
throat were just the latest attempt to take away what small degree
of real independence St. Clements had so recently won. He always
needed new ways to secure revenue, new avenues of trade and co-
operation.

A knock on his door brought Henri back to the present. '*Oui!*'
His French accent flowed like *pinot gris*.

The office door flew open and a well-built island man walked
in. 'Morning, Henri,' he boomed.

'Gates,' Henri smiled back at him. One of the things he loved
about being Prime Minister on St. Clements was that it was such a
small place that he knew most of the state employees. 'What brings
you here today?'

'Treasure hunters at the airport again.'

129

'*Merde*. When have we *ever* had any pirates, or even any rumours of pirates here on St. Clements? Have they got any money to spend?'

'Don't know. You ever heard of someone called Cold Steel?'

'A person?'

'No, man. A group. They say they's musicians.'

'Musicians? You mean Cold Steel, the heavy metal band?'

'Could be. You know I don't listen to that crap. Reggae's the sound for me.'

'Cold Steel? Here in Porte Juste?'

'Their passports are genuine.'

'And they're here for a treasure hunt?'

'It's what they said. I thought you might like to know.'

'*Merci,* Gates. We could well find a use for their talents.'

'They'd need to be better treasure hunters than musicians to find anything around here.'

'Perhaps, Gates, and perhaps that is something we need to find out.'

*

'What did you expect?' asked Johnny. 'They've probably heard that story a million times before.' After checking in to a crumbling hotel that overlooked the fishing harbour, they stepped out into the slow dusk. The heat and the day's travel leached their minds, and they came to a bar called Coconut Grove and collapsed into hollowed-out rum barrels that served as chairs surrounding a low driftwood table.

'More drinks, sirs?' The barman strolled up to them and chuckled once more. 'You know, Angelo here is a brilliant barber. He can give all of you gents a great haircut, do you a group discount, or maybe he'll just take a slice of your treasure once you find it.'

'Two bottles of rum,' growled Maxwell. 'And how about some music in this place?'

The barman laughed. 'Well, we're getting ready for Elvis' return, but maybe you guys could do a spot tomorrow night?'

'Yeah, right. Just get us the drinks.'

The barman walked away and Maxwell shook his head and stared thunder at Johnny. 'Can you believe this? We're Cold Steel, for Christ's sake.'

'Yes,' said Johnny. 'Cold Steel on a treasure hunt. I always said it was a stupid idea, and everyone on St. Clements thinks so as well.'

'But I've got the map.'

'Map, no map, a dozen bloody maps. It doesn't make any difference around here. They've heard it all before. But now we're here, why don't we just soak up the sun and enjoy the break?'

'Ozone gave us time out for that map.'

'No, they gave you time out, period. As long as you're all back in the studio when *they* say so, they really don't care if you find anything or not. That's a long way from them actually *believing* you.'

*

Closing time trundled over the band and Johnny waved unsteadily to the barman. Island rum soaked through his organs and bloodstream, and the sting of St. Clements' collective reaction to the band and the treasure hunt blunted his mood.

'You can't blame them.' His voice was slurred and they slowly weaved back to the hotel. 'They hear it all the time. Why should *we* be any different?'

'Because we're –'

'Cold Steel. Yeah, right. And that doesn't carry much weight around here either.'

They meandered back to the hotel. Walking through a rusting set of iron gates that were slowly being covered by grass and wide-leaved green plants, they swayed up to the chipped whitewashed building and drunkenly made their way to the louvered front door.

'Evening, gents.' A large policeman loomed up out of the darkness. Johnny yelped in fright.

'Holy shit,' he said, before inebriated politeness took over. 'Sorry, officer. What can we do for you? Look, I can vouch for these lads.' He indicated the band with a vague, drunken sweep of his arm. 'They've done nothing wrong.'

'You's summoned to see Mister Chevalier first thing tomorrow morning.'

'First thing?'

'Nine o'clock sharp, Government House.'

'Where's that?'

131

'I've told you where it is, man. Anyone on the island can take you there.'

*

The next morning, dawn trickled across the dark sky shortly after four o'clock, and with it, the harbourside came alive. Loud diesel engines rattled into life, dockers and boat crews shouted greetings and orders at each other, and vessels all along the wharf slipped free of their moorings and splashed out towards the open sea.

Sleeping through the tropical night's heat with closed windows was impossible for Johnny, so when the harbour woke up, he did too. He looked at his watch and a terminal hangover slam-dived around his visceral cavity and lit a touch-fuse of nausea. The logical conclusion to the night before slurried up his oesophagus, giving him just enough time to lurch his head over the toilet's chipped pan and empty his stomach's contents into its pallid water.

Unable to slide back into unconsciousness, he hammered on bedroom doors and dragged the band awake. Now alert and very low in mood, they spent the next four hours force-feeding themselves breakfast and coffee, then fighting to keep it all down before wandering limply around Porte Juste's narrow cobblestoned streets, looking for Government House. Johnny looked at the small, whitewashed buildings through bloodshot eyes before a skewed homing instinct led them back to the Coconut Grove.

'Morning, boys,' beamed Angelo. 'More rum?'

'Jesus, no,' rasped Johnny. 'We need to get to Government House. Where the hell is it?'

*

After the noise and bustle of the harbour and the day's range-oven heat, Government House was like an oasis of cool serenity. Thick stone walls shaded by palm trees kept the heat outside, while inside old wood-panelled flooring gave the place a relaxed, vintage feel. The only thing that was completely out of place was Henri Chevalier, who sat behind an old leather-topped desk, wearing jeans and a Hawaiian shirt, although his thinning hair tied back into a slick ponytail instantly endeared him to Johnny.

'Welcome, *mes amis,* to St. Clements.' His thick French accent and Johnny's screaming hangover made understanding him difficult.

'Johnny Faslane. I'm the band's manager.'

132

'It is a pleasure, *mon ami*.' Henri shook hands with Johnny and kissed each band member on the cheeks. 'But what is this I hear of your mission to our island? A treasure hunt?'

'I know you've heard it all before, mate.' Maxwell pulled out the map. 'But we've got real evidence that it's nearby.'

Henri scanned the map with polite interest, then handed it back and smiled. 'You would not be the first to come here with maps such as these. Of course I wish you all possible luck, but I must caution you to prepare for disappointment. There are better, more profitable ways to spend your time here. You know, *mon ami*, we have a magnificent new cricket stadium in Porte Juste. We would love to host you here for a concert. You could be assured of great support.'

'I don't know, mate.' Maxwell looked at Johnny. 'Our tour's just finished and we're due in the studio soon. Maybe once the new album's released?'

Henri smiled. 'Of course. But as to this enterprise, we have had many treasure hunters here, they have never found anything.'

'But this map is *real*.' Maxwell stared at Henri. 'It's real. I bought it in London from a guy who got it in Miami, and *he* said it was found on the American mainland near where Blackbeard settled down. The numbers on the back are a date in his log that gave a navigational fix to this island. The entry in the log says they were in open sea on that date, but the real bearing is an island.' He stabbed the map with his finger. '*This* island.'

'And is this island St. Clements?'

'No, mate, the one right next to it.'

'Ah, Iguana Island?'

'That's the place,' beamed Maxwell.

'It is a wildlife sanctuary.'

'Is that a problem?' asked Johnny.

'We have many native species on Iguana Island,' said Henri. 'And we allow no permanent human dwelling there. But from time to time scientific observers go there for short periods. We need to be sure that we do not disrupt the wildlife. If I were to know exactly what you planned to do, then maybe we can reach an agreement. And of course, were there to be some benefit for St. Clements as a whole, then that can only help everyone.'

'A benefit involving your new stadium, perhaps?'

133

'I must think of St. Clements in every decision I make, *mon ami*. I am sure you understand that. I also have to warn you about our neighbours.'

'Warn us?' asked Johnny.

'*Mais oui*. Here you have had the perfect welcome, and judging by the looks on your faces, sampled our island rum last night, *non?* But it is not so elsewhere. Iguana Island is on the western edge of our territory. International waters stretch for many miles, but other islands are not so friendly, especially Ancadia.'

'Ancadia?' said Maxwell. 'Never heard of it.'

'You surprise me,' said Henri. 'You wish to look for pirate's treasure? You say you are sure of the history, but you know nothing of the present. If ever a pirate crew became rulers of an island, then they would be Ancadians. There, they do what they wish, they care nothing for their island neighbours, and thanks to their deep-sea harbour they have powerful friends. There have been some attempted escapes by their own people, but their navy catches most of them, and they do not welcome unexpected visitors as we do. If you wish to visit Iguana Island, as long as you stay within the two-fathom line you will be safe, but I urge you not to go beyond it unless you wish to make friends with the Ancadians.'

'It looks like Iguana Island and no further,' said Johnny. 'So how are we going to get there?'

Chapter 19

Donnagh Fearneyhough, known by everyone on St. Clements as Skipper, pushed the dirty cloth cap to the back of his head and scratched greying hair with a greasy hand. 'Now, will you look at those stupid feckers?' He sucked on a bamboo pipe and thick, apple-flavoured smoke filled the small wood-panelled wheelhouse of his rusting recovery tug, *Andrea*. 'By feck, if anyone ever deserved to drown within sight of dry land, it's them.'

Six corpse-white men walked along the bustling wharf towards his corrugated iron repair shed. He held back a laugh once he saw what their balding leader was wearing.

'Do you not realise you're in the Caribbean?' he shouted as they came closer.

'What?'

'Leather trousers, for feck's sake? Have you fallen off your horse, sheriff?'

The five men behind him giggled, but as far as Skipper was concerned, they didn't look much better. Long hair, imitation football shirts and skinny legs poking out of market-bought shorts confirmed his suspicion that not everyone should travel.

'Are you Skipper?' asked one of them with a hooked nose and salesman's grin.

Skipper nodded.

'Great. I'm Maxwell. We're looking for a boat, and we were told you could help us.'

'You want a boat?'

'Yes.'

'Why's that? Is the island sinking? Because unless it is, I'd say you feckers would be better off staying put.'

'We're going to Iguana Island.'

'Really? You don't look like nature types to me.'

'We're not, we're –'

'So why should I let you feckers anywhere near a nature reserve?'

'Henri Chevalier said you might help us out.'

'Did he, by feck? Wait here.'

*

Johnny looked around, squinting under the sun's glare. Porte Juste was no hi-tech marina, and the only boats were either small traditional island trawlers, or handy-size cargo ships. Skipper walked inside his crumbling shed with a rolling gait as though he was aboard ship in a force ten gale. He emerged two minutes later with a scowl that only the most optimistic imagination could have called a look of approval.

'You might look like fecking idiots,' he growled, 'but at least you're telling the truth. Come with me.'

Moored behind the *Andrea,* and looking as though it might sink were it not for the lines securing it to the wharf, lolled a small cutter. Twenty years earlier it might have been new, might have been clean, and its mildew-stained panels might have shone white. The mast skewed to one side like an abandoned flagpole and the boom shifted on loose stays, all but redundant with no sails attached. The name *Friday's Fancy* was barely readable on the filthy stern.

'*That's* going to get us to another island?' asked Johnny. 'Jesus, it couldn't even get out of harbour.'

'Whatever you say, Captain,' said Skipper. 'It managed to get the last group over to Iguana Island, and back again.'

'It hasn't got any sails.'

'It's got an engine, Mister Twenty-first Century, it doesn't need any fecking sails. Take as long as you need getting used to it. If you can manage to clear harbour, you'll make Iguana Island in about a day. You'll get your provisions from the market. Come back with the boat in one piece, or don't come back at all.'

Maxwell looked at Skipper. 'Isn't there anything else, more...'

'Modern?'

'Well, yes.'

Skipper laughed a high-pitched giggle. 'All the money in the world doesn't always help, does it, lads? What you see is what the island has, I don't care how fecking famous you are. So unless you want to swim back to Jamaica and hire a boat from there, put up with it.'

Skipper swayed back to the *Andrea* and the band looked at *Friday's Fancy,* as though the power of vision would transform it

136

into a newer, cleaner boat that *might* make it back from a short voyage across a still pond.

'Let's get aboard, then.' Johnny led the band across a trip-hazard gangplank, onto the unwashed, slippery deck and down into the mouldy, student-like decor below. Crouching low, he moved around the low galley, past a tiny bench and table and through to the small cabins with stained mattress bunks. Back on deck, he saw what looked liked an old GPS device bolted next to the ship's wheel. 'At least we shouldn't get lost.'

'Yeah,' said Maxwell. 'As long as we know how to use it.'

'Best we start learning, then.'

*

The band's feet thudded around the deck's planking and they got used to the boat's dimensions, while Mike, the only one wearing a lifejacket, held the stays with white knuckles and moved as few paces as possible. He looked at the narrow strip of water between *Friday's* port side and the quay.

'Mike,' said Johnny. 'Are you alright?' He walked towards Mike, his movements causing the narrow ship to sway slightly. Mike stared wildly at Johnny and gripped even more tightly to the thin ropes.

'Keep still,' moaned Mike. 'Can't you feel the ship swaying? We'll turn over.'

'Don't be stupid,' said Johnny. 'Of course we won't.'

He placed a reassuring hand on Mike's shoulder. Mike squeezed his fingers, almost crushing them, before fleeing to the open hatchway in front of the wheel. His wild movements made the ship sway even more. He overshot the hatchway and came up against the starboard rail. His arms windmilled, he screamed as gravity took him and fell into the water with a loud splash.

'Man overboard!' shouted Maxwell.

Mike thrashed his arms, spluttered and drank the murky harbour water. His lifejacket kept his head visible, but his long, corkscrew hair soon flattened to his head. Maxwell picked up a kisby ring and flung it at Mike. The ring slammed into Mike's forehead and his arms instantly flopped out of sight.

'Oh, Christ, you've knocked him out.' Johnny jumped into the water and was pushed under as the rest of the band followed him, all landing on each other. Throwing up gouts of spray, they

137

surfaced and punched out to get away from each other. Maxwell grabbed the ring and dropped it over Mike's unconscious head, and between them they pulled and pushed him to the ship's side.

'Did anyone roll down the ladder?' asked Johnny. Blank stares told him they hadn't. 'Shit. Hold him here.'

He swam around the ship's stern and grabbed a mooring rope. His fingers slid on the wet hemp and he gripped tighter, slowly inching himself out of the water. Grabbing a touch hold in the pitted concrete lip, he scrambled up, wrapping his legs around the mooring rope and nearly castrating himself as he struggled ashore. Puffing like an asthmatic, he got up and ran across the gangplank and back aboard. Seconds later he stood at the rail, a few feet above the band. He saw the rope ladder neatly rolled up and he kicked it over the side, its thin wooden rungs clacking against the ship's planking.

And disappeared overboard…

'Nooooo!' shouted Maxwell.

'What?' said Johnny.

'It's not fastened.'

Maxwell left Mike with Vince, Andy and Joe, and duck-dived underwater. Ten seconds later he emerged with a sodden length of fresh hemp. He trod water and held his arm above his head, and Johnny leant over and grabbed it.

'Main mast,' coughed Maxwell. 'Double bowline.'

Johnny yanked on the rope and looped it round the mast, then tied a knot he hoped would hold. Maxwell was the first up the ladder, and with Vince, Andy and Joe pushing, Johnny and Maxwell pulled Mike back aboard. They rolled him onto his side and he puked up a mouthful of seawater, then groaned and rubbed his head.

'Fucking hell,' said Johnny. 'How far away is this island?'

'Textbook rescue,' grinned Maxwell. 'I don't know what you were worried about.'

Chapter 20

'What do you mean, you can't swim?' The band was squeezed around the small table in the ship's tiny galley that doubled as the main cabin. Johnny rummaged through the cabinets, found a pack of just in date beers and passed them round. 'You're built like a brick shithouse, Mike, I'd have thought you could swim the channel.'

Mike coughed saltwater sputum and his hands shook. 'Guess again.'

'Well,' said Vince, drip-drying onto the plastic flooring beneath his bare feet. 'You're going to have a shit time on this trip.'

'No way,' replied Mike. 'You've been on a plane loads of times, haven't you?'

'Yes, so?'

'So do you know how to fly? If the plane disappeared at thirty thousand feet you'd be fucked, right?'

'I guess.'

'Same thing here.'

'Apart from the fact that you went overboard when we were still tied to dry land,' said Johnny.

'I didn't drown, did I?' Mike rubbed his head where the kisby ring had knocked him out. 'You guys got me back aboard.'

'You were lucky,' said Johnny. 'I wouldn't like to do that in the middle of a storm.'

'Look, lads,' said Mike. 'The island's only a day away, Skipper said so. The lifejacket kept me afloat, and once we get going, I plan on staying below deck as much as possible.'

'Leave the work up top to the rest of us,' sniped Andy.

'What work? Besides, someone's got to cook, right? That can be my job.'

'The ugliest housewife afloat,' grinned Maxwell. 'There's a song in there somewhere.'

*

Sunset shimmered across the harbour's settled waters, and *Friday's Fancy's* hold bulged with fresh island produce, although the sting of the market sellers' reaction had left its scar. Good-natured laughter stalked them from stall to stall along the seafront. Polite curiosity about Cold Steel and what heavy metal meant gave way to uninterrupted scepticism about the treasure hunt. Johnny kept his thoughts to himself, and early the next morning, the ship's stained bows sliced through the surf.

The GPS beeped directions to port or starboard, and the cracked display screen gave a distance to their destination. Skipper assured them that as they would always be able to see either Iguana Island or St. Clements, they couldn't get lost. Henri had seen them off, and in between wishing them luck, he'd laid down strict rules. They were to anchor at the river mouth only, go ashore in one boat, and carry everything with them. They were to dig in just one place, and the treasure had to be offered to St. Clements after it was found.

'Jesus Christ,' muttered Johnny. 'That guy should be managing a band.'

'He's driving a hard bargain,' agreed Maxwell, turning the wheel a point to the north. 'But you've got to respect him for fighting St. Clements' corner.'

'And what are *you* getting out of all this?'

'The trip of a lifetime. Don't tell me you'd rather be stuck in the studio? Or haggling our next recording deal, or keeping us in line on tour?'

'You've got a point.'

'Course I have, and you know it. Besides, we don't *need* that treasure, any of it. If Henri can help us find it, then that's a fair enough deal.'

Johnny grimaced at the foaming waves and glistening reefs off their port beam. 'And how many more shoals like that are between us and it?'

'So we have to sail the long way around to get to our spot. It's no biggie; we'll get there. Another hour and we'll see where we're anchoring. Nothing can go wrong.'

*

The island lay visible for the rest of the day, and they circled to avoid the reefs, taking care to keep dark blue sea beneath the shallow keel. They approached a small cape on the island's southern tip, where lush virgin jungle bearded the entire island from behind its wedding band of gold beach.

'Look.' Johnny pointed to the west. 'What's that?'

The band followed Johnny's hand. Floating on the surface was a collection of red plastic floats supporting a tangle of green netting.

'Looks like a fisherman's lost a net,' said Maxwell.

'A St. Clements one?' asked Johnny.

'That net could have come from anywhere.'

'Hey, man,' said Joe. 'There's a ship out there, coming this way.'

Johnny looked and saw a small, plank-built fishing boat approaching, a black stream of exhaust smoke pluming from its funnel just behind the wheelhouse.

'Looks like he's come to collect his nets,' said Maxwell. 'What say we help him out and see who gets there first?'

Maxwell spun the wheel and *Friday's Fancy* slewed around, bringing a shriek from below as Mike lost his footing and clattered to the floor. The fishing boat's crew stood and waved from the prow of their own boat.

'Here,' said Andy. 'Is that another ship approaching?'

Johnny screwed his eyes against the bright sunshine and saw a black dot on the horizon getting bigger. 'Oh, shit. Guys, maybe we should turn around again.'

'What do you mean?' asked Maxwell.

'There *is* another ship arriving behind that fishing boat, and it doesn't look friendly.'

Maxwell stared hard into the distance. Johnny shaded his eyes and made out the angular, grey shape of a naval gunboat. It came towards them at speed, approaching the fishing boat at a much quicker pace than they were travelling.

'We ain't done anything wrong,' said Maxwell. 'And nor has that fishing boat. That other ship's probably coming to help.'

Johnny's heart hammered in his chest and his sense of disquiet percolated through his body. The fishing boat had reached the drifting nets and two crewmen were leaning over the edge with hooks, straining to bring them in. Intent on their task, they didn't notice the gunboat approach and a uniformed sailor jump aboard. On *Friday's Fancy,* they were close enough to hear the sailor jabbering in Spanish, and saw him drag one of the fishing boat's crew back from the rail and slap him around the face.

141

'Hey!' shouted Maxwell. 'Leave him alone, you bastard.'

The sailor turned to face the band. '*Vamos, hombre!*' he shouted at them.

'Bollocks,' replied Maxwell.

The sailor drew a pistol.

'Maxwell,' said Johnny. 'This isn't our problem. Let's go.'

'He's got no right,' said Maxwell. 'Besides, he's just telling us he can't get it up without holding a gun. He won't do anything.'

After a minute, with *Friday's Fancy* showing no sign of turning, the sailor pointed his pistol and fired three rounds into the water. Small hydro-fountains splashed over the bows and the gunboat appeared from behind the fishing boat, a bow-mounted chain gun pointed at *Friday's Fancy.*

'Jesus, Maxwell,' said Johnny. 'Their dicks are getting bigger by the minute.'

The gunboat trod water and continued to threaten them, while the sailor aboard the fishing boat shouted at the crew in Spanish and gestured at the netting in the water. Johnny looked at the band. Maxwell and Andy glowered at the gunboat, as though they could sink it with their poisonous stares. The gun-crew trained their weapon on them, and Johnny felt as though he could see right down its multiple barrels.

The fishing crew gathered in the netting, and under the gunboat's malevolent supervision, turned about and slowly chugged away. The gunboat followed, its aft gun trained on *Friday's Fancy.*

Chapter 21

They cleared the island's southern tip and watched the orange sun dipping beneath its pyramid skyline. Johnny joined the rest of the crew on deck as they looked across the short stretch of sea between them and the beach. It was a perfect untouched wilderness, with the setting sun perfectly framed by the palm trees.

'Bollocks to the treasure,' said Johnny. 'Why don't we just retire here?'

At half past four the next morning, a loud hammering on his cabin door matched the peristalsis kick in Johnny's bowels which reacted to the island food's high fibre content. Still half asleep, he rubbed a hand over the rough, unwashed stubble of his face, before grabbing a well-thumbed adult mag and stumbling to the heads. Two minutes later, the machine-gun knock followed him like a groupie on a mission.

'There's no time for that.' Maxwell's voice spooked through the plywood. 'We've got treasure to find.'

Slowly, the sun climbed above the blue horizon while the crew crammed a psychedelic painted dinghy with food, shovels and pickaxes. It bobbed alongside, filled almost to the point of capsize.

Perched at the prow, Johnny untied the securing rope before taking his place at an oar and the tide's gentle swell sped them on their way. They approached the island's narrow beach, and he looked over his shoulder and saw the mouth of a small river opening up to them.

'First landmark,' said Maxwell. 'Just where it's supposed to be.'

Once into the river, Johnny's hands slicked with sweat against the oar's smoothed wood. The rough-planked rowing bench quickly became uncomfortable, and his muscles ached as they pitched their strength against the current. Every time he pulled back, his thighs ricked in agony, while his arms felt as though they were being yanked out of their sockets. For two long hours, they struggled to get five miles upstream before the whooshing torrent from a fifteen-foot high waterfall stopped them dead.

Maxwell looked at the cloud of spray thrown out by the waterfall. 'That's as far as we row, lads.'

Sweat-soaked and hot, Johnny gasped and stood knee deep in freezing water. They dragged the dinghy through reed-infested shallows, while Maxwell unloaded their gear and stored it above the waterline. Johnny's rucksack bit deep into his shoulders, and the wisdom of wearing leather trousers sat heavily on his conscience.

Maxwell, though, wore his own pack as though it were nothing more than a knapsack. He strode along the grass-banked river's edge while Johnny picked up the rear, his cowboy boots causing his feet to ache abominably. Their path weaved into dense forest, and leaves and branches closed in on them before they came to an exhausted halt at what appeared to be the river's source, a collection of rock pools in a clearing surrounded by thick green vegetation.

Johnny dropped his rucksack to the floor and his spine felt like a released tension spring. He looked around. The steep rise they had just climbed gave him a good view. They seemed to be at the island's highest point, and if the map *was* correct, then somewhere directly between the western shore and where they were standing lay the possibility of an undiscovered treasure chest. 'Bloody hell, Maxwell,' he wheezed. 'We *must* have earned a break by now. Here, why do you think this place is called Iguana Island?'

As soon as Johnny spoke, a green scaly head appeared through the grass, and a long, dry body sped towards him at knee height. He stepped backwards nervously. 'I think I've just found out,' he stammered.

'Don't worry,' said Maxwell. 'They aren't dangerous.'

'How the hell do *you* know?'

The iguana snapped angrily at Johnny and advanced towards him. He turned and ran across the clearing with the iguana's high-pitched screech ringing in his ears. Wailing in fear, he sprinted towards the nearest tree, his fingernails sinking into the bark. He clawed upwards, hooked his arm around the nearest branch and rapidly pulled himself out of the angry iguana's reach.

Still keening in fury, the iguana spun around and hissed at the band. Johnny pulled himself up and pushed aside a living net curtain of green leaves. The band were slowly edging backwards, away from the iguana, leaving their kit where it was. The iguana charged, scattering the band in all directions; their screams of fear left audio vapour trails, which followed the trampled grass towards their individual tree-line sanctuaries.

With its tail twitching among the grass, the iguana flicked his head from side to side, his fury unslaked. He sniffed at the abandoned rucksacks, then ripped them apart, gorging on the food and splintering shovel and pickaxe handles between powerful jaws. He gave a final triumphant swish of his tail, then slowly disappeared into the undergrowth.

Slowly, Johnny's heart rate subsided. He shouted out into the jungle. 'Has that bastard gone yet?'

'Looks like it.' Maxwell's faraway reply fed back to him.

Legs trembling, and feeling sick with fear, Johnny slowly slid down the tree's rough trunk till his boots touched the soft, matted ground. He spun around, looking everywhere for a returning iguana. Their attacker had gone, and he ran towards the debris of their equipment, where the band joined him one at a time.

'Oh, shit,' fumed Andy. 'Our kit's trashed. What do we do now?'

'Carry on,' said Maxwell.

'Carry on? Are you nuts? That scaly handbag even ate our shovels.' Andy picked up a ruined pickaxe handle. 'And what are we gong to do for food?'

'Hey, man,' said Joe. 'It's their island.'

'And we've just been chased all around it, you stupid bastard. I think that tells us we're not welcome.'

Maxwell picked up the destroyed packs and piled them at his feet. 'Let's just see what we can still use.'

Two rucksacks remained intact, and much of the food hadn't been touched. The iguana seemed happy to have spread it all over the clearing once he'd eaten what that he wanted. Of the three shovels and two pickaxes, one shovel was useable.

'Right,' said Johnny. 'Let's at least try and find out if there's anything here.'

Two water bottles were undamaged and one was passed around before Johnny returned to his position at the rear of the column. He trudged along on footing that alternated between soft, loamy soil and tree-roots that spread like tripwires. Noises all around him jangled his nerves and he wondered what other animals made Iguana Island their home. Then he looked down at the ground at a narrow but still discernable forest track.

'This has *got* to be the path the Captain used on his way to bury the treasure.' Maxwell's words clanged in Johnny's ears.

For four hours that felt more like four hundred, Johnny stumbled onwards. Loose rocks conspired with the damp, slippery leaves that had fallen from the trees. Eventually, with the sun sinking low in the sky, Maxwell stopped and looked off to his right.

'That's it!'

Johnny's senses pushed through mists of exhaustion and he followed Maxwell's gaze. He saw a cave nestled into the hill, half obscured by dense vegetation. 'It's a cave,' he said.

'It's an 'X' on the map, and the treasure's right here.'

'Where?'

'Look.' Maxwell pointed at the cave and Johnny dropped his pack and looked. High up on either side of the cave entrance were two smaller openings. It was difficult for Johnny to make them out. Reeds and moss had blended the cave wall in with the rest of the undergrowth. 'This cave is the most skull-shaped cave I've ever seen. Captain Teach couldn't have picked a more obvious site if he'd tried.'

Johnny looked closely at the cave. It looked a bit like a skull, but only just. He shrugged his aching shoulders. 'Whatever, Maxwell. But if we don't find any treasure, at least we'll have a decent place to sleep.'

'Yeah,' grumbled Andy. 'But only *after* we've dug a fucking huge hole.'

They shuffled inside. Johnny fumbled with his lighter and brought the flame to the hurricane lamp's reeking wick. Bizarre shadows danced across the cave walls. He grasped the shovel and started to dig through the dry earth. The loose soil gave way, and he jumped into the quickly deepening hole, relieved after half an hour by Maxwell. The shovel ate away at the ground, and Johnny saw the hole getting steadily bigger.

With a dull clang, Maxwell's shovel jarred against a solid object. He grunted, dropped to his knees and scooped away the loose earth.

'Found it!' he shouted.

Chapter 22

Maxwell cleared more earth away from the dirt-stained top of what looked like a very old, tanned leather sea chest. As one, six sets of hands eagerly set about uncovering it, and after much hard lifting and even harder swearing, it was squeezed free from the ground and dumped on the cave's floor.

'Joe.' Maxwell stared at the chest's sand-crusted latch fastening.

Joe knelt down beside Maxwell. His long, greasy hair obscured his face and he stared at the corroded lock. 'It's pretty wasted, man,' he said. 'I think I need to blow it.'

'Blow it?' asked Johnny.

'Look, man,' said Joe. 'How did you *think* we'd get a locked sea chest open? It's been under the ground for three hundred years. There's no *way* I'd be able to pick it.'

'Hang on a second,' said Johnny. 'Blowing the lock, picking it. Never mind Maxwell and his nautical research hobby, what the bloody hell do *you* do in your spare time? This is a long way from the dope-smoking hippy who can barely even turn up for his own band's concerts.'

'We've all got histories, man. What did you do before Cold Steel?'

'I managed one metal band after another. What did *you* do?'

Joe shrugged. 'Had to pay for my weed somehow. Good job I never got caught, really, otherwise you'd have no one to open this chest, right?' He dug into his pocket and pulled out a grease-papered package. He peeled back the slick paper and revealed a damp putty-like handful. He gently laid it on a cleared patch of sand. 'It's starting to sweat, guys.'

'Jesus,' said Johnny. 'Is that –? Is that –?'

'Plastic explosive?' said Joe. 'Yeah, man.'

'And how long have we been carting that shit around with us?'

'Take it easy, Johnny. I picked this up at the market yesterday, and as soon as they found out it was for a treasure hunt the bastards doubled their price.' Joe turned towards the chest, shaped the explosive around the chest's lock and fumbled in his other pocket,

148

pulling out a tangle of wires. 'Okay, guys. I'm using the stuff, so you'd better get back.'

'Bloody right,' said Johnny. 'I'm not hanging around in here when there's bombs going off. It's been nice knowing you, Joe. I hope you survive all this.'

He turned and walked out of the cave. He found his rucksack in the darkness by nearly tripping over it, pulled out a torch and searched for somewhere to take cover. With pterodactyl-sized butterflies swooping around his stomach, he settled behind a collection of fallen tree trunks and wondered if they would withstand the blast. The rest of the band joined him, Maxwell last of all, blatant impatience stamped on his face.

'Bugger this waiting around,' he muttered after a minute's restless fidgeting. 'I'm going to see what Joe's up to.'

'Jesus, Maxwell,' hissed Johnny. 'Just stay put and wait for the bang. I didn't come all this way with you to see you get blown to bits.'

'You do what you want to mate, but I'm off.' Maxwell stood up and returned to the cave.

Johnny fidgeted, stood up, sat down, and repeated the process, fighting to decide what to do. Risk his life to drag Maxwell back, or stay alive and remain where he was? After ten minutes of indecision, Joe appeared, trailing a thin strand of copper wire behind him.

'Where's Maxwell?' asked Johnny.

'Back at the cave, man. He said he wanted to be the first person to see the treasure.'

'He's standing by the chest? Right next to the chest?'

Joe shrugged. 'Seems pretty dangerous to me.'

'Is he fucking nuts?'

'There's no telling him, man. His mind's made up.'

'Who said anything about talking to him?' Johnny stood up and brushed himself down. 'Come on, lads, let's drag that stupid bastard out of there.'

He strode towards the cave, followed by the rest of the band. Inside, Maxwell stood with his back to them, staring at the chest. Johnny placed a hand on his shoulder while the rest of the band pounced. The cloud of sand subsided and they lifted him clear of the ground and carried him out of the cave.

149

'What are you doing?' he screamed, writhing in the band's collective grip.

'Saving your life, you stupid prick,' said Johnny through clenched teeth. He fought hard to hold Maxwell's wildly kicking leg.

'But I want to see the chest get blown open!'

'The only thing getting blown open would be your head,' retorted Johnny, by which time they had reached their improvised shelter. Maxwell was thrown to the ground and sat on by the rest of the band. They struggled to keep him where he was, and Johnny looked over at Joe and nodded. He connected the wire to the detonator, and seconds later pushed the firing button.

Nothing happened. Mosquitoes buzzed contentedly around the band and jungle noises screeched and wailed all around them, uninterrupted by any sudden explosion.

'Is that supposed to happen?' asked Johnny.

'Is what supposed to happen?'

'Nothing, for Christ's sake.'

'No, man. Something's not right here.' Joe looked at the small detonator box, and then squinted at the wires running from it. 'Maybe I didn't connect it properly.'

'Maybe you're an idiot,' shouted Maxwell. 'Now get off of me, you bastards.' He wriggled free and stalked back inside the cave.

Joe slowly retraced his route, running the wires between his fingers and muttering to himself. He arrived back at the chest and fiddled with the small tubes of bare metal that poked out of the moulded explosive.

'So why didn't it work?' asked Johnny.

'I'm not sure, man.'

'Oh, Christ,' growled Andy. 'He doesn't know.' He picked up the shovel. 'Why don't we just bash it open?'

Maxwell pushed Andy away from the chest. 'Get back there, punchy.'

'Well, Joe's method isn't helping much, is it?' Andy squared up to Maxwell.

'Back off and cool down,' said Maxwell. 'He'll figure it out.'

'Bollocks.' Andy swung the shovel hard. Maxwell ducked, then bounced up and pushed Andy backwards. Andy was already off balance as the swinging shovel pulled him around, and

150

Maxwell's hands in his chest did the rest. Andy's arms spun like bilateral hamster wheels as he teetered over the hole, then fell into it, landing with a dry thud on the sandy floor, groaning loudly.

'He's still making some noise,' said Maxwell. 'He must be alright. How're you doing, Joe?'

Loud screeches from the darkening jungle made the band turn their heads in all directions.

'What's that?' asked Johnny.

Bushes rustled and rasping breaths accompanied multiple footfalls in the undergrowth. Wild, moving silhouettes approached them.

'Fucking hell,' shouted Maxwell. 'Run!'

While Andy sprawled at the bottom of the newly excavated hole, the rest of the band bomb-burst in compass-spread directions. Johnny tripped over a solid moving object at knee-height, fell face down in the undergrowth and picked himself up, fear propelling him onwards. He almost collided with a tree and his nails dug into the bark once more as he put as much distance between himself and whatever was below him, hoping it couldn't climb trees. 'What kind of hell is this place?' he called out, once he'd settled into the branches.

'It's definitely the animals' kingdom, man,' chirped Joe.

'That *really* helps. And what's going on down there?'

'Hang on a second.'

Johnny heard rustling at tree-height over to his left, and a narrow torch beam stabbed through the darkness. Moving in and out of the torchlight were multiple iguana shapes, prowling over the ground they now controlled.

'Oh, Jesus,' said Johnny. 'How long are those bastards going to hang around? And how many of them are there?'

Joe's torch beam moved around the small clearing in front of the cave entrance. Shapes moved in and out of the light, making it impossible to know how many iguanas stalked beneath the trees.

'Christ,' said Johnny. 'We'll never keep track of this lot with one bloody torch. Joe, see if the detonator's okay.'

The torchlight moved around the patches of sandy soil. 'It's not easy from up here,' he moaned.

'Do you want to go down there and try?'

151

Joe's beam moved more methodically. It fixed on the cave entrance, then moved back towards Johnny's abandoned rucksack, to the wall of fallen trees, and then to the small detonator, which was being closely examined by a bull iguana. Its black eyes looked at the thin wires and electrical box, he sniffed cautiously at it, then nudged the firing button.

A bright lightning flash exploded for a microsecond inside the cave, followed immediately by a sharp crack. A thick cloud of dust flew out from the cave entrance, and the iguanas shrieked even louder than the explosion and tore off into the jungle, letting a sudden silence blanket the area.

The sound of animals crashing through the undergrowth got further away.

'I think they've gone,' said Johnny.

'And they could be back any time.' Maxwell's voice filtered through the darkness. 'We need to make the most of it while they've been scared off.'

Johnny climbed down from his tree and the band congregated at the cave entrance. Inside, Andy stirred and climbed out of the hole. 'What happened?'

'Onstage suspension wires,' said Vince.

'Very funny.' He looked at the top of the chest, which had been sheared off by the explosion. 'Maybe Joe's not as stupid as he looks after all.'

'I had a bit of help from the locals, man.'

'Never mind that,' said Maxwell. He knelt down next to the chest, picked up the discarded hurricane lamp and looked inside.

Chapter 23

'Rocks.'

'What?' asked Johnny.

'Rocks. Fucking rocks.'

Johnny leaned forward and looked inside. The stained leather chest was crammed with dust-covered, non-descript rocks. 'No,' he said. 'That's not possible. You said. Maxwell, you *said* this was where the treasure was.' The constant sense of humiliation that had dogged him his entire life now landed on his shoulders with crushing force. He clenched his fists and shook his head. 'Jesus Christ. We could have been in the studio right now making a brilliant album, but instead we're on a deserted island surrounded by killer iguanas, and all we've got to show for it is a three-hundred-year-old chest full of rocks.'

'Sure,' said Maxwell. 'There *should* be treasure in this chest, but it doesn't look like a hoax to me. None of this looks new, and the lock certainly wasn't. I'd bet my life this chest was put down three hundred years ago by Blackbeard and his crew.'

'What, you mean he deliberately buried a chest full of rocks instead of his treasure?' said Johnny. 'Why would he do that?'

'To fool everyone into thinking this is where the treasure is. Meantime it's safely somewhere completely different.'

'So where are we supposed to look now?'

'I don't know, but I'm certain Blackbeard buried these rocks here. It also looks like we're the first ones to have ever got this far. That means his treasure is still out there somewhere.'

'*Where?*'

'Mate, I don't know. But come tomorrow morning we're burying that chest, then we're going back to St. Clements while we work it out.'

'We've come this far,' said Mike.

'Yeah, man,' said Joe. 'And it might only be rocks, but we *have* found something.'

'Which is more than anyone else has,' said Vince.

'Good lads,' grinned Maxwell.

Johnny raised his eyebrows and shrugged. 'What the hell. I might have known you guys would write this your own way.'

*

The solid-tyred cycle cab delivered a fracturing ride over Porte Juste's uneven cobbled streets, and Johnny was almost in tears by the time the squadron of converted bicycles dropped the band off outside Government House. A suited security man guided them inside and on to Henri's office.

'Maxwell, *mon ami*.' Henri stood up and walked towards Maxwell. 'Back so soon? So, tell me, how is your treasure hunt proceeding?'

'Well…' Maxwell stood at the front of the band. 'The map led us straight to a buried sea-chest, only there was no treasure in it, just a pile of rocks.'

'I told you. I told you this treasure hunt of yours would be fruitless. Rocks, *oui?*' He chuckled. 'So you have satisfied your honour, now relax and enjoy yourselves here. Look at our new cricket stadium. You have played open air concerts before, *non?*'

Maxwell shook his head. 'There's still treasure to be found.'

'Where? Where is this treasure? You had your map, you went where it sent you, and you found no riches.'

'But that chest, mate. It might not have had anything valuable inside it, but it hadn't been disturbed for years – centuries, even.'

'So?'

'So whoever buried those rocks buried something else more valuable. And this map and everything else, the chest, the rocks, it was all part of some plan to lead everyone away from the real thing.'

'Are you sure?'

'I know it, mate.' Maxwell's eyes burned like lasers. 'I *know* it.'

Henri smiled once more. 'Our agreement still stands? St. Clements displays this treasure if you can find it?'

'A deal's a deal, mate. We shook on it.'

'Then maybe I know someone who can help.'

154

Chapter 24

St. Clements University occupied a crumbling mansion house complex on the hill above Porte Juste, but Johnny had little time to marvel at the amazing view once he and the band climbed out of the prime ministerial minibus. Henri ushered them towards a carved stone staircase set into a grassed knoll that led up to one of the white buildings, shaded by palm trees, and Johnny's gaze took in the two naval cannons that guarded the entrance. To one side of the doorway stood a brilliant white flagpole, from which the skull and crossbones flew in the warm wind.

'Welcome, *mes amis*,' said Henri, 'to the Faculty of Marine Criminology.'

'Your university studies pirates?' asked Johnny.

'Of course. Although no such historical figures were ever known to inhabit St. Clements, this whole area was a crucible for piracy. Privateers, colonial expansion, slavery and raw conflict between the world powers defined life on these islands. We would be fools not to develop an awareness of our own history.'

Johnny followed the rest of the band into the hushed building. Inside, plush red carpets ran the length of polished wood floors. He looked up at the oak-panelled walls, where his eyes were met by the imposing stares of one infamous pirate after another, all of whom glared malevolently out at the world from their portraits.

Henri came to a halt outside a mahogany door. The nameplate in gothic letters said 'Professor Miles Deep, Dean of Faculty'. He knocked once and was called in by a booming voice. After the soft, ambient lighting in the corridor, Johnny's eyes suddenly squinted in response to the florescent glare that illuminated the small office.

A large wooden desk, full of antiques, dominated the room, while a dust-covered computer perched on one end, almost as an afterthought. Sitting on a stool that looked as though it would collapse at any moment was the biggest man Johnny had ever seen. Slowly, the man turned his immense bulk towards his visitors, and the stool's bearings squeaked in protest. Professor Deep faced them, and Johnny saw that he had a large head with no hair, and his moon- like face projected an equally massive smile.

155

'*Bonjour*, Professor Deep,' said Henri.

'Morning, Henri,' he replied, speaking with a slow island accent. 'And who have you brought with you this time?'

'Travellers from the old world,' replied Henri. 'They have an interest in the doings of Captain Blackbeard.'

'What? You're bringing treasure hunters here? Into my faculty? Don't tell me, they've found a map? They've stumbled across a unique combination of events? Henri, we've spoken about this. There were no pirates on St. Clements, *including* Blackbeard. There is *no* treasure buried here. And what the hell is going on with their hair?'

'They are musicians, *mon ami*.' Henri spread his arms wide. 'And artists, they suffer for their art, so perhaps we must suffer for their appearance.'

'And I have to suffer for them being here? Musicians, Henri? On a treasure hunt? Is it possible to find a more powder-brained combination?'

'They found something on Iguana Island.'

'No they didn't. There's nothing to find there. I reviewed the place myself before you made it a sanctuary. Surely you remember.'

'I remember. But since then, and since yesterday, these fellows *have* been to Iguana Island, and they *have* found something.'

Johnny saw reluctant curiosity jabbing at Miles. He looked at Maxwell and folded thick arms across a chest the size of a forty-gallon oil drum. 'So, what have you got?'

Maxwell brought out the map. 'I got this a few years ago.'

Miles looked at the crude drawing, and the faintly written numbers on the back. He pursed his lips. 'Colonial-era paper, similar style script. Have you seen these numbers on the back?'

'Seen them, worked them out, used them.'

Miles grinned, showing two rows of fluorescent white teeth.

'Well, you've got my attention. Tell me how this map led you to Iguana Island?'

'The date on the back. I took a leap of faith, assumed it was Blackbeard's and looked at his log that was captured when his ship was taken. The date written on the map is a navigational fix. The entry in the log on that date said they were in open sea, but the co-ordinates in the log gave us Iguana Island. To do that, you had to

156

put the map *and* the log together, and it's my guess that Blackbeard kept them both separate so that nobody would.'

'And you made the connection, and this connection led you to Iguana Island and a chest full of rocks? It seems a lot of trouble for anyone to go to.'

'Unless it was part of an elaborate plan to lead everyone away from the real treasure.'

'That's possible.' Miles sighed a deep breath. 'But you have to understand Blackbeard. He was a man who was quoted as saying he used to kill a crewman every day so that the rest would remember who he was. A man who lit brimstone below decks and put burning tapers in his hair before going into battle. He's not an easy man to predict or read.'

'But he *must* have buried his treasure.'

'Why? Because all pirates did that? No, Maxwell, they didn't.'

'So you think he went to all of this trouble to send everyone looking for a treasure that didn't exist if he had absolutely nothing to hide?'

'In short,' replied Miles. 'Yes. And if you hadn't turned up a chest full of rocks with this map I'd have laughed you out of here already.'

'But?'

'But, you may have a point.'

'All right! So what do you think, Miles – can you help us?'

'Well, let's see.' Miles stood up and waddled towards an overflowing filing cabinet, pulled open a drawer and rifled through the untidy contents. 'Damn computers on this island.' He glared at the abandoned machine on his desk. 'The only time they work is when we have a power cut.' He pulled out three bulging files and slammed them onto the desk, rattling the artefacts already there. 'So...' He looked at the map again. 'The date on this map tells us your priceless rocks were buried before Blackbeard began his New Providence career, and that both helps and hinders us.'

'How's that?' asked Maxwell.

'It helps us because it means we don't have to go searching all over the Bahamas, Florida or the Carolinas. But if he wanted everyone to think his treasure was on Iguana Island, he must have buried it before then, and that's our problem.'

'Why?'

157

'Because until he moved to New Providence, everything else about him is unconfirmed. We're not even sure what his real name was.'

'So if he *did* bury his treasure –'

'Assuming he actually *had* any, then yes, it's possible that because no one has connected this map with his log, then anything he had stashed away before the Iguana Island find may still be there.'

'So all we need to do is find out where he went before he dumped these rocks.'

'Not the easiest task in the world. We have no hard evidence of his moves at that time, and as you know, his ship's log was started at a point in the middle of the sea, probably with the express purpose of making him untraceable.'

'Isn't there *any* way we can find out where he went?'

'Maybe.' Miles leafed through the first file. 'This reminds me of something I read recently. Much like your map, much like the log, on its own it meant nothing, so I didn't follow it up. But now it might mean a little more.'

He inched through the closely written text in the files, turning the pages, going back to check what he'd read before ploughing on again. He muttered to himself and sometimes read aloud. Johnny wanted to scream at him to hurry up, to tell them what he was looking for, and he dug his fingernails into his palms while he forced himself to keep quiet.

'Got it,' said Miles. Everyone crowded around his desk, and Johnny tried to read the tiny text, which was upside down from where he stood. 'A report from a Spanish prefect.'

'What's one of those?' asked Johnny.

'A magistrate or governor.'

'And how did he know Blackbeard?'

'He was probably doing business with him.'

'Doing business with a *pirate?*'

Miles grinned again. 'Surprised?'

'Christ, yes.'

'Don't be. It was a lot more common than you think. Much more common than burying treasure.' He chuckled. 'In fact, Blackbeard even settled ashore in North Carolina for a period of time, a pardoned man.'

'No way.'

'Ask your friend here with the map.'

Johnny looked at Maxwell who grinned and nodded.

'So what did this prefect report?' asked Johnny.

'Well, it's not conclusive, but he talks about an Englishman he used to trade with. He mentions no names, and he says that after their trade was concluded, he was invited aboard the Englishman's ship to witness him destroy his home and sail away with his crew and possessions.'

'Why would he do that?' asked Johnny. 'Why would anyone do that?'

'We can't say for sure,' said Miles. 'But it may have been to prove to everyone that any acts of piracy in that area couldn't have been committed by the mystery Englishman because he had moved on. And until he decided to announce his presence somewhere else, no one would know where he was, or where he was heading. The prefect would have noted this as a favour for previous trade. What caught my attention was the final two lines.'

'What do they say?'

'The report says that the flames of their settlement could be seen from the ship, the men came aboard with a large and locked chest, and that their leader had a black beard.'

'Holy shit,' blustered Maxwell. 'That fits, that fits.'

'It *might* fit,' said Miles.

'Bloody hell,' said Johnny. 'It's worth checking.'

'Gets under your skin, doesn't it?' grinned Maxwell. 'So what do you think, Miles?'

'Well. *If* this is Blackbeard, then it's possible the chest he was seen loading aboard his ship *was* the chest full of rocks you found on Iguana Island.'

'And I bet at the time, no one looking at that chest knew what was in it,' said Maxwell.

'Probably not. Including you, three hundred years later. Clever move, and if I were him, I might not have left that base as deserted as people thought.'

'So you think there's something there?'

'I think there *might* be something there, *if* you're prepared to go and find out.'

'You think we're not?'

159

'This won't be some leisurely cruise to a nearby island,' said Miles. 'The prefect gave a very clear location for this place. And it wasn't just because his account described it as barren that no one has been there.'

'What do you mean?'

'Wait here.' Miles stood up, threaded past the band, and walked out of the office. He reappeared minutes later with a large bundle of charts under his arm, then cleared a space and unrolled them onto the desk. 'This is where you need to be looking.' He marked a large circle with a pencil. Johnny's spirits plummeted when he saw a multitude of small islands pebble-dashing the light blue specks in among the darker blue.

'Jesus,' he said. 'Look at all those islands. Look at all those *reefs*. How do we find what's left of a three-hundred-year-old house in among all that lot?'

'That's only part of your problem,' said Miles. 'This island is deep inside Ancadian waters.'

Maxwell looked at Henri. 'Didn't you tell us something about those guys the other day?'

Johnny's eyes flew wide open. 'Hang on a second, do the Ancadians speak Spanish?'

'*Oui*,' said Henri. 'Ancadia used to be a Spanish colony.'

'Oh, shit,' said Johnny. 'Maxwell, you remember that gunboat just off Iguana Island? They fired at us and boarded that fishing boat. They spoke Spanish. Henri, do you think they were Ancadians?'

'It sounds like them. Do you still want to go there?'

'What else can you tell us about them?'

'Ancadia is a police state ruled by a man called General Alpinos, a descendant of the old Spanish Empire. He rules his country with an iron fist, and were it not for the gold mines in his mountains and the deep-water harbour of his capital, the Americans would have deposed him long ago. Alpinos sells them cheap gold, and allows them use of the harbour for their battle fleet. It's an excellent staging post for their Central American operations. And for that, they turn a blind eye to the atrocities he inflicts on his own people. If he captures you, *mon ami*, I cannot help you.'

'So what about this particular island?'

160

Henri shrugged. 'Who can say? Nobody but the Ancadians knows anything about Ancadia. It is the way Alpinos has wanted things for years.'

Miles rifled through the charts and transferred points and bearings. 'I can detail where on the island you need to be looking. You need to anchor on the southern edge, cut uphill through the forest and you should come to a plateau that ends on a cliff. There you should find the site, or at least where it used to be. *If* it really was Blackbeard's old base, and *if* he actually did leave something behind, then you should concentrate your search there.'

Chapter 25

A slow dawn edged back the night sky and the galley's wind-up
alarm clock reverberated its shrill ring down the length of *Friday's
Fancy's* claustrophobic interior. With stiff muscles and blurred
vision, Johnny clambered onto the deck. Under a cloudless sky,
and with the fresh smell of the open sea in his nostrils, a strong
wind blew from the east and carried away the noise of the engine's
stuttering heartbeat.

Friday's Fancy's unwashed bows bucked and slid through the
waves. Johnny looked up at the mast, saw the Jolly Roger flying
defiantly in the wind and felt raw pride.

For the rest of that day and all of the next, they seemed alone in
the ocean's infinity. On the third day, bathed in brilliant sunshine,
the seascape changed dramatically. Johnny looked out on an area
infested with tiny islands, many of them little more than rocky
outcrops, intermittently hidden by the waves. He peered over the
ship's rail. The much lighter, almost sky-blue sea screamed out a
dramatic confirmation that it was getting a lot shallower. The
engine chugged more slowly and the ship decelerated to a nautical
crawl.

*

After two days of low-speed reef-skimming, Johnny's nerves were
wound tightly inside him as they inched through the coral, finally
coming close enough to row ashore. Cramped into the dinghy, with
boxes of food and digging equipment pressing uncomfortably
against him, he felt the rising sun already sending channels of
sweat down his body. He looked across the short stretch of water
to land. A thin strip of golden beach greeted the gently lapping
waves. Behind the fine sand growled a thick, seemingly
impenetrable forest, while off to the right an imposing hill
dominated the whole scene. Somewhere on that hill were the
remains of Blackbeard's home – or so Maxwell thought.

Johnny pulled against his oar, and soon his muscles strained
with the effort. By the time he heard the crunch of sand beneath the
dinghy's keel, his arms and shoulders were screaming in protest.

He dug some more, getting steadily deeper, hearing similar sounds around him where Johnny and Andy worked in unseen holes on either side of him.

What the hell am I doing here? he asked himself. *And for Christ's sake, how long will this trip to nowhere last?* He felt showers of dirt land on him, accompanied by cackles of laughter from Andy. He looked up, but saw just a pockmarked plateau. His hole got deeper, and so did his mood. When the hell would Maxwell give up on the whole idea? Christ, he was even looking forward to getting back to the studio and then going on tour again.

His shovel glanced off a stone. He cursed and scraped the dirt around its edge, then knelt to try and pull it out. He looked closer at the muddy brown object stuck fast in the clay.

'Sweet fucking Jesus,' he cried. 'I've found it.'

Mike threw his shovel out of the hole and cleared away more earth. The top of a sea chest, similar to the one on Iguana Island, started to poke into daylight.

'I've seen one of those somewhere before.' Johnny looked down from the lip of the hole. 'I wonder how many rocks are inside.'

'Just because you didn't find it,' said Mike.

'It's blind luck that you did,' said Andy. 'Was there a lifejacket and cooker in there as well?'

'Never mind that,' said Johnny. 'Let's open the damn thing.'

Johnny and Andy prised themselves into Mike's hole, ending up shoulder to shoulder. They tried to dig the chest free but there was barely enough room for one, and all they managed to do was hit each other with their shovels.

'For fuck's sake.' Mike jabbed outward with both elbows, stabbing into ribcages on either side of him with a muscle-fuelled olecronon. Johnny and Andy buckled and slammed into the sides of the hole. Mike grabbed Andy's ear and Johnny's follicular remnants, and smacked their heads together. 'Look, there's only enough room in here for one person, so fuck off out of *my* hole.'

His shovel bit into the clay around the rapidly emerging chest. His pulse raced. It was big: bigger than the one they had unearthed on Iguana Island. He excavated along the sides and down to the chest's bottom.

'You need a hand?' asked Johnny.

'No,' he growled. 'This is *mine.*' He piled up loose earth around the hole's lip.

'It's huge,' said Johnny. 'I'll bet what's left of my hair it weighs a ton.'

Mike brushed the last clod of earth from the chest and faced Johnny. '*Now* you can get your arses in here and find out.'

Johnny and Andy jumped in the hole and splashed sandy water over each other. They each grabbed a corner of the dirty sand-crusted chest and heaved. Slowly, they lifted it clear. Three hundred years of damp and soil had stained it a dirty brown.

'Jesus,' wheezed Johnny. 'There's no way we're going to be able to lug this bugger all the way down the mountainside. Time to call the others.'

Mike picked up two shovels. 'And next time we do a treasure hunt, we make sure there are phone masts nearby.'

*

Maxwell lay on the beach and felt the sun's warm infusion, while Joe's ganja fumes washed over him and made him feel peckish. He wondered if there was any sweet potato left over from the night before, but his laziness bombarded him into staying where he was. *You won't starve,* he thought to himself.

'You think they'll find anything?' asked Joe.

'Do me a favour,' said Maxwell. 'Johnny's probably reading them chapters from the health and safety manual, Mike will still be wearing his lifejacket and cooking them breakfast, and Andy will be starting an argument with the trees. I'd be surprised if they've done any digging at all.'

'Wait,' said Vince. 'You hear that?'

Maxwell strained his ears and heard a distant clanging. He sat up. 'Do you think?'

'Well, who the hell else is out here to knock a pair of shovels together?' Vince stood up. 'They've got something.'

'Well, they're not opening it without me being there.'

*

Half an hour later Maxwell stood, dripping with sweat and staring at the chest.

'Do you think *this* is the one?' asked Johnny. 'Because I'm damned if I'm doing any more digging.'

'Who did the digging?' asked Mike

'*Mike* found it?' said Joe. 'Hey, guys, looks like we owe the big man a sorry.'

'Save it,' said Mike. 'Joe, have you brought your stuff?'

'Er, not exactly, man.'

'So we need to get it down to the beach.'

'Even if we'd opened it here, we still need to move it,' said Maxwell.

'Assuming there's anything other than rocks inside,' said Johnny.

*

It took two long hours of foul-mouthed, ankle-twisting purgatory before they exited the dense forest and stepped onto the sunlit beach. Despite six able bodies carrying the heavy chest, Johnny's fortitude stumbled more often than he did, and he found out just how awkward it was to handle a big, heavy object over a roughly cleared forest path strewn with tree roots and thick, slippery jungle soil. His knees nearly gave way every time Maxwell's misplaced footfalls kicked into him, and he tried, and failed, not to do the same to Joe in front of him.

Finally, when they arrived at the beach, the chest was dumped onto the sand from shoulder-height, and Johnny rubbed his aching shoulders. 'Now then,' he said. 'What about this chest?'

'Well, man,' drawled Joe. 'I ain't even *thinking* about trying to pick the lock. We're smack in the middle of hostile waters, and there's no way you impatient bastards will wait, is there?'

'No,' said Maxwell. 'And we're due back in the studio soon, right, Johnny? So let's blow that thing open and get the hell out of here.'

'Well, okay,' said Joe. 'But I don't want no bullshit about you wanting to watch the explosion. I want a blast wall thirty yards away, and I want *everyone* behind it. That includes you, Max. Understand, man?'

'Sure.'

*

Behind the newly constructed blast wall of chopped and fallen-down palm trees, Johnny watched Maxwell fight a losing battle with his impatience.

'Jesus,' he snapped at Joe once he appeared with his thin strand of detonating wire. 'Can't you work any faster?'

169

'Yeah, man, I can blow that whole chest to pieces, and everything inside it. But if you don't want that to happen, then shut up and wait. It'll get done when it gets done, okay?'

Maxwell grumbled to himself before descending into a bad-tempered silence, while Johnny watched Joe's dextrous hands fly over the small detonator. Five minutes later, he faced the crew.

'It's done, man.'

'So blow the damn thing,' said Maxwell.

Johnny watched Joe's finger push the detonator. Suddenly, almost anticlimactically, he heard the muffled crack and the charge blew. Maxwell's frantic burst of movement the next second was much more impressive, and his speed left the rest of the crew standing.

Johnny ran around the blast wall and raced up to the chest. Hanging over it was a large cloud of sand. As the warm breeze blew in gently from the sea, the sand dissipated, and he once again looked at the chest, which was covered with a fine layer of dust. Maxwell dropped to his knees. Gripping the worn lid with both hands, he threw it open with a roar of exultation. Johnny and the rest of the band surged forward and looked inside.

Chapter 27

It was the treasure! Johnny felt a lightning bolt of triumph pulse through his body and he saw brooches, necklaces, bracelets, glittering jewels and precious stones.

It was the treasure! Maxwell screamed and whooped with delight and dug his arms deep into the chest, throwing handfuls of thick, heavy gold coins all over the beach.

It was the treasure! The rest of the band joined in, dancing in the sand and shouting themselves hoarse. Johnny's castle-keep retreat of reality and safety was blasted to bits by what they'd found. He had never really thought they'd actually find it, and now that they had, the unexpected success showed him just how good the unreal could sometimes feel. He sat down on a fallen palm tree and grinned. The heat, the tension and the exertion of recent days expressed itself in the band's near-hysteria, before gradually stilling. 'Okay,' said Johnny. 'So we've got the treasure. We're still only halfway there.'

'What do you mean?' asked Maxwell. 'We're done, we've won, we're the boys.'

'We're in the middle of Ancadian waters, reefs all around us, we've got a bloody heavy treasure chest on the beach and a leaking dinghy between us and *Friday*. There's plenty more to do.'

*

'Heave!'

The crew raised the full chest and as gently as they could, wrapped it in a second-hand football net purchased at St. Clements and lowered it into the dinghy. It settled into the gently lapping water, taking a disturbing amount of freeboard with it. Mike stepped aboard and looked nervously at the rest of the band, who were on the outside of the dinghy. They'd swim back to *Friday's Fancy* alongside the dinghy and just hope that it didn't sink with their newly found treasure.

'You'll be fine,' said Maxwell. 'A short trip across the water and we're done.'

Johnny saw Mike trembling as they pulled away from the beach.

'This leak's getting worse, man,' he said with a tremor in his voice.

'So do your thing,' said Maxwell. 'You found the chest, don't be the one that loses it.'

Mike filled up a plastic bucket and began throwing water overboard.

'Hey,' snapped Andy. 'In the water, not over me.'

'Sorry.'

The dinghy bumped against *Friday's Fancy*. Maxwell shot up the ladder and threw lines from the boom's end pulley down to Mike, who threaded them through the netting. His hands trembled as he worked on the knot.

'Get it right,' growled Maxwell. 'Drop it here and we're fucked.'

Mike fiddled with the rope, tying the knot, then undoing it and tying again.

'Get a shift on.' Johnny trod water by the side of the dinghy. 'This thing's sinking fast.'

'Done,' said Mike.

Maxwell heaved on the rope. The pulley wheels turned, the boom creaked and *Friday's Fancy* dipped to one side as the improvised crane took the chest's weight. Slowly, it lifted free of the dinghy, and Mike kept bailing and the freeboard got less and less, despite the chest now being completely clear. Both objects were now going in different directions. The chest was inched into the air, accompanied by pulley squeaks and creaking ropes and ship's timbers, while the dinghy gracefully disappeared from surface view, despite Mike's increasingly frantic bailing. It settled and then slowly sank beneath the coral reef waters.

'Shit, guys,' wailed Mike. 'Help, help me.'

'Calm down,' Vince swam over and pulled him towards the ladder. Hyperventilating, Mike climbed the ladder and disappeared below decks. Vince followed him up the ladder, with the rest of the band behind him.

Too big to be taken below, the crew reversed the netting, using it to secure the chest to the stern deck.

'Do you think we should have covered our tracks a bit more?' asked Johnny.

'You want to swim back ashore?' replied Maxwell. 'Besides, we've got a sunk dinghy that we'll never be able to hide. The only thing we can do is make best use of the light and start putting in some distance.'

Johnny stood nervously at the ship's rail and watched the bows come about. Slowly, they headed for the small opening through the razor-sharp reefs. He held his breath and they entered the coral and slid carefully through its jagged heart.

It took another two days of tortuous progress through the treacherous, shallow waters, and Johnny's nerves stretched when he frequently dwelt on their fate were they to become shipwrecked. At each dusk, they dropped anchor and he collapsed into an exhausted, fear-drugged sleep, while with the coming of dawn a few hours later, they again coaxed *Friday's Fancy* onwards.

After clearing the coral, with dark sea now beneath them, Johnny's spirits rose. Maxwell eased the throttle forward and they picked up speed. 'How far are we from international waters?' asked Johnny.

Maxwell looked up at the sky and then the sea around them, and squinted at the charts before staring myopically at the small GPS screen. 'Hard to say, but as long as we keep moving, by morning at the latest.'

Friday's Fancy kept a foaming bow wave through the deep blue all around them, her engine singing a rhythmic clatter that was almost musical. Dusk wrapped itself around them and Johnny turned to Maxwell.

'Did you hear that?' he asked.

'Hear what?'

Seconds later a column of sea, twice as high as *Friday's Fancy*, rose into the air just in front of the bows, immediately followed by a deafening crash and a thick cloud of seawater that covered the entire ship. It quickly cleared, and Johnny looked out to sea in terrified wonder. Only just visible in the darkening sky, a grey-painted cobra helicopter snarled towards them, its rotor blades oscillating like a mutant hornet's wings, while a viciously powerful searchlight stabbed through the dusk. Then, at the edge of visual range but closing fast, a sleek grey naval ship sifted into view. Johnny's heart sank to his cowboy boots and he recognised the Ancadian flag flying from its stern.

Chapter 28

The gunboat sliced through the sea, its searchlight holding them while the cobra dwindled into the night. Under the ship's beam, Johnny watched its crew lower a dinghy.

'Oh shit,' said Maxwell.

'Still feel like being a pirate?' asked Johnny.

'Maybe we should leave the negotiating to you, mate.'

The Ancadian dinghy came alongside, its motor buzzing like an angry wasp. A rope ladder flew over the rail and a grappling hook dug into the planking. Seconds later half a dozen soldiers swarmed onto the deck and pointed their guns at the band, herding them together. Another man then climbed aboard, armed with a pistol that hung from an ornate holster. Gold insignia and medal ribbons infested his dark blue uniform, and Johnny watched him look around *Friday's Fancy* with eugenic contempt. His eyes rested on the band, who stood huddled against the rail. He walked over, speaking to them in a heavy Spanish accent.

'*Buenos noches, hombres,*' he said. 'Who are you, and what are you doing here?'

Johnny took a deep breath. 'These guys are Cold Steel, the heavy metal band. And I'm their manager.'

'Cold Steel? Heavy metal?' He stared uncomprehendingly at Johnny.

'Yes, musicians.'

'Musicians?'

'Yes, we're –'

'And what are you doing here?'

'We were –'

'And what is that?' He pointed at the chest.

'Well, it's –'

'I don't *care* what it is!' he barked. 'What I care about is what you are doing with it, that you see fit to rob Ancadia of its sovereign possessions.'

'How do you know we're robbing you if you don't know what we've got?'

'I don't *need* to know, *hombre.*'

174

'Yes, you do.' Andy barged forward. 'We know our rights. Tell us what we've done, tell us what you *think* we've taken, and *ask* us if we'll help you out. We're not stupid, you know, *and* we've got lawyers.' He turned to Johnny and grinned. '*That's* how you handle this lot.'

The officer pulled out his pistol and pointed it at Andy's head. The other soldiers cocked their guns and levelled them at the band. Andy stepped back and gaped in terror. Johnny couldn't believe the sudden change in the Ancadians, or in Andy. This wasn't just a sailor accosting a fishing boat and firing random shots in the water, this was a gun in the face, and Andy, for all his pub-fighting belligerence, had never faced one before. He hid behind Maxwell, buried his face in his hands and started crying. Johnny ignored the Ancadians and stared at Andy.

Still pointing his pistol at the band, the officer barked an order. Three of the soldiers raced up behind them and started unlashing the chest, while the gunboat slid alongside, chain gun levelled at *Friday's Fancy*. A tubular tripod was expertly put together by the gunboat's crew, a line thrown over, and while Johnny and the band looked on impotently, the chest was hoisted away.

'So,' said the officer. 'We have removed your cargo, and now I shall escort you to headquarters where my commanding officer can question you further.'

He returned to the Ancadian dinghy, which took him back to the gunboat. The soldiers remained.

'Ambushed and robbed at gunpoint,' said Maxwell bitterly. 'The bastards.'

'Pretty ironic when you think about it,' said Johnny.

'What do you mean?'

'That's exactly how Blackbeard got that treasure in the first place. I mean, it's not like we're the real owners, any more than the Ancadians are. One way or another it's caused misery to someone. Maybe we're better off without it.'

'And you think *they* deserve it?' Maxwell stood at the rail and glared at the Ancadians.

'Like we can do anything about that.'

'We can't just give up.'

'What do you suggest? Right now all we can do is hope to Christ they let us go.' Johnny looked across the short stretch of sea to the Ancadian gunboat. The admiral was back on board and strutting around like a peacock on heat, directing *Friday's Fancy* via loudhailer. 'If that bastard's got a power trip, what do you think his boss will be like?'

Next to the Ancadian gun, a searchlight bathed them in bright light. Night fell, and Johnny's despair deepened. With an armed soldier at the ship's wheel, and under the gunboat's malevolent, ever-watchful eye, the other Ancadians were so sure of their own security that as the cool tropical night wore on they began to doze off.

With nothing to do, and absolutely no control over their immediate future, the band shuffled below. Johnny couldn't sleep, and was left alone on deck; time crawled more slowly than their progress through the cooling surf. As the dawn poured across the sky, he looked around, seeing nothing but vast, empty sea. He went below and joined the rest of the band in the galley. Stubbled faces and dark patches under their eyes spoke of collective insomnia.

'So what now?' asked Maxwell.

'I don't know,' said Johnny. 'As far as they're concerned, we were caught red-handed.'

'Bollocks. That treasure's been forgotten about for centuries, it doesn't belong to anyone. It's just chance politics that it was on Ancadian soil.'

'Well, they've got it now. And us.'

'But why keep us? They've got the chest.'

'Maybe they're taking us somewhere for a reason.'

'So a parlay might be on the cards?'

'Perhaps.'

A flurry of rapidly spoken Spanish erupted from the deck above them. They climbed outside, and Johnny's senses snapped alive. Directly in front lay a small island, gradually dominating the view as they approached. At its centre, a tall mountain reached upwards, while a dense coat of vegetation surrounded its lower half. On the seaward side, there were no coral reefs to deny man's sprawling presence, and the large bay on the eastern edge formed a massive natural harbour that had been enlarged by concrete breastworks.

They approached the island, and Johnny saw frenetic activity within the harbour. Small, heavily armed vessels came and went with astonishing regularity, while at anchor, he saw two ships,

176

much larger than the more numerous gunboats. Laying at rest at the stern of each was the streamlined, menacing shape of a cobra helicopter.

Johnny's gaze zeroed in on the Ancadian sailors. They had stopped what they were doing and were watching *Friday's Fancy*. He saw the hostility beneath their enquiring looks as they came alongside and tied up on the concrete quay. They were herded onto dry land, and Johnny's stomach knotted while the medalled officer alighted from his boat.

'Welcome to Chanderos Island naval base,' he crowed. 'This place houses the most potent maritime force in the entire Caribbean. I would give you a guided tour, but as you can imagine, we have many secrets we wish to keep.'

Chapter 29

Johnny stared at a foreboding block of cells. Surrounded by a high wall topped with barbed wire, it needed no explanation. Inside, his eyes swept across the dusty exercise yard, where he saw several floors of cells taking up one side of the barren compound. Rust wormed across the close-set bars and paint peeled from the walls behind them, exposing chipped and worn brickwork. He cast nervous glances at the listless prisoners inside. They came to an empty cell, and the rusty but still solid-looking door stood uninvitingly open as the band were shoved inside. The door closed behind them with a loud clang.

'So,' he said. 'Who thinks they can get a hotshot lawyer to come and get us out of here?'

'For fuck's sake,' said Andy. 'How can you joke about this?'

'Who's joking?'

'Yeah, right. How are you *really* going to get us out of here?'

'You think I can?'

'You were pretty good at solving our problems on tour.'

'And you're Andy Stains, hard-as-nails guitarist who burst into tears yesterday.'

'Look, mate,' said Maxwell. 'Just tell us what you think.'

'You want it straight?' asked Johnny. 'I think we're fucked. We've definitely lost the treasure, and we'll be lucky if these mad bastards don't shoot us.'

Before the band could respond, the cell door crashed open and two guards dragged Johnny outside.

*

Colonel Ronaldo Santos Mucama brushed an imaginary speck from his grey and blue naval camouflage uniform. He then glared at the straggly-haired, stupidly dressed prisoner being marched into his office. *Valgame Dios! Just like all the others,* he thought. Another sorry set of treasure hunters to fill his *encierro*. But after a two-month stretch, they soon lost any desire to go looking for hidden riches, and went back to their decadent homes with more sensible thoughts in their heads. They should thank him for giving them a reality check, although he doubted any of them would.

178

However, these *idiotas* had been lucky, until they'd been caught. They'd actually found something.

The brief radio message had alerted him to some of the story, but not all. His cold grey eyes shot armour-piercing hatred at his captive from behind an obsessively tidy desk. *This damned desk! I should be out there, especially now, when the action is just about to start.* His base job at Chanderos had been the worst insult to his years at sea, and he unloaded his bitterness and aggression on everyone around him, including prisoners. He could still sail, could still fight a ship, and he knew it. Instead, they gave that *pavo real,* Baptistos, a gunboat and an independent patrol. And despite being forty-eight, Mucama's bulk remained gym-hardened muscle, even if his close-cropped black hair was now peppered with grey, as was his thick moustache. A minute ticked by, and still he said nothing. Then he cleared his throat and spoke.

'Captain Baptistos informs me you were found in restricted waters.' His deep voice carried a heavy Spanish accent. 'You are lucky we didn't shoot you there and then. And what of these items you have openly stolen from Ancadia?'

Silence sucked at his words before the prisoner spoke. 'Look, mate.' His voice trembled. 'We didn't know we were in Ancadian waters.'

'So you just *happened* to find an island that just *happened* to be in Ancadian territory, where you just *happened* to find these artefacts?'

'Something like that.'

'You are grave robbers at best. At worst, spies.'

'Spies? Now, hang on.'

'Silence!' Mucama's gaze bored into him. 'First of all, who are you?'

The prisoner was scared, and so he damn well should be, but he held his eyes up. For all of his stupid appearance, he had backbone.

'We're musicians,' he stammered. 'Well, the other guys are. They're Cold Steel, the heavy metal band, and I'm Johnny Faslane, their manager.'

'Cold Steel? Musicians?'

'That's right.'

'And why are you here?'

Johnny held out his arms. 'You got us there, it *was* a treasure hunt. Look, if the loot's yours, take it. No harm done.'

Mucama looked at Johnny, and suddenly saw the potential. This balding *flaco* could give them the justification they needed, *if* Mucama could get him to talk. 'Where did you sail from?' He fired out the question.

'What?'

'It is simple to answer. Where did you sail from?'

Johnny folded his arms and said nothing.

'Immigration violation, two months,' said Mucama. 'Theft against the state of Ancadia, ten years. Espionage, thirty years if the judge likes you, death if he doesn't. And the judges here do not like *extranjeros.*'

'What?'

'Foreigners. The judges here do not like foreigners. Especially foreigners who steal from us and spy on us.'

'Look, mate. Do you really think Cold Steel have got the juice to be spies? They're just a metal band, and between you and me, much more of this shit and they won't even be that. Christ, one of them can't even swim. And if we really *were* spies, don't you think we'd have used a boat with a bit more guts?'

'I think you used the vessel you did because you thought to lower your radar signature, yes?'

'No.'

'Yes!' roared Mucama. 'You dare to argue with me? You *dare* to deny it? You will be tried tomorrow, with evidence as fresh as the morning. Justice is swift in Ancadia. Tell us where you base yourselves in the Caribbean, or face the consequences of your silence.'

Mucama watched Johnny's jaw firm up and his shoulders square. *He'll take time to break,* he thought. *Let's see what the others are like.* He barked out an order, and guards flew into the office and hauled Johnny out.

*

Johnny cast meerkat looks around him as his guards marched him past derelict, empty buildings with broken glass clinging to peeling window-frames, and warped wooden doors hanging off rusty hinges. The guards sped up and he was almost forced to run into the prison. The cell door clanged open, and under the gaze of several automatic weapons, Johnny was hurled inside and Andy was yanked out.

'Don't tell them a thing,' shouted Johnny, as Andy was taken away.

*

'It was St. Clements,' sobbed Andy. 'We stopped at St. Clements.'

Mucama laughed, unloaded his pistol and holstered it once more. This *coño* was even more spineless than Baptistos had said, which, coming from that painted jackanapes, was quite an insult. Mucama had checked Cold Steel on the internet, and on that point at least, they were being honest. But after watching one video clip after another that showed an endless procession of onstage disasters, he was amazed they'd achieved anything. They weren't spies, but by implicating St. Clements they had given him exactly what he wanted. 'You see,' he chuckled. 'We are really not so bad.'

'So that's it? You'll let us go?'

Mucama's laughter washed over Andy, and he saw him wilt even more. 'So soon? But we have only just got to know each other.' A little pressure and they'd all melt, just like this *endeble*. 'So, we know that you were supplied at St. Clements. And why not? Monsieur Chevalier is a friendly, welcoming leader. Perhaps he is even fond of your metal music, yes?'

'All he wanted was for us to do a concert and make his island some money.'

'And perhaps you had other historic sites to visit, perhaps find more riches, riches that have been hidden for centuries?'

'I don't know, man.'

'No?' Mucama unholstered his pistol.

'No, I swear. Maxwell knows all about that treasure shit, not me. Ask him, man.'

*

Minutes after Andy was sucked from Mucama's office, Maxwell was pushed through the doorway after first having his face rammed into the closed door. *He's tough,* thought Mucama, *like that first one. But we'll give him a bit of pain; he'll make a mistake.* Maxwell stood before Mucama, who made to speak, but Maxwell spoke first.

'We're not spies.'

181

'Oh?' said Mucama.

'Treasure hunters is what we are, mate, and that's all.'

'You have nothing else to say? So, you have what you came for? Well, you *had* what you came for. *We* have it now.'

'You haven't got it all.'

Mucama's eyes flickered and he cursed himself for revealing his eagerness. He covered it with a scowl. 'What do you mean?'

'Sure, we dug up that treasure, but it wasn't the only chest we were after.'

'There's more?'

'You bet.' Maxwell picked up a chair, pulled it towards him and sat down. Mucama said nothing. 'I'll tell you a story,' said Maxwell. 'Now, we found Blackbeard's first treasure chest, but after a few years he'd built up another one, and we know where it is.'

'Where?' Mucama snatched up a telephone and shouted into the receiver. A few minutes later one of his men entered the room, armed with a bundle of sea charts. Mucama rolled them out on the desk and glared at Maxwell. 'Show me.'

Chapter 30

The cell door screeched open and Maxwell was shoved inside.

'Well,' said Johnny. 'Andy blabbed about St. Clements. What did you tell them?'

Maxwell smiled. 'I made up a bullshit story about another stash of treasure. I think he's heading there right now.'

'Where's he going?'

'Some uninhabited island in the middle of nowhere. Not even in any territorial waters. Practically a straight line from here to there.'

'Doesn't sound too bloody clever to me,' said Johnny. 'Once he finds nothing there, he'll just follow his straight line back here and shoot us.'

'Where have you been, mate? You said it yourself; we're fucked. They've got the treasure, they think we're spies. Christ knows what they want with St. Clements, and the way I see it, we need to get ourselves out of here, get to St. Clements and warn Henri. We owe him that much.'

'And how are we going to do that, Maxwell? Once that Ancadian gets back with no treasure he's going to be even more pissed at us than he is right now.'

'Assuming he gets there, manages to stay alive long enough to have a good look around, and then gets back in one piece.'

'What are you talking about?'

'This particular straight line of sea's got lots of history. I know it all, but I was banking on him only knowing some of it.'

'History? What history?'

'The island I sent him to is uninhabited for a very good reason. It's radioactive. It was the sight of some of the earliest nuclear tests. Pretty common knowledge, but not that important in the big scheme of things. The warheads they tested weren't that powerful.'

'Which is hardly going to stop him coming back.'

'There's more to it than that,' Maxwell motioned the band closer and spoke in a staged whisper. 'Now, every bugger and his dog knows about that American naval base at Ancadia. But what too many people *don't* know about is what goes on underneath. Just offshore from here, there's an ocean trench three miles deep, and that's an ideal hiding place for submarines. It's called the Columbus Trench, and it runs from the Atlantic, to Ancadia, to Cuba, to America. And that old nuclear test island sits right next to it.'

'Fucking hell,' exclaimed Johnny. 'That trench must be like an underwater version of the Berlin wall. I bet there are more nuclear subs down there than anywhere else on the planet. I wouldn't go near the bloody place even if you promised me all my hair back.'

'Right,' replied Maxwell. 'And nor would anyone else. Leastways, anyone else who *knew* about it. Our general might be a mate of the Yanks, but I don't reckon they trust him enough to tell him where their subs hide out. And if he's a mate of the Americans, the Russians won't trust him either. A lot of the old tensions are still there.'

'So how did you find out all this?' asked Johnny. 'Back in the real world you don't even know who does your laundry.'

'France.'

'What?'

'In France, when we all took off and got arrested.'

'Hacking!' said Johnny. 'They wanted to do you for hacking. Something about French Intelligence.'

'You'd be surprised how much the French know.'

'You learned about this from hacking into French Intelligence? *You* hacked into French Intelligence?'

'Well, credit where it's due. It wasn't me that broke in, I just read what was there.'

'So the French know about this? They were told about it?'

'No, they stole the info from GCHQ after the British stole it from the Pentagon.'

'Jesus,' said Johnny. 'And now you know about it?'

'Well, mate, you might think it was wasted time and a shit concert in Paris, but some us did more than get flags tied to our dicks. Right, Vince?'

'Don't knock it,' said Vince. 'They were politician's daughters.'

'Christ,' said Johnny. 'So the Ancadians are heading into one seriously restricted area with a couple of warships, and they're doing it fast. Holy crap, they'll get blown to pieces.'

Maxwell grinned. 'Even if the subs don't sink him, you can be sure the American surface fleet will be alerted. He'll be a long time trying to convince them he's looking for buried treasure. Either way, he's out of our hair for a long time.'

Johnny smiled for the first time that day. 'So now, all we need now is a plan for getting out of here.' He stared through the bars, and time passed slowly in the baking, dusty heat. The sun gradually dipped behind the high mountain that dominated the island, and Johnny was suddenly shaken from his dream-like state by the cell thrown open for what he assumed was the exercise period. He led the band outside into the sifting dusk, and they cautiously inspected their new home. On one side of the floodlit courtyard, a plank of wood with holes in it stretched across an odorous pit. Toilet doors on Chanderos appeared non- existent, and Johnny was treated to the sight of Ancadian prisoners of both genders wiping their arses in public before going about their business. Next to the latrines, he saw what he thought were little more than rotting water pipes, but it was only when he noticed several inmates standing underneath them that he realised they were showers.

A diesel engine's low clatter, and high-pitched, rapidly spoken Spanish pulled Johnny's attention away. He watched as the gates were creaked open and a battered military truck trundled into the open space. The guards paced up to the truck, yanked down the tailgate and set up a flimsy plywood pasting table; then they climbed back into the truck and pulled out two large steaming vats which they planted on the table. Inmates gravitated to the back of the truck, holding out grimy tin plates.

'Looks like chow time,' said Johnny. 'Christ, it smells bad enough from over here. Wonder what it tastes like.'

'Doesn't look like we've got anything else to look forward to,' muttered Andy. 'Everyone else seems to be queuing up pretty quickly, I reckon we should as well.'

'That's it,' said Maxwell.

'That's what?' asked Johnny.

'That's our way out of here.'

'What is?'

'The food.'

'What? You mean we should eat that shit, get food poisoning and go to the infirmary?'

'You've been watching too many prison films, mate.'

'What then?'

'What Andy said. That food line is probably the highlight of the day around here.'

'So?'

'So suppose they don't get it? How do you think a riot would go down around here?'

'What?'

'It'll take the guards' minds off the truck for a while. Time enough for us to grab it.'

'Are you serious, Maxwell? What if –?'

'What if we're still here when that Ancadian gets back?'

'*If* he gets back.'

'Either way, it won't be good for us. He gets back, we're screwed. He gets in trouble out there, we're screwed as soon as they find out.'

'Oh, shit, Johnny,' said Andy. 'He's got my vote. What's the plan, Max?'

'Right. The only thing these lads have got to look forward to is their food. For all we know, they might not even get fed every day. We kick it over and they go nuts. Vince and Andy, watch my back while I do the business there. Johnny, you, Mike and Joe take the truck. As soon as we're all aboard, drive like hell.'

'And then what?'

'That's up to you, mate. I haven't thought that far ahead, I'm only a singer.'

'Jesus.'

'Are we doing it or not?'

'Yes,' said Andy.

'Hell yes,' said Vince.

'Nothing to wait here for,' said Mike.

'No choice, man,' said Joe.

'Well, shit,' said Johnny.

'Time's wasting with talk,' said Maxwell. 'Let's do it.'

Chapter 31

Maxwell strode towards the vats. He barged through the crowd, chased by a ploughed furrow of angry calls. Ignoring the anger, he planted his hands on the table edge and with a roar flipped it over. All attention switched to the upturned vats and their rapidly emptying contents, which were gurgling onto the dusty floor. A low growl of fury grew among the inmates, and the guards nervously fiddled with their rifles at the unscripted development.

A tin plate frisbeed towards Maxwell. He ducked, shouted again and ran into the gathered inmates, lashing out with both fists. A howl of anger rose and blows flurried outward like an exploding sandbag. Vince and Andy punched and elbowed through the snowdrift of prisoners towards Maxwell.

Johnny, Mike and Joe ran for the truck. The guards were watching the scrum around the now invisible table and slop vat, and showed no clear idea about how to restore order. Around the jail, fury built at the unspoken news that there was no food that evening, spreading like spilled ink on blotting paper. Joe vaulted the tailgate, howling vegetarian pacifist anger, and the smacks as he punched living beings for the first time in his life were drowned out by the building madness in the yard.

Johnny ran to the front of the truck where Mike, a step ahead of him, pulled out the driver and knocked him senseless with a hammer-blow on his head. He climbed into the cab.

'Do you know how to drive this thing?' asked Johnny.

'No, but I can roll a four by four.' Mike looked uncertainly at the truck's dashboard.

'Fucking hell. Can't swim, can't drive a truck. Bloody good job you can brain Ancadians. Shift over.'

Johnny looked frantically in the truck's cracked wing mirror. Maxwell swirled into view, emerging from the boiling mass of punching, kicking prisoners. He ran at a guard hovering impotently at the periphery of the madness and swung a roundhouse punch at his face. The guard swayed backwards and Maxwell's fist sailed through the air without connecting. He then countered with a rifle butt that whacked solidly into Maxwell's jaw. The dark-haired

187

singer dropped to the ground with a grunt, while Andy filled the spot where Maxwell had stood, kicked the guard in the balls and pushed him backwards. Vince grabbed Maxwell's ankles and dragged him towards the truck, while all around them the prisoners sensed the moment. They grouped around isolated guards and pulled their rifles away from them.

Andy and Vince grabbed Maxwell and chucked him over the tailgate, where he flop-landed in a groaning heap, before vaulting inside themselves. Sitting in the passenger seat, Mike looked nervously at Johnny. 'Can you drive a truck?'

'I can drive a car. How different can it be?' Johnny's hand flew over the gear levers and he gunned the engine. 'Diff lock, four-wheel drive. Oh, bollocks, Faslane, just keep it simple.' He crunched the gear lever into first.

The disturbance had drawn Ancadians from the rest of the base. Whistle blasts and spaced rifle shots trumpeted a return to order.

'We need to get out of here, man,' said Mike. 'Right fucking now.'

Johnny stamped on the plate-metal clutch and yanked the gear lever through the shift. The truck's engine coughed and screamed and they shot towards the rapidly closing gate. Two guards scrambled to close it while a third unslung his rifle and levelled it at the truck. Johnny pushed the accelerator and gripped the steering wheel tight. The gate clattered shut and the guards scrambled aside.

The truck rammed the gate, and Johnny's chest whacked into the steering wheel. The back wheels lifted off the ground and the truck's heavy nose drove hard into the steel and wire obstacle, which bent outwards with a grinding shriek. They bounced back and Johnny heard shouts from the band.

'That's some fucking gate,' said Mike.

Johnny forced the gearshift into reverse and they shot away from the gate. He stood on the brakes, crunched into first and they thundered towards the skewed, wounded gate. The front wheels mounted the sagging metal mesh and bent steel tubes. Johnny fed the engine's power and they slowly drove onward. They crunched onto the potholed roadway beyond and Johnny and Mike whacked into each other. Johnny floored the accelerator and they sped away into the spreading darkness.

Loud staccato cracks rattled, and bullets smacked into the truck. The windscreen starred and then disintegrated. The tyres took a hit and they lurched to the left. Johnny wrenched the wheel to the right, pulling with all his strength against the manual steering, which was bogged down by bullet-shredded tyres. He cursed and forced the gear lever through the numbers, and kept his right foot planted firmly on the accelerator. They pulled away from the jail house and pinballed along the dusty, rutted road.

'Jesus, man,' said Mike. 'Those bastards were shooting at us.'

'No shit,' said Johnny. 'Has anyone been hit?'

'What? You mean shot?'

'Yes, Mike, I mean shot.'

'Well, how are we going to know?'

'Climb into the back and find out. We're sure as hell not stopping to check.'

Mike looked uncertainly at Johnny. 'Do it,' he snapped. 'They'd do the same for you.'

Mike nodded jerkily and clambered through the canvas, while Johnny powered the truck through a decaying, unguarded barrier. The headlights stabbed into the murky forest and the road dwindled to a narrow, uneven dirt track before vanishing completely. Johnny eased on the brakes, then switched off the engine and lights. The night beat down on him, and he felt his panic rising. They were fugitives on a hostile island with no way off, and sooner or later the Ancadians would come looking for them. Soft moonlight filtered through the trees and Johnny climbed out of the cab and walked to the back of the truck.

'Is everyone okay?' he asked.

'Is that you, Johnny?' asked Mike. 'Why have we stopped?'

'Because the road's stopped.'

Mike's head appeared over the tailgate, his bushy corkscrew hair silhouetted against the night sky. 'So what do we do now?'

'First off, is everyone alright?'

'Maxwell's waking up now.'

'Any broken bones? Can he walk?'

Another head poked over the tailgate. 'Ask me yourself, mate. My jaw hurts.'

'Well,' said Johnny. 'You can still talk, so you can't be dying.'

'Those bastards were shooting at us.'

189

'That's because we started a riot and broke out of their jail. Of *course* they were shooting at us.'

'So how the hell are you going to get us out of this mess?'

'Down to me again, huh? Because being boarded, taken prisoner and then doing a jailbreak is what I deal with every day.'

'Quitting when it gets interesting, are you?' asked Vince.

'Bollocks am I. Now get your arses out of this truck. Right,' Johnny looked around him while the band clambered over the tailgate. 'This looks like the only road out of that base, and they saw us driving along it, so sooner or later they'll come looking for us. Which means we need to get a long way from both the truck and the road.'

'Head to the hills?' asked Maxwell. 'Live off the land?'

'Fucking hell, listen to Grizzly Adams here.'

'So what *are* we going to do?'

'Get the hell off this island.'

'I forgot we had a private jet waiting for us. Lead the way, mate.'

'We're not flying out of here.'

'What, then?'

'The only way left. We'll take a ship.'

Chapter 32

Johnny led the band through the undergrowth in a slow, single-file, longhaired snake. He gauged their direction by going downhill, figuring it would eventually lead them to the sea. After forty minutes of hard marching through the dark primeval forest, they approached a decaying barbed-wire fence that stretched along a clearing being slowly reclaimed by the trees. He wiped a sheet of perspiration from his forehead and squinted at the harbour lights. 'Right turn, lads.'

'What?' said Maxwell. 'The sea's that way.'

'How else do you think we'll find a boat?'

'But we'll have to –'

'Swim?'

'Er, yes.'

'Get used to that thought.'

On through the night Johnny marched, his tense nerves screaming at him in the silence. Underfoot vegetation snagged at their feet, and this time they had no machetes. After the longest hour of Johnny's life, just when he was beginning to think it would last forever, his footsteps crunched onto a stony beach. The cool sea breeze caressed his sweating body, and after a few seconds, he looked out at the dark, featureless seascape in front of him, seeing nothing but empty water. Small waves lapped against the shore, and as the wind cooled him down, his trousers stuck to his legs and he began to shiver. He looked in all directions, but the sea was devoid of activity. The vast multitude of pebbles on the beach stretched away to their left, forming a sharp spur. On one side of the spur was open sea, and on the other was the harbour. He squinted into the distance at the pinpointed lights.

'Not much happening over there,' he said. 'It looks like their boats have all shut up for the night. With a bit of luck they're searching for us inland.'

'Aren't you forgetting something?' asked Maxwell.

'You mean Mike?'

'Yeah, he can't swim.'

'I know that.'

'So?'

'So he wore a lifejacket on board *Friday's Fancy,* didn't he? Go back to the woods, get two great big logs, shove them under his arms and we'll drag him along.'

'But we –'

'Don't have a choice, man,' said Mike.

*

Six heads pac-manned silently along on a slow, nerve-stretching swim towards and then around the spur's protruding end. They bobbed along in the water like hairy apples, and Johnny led them towards a gunboat's seaward shadow. 'Still with us, Mike?'

'Whose bloody idea was this, anyway?' Mike's reply spluttered through the darkness. 'I swear I'm not even standing under a shower again once this shit's over.'

'You're doing well,' said Johnny. 'Now, we're safe in the shadows, and *Friday's Fancy* is just over there. All we have to do is make our way to it from one boat to the next.'

He led the band through the harbour's black waters, dragging a choking, gagging Mike with them until ten minutes later they were treading water inside *Friday's* shadow. 'Maxwell,' said Johnny. 'You're always going on about pirates. Make like one now, shin up that anchor line, then throw down the rope ladder.'

Maxwell felt his way along the wooden hull and was soon swallowed up in the night.

'You think he can do it?' asked Andy.

'All he's got to do is climb one rope and chuck down a ladder,' said Johnny. 'It's not Olympic knife-throwing.'

He looked up as he heard the sound of wood scraping along the ship's planking. His vision filled with the ladder's irregular shape as it came straight towards him and smashed him in the face.

*

Slowly emerging into painful consciousness, Johnny lay on his back and stared at the stars.

'Is he dead?' asked Andy.

'No chance,' said Vince. 'He's probably got a clause in his will sending us back to the studio before he kicks it.'

'That's not a bad idea,' mumbled Johnny. 'Are we all aboard?'

*

'You have got to be joking, Maxwell.' Johnny hunkered in the galley and slowly drip-dried.

'We came for the treasure,' replied Maxwell. 'We're not leaving without *trying* to get it back.'

'Christ, we've got to make the most of every bit of darkness. We need to leave right now.'

'Not without the treasure.'

'We don't even know where it is.'

'You do.'

'I fucking well don't.'

'But you could. You're a manager, you know about safety, security, all that shit. If you were an Ancadian, where would you put it?'

'Look, Maxwell, we don't have time to piss around on guesswork.'

'So just give us one guess. Come *on*, Johnny. We didn't go through all of this just to run away. If we do have to leave here empty-handed, at least let's be able to say we tried to take the treasure with us. We can't let those bastards just have it.'

Johnny looked at the five sets of eyes boring into him. 'One guess. And then we're out of here, whether we find it or not.'

'Deal,' said Maxwell.

Johnny put his elbows on the table and rested his head in his hands. 'Well. That treasure would make a saint sell his own mother, and if the Ancadians are smart, they're telling as few people as possible. The crew on board the ship that took us know about it, and they've seen it as well. But maybe no one else has. They can't stop the rumours, but the best way to stop anyone else from seeing it is to keep it where it is.'

'You think it's still aboard their ship?'

'It makes a lot of sense. It's also easier to keep secure. The only way on and off is by a gangplank when it's moored. If they're really twitchy they can anchor offshore.'

'So what do we do now?'

'What do you mean, what do we do now? I've given you my guess, now let's get out of here.'

'Not until we try for that chest.'

'So now you want me to come up with a plan that'll get us right back where we started: locked up?'

193

'Only if they catch us. If it looks like going tits up, we'll up anchor and haul out.'

'It might be too late by then.'

'It won't be, trust me.'

'Trust *you?*'

*

'This is fucking insane,' hissed Johnny.

'I'm with you there, mate,' whispered Mike.

'Then why the hell didn't you say something when we were on the ship?' They crouched behind a low wall on the wharf, ten feet from a gunboat's gangplank. 'Now we've got to board this gunboat and we don't even know if it's the right one. Christ, why didn't I keep my big mouth shut?'

Maxwell and Andy crept along the Ancadian gunboat's gangplank. Johnny had to hand it to them, they were definitely quiet. They snuck aboard and vanished into the shadows and a guard sloped past them, half asleep with his rifle slung. Like silent ghosts they rose up behind him. Maxwell placed a hand over his mouth and pulled him backwards while Andy raced round the front and slammed a fist into his stomach. The guard grunted and sagged and Maxwell and Andy dragged him across the gangplank. The rest of the band each grabbed a part of him, and they scuttled back to *Friday's Fancy*.

*

The guard looked up at the band and was almost incontinent with terror. They slammed him down on the galley's table, ripped his rifle away and each held a limb. Maxwell grabbed his throat and breathed over him.

'Where is it, mate?' he hissed.

'*No entiendo, Senor*,' he sobbed. '*No entiendo.*'

'Does anyone speak Spanish?' asked Johnny. 'I don't think he knows any English.'

'Sure he does,' growled Maxwell. He glared into the guard's eyes. 'The treasure. The treasure. Where is it?'

'*Tesoro? Tesoro?*'

Maxwell grinned an evil smile and looked at Johnny. 'See, he's practically bilingual.'

'Are you sure tesoro means treasure?'

'What else would it mean?'

194

'Shit, Maxwell, it could mean testosterone for all I know.'

'Where?' Maxwell whispered malevolently at the guard, his eyeball almost making physical contact. 'Where tesoro? Where?'

'Fernando,' the guard stammered. 'San Fernando. San Fernando.'

'San Fernando,' said Johnny. 'The place, the boat or the person?'

'The fucking boat, according to you,' snapped Maxwell.

'According to my best guess. Christ, Maxwell, the only time you ever do what I say without an argument and it's the one time I wish I hadn't said anything.'

'Look, we'll just scoot along the quay. If we find a boat called San Fernando, we'll nip on board and see what we find.'

'And what about him?' Johnny pointed at the guard.

'We can't let him go, man,' said Joe.

'What? So we have to kill him?'

'Shit, Johnny,' said Maxwell. 'No one's killing anybody. We'll just hold him here till we get back, then decide what to do.'

Johnny picked up the guard's rifle. 'Well, seeing as none of us know how to use one of these, I suggest we chuck it over the side. We can leave Mike here to growl at the guard in case he tries anything, and the rest of us look for this mystery boat before someone misses the lone ranger here.'

Chapter 33

Johnny led the band onto the quayside and felt sick with fear. They
trotted along the wharf, and in his mind he saw hordes of
Ancadians hiding in every shadow. They took cover next to a large
pile of mooring ropes beside a gunboat and scanned the barely
decipherable nameplate.

'General Miguel san –'

'Not this one,' whispered Maxwell.

They crept past a low-domed grass circle with a ceremonial gun
in the middle, slipped into the shadow of a deserted, padlocked hut
and came to the next one.

'Christobal y Maria –'

'Next!'

Their footsteps bounced on a wooden walkway. Moonlight
reflected off the harbour's still waters and Johnny felt horribly
exposed. They broke cover, easily visible to anyone around them,
then hid behind a collection of crates and boxes near the next
gunboat's stern.

'San Fernando,' hissed Maxwell. 'That's it, that's it!'

Johnny grabbed Maxwell's shoulder and pushed him to the
ground. 'Keep a lid on it, for Christ's sake. Now, let's see what we
can see.'

'It's there, it's there. Look.'

Johnny elbowed Maxwell in the ribs and he grunted and sat
still. Johnny gazed at the ship's stern. Still in its cargo netting, and
apparently still hooked up to the hoist, sat the chest. 'Back to the
ship,' he said.

'But –'

'*Back* to the ship. I've got a plan.'

*

Each armed with a boat hook, the crew grabbed at Ancadian ship
railings and noiselessly pulled *Friday's Fancy* along the line of
equally silent gunboats. They crouched low and passed the sleek
outlines, although close up Johnny saw rusted panels and cracked
portholes.

'Are you sure this is going to work?' asked Maxwell.

'No,' hissed Johnny. 'I think getting out of here right now is going to work.'

'Hey, this is *your* plan.'

'Better than running mob-handed aboard one of their boats. *Not* better than leaving.'

Friday's Fancy trickled up to the *San Fernando* and Maxwell and Andy leapt over, securing both ships together with lines. Joe followed them, bent double with a loaded rucksack. While Maxwell and Andy's hands flickered over the cargo netting and hoist, Joe fiddled with his pack, then lowered it down an opened stern hatch. Trussed up, gagged and wearing a life jacket, the captured guard swung between Mike and Vince. Back and forth they pendulumed him, then threw him over the short space between the two ships. He landed with a thud and a muffled moan on the gunboat's decking. Andy and Maxwell turned a creaking handle on the hoist and the chest slowly lifted off the deck.

The hoist's spars bent slightly as it took the chest's weight, and the gunboat swayed with added buoyancy. Johnny feared that even the slightest movement would attract attention. He was amazed that they'd got this far without being discovered. The chest floated in the air, levitated between the two ships and then slowly kissed *Friday's Fancy's* planking. Mike and Vince lashed the chest to the deck, Maxwell, Joe and Andy leapt aboard and Johnny released the lines.

'*Parar! Quién está allí?*'

'Shit!' said Maxwell. 'How long till it blows, Joe?'

'One or two minutes, man.'

Maxwell swung the wheel and *Friday's Fancy's* engine burped into life and pulled them around towards the harbour entrance. Aboard the *San Fernando*, loud voices and stamping feet broke the night's stillness.

*

Seconds stretched out tighter than a guitar string, then loud shouts of dismay soaked through the Ancadian ship once Joe's explosive rucksack detonated deep inside the *San Fernando*. Maxwell turned the wheel and they slid out of harbour. Johnny looked back. The *San Fernando* stood motionless at the wharf, a cloud of smoke rising into the night from her aft hatch, while a thin stream of

197

Ancadians headed towards the shore. 'They aren't firing back,' he said. 'Do you think we cut their electrics?'

'Must have,' replied Maxwell. 'Elsewise they'd have sliced us to nothing.'

Friday's Fancy plunged into the deeper seas and undulating waves of open water. Maxwell peered at the chart, lined up a ruler, then pressed buttons on the GPS. He cast a look over his shoulder and the high mountain in the middle of Chanderos began to dip gradually into the horizon. Soon the harbour lights vanished and just the moon and stars lit their way. Maxwell swung hard on the wheel and Johnny almost fell overboard as the ship spun like a ballerina. 'I wonder why they aren't coming after us,' said Maxwell.

'No idea,' replied Johnny. 'But it won't last. Jailbreak, beating up their sailors, bombing one of their ships and then stealing back the treasure they took from us. They'll be coming, count on it.'

'We could lead them a right chase around here.'

'In your dreams, Maxwell. We're getting the hell out of sight before dawn, and only moving at night. We'll never outrun them if they see us. You've looked at the charts?'

'Yes.'

'So find us an island big enough to hide out on during the day.'

Chapter 34

Captain Baptistos slept the dream he wished he were living. Decorated by Colonel Mucama for capturing the foreigners, given a command post ashore – and the only time he went to sea was for ceremonial duties, a long way from the *San Fernando* and her terrifying crew. He thought he'd been clever by surrounding himself with the toughest brigands the navy had, just to keep him safe, but their murderous efficiency and the zealousness of the first mate horrified him. The sooner he was free of them, the better. And in his dreams, he always was.

Dragged from his world of comfort and security by a loud kicking against his bunk's metal panels, Baptistos stared at the nightmare face of first mate Castros, whose pale green eyes seemed to bolt straight through him. Castros wore a gold metal hoop in his left ear, and no one, not even Mucama, and certainly not Baptistos, had the nerve to tell him to take it out.

'You're wanted on the bridge,' he growled.

Castros only ever called Mucama 'Sir', and that was just when people were watching. Baptistos pulled a tailored jacket over his silk pyjamas and laced up his doeskin boots before walking to the *San Fernando*'s spartan bridge. 'What's happening?' he stuttered.

'Intruders,' said Castros. 'There.' He pointed off to port, where *Friday's Fancy,* clearly visible under the moonlight, made way. 'The gringo ship we captured. It came alongside, they dumped one of our men aboard and made off with their cargo.'

'They did what? Castros, how could you have allowed this to happen?'

'Because you stood the crew down, *Sir.* We have a night watch aboard, and little else.'

'And you think to allow those bandits to escape with their ill-gotten gains? Oh, Castros, you have much to learn if you ever wish to rise beyond your current rank. Start engines, switch on the searchlights, and when we have power in the guns, blow the *bastardos* out of the water.'

'That'll take time with a sedentary crew.'

'Then move faster. Must I explain every move to you, Castros? Really, sometimes I wonder how you ever achieved your fearsome reputation. We must face down these brigands and chastise them forcefully. Do it!'

A sharp explosion at the stern rocked the *San Fernando*. Smoke rose from the aft engine hatch.

'*Caramba Pablo*,' wailed Baptistos. 'They've opened fire! We're hit. Abandon ship, save yourselves. Get ashore now.'

'What of the enemy?' asked Castros. 'They aren't armed. I'll investigate the explosion. We may be able to make way.'

'You mad, suicidal fool. You think we can fight in our stricken state? Our duty is to save our brave sailors' lives.'

'But they'll escape.'

'And how far will they get? That yacht moves at a crawl. No, Castros. I won't endanger our boys. We go ashore and await further orders from Major Aguila.'

*

Twenty minutes later, a hastily woken Major Aguila sat in the harbour master's office and glared iced venom at Captain Baptistos, who squirmed under his baltic gaze. Castros stood behind Baptistos like an immovable tree trunk and stared over Aguila's head. 'These criminals must be hunted down,' hissed Aguila. 'How many ships can we mobilise?'

'Six,' said Castros. 'Seven, once the *San Fernando* is repaired.'

'How long will that take?'

'Four hours. The internal damage is cosmetic, but we have to test the hull's integrity.'

'Four hours? You've got two.'

'Major,' said Baptistos. 'I protest.'

'You *obey!*' snapped Aguila. 'These *bastardos* have humiliated us. They steal historic artefacts from our soil, escape this base, raid our ships and make off with their booty. We shall extend every effort to stop them, and that includes you, Captain, *and* your ship. You will be ready to sail when I have said, not a minute later.'

'And what are our rules of engagement?' asked Castros.

'There's no point bringing them back here. Find them and stop them. When Colonel Mucama returns from his mission I want to report a success to him.'

*

An island's dark silhouette rose in front of *Friday's Fancy*'s gently pitching bows, and Maxwell pointed to a beach only just visible as the black waves lapped against it. 'That goes around the whole island, and it's narrow.'

'So?' asked Johnny.

'So this island's got deep water all the way up to it, which means we won't run aground. And that there gap in the beach is a river mouth leading us right into the island. Five minutes and we'll be totally hidden from view.'

Maxwell turned the wheel, and *Friday's Fancy* glided a hundred yards upstream. For the first time since their capture, Johnny felt safe. There was still no sign of the dawn, and the tall trees on either side of the riverbank formed an impenetrable canopy. He could smell the musty swamp on either side, and he was left with an overpowering feeling that he was as far away from civilisation as he could possibly be.

His attention was abruptly drawn to the bows, where Vince and Andy heaved the sea anchor overboard. It landed with a loud splash, and he felt it take hold of the mangrove roots, bringing them to a dead stop. Maxwell cut the engine and the sounds of water lapping against the riverbank and crickets in the reeds invaded Johnny's ears. He picked up a coiled rope and climbed overboard. He struck out for the muddy bank, and dank, pungent swamp water soaked through to his skin. He could almost feel his boots and trousers being dyed ditch-slurry brown, and after a few dog-paddle strokes, his feet touched the riverbed. Unseen tree roots hindered his movement and he slithered onto land and secured the line to a tree trunk. Then, grabbing the rope, he pulled himself back aboard.

*

Lying in his airless cabin, the island's rising temperature woke Johnny up, his body sheened with a fever sweat. Then he heard the helicopter engines and fire-panic blazed through his body. He pulled on his damp leather trousers, forced pasty feet into shrink-wet cowboy boots and stumbled through to the already cramped galley.

'What's going on?' he asked.

'A helicopter,' whispered Maxwell. 'Buzzing the island, looking for us.'

'Shit, do you think they've seen us? And why are you whispering? They can't *hear* us.'

'Well, as long as we stay put, they won't see through the trees. We can't see them either.'

'We can't stay here for ever, man,' said Joe.

'We're not,' said Johnny. 'As soon as it gets dark we're out of here. The longer we stay out of sight, the bigger an area they've got to cover looking for us, and if it's dark, we've got a fair chance of slipping away.'

'And if we're seen?' asked Maxwell.

'Then we're screwed.'

*

Twilight settled around them, and Johnny clambered over the side and untied the moorings, landing with a squelch into thigh-deep mud. 'Bollocks,' he said.

'What's up?' Maxwell called down from the deck.

'Where's the river gone?'

'I can't see shit up here, mate. What are you talking about?'

'It looks like the tide's gone out, and it's taken the river with it.'

'Well, it can't have dried up completely. Get those ropes untied and let's get moving.'

'They *are* untied. We're stuck.'

'What do you mean?'

'We're up to our spuds in mud.'

'What?'

'It's time to get out and push.'

*

'Harder. Come on, lads. We'll never get out at this rate.'

'Why don't you get down here and help us?' grunted Johnny. He and the rest of the crew strained against the cloying mud and slipped against the ship's slicked stern.

'Someone's got to steer this thing, ain't they?' replied Maxwell.

Johnny pushed against the slowly moving hull, while on either side of him in the darkening dusk, the rest of the band did the same. Inch by inch they moved her free from the toffee-melt mud. Johnny groaned and fought to pull his legs clear, and the stench of disturbed swamp gas rising with each footstep made him gag. Slowly, just as their muscles ached and then failed, they felt the ship start to move more easily and she floated free in the river's lower reaches.

Friday's Fancy slid forward. Johnny's arms spun but his legs remained stuck fast in the glutinous mud. He pulled hard on each leg, falling flat on his face, barefoot and his whole body the same colour as the mud all around him. His cowboy boots were nowhere to be seen.

'Hurry up, man.' Joe slopped past him. 'Our ride's getting away.'

'Not without my boots.' Johnny plunged his arm into the sucking, damp holes where his legs had been, his fingers questing for the soaked leather. He yelped in pain at what felt like a hundred needles lanced into his hand and outstretched arm. He pulled free and felt moving, clicking objects clinging to him, nipping him painfully.

He shook his arm to get the small crabs off of him, and fresh rivulets of pink, sharp-clawed crabs erupted from the foot holes in the mud. He moaned in dismay, turned and struggled after *Friday's Fancy,* now free-floating down the river and entering the sea around the island. 'No. Stop,' he cried. 'Wait for me, wait for me. Crabs! Crabs! Fucking crabs!'

The rest of the band were already clear and swimming towards *Friday's Fancy,* while Johnny waded through the crab-infested, sticky brown nightmare. Each time he pulled himself upright and tried to scrub himself free of tiny pink crustaceans, one of his feet would slip and he'd back-slap into the slime once more. He swam, crawled, slipped and slithered towards the water, his whole body becoming a mass of tiny nip marks where the crabs latched onto him.

He splashed into the water, then kicked and struck out towards *Friday's Fancy,* the crabs finally unlatching from the hundred stinging mini-wounds all over him. He reached for the rope that had been thrown over the side and pulled himself aboard.

'About time, too,' drawled Maxwell, as the engine coughed into life. 'The break's over, mate, now clear that mud off the deck.'

Chapter 35

The cold grey dawn greeted Johnny over the seascaped horizon, and he wished it was still night. Emptiness yawned at them from all directions, and the temperature quickly rose. The rising sun burnt away the cool mist, and Johnny knew they'd be able to see anybody coming from a long way off, but it also made them highly visible.

'Looks like the wind's coming back.'

He followed the direction of Maxwell's finger and saw that where there had once been blue sky, an enormous bank of clouds had suddenly built up. Small, angry squalls rippled the sea, creating dark waves.

'We *need* that wind,' said Maxwell. 'And rain. It'll cut down on the Ancadians' visibility, and high winds'll hopefully keep their helicopters on the ground.'

'Never mind that, man,' said Joe. 'Look over there.'

Johnny looked aft. A drab grey patrol boat whispered into view. Its front-mounted cannon pointed straight at *Friday's Fancy*. It began to overhaul them and the changing weather announced itself with a chill wind.

'Can we lose them in the storm?' asked Johnny.

'We can try.' Maxwell spun the wheel and the Ancadian gunboat bore down on them. Johnny noticed it was a different type to the one that had captured them, and he stared down the barrel of a true ship-killing front gun.

A white puff of smoke blew a perfect ring around the gun's muzzle, and seconds later Johnny was thrown to the deck by a crashing explosion less than six feet from the starboard beam. A huge column of water erupted into the air and splashed on the deck, soaking them all.

'Fuck me, that was close.'

Maxwell swung the wheel and Johnny looked back at the Ancadian ship. It leaned over and it corrected its course, and the gun crew adjusted their aim. Another puff of smoke and the shell shrieked overhead, while *Friday's Fancy* dropped into the increasingly heavy waves.

Johnny threw himself into the galley and ripped open the equipment locker. He pulled out a handful of lifejackets, threw one over his head and stepped past Mike.

'What's happening, man?' he asked.

'The Ancadians are correcting their aim,' replied Johnny bluntly. He shouldered past Mike and climbed onto the deck. Another shell crashed into the sea just feet to starboard. More water soaked him and he pushed a lifejacket into each band member's hands.

'Do you reckon we'll need them?' asked Maxwell.

'What do you think?'

Maxwell zipped up his lifejacket, looked behind him and worked the wheel, trying to keep them stern-on to the Ancadians and present less of a target. 'They're getting closer,' he said.

Another puff of smoke from the Ancadian gun.

'That's bad, right?' asked Johnny.

Before Maxwell could answer, the entire stern was lifted clear of the water, then disintegrated in a shower of wood splinters. Free of the aft deck which now no longer existed, the chest dropped into the foaming water where the back of *Friday's Fancy* had once been, and disappeared from view. Disconnected from the now shattered rudder, the wheel spun uselessly and with nothing to push against, Maxwell fell into the galley on top of Mike. Johnny was slammed face down onto the deck once more, and *Friday's Fancy* ground to a sudden and sickening halt. He struggled to his knees and looked behind him. They were no longer skipping among the growing waves in a desperate attempt to escape the Ancadians; they were crippled and not moving.

'Overboard,' shouted Johnny. 'Get off the ship. Now.'

'Are you crazy?' asked Vince.

'The ship's finished, and if we stay aboard, so are we.'

A second boil-spout of water flew a hundred feet into the air, this time off the port side. Johnny grabbed Vince and threw him into the seething waters around the stricken ship. Joe and Andy didn't wait to be pushed; they jumped in alongside Vince. Johnny turned and clambered back towards the galley, looking for Mike and Maxwell among the splintered ruin of the ship's stern, which was now rapidly settling beneath the churning sea.

Another shell screamed overhead, so close it rammed Johnny facedown into the doomed planking, then threw him into the air as it landed and shattered the bows. He was sucked under the water, then dragged to the surface by his lifejacket. He coughed and puked diced-carrot seawater, then rubbed his eyes. *Friday's Fancy* had been blasted into a random collection of splintered wood. Joe, Andy and Vince clung to a flat, jagged remnant of deck and Johnny struggled towards them. 'Where the hell are Maxwell and Mike?'

'They were below when the ship got hit,' said Vince.

A small, upturned remnant of hull bobbed between the waves, alternately appearing and vanishing from view in the now malignant sea.

'Wait here,' said Andy. 'Vince, with me.'

Vince and Andy struck out towards the small floating piece of wreckage. Joe and Johnny clung to their own improvised life-raft while a rain squall guttered down on them and the waves tried to pull them from their barely floating handhold.

Johnny looked back to see where the others had gone. He shouted into the storm, his voice drowned out by the howling wind. Out of the foam-flecked gloom he saw four struggling figures. They bobbed through the swirling surf, kept afloat by their life jackets. Johnny and Joe screamed and waved them on. Slowly they splashed towards the improvised raft. Mike blundered through the tortured seas with awkward but independent strokes of his own.

'Hell of a time to learn to swim,' choked Johnny. Mike gripped a chunk of wreckage and shivered.

'Yeah,' he choked. 'We'll be doing it synchronised on the next tour.'

'Better than the last bloody solo you did,' spluttered Vince.'

'Max and me would be drowned if it wasn't for you two,' coughed Mike. 'Thanks, lads.'

'You'd have only come back to haunt us,' hacked Andy.

'Hey, man,' said Joe. 'They've gone. The Ancadians, they've gone.'

'What?' Johnny looked around him. In the dwindling visibility all he saw was sea and driving rain. 'Where are they? They sunk us. Don't they want us?'

'Why should they?' asked Vince. 'They just wanted us out of the picture, I guess now the sea will do that for them.'

'So, Johnny,' panted Maxwell. 'What's your plan?'

*

Dark clouds hosed torrents of rain onto the band and they were thrown around the boiling waters that surrounded their wreck-raft. Visibility had been smothered down to fifty yards, while the small wedge of wood they clung to had just enough room for one to climb onto, although they could never dry out in the midst of the heaving storm.

The hours oozed past, night fell, and Johnny wondered how long they could hold onto their small piece of wreckage, and how close they were to any shipping lanes. Through the night, the storm battered down on them, and they clung to the swollen rope fragments and slid and slipped on and off the raft. The following dawn brought little cheer with low clouds scudding across the sky.

Johnny's night vision slowly retreated and gloomy sunlight swept the night beyond the heaving seas. He gradually became aware of a slightly quieter wind, and a lessening of the rain. Looking up, he saw grey clouds give way to lighter ones. The visibility increased, the rain stopped, and the clouds thinned and dispersed.

The sun warmed the band, comfortably at first, then with a burning heat as it beat down on their shelterless floating island. Johnny's sparse hair left him feeling like a struck match. He squinted up at the sky, then felt his heart rate speed up.

'Hey, look,' he cried. 'That's a plane. It's a plane.'

A small white speck flew far above them against the now blue sky, sailing through the air in silence. Gradually it approached. The band waved their hands, Johnny climbed onto the small stamp of wood and jumped up and down, and they all screamed their tonsils bloody. The plane circled them, still at height, before disappearing into the eastern sky.

'Do you think they saw us?' asked Maxwell.

'Sure,' said Johnny. 'They've got downward-facing, stealth-proof, wood-seeking radar, thermal-imaging pickups, binoculars and sonic sensors. They're bound to see us.'

'Really?'

'I don't bloody know. What am I, Top Gun?'

207

'Easy, mate. I was only asking.'

'Sure.' Johnny jumped back into the water and Mike climbed onto the raft in his place. 'Hell, even if they did see us, and even if they are sending help, it's not going to get here anytime soon. We're in the middle of nowhere, and we don't even know where here is.'

*

The sun climbed into the shimmering, empty sky and the band roasted. Johnny's thirst built and he felt his tongue start to swell. He felt dizzy and sick, and the first wisps of real fear crept through him. *We can't take much more of this.*

The sea calmed to a dark blue plate in all directions. Johnny vision blurred and starred. He was no longer sure what he was seeing. His ears started buzzing, made worse every time he got seawater sloshed over his head. The buzzing turned into a roaring, rhythmic, chunking rattle. Nothing registered in his tortured mind, nothing made sense, not even the whoops and cheers of the band, not the approaching, clanking, engine noise, and not the grey, greasy wall of slightly rusting metal that now towered over them.

Chapter 36

Skipper pushed the throttle forward and felt *Andrea*'s responding vibrations rattle inside his head. He smiled at her feel, knowing that anyone else would have been terrified, convinced she'd be about to shake apart, but not Skipper. He knew her, knew her limits, knew her too well. He coaxed her out of Porte Juste's small harbour and laid a course on the co-ordinates he'd been given. *And just what in the name of God have those fecking idiots been up to now?* he thought.

Five hours, three chicken sandwiches and two pints of black coffee later, Skipper looked up from his dog-eared spy novel and saw a floating chunk of wood and tangled rope, surrounded by a microbe-ring of soaked humanity, all of which was slowly being fricasseed by the burning sun. He pulled the wheel round and set a line for them, slowing down to an idle. He slowly approached and threw a scramble-net over *Andrea*'s side.

'I always said that boat had an unlucky name,' he shouted down to them.

*

Barefoot and missing his cowboy boots, Johnny felt his leather trousers drying and cracking in the hot sun. He and the band lay on *Andrea*'s tiny cluttered deck. Coiled ropes and crates of tools made it an uncomfortable platform to lie on, but nobody was complaining.

'So we lost the treasure, *again,*' said Vince. 'What was the point of all this?'

'Maybe we could find it, *again,*' said Maxwell.

'What? We've been shot at, slung in jail, had our ship blown out from under us and left for dead in the middle of the sea. It's straight back to the high life for me, mate. I just hope they've got a decent hotel somewhere on St. Clements.'

*

The sun slowly traversed the sky and started to cast longer shadows across *Andrea,* making it easier to walk barefoot on the cooling metal deck. Late afternoon gave way to early evening, and the welcome sight of Porte Juste was just visible below the sunset.

Andrea's clanking, smoking engine inched them into port. The waterfront's bleached white buildings reflected the setting sun, while behind them the dark forested interior surrounded the city on all sides like a green lava flow. The extinct volcano on the island's far side was easily visible, rising above everything else and dominating the island landscape.

They approached the harbour's granite block walls, chugged through and tied up beneath Skipper's repair shed. Johnny stared at the wharf, and was dazzled by the familiar Hawaiian shirt and faded jeans of Henri Chevalier.

'Bonjour, *mes amis*,' he said, as *Andrea* gently kissed the wharf's rubber-tyred fenders. 'You seem to have left your ship behind.'

'We wouldn't want you to think we were being possessionist,' said Maxwell.

'Especially when it was only borrowed. And the treasure? Did you find it?'

'Yes, and no.'

Henri laughed. 'Easily found is easily lost.'

'There was nothing easy about finding *or* losing it, mate.'

'You can tell me all about it tonight, *mon ami*.'

'Tonight?'

'*Mais oui*. You are the guests at my residence.'

Henri ushered the band ashore and then into a black minibus with the St. Clements coat of arms neatly painted on the side. '*Mon ami*,' he whispered to Johnny. 'You are destitute. Can I offer to resupply you?'

Johnny looked down at his cracked leather trousers and bare feet. 'Some new clothes might help.'

'And the settlement?'

Johnny smiled. 'From one manager to another, huh?'

'You return to us empty-handed. You lose a ship. A St. Clements ship.' Henri shrugged. 'We need to negotiate.'

'Negotiate?'

'I was expecting to be able to exhibit a recovered pirate's treasure, so as to perhaps bring some revenue to the island, maybe enough to replace your losses. Alas not. So now you have become troublesome guests requiring a rescue. I would say that you owe us.'

210

Johnny sighed. 'Okay, Henri, get me an international phone link and I'll wire over some money for our clothes.'

'*Très bien.* We can discuss other matters later.'

*

'They're white,' said Vince.

'They're cowboy boots, they're cool.' Walking along Porte Juste's bustling market street towards the waiting minibus, Johnny stared at the rest of the band, straggly-haired, all wearing rope sandals, sack T-shirts and shorts. As far as he was concerned, they looked like lost disciples, despite the designer labels that clung to their clothes like limpets.

'A free wardrobe from Henri,' said Vince. 'And all you could get was them stupid boots and the same clothes you always wear. This is the Caribbean, man. You've got to get with the locals.'

'None of this is free,' said Johnny. 'We're in hock to Henri for the clothes and a replacement ship for Skipper, and that's just the start of it.'

'What?'

'Look, it's not like we've done him or St. Clements any favours, is it? We lost the treasure, the Ancadians know that St. Clements helped us, and we needed Skipper to rescue us after we got sunk. And it was *his* ship we lost as well.'

'So what are you saying?'

'We owe Skipper, we owe Henri, and we owe the island.'

'And what do they all want?'

'Henri's not saying, yet. That'll happen tonight.'

*

The minibus whispered to a halt on Henri's large driveway. Johnny's feet crunched on light-coloured gravel and the band were ushered inside and introduced to luxury, presidential style. The white walls of the spacious, open rooms gave an impression of sheer size, and the solid wood furniture gleamed under the tropical sunlight that poured in through large windows. The thick walls kept out the baking heat, and large fans hung from the ceiling and spun slowly, providing a cooling downdraft on Johnny's damp body. After passing through one enormous room after another, Henri smiled a welcome at them as they halted in a reception room, which opened out onto a large garden.

211

At one end of the room was an oak dining table, pebble-dashed with a hot and cold buffet, while underneath it stood a row of cool boxes, filled with beer cans. The packs of ice surrounding them radiated refreshing coolness.

'Enjoy, *mes amis*, and tell me your story. I notice that you did not arrive back at Porte Juste in the same style as you left. So what exactly *did* happen to your ship?'

'Sunk,' said Maxwell. 'And the treasure with it.'

'So you found it? It was there?'

'Exactly where Miles said it would be.'

'And then you lost it?'

'Found it, lost it. Twice.'

'Twice?'

'You were right about the Ancadians, mate.'

'You met them?'

'Let's say they met us.'

'*Mon ami*, I need to know. They are our neighbours, and they are bad neighbours. What happened?'

'After we got the treasure, they grabbed us.'

'And sunk your vessel?'

'Well, not exactly. They took us to some naval base and locked us up. We escaped, took the treasure back, they chased us, then sank us.'

'And that is all?'

Maxwell looked at Johnny.

'Is that all?' repeated Henri.

'We might have indirectly caused a few casualties in order to get away,' said Johnny.

'Oh? How?'

'Well, they were about to shoot us, or at best put us away for years, so we had to come up with a way to delay them, and Maxwell made up a story and sent them off on a false trail.'

'Where did you send them?'

'An island,' said Maxwell. 'Sitting over the Columbus Trench.'

'*Merde!* You did not? The Columbus Trench?'

'You know about it?' asked Johnny.

'Of *course* I know about it. I'm the Prime Minister of a former French colony. La France may be our old masters, but they still wish to be our friends. Now, I don't know everything about it, but I

212

know enough to keep my people away from there. The Americans, however, do not trust the Ancadians enough to tell them *anything* about it. You sent them to the Columbus Trench, which means they won't be coming back. Which probably explains why they sunk your ship, which in fact wasn't your ship. It is a good job they didn't know you berthed here first.'

Johnny looked at Andy, who blushed viciously and stared at the floor.

'I see,' said Henri.

'Henri,' said Johnny. 'We had no choice.'

'No choice? No choice at all?'

'What else could we have done?'

'Maybe you could have come up with a plan that did not involve sending their navy on a suicide mission.'

'We were on the spot, Henri, under pressure.'

'And your slip of the tongue regarding St. Clements?'

'Look,' said Andy. 'That mad bastard had a gun on me. Hey, I'll fight anyone in a pub, but that was crazy.'

Henri sighed. '*Oui, oui.*'

'So what happens now?'

'*Damne,*' said Henri. 'I had intended to talk to you about arranging a concert here in St. Clements. But now you are too dangerous to have around, and the less anyone knows about you ever having been here, the better. So tonight, you shall stay here, and tomorrow morning you will fly home. The Ancadians think you are dead, and I do not know what they will do next, but it will not help any of us if you suddenly appeared on our island.'

*

Early the next morning, Johnny woke up and stared at the silken cover atop his bed, wondering how the mere manager of a heavy metal band had just been asleep in the guest bedroom of a head of state, even if it was only while he waited to be kicked out of the country. He sat up and pulled on the beige suede jeans he'd bought the day before along with his white cowboy boots, completing his look with a Cold Steel T-shirt. Just as he was wondering what to do about breakfast, the door burst open and Maxwell rushed inside.

'Forget about the flight home,' he said. 'We're in trouble.'

'Because that's so unusual, isn't it?' said Johnny. 'What's happened now?'

213

'Best we talk to Henri downstairs.'

Johnny shuffled downstairs into the large reception room, where the rest of the band sat with dazed expressions on bed-sized sofas and watched a large screen television. Henri stood and looked at the screen with a scowl like a tropical storm. Johnny's eyes moved to the screen and he fought a sudden surge of nausea.

'Holy shit, is that St. Clements on the news?'

'Yes, *mon ami*. And those are Ancadian gunboats just offshore. Walk to the seafront and see them for yourself if you like.'

'Fucking hell.' Johnny squinted at the screen. 'How many boats have those bastards got? How long have they been there? Have they said what they want? What do we do now?'

Henri switched off the television, threw the remote onto the sofa and collapsed into its soft, pliant cushioning. 'Well, we can no longer fly you out of here. They have guns trained on the airport, and threaten to shell the runway if we attempt any flights. Their gunboats also blockade Porte Juste. We are all trapped on the island.'

'But that do they want?'

'They want St. Clements.'

'What?'

'Oh yes. They always have. They've made no secret of it, and this may just be the first of many such acquisitions.'

'But –'

'As soon as they knew you stopped here on your way into Ancadia, they had their excuse. In their eyes we helped you, and in sending them to the Columbus Trench, you became criminals and we are the ones who aided you, possibly even assigned you there.'

'Oh Christ. So what do we do now?'

Henri looked at Johnny and his eyebrows climbed into his receding hairline. 'We?'

'Hell, yes, we. Jesus, Henri, we've just unleashed an entire shit-storm onto your shores. We're responsible, we owe you. Right, lads?' Johnny looked around at the band. None of them met his gaze and his anger built. 'Look, you ungrateful bastards. If it hadn't been for St. Clements we'd never have found the treasure in the first place. Wasn't that the whole reason for coming here? If it weren't for St. Clements we'd also still be clinging to a chunk of wreckage the size of a record player. And if it weren't for *us*, the

214

Ancadian gunboats wouldn't be lying offshore. But it's not just us that are in the firing line now; it's everyone on this island. Henri, what'll happen if the Ancadians realise we're here and not drowned?'

'They will probably demand that I hand you over?'

'And then?'

'I suppose you will be shot, and the blockade will continue. They were always coming for St. Clements, *mon ami*, you have just made it happen sooner.'

'Oh, for Christ's sake,' said Maxwell. 'Look, Henri. No one's going to shoot us. Whatever they think we've done, we're still Cold Steel. We're in the public eye, we'll be safe.'

'You will not be safe,' said Henri. 'And you will stay here until this matter is resolved.'

'Have you got any idea how that might happen?' asked Johnny.

Henri spread his arms wide. 'At this moment, I do not. Apart from giving in to their demands and signing the entire island over to Ancadia.'

'So what's stopping them from invading right now? They've got us surrounded, why not finish it?'

'Because they can't,' replied Henri. 'They have the most powerful sovereign navy in the Caribbean. Their boats are especially designed to move quickly from island to island and sail over the shallowest reefs. They are small, but they have the newest weapons, and a lot of them. However, they are not geared towards an invasion. In addition, our ground forces are well equipped and fully trained to defend the island. They have already been mobilised and would make invasion a costly option for the Ancadians.'

'So it's a stalemate?'

'For the time being.'

'Well, that's alright then. All we've got to do is wait for them to get fed up and go home. Anyway, isn't there some sort of international law against this kind of thing? Surely the UN or someone like that will get involved.'

'Not without a good reason, *mon ami*. At this level there are many shades of grey. America is Ancadia's ally, and their government will not help us. The rest of the western world sees us

215

as a competitor economically, and would shed no tears if our exports were halted to their benefit. We are on our own.'

Johnny felt sick. 'So what are we going to do?'

'We have time, *some* time. But we are cut off, and sooner or later the people will starve. As long as that takes is as long as it takes to find a way out of this. We need help from the outside world. Our communication channels are open, and perhaps I can negotiate a deal with our competitors in return for their support.' Henri sighed. 'And ultimately their control. We may lose a lot of revenue in the process, and much of our income will go abroad, but it seems to be the price we must pay for at least some of our freedom.'

Johnny clenched his teeth and forced his mind into gear. The more he thought about it, the more it seemed that high-flying diplomacy differed very little from the scheming machinations of the music business.

The music business? Suddenly, the organisational dynamo within Johnny's mind came alive. 'Yes, Yes. Yes! Fucking YES!'

'Are you all right?' Maxwell looked at Johnny.

'Watch this face,' said Johnny. 'I've got a plan, and it's going to work. We're going to do the last thing they expect, and we just can't lose.'

'So let's hear it.'

'We do the one thing we do best. Henri's already said it, so let's do it. We'll play a concert right here in St. Clements. The Ancadians think we're dead so they won't see it coming, and Henri says our communication links are open. We'll announce it, and satellite and internet feeds will beam the news *and* the concert right around the world. If we sell this right, *nobody* will want to miss it. The whole world will be watching, and when they are, we're going to tell them exactly what's going on here. If we can do that, *if* we can raise a loud enough voice of indignation from the people watching, *if* we can rock their consciences from mere thought into action, then *maybe* they'll be able to shame their leaders into acting on St. Clements' behalf. Will *that* be enough to change world opinion, Henri?'

'It might be, *mon ami*. It also might not. But you are right. If we can raise the popular support across the world, then the politicians will have to act.'

216

'And to do that,' said Johnny, 'we're going to need one major metal gig, the concert that beats them all, that nobody will want to miss. Twenty years from now, we want people to ask each other what they were doing when Cold Steel played St. Clements. It'll need to be on every phone, TV and computer screen on the planet. We'll use the cricket stadium next to the harbour, and then when everyone's watching we've got to lay it on the line about what's happening here. But until the night of the gig, the rest of the world will have to think we're doing a concert and nothing else.' He stared razor blades at the band. 'Even if they point a gun at you. Right, Andy?''

'*Très bon*,' said Henri. 'We shall make the announcement this afternoon. I had already called a press conference to give our response to the blockade. After I have done that, the world's media are yours.'

Chapter 37

'Randall Spitz.'

'Randall, it's Johnny.'

'Johnny? Johnny? Do I sound like a goddam address book? Johnny who?'

'Johnny Faslane.'

'Johnny Faslane?' Randall sat up and gripped the phone. 'Holy shit, Cold Steel Johnny Faslane?'

'That's right.'

'What do you want now, you little prick? Have your boys got into an even bigger pile of crap? You only seem to call me when there's trouble. I'm like your goddam mother.'

'The band want to do a concert.'

'They want to what?' Randall put down his iced tea and reached for his sunglasses. 'Hang on a second. Cold Steel, Cold Steel. Yeah, I got it. You bastards are due in the studio after your goddam sabbatical in the Caribbean. There's nothing in *your* script about a goddam concert.'

'We'll still be in the studio on time. This is just something we've got to do.'

'Which means someone's making you do it, right?'

'It's a long story.'

'Does it involve Ozone?'

'No.'

'Then I don't give a good god damn who's got a monkey wrench around your balls. What do you want from me?' He picked up his drink.

'Live broadcast rights.'

Randal spat iced tea over his spotless veranda. 'You want what? Live rights, you son of a bitch? When the fuck did Cold Steel join the live broadcast league?'

'The band can handle it, Randall. They proved that on the European leg of the tour.'

'*You* proved it, you bastard. Those jerkoffs would be cleaning park benches right now if it weren't for you. So, what's going down?'

'We're doing a special show in St. Clements.'

'St. Clements? Jesus, isn't there some kind of war going on down there?'

'We're not involved in the politics, Randall. The band are just here to do a show.'

'You'd better be, you son of a bitch. If I hear you assholes have gotten involved in a war, then it's over, but for real. You cocksuckers will wish you'd died in that goddam war. But you're wanting my say so before you go ahead, and that shows respect. I like that. So you want the right to play? What does Ozone get?'

'Cold Steel's live album and enough video footage for a movie release.'

'Okay, you've got my interest. When's the show?'

'A week from now.'

'A week? You're shitting me. You think you'll put this together in a week. Hey, Johnny.' Randall pronounced Johnny's name with a Brooklyn family accent. 'You're good, you proved that in Europe, but a week?'

'I can do it, Randall, and so can the band.'

'Just don't get your asses shot off in that goddam gunfight down there.'

'Worried about us, Randall?'

'Hell no, I'm just protecting Ozone's investment. And if you fuck this up, you'll wish you *had* been shot.'

*

Despite the cool comfort inside Henri's house, Johnny felt like he'd sweated half his body heat away as the day wore on. Like a super tanker approaching a rowing boat in the dark, the press conference loomed ever closer. Henri was due to speak first, and then the band would face the media. Johnny stood in front of them like a prison guard on death row. 'We don't have time for details,' he said. 'So let's keep this short. Henri goes out there first to say what he has to say, then it's your turn. You mention the concert and nothing else. Not a word about the Ancadians, or the treasure.'

Henri pulled back a curtain and slid open the glass doors, while Johnny hovered out of sight. Aside from the security men that held back the reporters, the patio was clear, and there was a spring in Henri's step that seemed to surprise many of those watching. 'Ladies and gentlemen of the press,' he began. 'Let me begin by thanking you all for being here in such large numbers. I am flattered that there is such interest in the affairs of St. Clements. Now, as I am sure you are aware, we are currently embroiled in a disagreement with our neighbouring nation, Ancadia. This will surely come as no surprise to you, since their Navy is now clearly visible from any point on the island. However, I call on us all to consider the consequences of our actions, and in the days to come, search for a peaceful conclusion to this matter.'

There was a two-second pause before the questions came like a hailstorm.

'Henri, why is St. Clements under blockade?'

'A local trade disagreement; surely it will remain a small matter.'

'Are you going to resign, *Monsieur*?'

'I am Prime Minister only for as long as the people wish me to be.'

'Will St. Clements be invaded?'

'We are ready for every eventuality,' he smiled.

'Are you ready to negotiate?'

Henri held up his hands. 'All lines of communication are open. I would remind everyone here, though, that we are surrounded by a hostile power. We have not retaliated, and we seek a peaceful resolution to this problem. And even as I appeal to the leaders of the world for mediation, let us put such things in their true perspective, and turn instead to matters which really do deserve the complete attention of the world. For some time now, St. Clements has been the grateful host to one of the world's legendary entertainment acts. And now, to announce their latest plans, it gives me the greatest pleasure to introduce you all to the truly magnificent Cold Steel.'

There was a second's silence at the unexpected change in subject, and then the band erupted into view from behind the curtains and swaggered onto the patio. Maxwell beamed his best shit-eating grin at the bemused reporters as though it was a world tour opening night.

'So,' he said. 'We've been out of circulation for a little while now, thinking about our next move after Beer Doctor, and we know you lot want to know what it is. Now, here on St. Clements, the place is great, the people are great, and we want to thank everybody here for their hospitality, the only way we know how.'

'One week from now, we'll be playing a concert at the Porte Juste cricket ground for the people of St. Clements, and it'll make the Beer Doctor tour look like small change. I'm telling you straight, everyone'll want to watch it, and if you miss it you'll kick yourselves for the rest of your lives, because I promise you this, nobody will ever do a show like this, *ever* again.'

A further two seconds of bemused hush before the questions started.

'What made you want to perform here at this time, Maxwell?'

'Gratitude,' he replied. 'Appreciation of hospitality, nothing else.'

'That seems like a strange thing to do in the middle of a blockade?'

'What blockade? We're staying out of the politics.'

'Any new material for the concert?'

'Maybe.'

'What kind of effects have you got planned?'

'You'll have to wait and see.'

Johnny saw the reporters' frustration rising at Maxwell's evasive answers. Vince turned towards Johnny, who nodded. He nudged Maxwell.

'Anyway,' he smiled. 'I'd love to stay and talk with you lads, but we've got a show to get ready for.'

Maxwell led the band back inside the house, and seconds later Henri took the podium.

'Maxwell Diabolo, and the brilliant Cold Steel, who will be playing at the cricket stadium in one week.'

Henri remained outside and the media attention swept back to the blockade. For the time being, the concert was seen as a strange irrelevance. Johnny turned to the band.

'Right, the first thing you lot need to do is start rehearsing. You've got a week to come up with a set list and play it perfectly, and while you're doing that, I'll be putting it all together.'

'Sounds like you've got it under control.' Maxwell pulled open a beer. 'I ain't worried about a thing.'

'That's because you're too stupid to worry,' said Johnny. 'Right now, you haven't even got instruments.'

'I guess you thought about that before you came up with this whole idea.'

'I've got a few plans, but they need to come off first time.'

'So where are we going to rehearse? If you've got to build a stage from scratch over at the cricket ground, we can hardly strut our stuff in between builders and scaffolding.'

'The St. Clements National Steel Band have got a recording studio somewhere on this island. It's a converted plantation house with guest accommodation, so you can doss down there for the night.'

'Okay, but we can't practice without instruments.'

'You just get yourselves over to the plantation house and get a feel for the place,' said Johnny. 'One of Henri's security men will drive you there, and I'll head into town for instruments.'

'Now?'

'Now. And get there by yesterday.'

Maxwell finished his beer and stood up. The band left, and Johnny looked out onto the patio, where it seemed that Henri was winding down the press conference. He stepped outside, expecting to attract no attention at all.

'Johnny Faslane.'

Johnny's head whipped round at the familiar voice, and he looked, wide-eyed, at the easily remembered waterfall of raven hair surrounding a heart-shaped face.

'Rachel,' he stammered. His heart trip-hammered inside his ribcage. He hadn't seen her since the UK leg of the tour. 'What are you doing here?'

'Looking for a missing metal band,' she smiled. 'I've been one step behind you all the time.'

'What? How?' *Christ, does she know about the Ancadians?*

'Well, maybe not one step. Maybe not all the time.'

'And you tracked us down to here?'

'That was the easy part. When a band drags back their reputation from the brink and re-invent themselves in mid-tour, then disappear straight afterwards with no explanation, don't you think that *might* make us curious?'

'Us being the media?'

222

She smiled and Johnny felt his knees turn to marshmallows. 'Us being the well-meaning bringers of information to your need-to-know fans.'

For a second, Johnny forgot the blockade, the danger, and his near-drowning, and laughed. 'Well, Rachel. It's good to know you came looking for us for all the right reasons. So how come you found us?'

'A contact in the UK told me about your flight to Jamaica. A contact *nowhere* near Jamaica got me the passenger manifest for your flight here. Everybody I spoke to on the island said a bunch of hairy musicians were here on a treasure hunt, and there the trail went cold, until I clocked your sun-baked buns being brought ashore yesterday. And now there's a blockade and I can't go anywhere, *and* I'm missing some serious gaps in your story. So what's going on?'

Johnny shrugged. 'Like the band said. St Clements has been good to them, and they want to repay the kindness.'

'Nothing else?'

'Like what?'

'I don't know.' Her cobalt eyes impaled him. 'Anything to do with the blockade?'

'How can a blockade have anything to do with Cold Steel? They're a band, not diplomats.'

'You sure?'

'Look, Rachel, it's very simple.' He returned her ice-wall stare. 'Cold Steel really needed to get away from everything after the Beer Doctor tour. That meant disappearing completely and not telling anyone where they'd gone, hence St. Clements.'

'And this treasure hunt?'

Johnny spread his arms wide. 'Do you see us carrying any treasure around?'

She laughed again, and Johnny couldn't help noticing the open neck of her white blouse. He felt his judgement slide.

'If you *weren't* on a treasure hunt,' she said. 'Why did you tell everyone on St. Clements that's what you were here for? And that rickety tugboat you squelched off yesterday didn't exactly look like a floating Hilton. It looked to me like you were in a bit of trouble.'

Johnny wondered what else she'd seen. Nothing, surely. Not unless she was embedded on an Ancadian gunboat as well. Jesus, why hadn't they been more cautious when they'd first arrived? How many other reporters had tracked them to St. Clements? He looked at her and forced a confident smile. 'None of that's got anything to do with the gig. Surely that's a newer, more important story?'

'Maybe, but still less of a scoop than the other event happening around here.'

'Well, I'm really busy right now. Can we talk about this later?'

'I've heard that before.'

'I mean it this time. Hey, where am I going to run to?'

'Are you going to say more than two words about the band?'

'Maybe,' he teased. 'Depends how persuasive you are.'

'You may regret finding that out.' She smiled and handed him a card. 'Or maybe you won't. I'm at the office till eight, but my mobile is never off. Call me when you're ready.'

He buried her card deep in his hip pocket and she walked back towards the departing group of reporters. Johnny followed Henri inside.

'*Sacré bleu.*' Henri cracked open a beer and sat down. 'Dealing with those vultures turns my stomach. All they care about is the sensation. They would love to see this erupt into war, or occupation. Anything to boost their ratings.'

'The music press are just the same.' Johnny thought about Rachel as he spoke. 'But hey, let's make sure this thing turns out the way *we* want it to.'

'*Mais oui.* The band have left?'

'On their way right now, and I'm just about to head into town to get some instruments. What's the best way to get there?'

'Go out of the front door and turn left. There you will see the bicycle shed. Help yourself to one, then go to the end of the drive and turn right. As long as you keep the ocean to your front you shall arrive at the marketplace.'

'Haven't you got a spare car?'

'Of course, but the roads of Porte Juste are narrow and crowded. Believe me, you will be no slower on a bicycle, you will not be polluting the environment, and you will also be getting a lot fitter.'

Johnny wasn't entirely convinced. He grimaced. 'See you later.'

'*Au revoir*. I must go to Government House, but on your return, please make yourself at home.'

Chapter 38

Under the shade of several closely cultivated Bahamian pines,
Johnny found a large bicycle shed filled with bikes, ranging from a
brand new mountain rider to flat-tyred butcher's bikes that were
slowly rusting back to nature. He took a deep breath and picked
one out, realising the drive's loose gravel was a far from ideal
medium on which to reacquaint himself with the forgotten art.
With his knees sticking out at right angles, he managed to swerve
onto the road, where he headed towards the marketplace.

Old white buildings crowded around him as he pedalled into the
small town square, skidding over uneven cobblestones. Porte Juste
had a timeless quality, added to by the lack of cars among the mass
of pedestrians and mostly antique bicycles that infested the narrow
streets. Ten minutes after leaving Henri's, he emerged into the
bustling seafront marketplace. It was late afternoon, but the boats
moored on the wharf were still unloading their cargoes, and the
stalls next to them overflowed with basic commodities. He
threaded through the milling crowds to the far side of the
marketplace, where a narrow street beckoned him in, leading to a
meandering array of shop windows. He propped his bike against a
whitewashed wall and walked into the shaded lane of a Caribbean
souk.

He almost walked past the Porte Juste Rhythmic and Musical
Emporium before stepping back, looking closer at the small-square
windows and opening the creaking door. Steel drums, acoustic
guitars and woodwind instruments greeted him. *Just one electric
guitar and amp, please,* he thought. At the back of the shop sat a
small, wizened black man of about sixty, perched on a high stool,
with a small cigarette attached to the corner of his mouth. His hair
was silver around his small ears and in his black, parchment-dry
hands was a Les Paul custom guitar, on which he was playing the
most unbelievable blues Johnny had ever heard.

*

The shop owner's fingers danced along the guitar's fretboard. He
pressed down on a string and the sustain razored through the shop.

226

Looking up at the strangely dressed visitor, he smiled. 'You like good sounds?' he asked.

'It's my job.' The visitor's guileless smile and thinning hair were offset by his obvious appreciation for music. For the shop's owner, there was nothing more important.

The pale, skinny man held out his hand and smiled again. 'Johnny Faslane, manager for Cold Steel.'

'Cold Steel?'

'Yes, the heavy metal band. We're playing at the cricket ground next week.'

'I heard something about that on the radio. Heavy metal, you say?'

'Sure. You like it?'

'You play blues with that?' He diplomatically avoided a more direct answer.

'It's where all the best metal started.'

'I like your respect.' He smiled with tobacco-stained teeth. 'My name's Chuck, and welcome to the finest music shop on the island.' Johnny looked around uncertainly. 'Well,' Chuck admitted. 'It's the *only* music shop on the island.'

Johnny's smile became more forced. 'Chuck, I need instruments for the whole band, and I need them today. The concert's in a week and the band need to rehearse. What do you say?'

'What do you need?'

'Electric guitar for two, bass, drums. If you've got microphones and amps, I'll take everything you've got.'

'Well, you're not having *this* one.' Chuck put his guitar to one side. 'I'm the only one who's ever touched it.' He moved slowly around the shop, looking intently at the instruments on display. He saw Johnny's impatient, almost despairing look. Sighing, he disappeared into the stock room and emerged with an electric Spanish and a battered telecaster.

'Jesus.' Johnny's face dropped. 'The tele might be alright but that Spanish will hum like hell onstage.'

'You want it straight away, friend, then this is what I got. In a day or two I might have something else for you.'

'If that's what you've got right now, how can you get anything else past the blockade?'

227

'We'll build it.'

'Build it?'

'Follow me.'

Chuck walked through to his workshop and switched on the light. An unshaded incandescent bulb swung back and forth in the gentle breeze from the opened wire-mesh window. Two half-completed solid body guitars rested on the scarred solid-wood workbench. 'These two are a bit of a hobby of mine,' he said. 'But if you're needing things in a hurry, we can talk overtime.'

*

'It's second-hand,' whined Vince.

'Yes,' snapped Johnny, still on edge after the slow drive to the plantation house in a rusty van, which reeked of petrol fumes but didn't stop Chuck from smoking for the whole journey. 'And so is everything else in this gig.'

'At least it looks like an electric.' Andy stared in dismay at his Spanish. 'Which museum did you get this from?'

Johnny looked at the band, who returned his stare with barely concealed anger. He could understand it, despite the encouraging start. The plantation house exterior had impressed everyone. Ground- and first-floor terraces wrapped around the whole building, offering shade throughout the day, and the brilliantly white painted woodwork matched the white rendered stone structuring. Inside, there had been heavy investment in modern recording technology. 'Look,' he said. 'If we're going to drag this concert up to what I *know* you can deliver, you guys need to be flexible.'

'We're flexible enough to agree to it in the first place, man,' said Joe, with undisguised disappointment at holding a Beatle bass.

'Look, these are just for you to work on the set list. You can have any type of instruments you want.'

'How's that, man?'

Johnny pointed at Chuck. 'Chuck here builds instruments from scratch. Tell him what you want and he'll do it. Right, Chuck?'

'I want a twin-set, single-coil pick-ups set in wax inside a tin,' said Andy.

'I want two uncovered humbuckers,' said Vince.

'Maxwell,' said Johnny. 'Have you got hard copy of any Cold Steel? Let Chuck have a listen, he'll know what you need from him.'

'And what am I supposed to do with this shit?' Mike stared up at Johnny, surrounded by a random pile of drums, cymbals and a sprinkling of unconnected mounts.

'Haven't you ever set up a drum kit before?' asked Johnny.

'Sure, but not for a while.'

'Roadie's job now, is it?'

'Yeah, along with every other band that makes it, what's your point?'

'No roadies here,' said Johnny. 'And a drum kit to set up. Deal with it.'

'So what are you going to do?' asked Maxwell.

'Let's get you lot sorted first,' replied Johnny. 'Talk to Chuck, and tell him what you want. The more he knows, the more he can help. He can go back in his van, and I'll use your driver to take me back to Porte Juste.'

'What for?'

'Absolutely everything else.'

Chapter 39

Johnny walked along the sunset-drenched seafront for quarter of a
mile until he reached the newly built St. Clements national cricket
arena. The white-stoned circular stadium spread before him like an
enormous scarab, while above the main gates hung a huge
electronic screen that flashed images advertising the gig. Johnny
saw that when it came to both cricket and steel band music, St.
Clements wore its emerging wealth with proud, well-earned
ostentation.

He walked past a pair of large wrought-iron gates, and on
through an archway that served as one of four entrances into the
arena. Inside, the ground displayed a flawless cricket pitch.
Illuminated by the floodlights, the turf was already being covered
over with a sea of plywood boards, designed to protect it from the
trampling of thousands of feet on the night of the concert. Johnny
had decided the band would perform in the round, which put the
stage in the centre of the pitch.

He wandered into the ground, through the stadium's vast
network of corridors before chancing across the supervisor's
office, a small space no bigger than a staff toilet squeezed beneath
the lower tier grandstand. Windowless, and with no direct view of
the ground itself, its chipboard door was wedged open, and the
sounds of a heated telephone conversation emanated from inside.
Johnny nervously poked his head around the doorway, and saw a
large, heavily built man, who looked like he'd been chiselled from
solid anthracite. He was planted behind a desk that was full almost
to the point of collapse beneath sheaves of paperwork, and he had
a firm grasp on a telephone receiver, into which he screamed a
manifesto of dockside abuse. He slammed down the receiver and
glared poisonously at Johnny.

'What do *you* want?' he barked.

'Bad phone call?' Johnny crept into the office and the
supervisor motioned him to take a seat. 'I'm Johnny Faslane, Cold
Steel's manager. We're playing a concert here next week, and I
thought it would be good if we talked about pyrotechnics, crowd
control and the like.'

'Concert, concert, that's all I've bloody heard about since the damn thing was announced. Your idea, I suppose?'

Johnny considered the risks of name-dropping. 'Henri Chevalier's backing it.'

'I thought he might be. It sounds like the kind of nonsense he'd dream up. Sometimes I think we'd have been better off with the old lot in charge.'

'It's not *his* fault there's a blockade going on.'

'No, but it's down to him to sort it out, and there's no aircraft carrier to call on anymore. Look, we all know this is part of some plan to get the publicity coming our way, and who knows, maybe Henri'll be able to win a few friends. But a heavy metal concert? If you ask me, he'd be much better off with a cricket tournament or a steel band show. That's what we're really known for. Still, he says I have to co-operate.' He reluctantly held out a hand the size of a boar's haunch. 'Fletcher Christian's the name.'

'Fletcher Christian?'

'Have you got a problem with that?' he demanded. 'A word of advice, don't even think about mentioning the Bounty, and if any of your boys take the piss, I'll drag them out back and give them the hiding of their lives, okay?'

Johnny held up his hands in silent agreement.

'Anyway.' Fletcher leaned back on his chair, revealing a wide expanse of gut that even wobbled aggressively. 'Whether I like it or not, you've got a free rein regarding the ground and its facilities.' He pointed at Johnny as though aiming an offensive weapon. 'But Christ help you if you damage my ground.'

'Hey, Fletcher, we're all on the same side. Let's just make sure this concert really is something to remember.'

'For the *right* reasons. I read some high old stories about this band of yours. Puking onstage, flying around on harnesses and knocking each other out.'

'That's all in the past, Fletcher, believe me.'

'Believe *you?* Why?'

'Look, mate. You don't like Henri, you don't like the band, and you don't seem to like me, but there's nothing any of us can do about it. We've *got* to work together. All those things about the band, sure, they happened, but they didn't happen again. That was Cold Steel at a low point, and they haven't been there since. Beer

231

Doctor went platinum in every European country they played in. These guys know what they're doing, so have a bit of faith. Whatever Henri wants us to achieve, we can do it.'

'Who knows what Henri really wants? If it was up to me, I'd hunker down and let those bastards do their worst. But it's not my show, *this* is.' He stabbed his desk with a finger. 'So what about your stage?'

'In the round.'

'What? You think I'm stupid? Haven't you seen the boards on the pitch? I *know* it's in the round. What else can you tell me about it?'

'Nothing. Until it gets built, that's all I've got so far.'

'You'd better get a move on then, hadn't you?'

'Who do you think's the best person to build this damn thing?'

'Skipper's your man, no doubt.'

'I thought he was just a boatman.'

'You thought wrong.' Fletcher dismissed Johnny with a curt nod, before picking up the telephone and shouting into the mouthpiece.

*

Inside Skipper's harbour-front shed, the unfinished hulls of two fishing boats glowed faintly under the pale moonlight that shone through the skylights. Johnny crept around, looking for any sign of life.

'Skipper,' he called.

'It's a bit fecking late to be asking me to work.' Skipper's high-pitched voice whistled unseen behind him, making him yelp in fright.

*

'So that's the situation,' said Johnny. 'Do you think you can do it?'

'Never mind that. Will Fletcher Christian let me get on with it without fecking interfering every two seconds? Do this, don't do that. The stupid bastard should have shipped out with the last governor.'

'Look, Skipper, we need to forget about all that, at least for the next week. Can you do it?'

Skipper puffed on his pipe. 'Maybe, but I'll give you no promises. You want a stage? What else?'

'A sound and lighting system that'll be seen from the moon, and loud enough to deafen everyone for miles around.'

'Fecking hell, not much then. Are you sure, Johnny, are you *really* sure you can pull this off?'

'We're sure as hell going to try.'

Johnny stood up and walked out of the yard, back towards the deserted marketplace. Half an hour later he arrived at Henri's. He stepped through to the reception room and saw Henri sitting by himself, drinking a beer.

'Hey, Henri.' Johnny cracked open a beer and sat down. 'How are we doing?'

'As expected.' He shrugged. 'I have been speaking to politicians and leaders across the world. They make noises of sympathy, but they will not help unless I sign the economy of St. Clements over to them. If the concert does not produce the desired results straight away, it is an option I shall have to consider, because a few days after that, our food and oil reserves will start running out.'

'We've got our balls to the wall and no mistake. But don't underestimate the power of live music, especially when Cold Steel are dishing it out.'

'In your musical world, I suppose the concert will be very big news?'

'That's the plan.'

Henri smiled. 'I was asked a few questions about it when I spoke to my opposite numbers.'

'What did you tell them?'

'I said it was something that we had been working on for some time, and left them to draw the conclusion that it is a farewell gift from myself to the people of St. Clements.'

'Christ, Henri. I hope we can pull this off.'

'Tell me the truth, *mon ami*. What are our chances?'

'I don't know, Henri. I just don't know. The band are rehearsing, but the stage design and construction can't be promised. It's a lot of work to cram into a short time.'

'It is a start.'

'It is, but *everything* has got to come together inside seven days, and we can't even afford a *single* ball to drop from the sack.'

'What more can we do?'

'We still need a lighting rig and sound system, and they've got to be damn good. Just putting the lights together takes weeks, let alone the time it takes to design the bloody thing. We'll also need speakers a damn site bigger and more powerful than anything Chuck's got. For all that to appear in a week, we need some serious industrial output.'

Henri finished his beer. 'Tomorrow morning we shall go to the industrial estate on the other side of the island. We shall see what can be achieved.'

Johnny looked at his watch and his thoughts strayed towards Rachel. Rachel. He hadn't forgotten about her all the time Cold Steel were touring, and now it seemed that she remembered him. But why? He had her office number in his pocket, and he wondered if she was still there. He reached for the telephone and dialled her number. For long, frustrating seconds it rang, and then he heard the static click of a re-route and pick-up. Her deep voice purred down the line and hammered a virtual centre-punch between his eyes.

Chapter 40

Sweltering in the unconditioned office space, Rachel Shaw sat at her desk, oblivious to the insane activity as reporters all around her reacted to the Ancadian blockade. With St. Clements' airport now closed, they gloated about the exclusives they'd be getting, while she felt relegated to second league for trailing Cold Steel to St. Clements and then being told to cover the concert.

Cold Steel. Ancadia. Cold Steel. Ancadia. Were they separate stories? She'd seen the news stream of the Ancadian reaction to the concert. They seemed as bewildered and surprised as everyone else, but there was something more. Was it fear, anger? She wasn't sure, yet. Who did she know in Ancadia? No one, but she had plenty of connections on the mainland who did. A few phone calls might turn on some lights. And Cold Steel, who did she know there?

Johnny Faslane.

She'd have had to be blind not to see that he liked her. *Then why didn't he call?* She couldn't remember the last time *that* had happened, and now she saw him as a challenge. When she needed to be, she could be as ruthless as an inquisitor after a confession, but there was more to Johnny than just a source: she also liked him, and she didn't know why. Maybe it was because he didn't just surrender to her, maybe his loyalty to the band confirmed that inner strength which she always admired; she just didn't know. He'd been tight-lipped at the press conference, but that was to be expected with his band right behind him. *Get him on his own; he won't know what's hitting him.* Well, that was the plan.

The island's dial-up internet connection slowed her research to an almost geological timescale, and with little about the concert to write about, she pieced together the history of Ancadia's military power in the region. *Why* were the Ancadians blockading St. Clements, and *what* did Cold Steel have to do with it? She knew Johnny would call her, and she knew she'd get some answers from him.

At half past nine that night, she felt impaled by rejection. Had she misjudged him? Was *he* using *her?* She flicked the switch on

235

her desk phone, re-routing all calls through to her mobile, and slowly walked out of the building.

Forty minutes later, a hot shower made her flawless skin tingle against the hotel towel, and she relaxed on the sofa with a drink. She examined everything she knew so far. The faint glimmer of a connection between Henri Chevalier, Cold Steel and the Ancadians was just beginning to coalesce in her thoughts, when the insistent ringing of a mobile interrupted her.

'Hello.'

'Hi there.' She recognised Johnny's voice. 'Remember me? What's happening?'

'Well, you and your mates sure know how to keep a girl busy. This concert has stirred up a whole cauldron of interest in the music world.'

'You can't have a good gig without it.' Damn him, she thought. He doesn't even *sound* nervous. 'So does this mean you'll be working all night,' he said. 'Or do bad penny reporters get *some* time off?'

'Oh, so now I'm a bad penny?'

'No, I just meant-'

'Quit while you're ahead, Johnny. I was just thinking to myself what a good time this would be to head out for a drink. The only trouble is I've got no one to escort me. What's a girl to do?'

'Stay there and I'll be right over. Where are you?'

'I've long since gone home. Why don't we meet for a drink at The Old Sea Dog?'

'Where the hell is that?'

'You'd better find out.'

*

Dressed simply and for the climate in black walking shorts and a white top, Rachel stepped out of her hotel. In the short time that she had been on St. Clements, The Old Sea Dog had become her local. It was less than two hundred yards from her hotel, and every time she looked at it, she was grateful that she didn't judge by appearances, a reflection that carried added punch as she thought about Johnny. Made entirely of discarded ship's planking, the place looked in danger of immediate collapse. Once through the rickety front door, though, Rachel was taken to a world where the lights were low, and the loud, throbbing music combined with the

236

smoke-laden air. She sat down at a window table and looked out to sea, ordering a beer from the coyote barmaid who undulated up to her table.

Her beer arrived, ice cold and dripping condensation onto the unvarnished table. She sipped her drink and kept an eye on the driftwood front door, eventually seeing a flustered-looking Johnny arrive. She watched him search for a full minute before he noticed her. He grinned and sauntered up to her table while she held back a smile at his appalling dress sense: his black T-shirt and beige leather trousers clashed terribly with his white cowboy boots. But there was something about him, something inherently decent that she was shocked to discover attracted her.

'Hi.' He sat down and ordered a beer. 'You're looking good.'

'Thank you. So how are the preparations for the concert going, and how long have you *really* been planning it?'

'It's nice to see you, too. Sorry I didn't get back to you earlier, I've got a concert to organise.'

'So I gather, but you didn't answer my question.'

'Which one? I counted two.'

'Answer them both, you evasive son of a bitch,' she smiled, not angry with Johnny at all, and enjoying the conversation. 'I *know* there's more to this than just a bloody concert, a lot more. One thing about me is my persistence, and I'll be hanging on every word you say till you slip up.'

'If you say so.' His smug expression infuriated and challenged her at the same time. 'Anyway, I don't know about you, but I've had a hell of a day, and all I want to do right now is relax. You know, *you* might do the same if you loosened up and enjoyed your beer.'

'Relax all you want, but *I'm* still working.'

'What, interrogating me?'

She smiled again. 'You know more than you're saying.'

'And I suppose you're going to get me to talk, right?' He smiled back at her.

'Treasure hunts, Ancadians, you being rescued from the sea, there's *plenty* for us to be getting on with. And that's before we talk about the timing for the show.'

'The gig and the blockade are pure coincidence.'

'Did I mention the blockade? And I don't believe in coincidences.'

'Me neither, and if you want to know about the gunboats, talk to the Ancadians, they know more about it than me.'

'I don't suppose it matters much.' She speared him with her direct stare. 'Henri won't last much longer unless he gets help.'

'Do you think he will?' There was obvious concern in his voice.

'Unlikely.' Her glossed lips curled downwards. 'He's worked wonders at diversifying St. Clements, but the big industrial powers would eat St. Clements for breakfast if they could. Every time Henri meets up with politicians from other countries, he has to fight to negotiate trade deals with the rest of the world, deals that don't allow foreign takeovers of St. Clements. At the same time, he still has to keep them sweet enough to stay friendly.'

'And now?'

'The blockade's a game-changer. Henri *needs* outside help, but it'll come at a price.'

'What do you think will happen?'

She arched her perfectly shaped eyebrows. 'It's not my assignment, I really don't know too much about it.'

'*Now* who's being evasive? What are you hoping will happen?'

'I'm not hoping for anything, Johnny. If Henri's going to make any progress, it's not down to me.'

'But you know what he's up against. Don't you care?'

'Hey, I'm a reporter, in case you've forgotten. All I care about is the story. But I do have *some* passions in life, and right now I need another beer. So are you going to get me one, or are you the kind of guy who just sits there drinking it all for himself?'

*

Johnny had no answer for Rachel's direct attention. He came back from the bar with two beers and watched her lift the bottle to her lips. His world telescoped down to her image, and he became oblivious of everything around him. His vision wandered over her outline before guiltily returning to her face.

'I can tell your eyes are off work,' she teased him with a cheeky grin.

'Perhaps.' He resisted. 'But the rest of me stays at the office.'

'Why?'

'Oh, come on, Rachel. You're a reporter: you're probably only talking to me to find out if I've got any information. Christ, it's not like I'm Jon Bon whatever.'

'And it's not like I'm having a drink with him, either.' She edged forward. 'And I could do, if I wanted.'

'So there's more to me than my mind?' he half-joked.

Her body pulsed with laughter. 'Maybe,' her hand brushed his forearm and he saw stars. 'Look. If you're going to spend all night worrying about my motives, then we'll both be missing out. The job will still be there in the morning. We can always go back to work then.'

'I guess that's as close as we'll get to a truce. So what else do you want to talk about, if not the band, the concert and the Ancadians?'

'What about you, you and you?'

*

Having talked about him, him and him, Rachel was still around. Incredibly, amazingly so. And both of them slightly, happily, gigglingly drunk. Johnny was amazed that he'd even shown enough balls to suggest a drink back at Henri's and his look of sheer astonishment had made Rachel laugh even more.

Despite it being dark, the suited security guard stood anonymously behind his sunglasses and nodded to Johnny. He and Rachel walked past the sold oak door that fronted Henri's residence, and at the foot of the deserted staircase he turned to face her.

'Rachel, I –'

His words evaporated as she devoured him with a kiss. Her strong hands kneaded his back, and his legs went weak at the scent of her lemongrass perfume clouding around him. He held onto her, as much for stability as anything else, and desperately unsure if this was actually happening.

She pulled away, panting quietly and looking around the hallway with belated modesty. She faced him, running her long red fingernails gently down his face.

'Don't tell me you're sleeping on Henri's sofa,' she said, her voice low and uneven.

'No,' he stammered, and pointed to the staircase with shaking fingers.

She looked at him and smiled. Then, walking backwards, she pulled him by the hand and they climbed the sweeping staircase. She led him past one room after another, before Johnny quietly announced that they were outside his. They had barely stepped over the darkened threshold before she slammed the door shut and pushed him against it. He felt her fingers pulling at his clothes, while his own hands roamed urgently over her body, shaking uncontrollably, and fighting a desperate battle against tiny hook and eye fastenings.

'Oh God,' he said, his voice a ragged whisper. 'Why are women's clothes always so bloody difficult to pull off?'

She chuckled. She'd already relieved him of his T-shirt, and his leather trousers were just seconds away, while Johnny had only managed to pull up her top to reveal little more than a finely muscled abdomen. She held her lips close to his ear. 'Come with me,' she whispered.

She kicked off her toe-post sandals, and barefoot, she gently led him through the darkened room towards the bed.

'You mean you're not tired?' he asked.

'Are you?'

'No,' he grinned.

She turned him around so that his back was to the bed. Gently edging him backwards, he felt his knees come up against solid wooden framework. She pushed him again and he was forced to sit down on the mattress. Soft moonlight penetrated the shutters, casting just enough light for him to see her standing before him, her long black hair a wild tangle of darkness that framed her face and fell over her top. Slowly, she circled her hips; her hands crept up the front of her thighs before she eased off her shorts.

Johnny gasped at the sight of her flawless legs. He sat on the bed, a building erection uncomfortably lodged within his trousers. She pulled her white top over her head and cast it aside to land in an untidy heap on top of her shorts.

Under the gentle light, her tanned flesh seemed bright, almost white, making her bra nearly invisible. The curves of her figure narrowed to a slim waist, with the tiny patch of her thong forming a neat, triangular shadow. Johnny stared at her like a faithful pilgrim, his breathing deep and ragged, and the hammering in his ears almost deafened him.

240

'Oh, my god,' he groaned. 'I've died and gone to heaven.'

'Not yet, that part comes later.'

The hours of darkness rolled past, and with them, Johnny's physical limits. But he didn't care. This was sex like he'd never known before, and only when the dawn's faint light gently sifted through the shutters did Rachel allow his exhaustion to catch up with him. With one last ragged scream, she threw her body on top of his, rested her head on his shoulder, and breathed warmly into his ear.

'I just knew there was more to you than the story,' she whispered.

Johnny, though, had already fallen asleep.

Chapter 41

The baking midday sun beat on the closed shutters, and Johnny drifted back into consciousness. Still dreaming of the night before, and wondering how it had actually happened, he smiled and rolled over, expecting his arm to rest on Rachel's firm curves. Instead, his outstretched limb landed on the crumpled sheet where she had once been. He sat up and looked at the bed, then heard a familiar chuckle behind him. He turned round to see her sitting calmly on a chair, fully clothed. Johnny ran a hand through the untidy mess of what was left of his hair, before feeling the rough rasp of his stubble.

'So, you've finally emerged.' Her lips widened into a smile. 'Your former French host has been knocking on the door for the past two hours.'

Johnny groaned, groping for his wristwatch. He shook his head from side to side. 'Oh, shite.' He threw himself off the bed and scrambled for his clothes. 'I should have been out of here hours ago.'

'What's the hurry?'

He wobbled on one foot as he tried pulling on a cowboy boot. Her cobalt eyes stared at him from beneath her straight-line fringe, and a small, cheeky grin turned up the corners of her mouth.

'You think we should stay here?' he asked.

'Do you?'

He looked at her and nearly lost himself. 'Hey,' he slurred. 'If it was up to me, yes. But it's not, and as much as I'd really love it to be, this isn't some kind of island runaway for either of us. I've got a concert to get off the ground, and you –'

'I've got to find out what it is you're not telling me.'

'I've got nothing to hide.'

'Which has got to be the *worst* thing to say to a reporter.'

He retreated to the bathroom and sprayed the top half of his body with cheap deodorant before returning to the bedroom and pulling on a T-shirt. 'Look,' he said. 'You've got your job and I've got mine, and right now there's a lot of things I just can't talk to you about.'

'I don't want you to give in to me, Johnny.'

'Then what *do* you want?'

She smiled. 'You've managed bands for a long time, but until you took on Cold Steel you didn't have much to do with the media, right?'

'So?'

'So you're new to this game, and you need to learn how to be a player. I can help you.'

'Why would you do that?'

'Bands need publicity, and a friendly reporter is better than a pissed-off one.'

'And you get all the exclusives, right? Haven't you got enough to keep you busy with this blockade?'

'That's not my assignment, Cold Steel are.'

'Disappointed?'

'Depends what I find out.'

'Look, there's no way I can let you or anyone else have unrestricted access to this concert just yet. But it's just possible that I could let you interview the band later on today.'

'When?'

'I'll give you a call. There's a few things I've got to take care of first, and don't ask what they are because I'm not telling.'

*

Johnny and Rachel left Henri's house and walked together to the end of the gravel drive. She turned left, and he turned right, and like a pair of duellists they stepped away from each other. Johnny strode along narrow pathways to Government House, where he was seamlessly ushered through to Henri's office. Locked in a telephone conversation, he motioned for Johnny to take a seat.

'You stinking piece of *merde*,' he grimaced at the phone, once he'd replaced the receiver. He turned to Johnny. '*Bonjour*. I have just been on the telephone, and we are still on our own.'

'Any reaction to the concert?'

'Some interest, *oui.*'

'As long as we've got an audience, leave the rest to the band.'

'How are the preparations proceeding?'

'You said you could help with sound and lighting.'

'*Après vous.*' Henri picked up a mobile phone from his desk, before following Johnny out to the car park.

243

'So where are we going?' asked Johnny.

Henri switched on his mobile, threw it into a jeep's glove compartment, then jumped behind the wheel. 'We are headed to the industrial estate on the other side of the island. I am taking the pressures of time quite literally, and so we are going there fast. Buckle up, *mon ami*.'

Henri crouched in the driver's seat with a look of insane exultation. Johnny fastened his seat belt and gripped the roll cage, and the jeep was thrust into tight curves and narrow roads. After the second fly splat-died against his ocular membrane he kept his eyes closed: better to endure Henri's wheelspin driving without having to see it. An infarct-inducing ninety minutes later, they arrived on the far side of the island, a barren, rocky wasteland, with Nissen hut offices and rusty-wall factories sprouting from the volcanic landscape.

'What would you do for sound if you were not here?' asked Henri.

Johnny thought about the Soundsphere rig that had followed the band right across Europe. 'Christ, it was all done with a phone call, and someone else did the legwork. And I thought *that* was difficult.'

'We must use what we have. Where else might we find this light and sound? What other endeavour uses them?'

'Live entertainment. Any type I suppose. Concert, theatre, maybe even sporting events. But we *need* volume, Henri. It has *got* to be loud, really loud. And for that we need big speakers. And not just that, the band need monitor speakers onstage, and it all needs to be linked to a central station.'

'So for that we will need an electrician, *non*?'

'Christ, we'll need more than one, especially if we're cobbling it together from off-cuts. Jesus, maybe we can't do this.'

'We can, *mon ami*, we can. Come with me.'

Henri walked downhill, towards the seafront with its pothole collection of rusting sheds and workshops. A headland and remnant palm forest obscured much of Johnny's view until they reached the quayside and turned a corner.

'Holy shit.'

Standing in front of Johnny, climbing eleven storeys into the air and barely floating next to the rubber-tyre wharf, wallowed the gradually dissolving remains of the rear half of what might have once been a cruise liner. Workers, appearing ant-like next to the huge maritime cadaver, swarmed over her to the sound of hammers, power tools and grinding metal.

'They sail around the world,' said Henri. 'But there are just a small number of places where these mighty ships end their days. We are one of the very few breakers of this size of ship in the western hemisphere. This is the third liner we have taken in. The other two have been reduced to their constituent parts.'

'I don't follow,' said Johnny.

'*Mon ami*, do you know how many entertainment rooms, stages, cinemas and theatres even one of these ships has? And do you know how many speakers that requires?'

'And you've got them here?'

'From all three ships.'

'All right. Now, we need to get them all to the cricket ground, mould them into one system, wire the whole lot together, *and* get someone to control it.'

'We shall be busy.'

*

Back at Henri's, Johnny wolfed down his lunch and phoned the plantation house.

'Who is this and what do you want?'

'Maxwell, it's Johnny.'

'So?'

'Good to talk to you, too. How's it going?'

'We've got a set list, Mike's managed to piece a drum kit together, Chuck says he'll be here sometime today with guitars. How's the venue coming on?'

'Slowly.'

'I hope you know what you're doing, mate. If we fuck up here we'll be the laughing stock of the entire business. Which will be nice, just before the Ancadians get their hands on us.'

'I guess we'd better not fuck up then.' Johnny hung up and walked outside, grabbed a mountain bike and pedalled to the cricket ground. He flashed his ID to the uniformed policeman at the gates and walked towards the pitch. Along the edge of the stands were draped hundreds of banners, emblazoned with the skull and crossbones. At ground level the turf had been covered with boards, while right in the centre yawned an empty space where the stage was supposed to be. He walked up to Fletcher, who simmered at no one in particular. 'I'm doing my bit,' he fumed.

'Have you heard from Skipper yet?' asked Johnny.

'Sure. I've *heard* from him, but I'm telling you, Johnny, you need to keep an eye on him. This wouldn't have happened if we'd stayed as a colony.'

'Unless we start seeing some action soon, you lot might be a colony again. Did Skipper say how much time he needed?'

'To build one stage in the round? One stage in the round, I might add, that the band have to access and exit from unseen? There are no underground tunnels here.'

'Isn't there anything? Christ, the last thing the band want is to sit and sweat under a stage for two hours before going on.'

'There's a sewage main.'

'A what?'

'A sewage main. It's do-able, if your boys are happy to wade through it.' Fletcher laughed. 'Hell, I'll even let you dig a hole in my cricket pitch if that's your plan.'

With Fletcher's laughter ringing in his ears like the bells of Gashadokuro, Johnny stalked towards Skipper's seafront shed. He'd expected, he'd *needed* more forward movement than was happening so far, and he felt control being skinned back from him. His stride picked up in response.

*

'Fletcher's full of shit, just like that fecking sewer,' said Skipper. 'We're making progress.'

'That's not what he's saying,' replied Johnny. 'And how come you guys don't like each other anyway?'

'He's stuck in the past. Thinks we should still be a colony.'

'Could that be a problem?'

'Not if you handle him right,' said Skipper. 'Let him think he's got one over on the rest of us, and he'll be mahi mahi in our hands.'

Johnny pressed his head with both hands. 'Jesus, mate, I don't have time for this intrigue shit. I've got enough to worry about.'

'I'll talk to him, tell him we're going to have to use the main sewer as an access point. He'll be happy with that, he thinks it'll put you boys in your place.'

'You tell Fletcher, I'll tell the band. They'll be overjoyed.'

*

'A fucking sewer?' screamed Maxwell. Johnny held the phone away from his ear and Maxwell's indignation climbed the decibel scale. 'You want us to walk along a sewer to get to the gig?'

'You can always parachute in.'

'Fucking hell, mate. I'd *much* rather just have the stage at one end of the stadium, like most gigs.'

'This *can't* be like most gigs, Maxwell. We need to be different in every way, and that means a stage in the round, and that means an underground walk to get there. The only access route we've got is the sewer main.'

'And I suppose us turning up covered in shit will fire up the crowd.'

'I've had a chat with Skipper. You'll be wearing top to toe survival suits. They might get covered in crap but you won't.'

'How did I let you talk us into this?'

'Yeah, loving how the treasure hunt turned out as well. Look, that's the plan, we're doing it, and we've got no choice.'

Johnny hung up his phone and turned to Skipper. 'Bunch of pussies,' he grumbled. 'It's not like they've got to eat it. So how about a special effects ship? It's essential for Cold Steel, can we do?'

'Jesus, Johnny, let me build the fecking stage first.'

'We don't have time for delays, Skipper.'

'I'm not delaying. Look around you.' Skipper's half dozen workers dripped sweat as they slotted and nailed boards together, pieced the segments to form a whole, then dismantled them again to transport them to the ground. 'We'll do our best, but this is St. Clements, not the industrial heartland of fecking anywhere. We've got to go with what we have, and first things first mean we build a stage, right? Besides, the last spare ship we had around here got blown out of the fecking water with you lot aboard it.'

*

Johnny walked back towards the cricket ground through a heat-haze dust cloud and Skipper's crew drove past him in two rickety

247

pick-ups containing the embryonic, disassembled stage. By the time he arrived on the board-covered pitch it had begun to mushroom into reality. Fletcher scowled.

'The sewer main runs directly below the south-facing wicket point,' he said. 'Take up a square yard of artificial turf and there's a manhole cover beneath that. I hope you know what you're doing.'

'We'll find out next week,' replied Johnny. 'Right now, we need some exposure. I'm getting a reporter in here.'

'What? Are you crazy?'

'Look around, Fletcher, what's to see? The stage has barely started. All she'll see is where it's going to be.'

'She?'

'Sure. Didn't they have female reporters when St. Clements was a colony?'

'Yes, and plenty of men who thought between their legs when they got within ten feet of them.'

'One day, Fletcher, I'll meet someone you actually like.' Johnny picked up his phone and dialled Rachel's number.

'Hello,' she purred.

'It's Johnny. I was wondering if you'd like a sneak preview inside the ground.'

'Me and who else?'

'Just you.'

'Promise?'

'I'm just playing the game.'

She laughed. 'I'll see you in ten.'

He switched off his phone and turned to Fletcher. 'She'll be here in about ten minutes. Now, she's the only journalist getting in here before the gig, and she won't be coming again. So we answer her questions as vaguely as possible, and no mention at all gets made about the Ancadians or what happened to *Friday's Fancy,* right?'

'Not much point in her coming then, really,' observed Fletcher.

'It's all about exposing the right amount. We want the world to see a stage being built, a lot of groundwork going in, but all the details need to remain a mystery. That way they'll be curious enough to tune in next week.'

248

Johnny sauntered towards the main gates and stood in the shade. Across the car park his eyesight was riveted by Rachel's purposeful stride.

'Hello.' Her low voice poured hot oil on his senses. 'So what have you got for me today?'

'An exclusive look inside the stadium, but make the most of it, because it's the only time. After today, health and safety regulations kick in and you won't be allowed.'

'You mean after today you're hoping to have more stage effects in place, and you don't want anyone to see them before the concert?'

'Well, okay,' Johnny grinned. 'But it's a damn sight more than we're showing anyone else, *and* I'll throw in an interview with the band.'

'Well, then, why don't you show me around this far from completed and totally unrevealing venue?'

Johnny spread his arms wide. 'You've got unlimited access. Go anywhere you want, *ask* anyone anything you want.' He walked over to where Fletcher and Skipper glared at her. 'Look, lads,' he said. 'Don't worry, she's only getting ten minutes, and if she's not bored by then, I'll drag her out.'

'I hope you're right,' muttered Fletcher.

'Once she sees there's nothing here, all she'll want to do is get the hell out and see the band.'

Six minutes and forty-three seconds later, she came over to Johnny and bluntly announced that she'd seen all she wanted to. 'Or, more accurately,' she continued, 'I've seen all there is to see right now. There's going to be a lot more here in twenty-four hours.'

'I did say there wouldn't be too much,' Johnny smiled. 'At least you're about to meet the band.'

'And I'm *bound* to get more information from that bunch of hairy layabouts than you lot.'

Chapter 42

Johnny climbed warily into the passenger's seat of Rachel's jeep. She gracefully folded herself behind the steering wheel and smiled at his obvious nervousness. 'Have you been driven anywhere by Henri?' she asked.

'Why do you say that?'

'Not everyone around here drives like him,' she said. 'The only time you'll be in any danger on this trip is if you make any unwise comments about women drivers.'

'I'm not saying a word.' Johnny stared ahead and gripped the dashboard. The jeep roared into life and she expertly guided it out of the car park.

Unhampered by the almost toxic levels of testosterone that handicapped most men the second they got behind the wheel, Rachel's driving was cool and precise. The jeep came to a controlled stop at the plantation house and they walked through the entranceway's faded grandeur. Powerhouse drumming accompanied by the thunderous riffs of two electric guitars driving into Cold Steel's last number one, Chasing the Sunset. The sounds quickened Johnny's step and heart rate.

Maxwell strode around the studio's small floor space as though he owned the whole world, with the rest of the band planted around the cramped room. His voice pitchforked piercing vocals into Johnny's ears before Chasing the Sunset thudded into silence. He then felt Maxwell's mocking gaze as he and Rachel slowly approached. 'I hope you haven't got any hidden microphones,' he drawled. 'I'd hate to have to strip-search you.'

Johnny cringed and Rachel released his hand and flick-switched her attention to Maxwell. 'I don't need hidden microphones. I'm a reporter and everyone knows it.'

'Then I'd better be careful.'

'Worried you might say something that'll get you into trouble?' she asked.

'I'm always in trouble, sweetheart. It's part of being in a band.'

'And what about the trouble you've gone to in organising this concert?'

'That's Johnny's territory, but he's got it under control. We've had the whole thing planned for months.'

'Oh? Planning on thanking the people of St. Clements before you'd even been here? That *is* the reason for the concert, right?'

Johnny barged in. 'It's simple, Rachel. We knew we were coming here after the Beer Doctor tour, and we knew what great hosts St. Clements would be. A thank you concert was always going to happen.'

'So why leave it till a week beforehand to announce it? How can you hope for the publicity, the coverage to make it a success?'

'This is Cold Steel's concert, and they want to play it their way. If we'd gone through the normal channels at Ozone Records, they'd have killed the whole thing with commerciality.'

'And what about the blockade?' asked Rachel. 'The concert was announced *after* the blockade happened. Why not keep quiet about it and come back when it's all settled down?'

'Yeah, right,' scoffed Maxwell. 'We're stuck here, love. There's no *way* the Ancadians are letting us off this piece of real estate.'

'Oh? Why's that?'

'Well,' Maxwell back-pedalled. 'They're not letting anyone off the island, not just us.'

'You're nothing to do with St. Clements, and that's who they've got the quarrel with. I'm sure Ozone, or your manager, or even the British Government could do *something* to get you out of here if you wanted to, if you *really* wanted to.'

Maxwell shot a nervous glance at Johnny, which he knew would be picked up by Rachel and set her inquisitive mind whirring into directions he didn't want her going.

'That's irrelevant,' said Johnny. 'The concert's announced, the organisation's under way, and it's either here or nowhere.'

'*Nothing's* as simple as that,' said Rachel. 'Apart from heavy metal bands. So what about this treasure hunt everyone on the island says you came here for?'

'Can you see any treasure here?' Maxwell spread his arms wide.

'Didn't you find any?'

'It seems not.'

'But you *were* on a treasure hunt?'

251

'We'd heard a rumour that there was an old pirate settlement on Iguana Island.' Johnny spoke up.

'Iguana Island? The animal sanctuary?'

'Iguana Island, which is a part of St. Clements.'

'And you feel the need to emphasise that? Did you go anywhere else?'

'No,' snapped Johnny. 'Henri did us a favour, let us look around the island, as long as we respected the wildlife and environment, which of course we did. That's one of the reasons we're doing the concert here, which is probably a much more interesting subject to stick to.'

Rachel smiled and turned to Andy, Vince and Joe. 'So will you be playing any new material, or will your songs be as old as those instruments you've got?'

'What, these?' Andy slapped his Spanish. 'We always rehearse with these, right, lads?' Vince and Joe nodded like burglars in denial. 'If we can sound good on this old stuff, then we'll be fucking knockout with our proper gear.'

'Wouldn't you be better off getting familiar with the instruments you'll be using at the concert?'

'Look, love. Don't tell us how to do our jobs, right? We're not telling you how to interrogate people.'

'You don't need to, I've found out all I need to know already.' She turned to face Johnny. 'Thanks for the interview, I'll wait for you outside.'

*

Johnny watched Rachel leave and felt his loyalties pulling him in opposite directions.

'Where did you meet her?' asked Maxwell.

'At the press conference after the concert was announced.'

'Judging from the looks you two were giving each other, I'd say she gave you a *real* interview last night.' The band erupted into ribald laughter.

'That's my business.' Johnny blushed furiously. 'How are the rehearsals going?'

'Better if we had decent instruments,' said Vince. 'Unless you believed what Andy was saying to your bird?'

'She's not my bird,' he snapped. 'Anyway, you sounded pretty good to me.'

'You're joking, right?'

'You sounded good. But don't worry, Chuck's coming over today with guitars, made to measure.'

'And how long do we have to ponce around in here?' asked Maxwell. 'We need to see the stage, get a feel for it.'

'It's being built as we speak. As soon as enough of it's put together you'll be there.'

'Today?'

'I hope so; tomorrow at the latest.'

'Jesus, mate. We're cutting this fine.'

'I know.' Johnny's hands flapped like a manic seagull. 'Look, just keep rehearsing, Chuck's on his way with some more instruments and I'll get you to the ground as soon as the stage is done.'

*

Rachel sat in the jeep and waited for Johnny, the hot sun warming her bare legs. She sensed more, much more than was being said, although getting it out of Johnny might be harder than she first guessed. *Not like those jackasses in there,* she thought. *They'd have imploded after Andreas if it wasn't for Johnny, and I bet none of them realise it.*

Johnny Faslane. In no way handsome, although his thin, wiry body did have an unexpected strength. His nervous surrender to her the night before had felt like taking his virginity, although his sheer stamina and unexpected skill told a different story. It mixed uncomfortably with his stubborn refusal to give her the information she wanted – unlike the band, who had been woefully transparent – and left her controlled by her own unruly desires, guilty of a self-accused crime: emotional involvement with a source. And that made her job, getting information, much more complicated.

He emerged from the house and climbed into the jeep. 'Are we still paying your game?' he asked.

She started the engine and they set off towards Porte Juste. 'You're better at this than you think.' She smiled at him.

'Too bad the band aren't.'

'Oh? What did they say?'

'Never mind. Just don't expect me to say any more than *they* already have.'

253

'And where would be the fun in that?' She threw the jeep into a blind corner and the wind tangled her hair around her face. 'I'd bet my life there's more to this concert than you're letting on, but I know you're not going to give it to me on a plate.'

'Jesus, this really is a game to you, isn't it?'

'The best and only game worth playing.'

Chapter 43

'You call this a stage?'

'No, Maxwell, I call it a start. Look around you.' Johnny flung his arm to one side. Beneath a dust cloud of their own creating inside the cricket ground, Skipper's crew were making as much noise as the band as they hammered and sawed at boarding and planks. Dusty pick-up trucks trundled in and out, dropping off battered speakers and spotlights that had been scavenged from the corpses of the scrapped cruise liners. 'No one's standing still on this. Have you got your set list worked out?'

'I suppose so,' he grumbled, kicking a random length of wooden beading.

'Good, have we got sound, Skipper?'

Skipper dropped an armful of steel tubing. 'What?'

'Sound, have we got sound?'

'Jesus, do I look like a fecking electrician?' He stomped off towards his crew and returned with an overall-clad worker. 'Ask him,' he snapped. 'I'm busy.'

'I'm Circuits, the electrician.'

'So what's the news?' asked Johnny. 'The band need to rehearse and they need sound.'

Circuits looked at the haphazard clumps of speakers and seemingly unrelated knots of wiring of varying lengths and thickness. He rubbed his stubbled chin and put his other hand into his overall pocket. 'One hour,' he said.

'Can't you do it any quicker?'

Circuits stared at Johnny. 'Can *you* do it any quicker?'

'Hey, I'm not an electrician.'

'No, but I am, and I say an hour.'

'Beer break, lads,' roared Maxwell. 'We'll see you in an hour, Johnny. Make sure you've got those guitars by then.'

*

'Are you sure it'll work?' Andy looked at the battered guitar with a collection of pick-ups inside a wax-filled tin.

'It's what you said you wanted, right?' Chuck's cigarette flicked up and down as he spoke. 'You can always stick with the Spanish.'

'It was good in its day, but after you made this one especially for me, what can I say?'

'You might like to start with "thank you",' sniped Johnny.

'Hey, that goes without saying.'

'It always does with you. How's yours, Vince?'

'Happy as hell,' he beamed, stroking the large humbuckers in an otherwise pedestrian jaguar body. 'Joe?'

'Never thought I'd be playing a through-neck mustang, man. When do we get to try them?'

'What's happening, Circuits?' asked Johnny.

Circuits walked over to a portable junction box with a length of cable wider than his wrist. He forced it into a spare connection point, jammed the wires in place, then secured them with a few stiff turns of a screwdriver. An even thicker cable snaked out from the junction box towards the distant main stand. He flicked a thumb-sized switch, and static buzzed through one of the large speakers with a solid thump.

'Feel that juice, boys.' Maxwell grabbed a microphone stand and wrapped the cable around his wrist. 'Any chance of a wireless, Johnny?'

'Ask the Ancadians,' he shot back. 'Now get on with it.'

'Sinners Sanctuary, boys.' Maxwell's thick voice boomed through the speaker. 'That's what this place is to us, so let's play it like we mean it.'

Mike tapped out the beat and Maxwell's body moved in time. He held the mic and hummed, then sung the first verse, gently to begin with, then louder and louder. Joe's bass added depth to Mike's playing and Johnny looked eagerly at Vince and Andy. Fingers blurred along vintage fretboards and the modified guitars solidified the sound. Riffs bounced off vocals and Johnny tapped his feet to a different, earthier sound than the slick production of the Beer Doctor tour.

Circuits checked the cables and patted the large speaker affectionately, then looked at Johnny and smiled before selecting another speaker at random and directing its placement next to the first. All around the band, Skipper's crew slowly expanded the stage while the band continued to play.

It's looking good, thought Johnny. The sun beat down on the still air inside the ground. *We just might be able to pull this off, as long as nothing goes tits-up.*

He looked up at the stage and noticed a missed note from Andy. Then he saw the pick-ups moving around the halved tin that had been packed with wax. Thick, clear fluid dripped across the guitar body and Andy looked down. Hot wax touched the power lead and suddenly ignited.

'Oh, Jesus.' Johnny ran forward and jumped onto the stage. The rest of the band were still playing, but Andy clawed at his now blazing guitar, the entire block of sealing wax in flames, generating a noxious black cloud while the guitar's lacquer coating started to burn.

Scrambling onto the stage boards, Johnny gripped the burning guitar. Andy wriggled free of the shoulder strap, Johnny unplugged the guitar and threw it off the stage, then jumped down and stamped on it. Circuits rushed over, brandishing an antique cruise-liner fire extinguisher. He pulled the trigger and off-white foam squirted all over the guitar, then Johnny. The flames diminished and a reducing cloud of smoke rose over the instrument's remains. Johnny turned and climbed back onstage.

'Are you alright, Andy?'

'Fucking hell,' he moaned. 'My guitar's cooked.'

'Mine's okay,' said Vince.

*

Chuck's cigarette end sprinkled ash over the foamed remains of the modified guitar. 'Your boy sure made a mess of this. Didn't he like it?'

'He didn't *want* to trash it,' said Johnny. 'The wax melted and caught fire.'

'That's because it was a stupid idea.'

'Why didn't you say something?'

'Would he have listened?'

Johnny paused. 'Probably not.'

'So this time we don't give him the choice. Look, I've heard enough of their music to know what they want. Give him the

257

Spanish and I'll rework the telecaster in time for the concert. It'll sound the way he wants it to.'

'Promise?'

'As long as they don't set fire to anything else. I've got no more spares.'

*

Rachel drummed her painted nails on the acrylic desktop. Cold Steel, Ancadia, St. Clements. There was more to this than her own frustration at seeing her story sidelined. Cold Steel had no reason to stay in a potential war zone, and as far as she was concerned, that meant someone wasn't telling her the whole truth.

Which was what she liked. Nobody wanted it handed to them like a burger bar ready-meal, and the reticence of everyone in the world to tell it straight was what kept her in a job. She picked up her phone, scrolled through the contact list and selected a number.

'Snowball,' she said. 'How's my favourite snoop?'

'How's your *only* snoop?'

'Don't give me that. A girl with my connections gets her information from all kinds of sources.'

'Then why do you keep bothering *me*?'

'Because you're the best. But don't get cocky, there are plenty of other snouts out there.'

'Sure there are. So what do you want? Where are you? Are you following a real story this time, or more celebrity gossip?'

'Ever heard of St. Clements?'

'Not until two days ago. Are they treating you nice?'

'As always.'

'Yeah, until the shooting starts or you piss someone off, and I know what normally happens first.'

'I don't know what you mean.'

'You do. So what do you want?'

'Eyes and ears.'

'Where?'

'Right here, and maybe Ancadia as well.'

'Maybe?'

'Has anything unusual happened in Ancadia recently?'

'You're not too much of an expert on them, are you?' said Snowball.

'What do you mean?' asked Rachel.

'*Everything* about the Ancadians is weird. They've got the biggest navy in the Caribbean, for no reason: none of their gold is sold on the open market, Uncle Sam has got open access to their deep water harbour, but nobody, not even their powerful friends, are allowed into their other ones, of which we think there are five.'

'You *think?*'

'Like I said, they're not your typical tropical backwater boys.'

'Well, has anything else happened in that area?'

'The main thing they're doing is what you can see right now, without needing to call me.'

'Look, Snowball. There's always a hidden part to every story. Can't you just *try* and find out for me?'

Snowball sighed. 'You want radio or satellite checks?'

'Both. Come on, surely you know me by now.'

'You just be careful your curiosity doesn't get you into trouble. No one's going to pull you out of the pan over there.'

'Worried about me?'

'Worried about my payment.'

'Now *that* I can understand.'

'Call me in twenty-four hours, I should have something for you then.'

'Snowball, you're the best.'

259

Chapter 44

Chaotic activity coalesced into routine. Onstage, the band rehearsed, while around them the cricket ground transformed into a concert venue. Under Skipper's acid commands and Fletcher's growling presence, the stage slowly, very slowly, grew, developing just fast enough to keep Johnny's nerves from pinning him to the plywood boards that now covered the pitch.

A steady if creaking and rickety procession of pick-ups dropped off haphazard mounds of ship's speakers, thin metal tubing and unconnected spotlights, leaving Circuits to construct a workable system from the assorted redundant pieces that he been dumped at his feet. At the same time, Chuck laboured on the remaining guitar body, trying to make it compatible with Andy's needs.

Offshore, the Ancadian Navy lurked, enforcing the blockade and threatening all flights, so isolating the island. The people of St. Clements could communicate with the rest of the world, but they couldn't leave.

Each morning, Johnny and Rachel woke up together, leaving Johnny bewildered at their relationship. He knew she was using him, trying to get what information she could. He also knew that if he told her everything, not only would it place him and the band in danger, there was a more than even chance that he'd also never see her again. He wasn't so naive to think that she had feelings for him, but as much as he tried to tell himself that she was a professional, that she was playing him, hope still flared inside him every time he saw her smile, or when he thought about the nights they spent together.

'Time for the dress rehearsal yet?' she asked, nibbling his shoulder and pressing her body against his.

'What?' he asked. 'Us or the band?'

'You decide.'

He kissed her and then sat up. 'If only there was a concert that could organise itself.'

'Problems?'

'You'd love that, wouldn't you?'

'So give me something else to report. Like why St. Clements for the concert? What were you doing here in the first place? What's with you and the Ancadians? Because, Johnny, I *know* there's something going on.'

'All in good time.'

'Lucky for me you're not my only source of information.'

'About what?'

'Hey, you're not telling, I'm not telling.'

Johnny stood up and got dressed. 'To hell with this game you want me to play, Rachel. We've both got work to do.'

*

Johnny pedalled round a road-kill corner towards the cricket ground. The closely packed white buildings all around him gave way to the seafront's open space, and he saw the rising smoke cloud and cursed. He furiously sped up, feeling his thigh muscles burn, and he barely slowed down for the guard who approached him at the gates and asked for his ID. He jumped off the bike, which spilled to the ground, raced through the empty stands to the pitch, then stopped and sank to his knees before getting up and stumbling towards the remains of the stage.

The smell of charcoal mixed with plywood glue stung his nostrils and he looked at the fire-blackened space where the just-completed stage had once been. At the centre, strips of burnt and still burning wood glowed red.

'I knew something like this would happen.' Johnny spun around and saw Fletcher's ebony bulk looming behind him.

'What do you mean, you knew?' asked Johnny. 'We had security. *You* had security.'

'I can keep everyone safe during an event,' said Fletcher. 'But keeping a ground empty in the middle of the night...' He shook his head. 'Not easy.'

'Bloody hell, our stage has been torched and you make it sound like you were expecting it.'

'Now that it's happened, I'm not surprised.'

'What? Jesus, Fletcher, what else wouldn't surprise you?'

'A bit of sense at the top would be nice. Maybe now Henri will call this whole farce off. He can't win against the Ancadians, and he's risking all of us by trying.'

'He's got no *choice!* He's got to stand up to them or St. Clements will lose any freedom it's got.'

'If Henri hadn't played things so damned independently from the start, then maybe Ancadia wouldn't be interested in us right now. Sometimes it's better to have a big friend than be all alone.'

'Ancadia isn't friendly, Fletcher.'

'Oh, really? And how do you know?'

Johnny checked as though hitting a wall. 'I know. That's all.'

'Well, it doesn't matter, there's no way the concert's going ahead now.'

Something in the way Fletcher spoke, his absolute certainty of failure, sparked an insane determination in Johnny. 'No way,' he growled. 'This concert is happening. We'll make good all the damage and we'll put on a show that'll make the whole world sit up.'

'You've got two days, Johnny; you'll never do it.'

'I don't do never, Fletcher. I *never* have.'

*

'It's a fecking shame, Johnny.' Skipper shook his head and pushed his greasy cap to the back of his head. 'It took everything we had to get this far. I just don't see how we can rebuild it in two days.'

'You got the first one built in three, surely it's possible.'

'We had a lot of it already assembled; we just modified what was in place. My boys worked like slaves on it. From scratch? In two days? You're asking the impossible, we just can't do it.'

'We can't just give up. We've got to *try.*'

Skipper sighed.

'Circuits,' said Johnny. 'How much sound and light did we lose?'

'Speakers and lights held up pretty well. I'm not sure about the cables, but the connections are gone.'

'Have we got any spares?'

'I don't know.' Circuits looked around at the lines of smoke. 'Maybe. That junction box we had was the only one that really worked properly.'

'Is there any way around it?'

'I might be able to repair another one, *if* there's a spare on any of the ships.'

'And if not?'

262

Circuits scratched his head. 'Then we'll need a lot of people all around this ground, flicking switches at exactly the right time.'

'Okay,' said Johnny. 'Stay here and see what you can do. Right now I need just one speaker for the band to practise through. Once you've done that, it's a salvage operation all the way. When the band get here, tell them to plug in and rehearse on any spare part of the ground they want to. I need to talk to Henri.'

*

Rachel's hand blurred across her notepad and she gripped her phone and listened to Snowball. 'That's unbelievable,' she whispered.

'Only if you can put it all together,' he warned her. 'And *only* if it's true.'

'How the hell can it *not* be?'

'Be careful, Rachel. I know how you like to run with a story. Just make sure you know the whys this time. This is more than just show business gossip.'

'Am I telling you how to do your job?'

'That's because I've just *done* my job by telling you all this.'

'You're giving me more than my source here is, that's for sure.'

'You're welcome. So how about this drink you keep promising me?'

'After the next story, I promise.'

*

'It *might* be ready on time? What the hell does that mean.'

'You want me to say it again?' Chuck put down his screwdriver and looked at Johnny. They were sitting on the low wall separating the seats from the pitch. Chuck had based himself there to run adjustments on Joe's and Vince's guitars in between rebuilding the telecaster for Andy. The rehearsals were far enough away for them to hear each other.

'Jesus H,' hissed Johnny. 'This gig is going right down the tubes. Stage burned to the ground, electrics melted, and only one guitar ready.'

'We've still got a day before the concert,' said Chuck.

'At this point we should have *everything* ready, not patching up fire damage and repairing everything else from scratch.'

'You want to quit?'

263

'Christ, no. No. We can't. Jesus, Chuck, are we just plain nuts? If this doesn't happen we're finished, all of us.'

'What do you mean?'

'Oh, fuck it. Where's the harm in telling you? I guess we're screwed anyway.'

Swaying on the brink of confiding to Chuck, Johnny looked up and saw Henri leading a long column of roughly dressed, easy-walking men into the ground. The new arrivals walked towards the slowly resurrecting stage and Henri approached Johnny.

'*La délivrance, mon ami.*' His smile equalled his atomic-bright shirt. 'At the last moment, our crisis becomes a solution.'

'Where did you get these lads from?' asked Johnny.

'Our friends offshore have closed down the fishing industry, so we bring the fishermen inland.'

'They won't catch many in here.'

'*Non*, but they will help build a stage so much quicker, yes? They will allow Circuits to connect the speakers and lights so much faster, *oui?*'

'Bloody hell, Henri, that's genius. Shit, this is going to make all the difference.'

*

'I don't care,' said Andy. 'I'm not touching it.'

Two hours after the fishermen had started to help with the stage, Chuck brought the modified telecaster over to the band. Johnny gaped as Andy refused to even hold the guitar. 'It's what you said you wanted, Andy.'

'No. What I wanted caught fire and melted.'

'You should never have asked for it in the first place.'

'And what makes you such an expert?'

'He's not,' said Chuck. 'But I am, and I agree with him.'

'Yeah, and you're the odd-jobber who made it. Just like everything else in this deal, man. A load of bollocks.'

'There's nothing wrong with this guitar.' Johnny heard an edge to Chuck's voice.

'If it's that bloody good,' said Andy, 'you play it.'

Chuck nodded slightly, unplugged the Spanish and hooked up the telecaster to the speaker. Andy folded his arms and watched with a smug grin, expecting Chuck to ring in a few strums, just to show that it worked. With the cigarette glowing at the corner of his

264

mouth, Chuck's small fingers settled on the fretboard while he held a chipped plectrum to the strings. Suddenly his left hand blurred down the fretboard and corrosive blues burned from the still random pile of speakers. Johnny hid a smile and saw the band shoot stunned looks at the little man before them, an unassuming shop owner from a forgotten Caribbean island who created magic with a shoestring-modified antique guitar. Like everything else, it should never have worked, but it did. Maxwell grinned and picked up the microphone.

'Let's give this lad some company.' His voice tidal-waved from the speakers. 'Cold Steel can play the blues; it's where metal came from in the first place.'

For the first time in a week, Johnny forgot about the Ancadians, the concert, the pressures, even Rachel and her incessant questioning intermixed with amazing sex. He stood and listened, and Cold Steel amazed him once more, this time with their till then unknown ability to play blues. Chuck led them into the music, and at first they supported him with a solid bass and drum line. Maxwell played his voice with a low pitch, bringing torrents of emotion into his singing. Vince played a firm rhythm line before matching Chuck's playing with delta and Detroit blues. Andy picked up the Spanish and joined in as well, leaving Johnny silenced and motionless.

Chuck's hands shuddered to a halt and he smiled lightly. 'Still think it doesn't work?' he asked Andy.

Andy grinned and handed the Spanish to Chuck. 'Want to swap?'

Chapter 45

Snowball's satellite images and radio intercepts weren't complete, but they didn't need to be. The radio feed gave it away. How many musicians were sailing the Caribbean, especially around Ancadia? Who else could the ship-to-shore messages be referring to? And was it them who escaped, them who were condemned by the message? 'Stop them but don't bring them back.' Rachel was certain of it. But like Snowball said, why? Why were Cold Steel sailing in Ancadian waters? Why had they been captured? See previous question, but then why stop them with such force? And how had they escaped a modern naval fleet? Had they been on a mission for St. Clements? She didn't have the answers, but that didn't matter. In fact, it was better. Put out an article asking the questions before the concert, and reveal the answers afterwards.

She looked back at her hastily written copperplate handwriting, then her ruby fingernails blurred over the keyboard as she typed, the words appearing on the screen almost as quickly as she thought them. *Johnny Faslane,* she thought, *he hasn't said a damn thing to me about this all week. And after all I've done for him.* She grinned and thought of their nights together. Maybe he was learning the game quicker than she was teaching him.

'Still working?'

She looked up and saw Johnny standing in the desk booth, still smiling that damn mocking grin, screaming out control while the rest of him yelled insecurity. What *was* it about him?

'Well, you know,' she stammered. 'The news doesn't work nine to five, so I can't either.'

'What's the latest?' he asked.

'A major military blockade, and a minor concert tomorrow night.' She looked at her laptop screen and quickly folded it down.

'Rachel.' Another reporter pushed past Johnny. 'There's a call for you on my desk.'

'Can't you put it through to my mobile?'

'We've had no signal for the last hour; where the hell have you been?'

'Okay, I'll be there.' She stood up and walked past Johnny. 'Don't move,' she said to him. 'At all.'

*

Johnny walked towards Rachel's desk and flipped up the screen, knowing he couldn't stop himself. Maybe she'd even staged it to see how he'd react. He didn't care, and there was a lot more to lose than just great sex if she had the goods on Cold Steel. Right now, the band and St. Clements needed good and bad and nothing in between, and Johnny knew that the treasure hunt, their capture and escape was nowhere but in between. If she'd found out everything, she was only doing her job, but Johnny was only doing his by stopping her. He sat down and read her piece, and as he did he felt the gods of doom suck out his insides.

He read the final paragraph and churning nausea desiccated his body. God, but she was good. It wasn't the whole story, but between her source and her own sharp observations she'd managed to fill in most of the gaps. If Ozone found out about any of it before the concert, there wouldn't be a concert. And if that happened, St. Clements was finished. And if that happened, so were Cold Steel. For any of them to have a chance of getting out, Johnny had to keep it between Ancadia and St. Clements. How the hell was he going to do that?

'So you moved?'

He felt his soul being dragged into her eyes, and knew her sense of betrayal matched his. A sudden Berlin wall of mistrust flickered and solidified between them, instantly replacing the gentle game of questions and no answers. He couldn't be angry with her. He knew there was every chance she'd find out, but there was no way he could let her release the article.

'I see you've been busy,' he said.

'So have you.'

He looked down at the screen. 'I don't suppose there's much point in deleting this?' he said. Rachel shook her head. 'You could probably re-write it all?' She nodded. 'So what are we going to do about this?'

'You tell me.'

'I can't let you put this story out.'

'Not ever?'

'Not yet.'

267

'You're still playing the game, Johnny,' she smiled. 'That's the best hook you've thrown so far.'

'I'm not playing games anymore, Rachel.'

'Oh, but you are. And you're better than you think. How much of that is true?' She nodded towards her laptop.

'I can't tell you.'

'Ever?'

'Yet.'

She raised her eyebrows. 'So what are we going to do until then? You going to kidnap me, tie me up?' She giggled. 'Perhaps we should have talked about this when we were alone together.'

Johnny remained focussed. 'You want the story? The whole story?'

'You know I do.'

'Then you'll have to wait until after the gig.'

'Why?'

'You've just got to trust me, Rachel. The concert is more important than what we did to get here. Sure, it's connected, but that's all you're gong to find out until we're ready to tell you.'

'And when will that be?'

'The day after the concert. Either way, it won't matter by then.'

'The day after the concert,' she repeated. 'You'll tell me everything?'

'I promise.'

'You've got a lot riding on that word. And what are you going to do until then?'

He laughed. 'What I'm *not* going to do is let you out of my sight.' He handed back her laptop. 'You're coming with me.'

'Where are we going?'

'Back to Henri's.'

'You're taking me to see Henri, and the band?'

'No, I'm keeping an eye on you to make damn sure you don't go running to your paper before we want you to. I sure as hell can't shoot you.'

*

'Trouble.' Henri's voice was strained as Johnny and Rachel walked through the front door. Camouflage-clad soldiers were moving quietly around the house, while Henri looked suspiciously at Rachel.

268

'You know what they say about keeping your friends close,' said Johnny.

'And your enemies closer still. Which is she?'

'A friend,' said Rachel. 'Come on, Henri, I've been here every night. What's going on? What's your army doing here?'

Henri looked at Johnny. 'Is she a trusted friend?'

'She will be after the concert.'

'And what do we do until then?'

'Keep an eye on her.'

'That's all?'

'Jesus, Henri, I didn't bring her round here to have her locked up. All she needs is a security man on her tail to stop her from using her phone, laptop or the internet.'

'Peeler.' Henri summoned a security guard. 'Escort *Mademoiselle* to the kitchen and see she is fed.'

A silent, suited guard led Rachel away. She glanced accusingly at Johnny as she was walked out of sight. 'What *are* all these soldiers doing here?' he asked.

'The Ancadians are coming to visit.'

'Holy shit. They're invading? But I thought you said they wouldn't. You said they *couldn't*!'

Henri shrugged. 'They are on their way here. We received a radio message saying they want to talk.'

'So why all the guns?'

'Suppose they don't want to talk when they get here?'

'Fuck me.' Johnny looked around and fear knotted his guts and turned his bowels to jelly.

'This lady friend of yours,' said Henri. 'You have told her nothing?'

'*I* haven't told her anything, but some other bastard has.'

'What does she know?'

'She knows we were in Ancadian waters, she knows we were held by them and she knows they tried to kill us.'

'*Merde. Mon ami*, that whole treasure hunt of yours was a fiasco. If the details get out before we can put our case to the world, it will make a simple argument very complicated.'

'I know, and if Ozone get wind of it they'll stop the concert, and the band. I guess bringing her here when the Acadians are coming isn't very helpful either.'

269

'No, but you could not leave her alone. For all that you may have pulled at her emotions, she has a job to do.'

'I've promised her the whole story after the concert: it won't matter by then. By that time we'll either have some help or we won't.'

'On that I agree. Now let us await the arrival of our guests.'

They walked through to the large reception room where the band had already congregated. They shot nervous glances at Johnny, who looked with equal trepidation at the armed men prowling around the flat gardens beyond the opened veranda door. The last time Johnny had stood there was at the press conference announcing the concert, and now this was happening. *Jesus, this is getting way too real.*

Barely audible above the crickets' evening chorus, but getting louder all the time, Johnny heard the approaching aircraft. The noise of its engines increased until it became deafening. Johnny, Henri and the band looked outside; the entire garden was lit up by floodlights. With a roaring crescendo of sound, a grey-painted Eurocopter passed low over the house, its massive downdraft blowing great clouds of dust through the open doors.

Soldiers slipped past them and took up station around the slowly descending aircraft, alert for whatever may have emerged from the helicopter. A side door slid back and a helmeted crewman looked outside. Small tyres touched down on the grass, the airflow flattened the vegetation and plastered the watching soldiers' uniforms against their bodies. With the landing complete, the engines switched off, their high-octane thunder slowly receding into silence.

Camouflage figures, similar to Henri's soldiers, dropped from the Eurocopter's cabin, rolled on the ground and took up fire positions. A steroid-bicep standoff quickly tensed as troops from both sides faced each other, gunsight to gunsight. Tension crackled around the floodlit garden and another man stepped out of the helicopter, clad in a dark-green uniform that swam with gold braid and medals. He looked mockingly at the St. Clements soldiers like a Capo watching morning parade.

'It is Alpinos,' whispered Henri.

'What does he want?' asked Johnny.

'I do not know.'

270

Sneering and now flanked by his guards, who were themselves within a cloud of escorting St. Clements troops, Alpinos walked inside. He stared down his long nose at the band, his drooping brown eyes lingering on Vince with his own Hispanic features, slicked-back hair and beard.

'What are you looking at?' rumbled Vince.

Alpinos' bodyguards formed an instant barrier between him and Vince. Henri's troops turned towards Alpinos, who cracked a crooked smile and spoke rapidly. Johnny heard the word 'Fernando'.

'The *Fernando*,' said Vince. 'That's right. We trashed that pile of shit when we broke out. What a bunch of pussies.'

If Alpinos didn't understand Vince's words, his scowl and squared shoulders needed no translation. His men reached for their weapons, Henri's reached for theirs, and Johnny heard the sound of gunbolts being slid back.

Alpinos and Vince stood motionless, eyeballing each other while both sets of bodyguards readied their weapons and watched for movement, waited for an order to fire. Johnny's heart went into trip-spasm. The seconds slowed down and tracked past like cold vegetable extract. His throat constricted and his mouth opened and closed like a beached goldfish. Alpinos slowly transferred his eugenic stare towards Henri.

'Is this a friendly way to conduct negotiations, Henri?' he asked, his Spanish inflections matching Henri's French ones.

'Negotiations?' spat Henri. 'While your gunboats lurk off our island, and you come here armed?'

Alpinos smiled, gestured to his troops to stand easy and looked at the band once more. 'Monsieur Chevalier already knows me, but let me introduce myself to the rest of you. I am General Miguel Alpinos, El Presedente of the Free Republic of Ancadia, and I come to you with a vision of the future.'

'This will be interesting.' Henri stifled a yawn. 'It has been a long time since I heard a piece of *merde* do some talking.'

Beneath the cap's low peak, the General's olive skin flushed. His thick neck swelled, and his black moustache bristled. 'Your words are as empty as the resistance you offer us,' he said quietly. 'My armada surrounds your tiny island with impunity, and at my orders I could unleash a firestorm that would destroy you all. You must know this is so, but there is another way. A peaceful way.'

'You offer peace at the end of a gun?'

'How else will you listen?'

'I won't listen at all.'

'No?' Alpinos chuckled and strolled around the room on smooth-soled, gleaming leather jackboots. He glared at Vince. 'Well, why don't you send my ships away? Why don't you ask these saboteurs that you are harbouring how harmless we are? Why don't you ask them how to disable my fleet? Engage their martial talents to sink us.'

'We've done it before,' muttered Maxwell.

Alpinos shot across the room like a parody ballet dancer and quivered before Maxwell. 'Yes, you have. And how you escaped without damage, yes?' Maxwell opened his mouth but Alpinos interrupted. 'No. We blew your ship out of the water and left you for dead. And so we thought you were until you announced this ridiculous concert of yours. An altogether kinder fate than the one you sent my cousin to.'

'Your cousin?' asked Johnny.

'Do not plead ignorance,' barked Alpinos. 'Colonel Ronaldo Santos Mucama, the commandant of Chanderos. Perhaps you have already forgotten? Perhaps you deny your involvement?'

'The last I saw of that guy,' said Johnny, 'he'd chucked us in jail.'

'For violating Ancadian territory, for stealing Ancadian national treasures. And the lies you told him about further treasure sent him to his death.'

'His greed sent him there, mate,' said Maxwell. 'Sure, we found that loot, and your man took it from us, but he was happy enough to go looking for more.'

'While at the same time you used violence to escape from us. And you return to the nation that supported you from the start.'

'We stopped here for supplies,' said Maxwell. 'Nothing else.'

'Lies! Like the lies to told to Colonel Mucama. Confirmed by your silence. If you are so good and we are so evil, why did you not make much of your unjust incarceration?'

'Like you told the whole world about sinking an unarmed ship?'

'An irrelevance. Just like everything about you, you fools. You think we cared about you, or your pathetic treasure hunt? All we cared about was who supported you, and we had an ample confession from one of your own.'

Johnny turned to at Andy, who flushed and looked at the floor.

'Did you really need an excuse?' asked Henri. 'You have made enough threats in the past.'

Alpinos smiled permafrost and turned to Henri. 'It's true, my vision for these islands is no secret. And here you stand on St. Clements, while the whole world will watch us tear you apart.'

'The world will never allow it.'

Alpinos laughed. 'You think so? You think our big friends will step in to protect your precious freedom? Henri, you are deluded. We sell them cheap gold and we allow them to use our deep-sea harbour. They value these things, and because of that, they will not hold us back. Believe me, Henri, you will get no help from them.'

'If we are so defenceless against your might, why do your victorious forces not wade ashore right now? Why come here like a thief in the night?'

'I do not need to waste Ancadian blood to subdue St. Clements.'

'No?'

'No. And we both know it. All I need to do is wait. Food, water, electricity: sooner or later you will run out of one of these and your people will not stand to be starved on account of your pride.'

'You will have given up long before then.'

'We will not,' growled Alpinos. 'We shall stay until victory. But how that victory is won is down to you, *amigo*. How many lives are thrown away needlessly is down to you. If it had not been for your toy soldiers here, this would have been over already.'

'Oh?'

'Yes. Why else would I set foot on this miserable island, if not to have you removed? Don't look so stunned, my friend. Had we been able to do it quietly, even now you would be sailing to Ancadia, I would be acquainting myself with your rustic comforts, and this crisis would have been averted.'

'So why the change of heart?'

Alpinos laughed. 'Henri, I am the visionary here, I am the one who is invaluable. It is not for me to place myself in harm's way.

273

Had we landed unopposed, the island would have been mine. Since you choose to contest my will with your toy *soldados,* we shall grant you this round, but it will only forestall the inevitable. You cannot resist me. Why, you cannot even organise your concert without the stage being burned to the ground.'

'Nothing to do with you?' asked Johnny.

Alpinos spread his arms wide. 'What can you prove? Can I prove that you sent my cousin on a suicide mission?'

'Either way, it's been rebuilt,' said Johnny. 'And the concert goes ahead as planned.'

'Perhaps. Perhaps not. Who knows what new disaster may befall you before tomorrow night? But it will be your last flourish, Henri. When the concert ends, your time as Prime Minister ends. The last decision you make will be if you have the courage to stand aside with dignity, or if you leave me the choice to either starve you or unleash my forces upon you.'

'Big words, Alpinos,' said Henri. 'But you do not intimidate me so easily. All you want is an easy victory. I will not sell my people down the river, and if you think you can overcome my defence forces, you would have invaded before now. You cannot take St. Clements by force, and you will soon realise that and go back home. Now, if you have nothing else to say, you are uninvited guests in my house, and my friends here need to rest.'

'You are stubborn, Henri.' Alpinos shrugged. 'I hope your people appreciate the concert tomorrow night. Do the right thing, or it will be their last chance to enjoy life for a very long time.' He turned and walked out to the patio, followed by his soldiers and flanked by Henri's. The helicopter's engines whined into life, then rose to a deafening roar. The helicopter flew over the house, and in the silence that followed it into the night, Johnny sat down.

'Well, shit.'

'*Mon ami*?'

'We've got no chance. Why did we even try?'

'*Vraiment?* It is words, words and no more. So they have told us their grand plans, but what else has changed? They cannot invade.'

'They managed to sabotage the stage, maybe they'll do it again.'

Henri smiled. 'They show their hand. Captain Boots.'

One of Henri's soldiers thundered over to him, stomped to attention and threw up a continuity-perfect salute. 'Sir!' he screamed, louder than the recently departed helicopter.

'Take your squad to the cricket ground,' said Henri. 'Make sure the stage and all other equipment remains safe.'

'Yes, Sir!' Captain Boots barked a rapid set of orders and the soldiers trooped out of the house. Johnny heard the sound of rubber boot-heels crunching along the drive and away into the night.

'So,' said Henri. 'The concert still goes on.'

'The concert *might* go on.'

'But you told Alpinos. I have seen the stage taking shape myself.'

'What else was I going to tell that bastard?'

'Well, you'd better tell *us,*' said Maxwell. 'We're going to be the sorry souls onstage tomorrow night. Is there any point in even showing up?'

'Okay,' said Johnny. 'We know the stage got torched the other night. That was the easiest thing to rebuild, thanks to Henri getting the fishermen on side. That made all the difference.'

'So what's the problem?' asked Maxwell.

'The electrics.'

'Everything electric?'

'The cables were insulated and fireproofed because they came from ships, but the connections, junction boxes and switches didn't make it. Circuits has performed miracles putting it all back together, and he thinks the sound and lights should work.'

'It *should* work? Jesus, can't he test it?'

Johnny shook his head. 'It's too risky. There are no spares, no back-up systems. If he fires it up and it blows, we've got nothing else to use. He's as sure as he can be that it's good, but until tomorrow night none of us will know.'

Chapter 46

At ten o'clock, Johnny woke up in a haze of fatigue and tension. Alone. After Alpinos left, Rachel had been brought in from the kitchen, glared sheet-ice at Johnny and demanded solo sleeping quarters if they were going to keep her overnight. He shrugged, trying to convince himself he didn't really mind. He'd known their relationship had to reach a crisis at some point; they were both after different things. Maybe it was better this way. Instead of trying to keep her happy *and* uninformed, he could just focus on his job, which right now he needed to do more than ever.

Doubting questions machine-gunned through his mind. Would the lights work? Would the sound work? Holy shit, would *any* of it work? Had Captain Boots and his men kept the place safe overnight? Had the Ancadians tried anything else? Was there someone on the island helping them?

He rolled out of bed and climbed into his clothes. Outside the room next to his stood one of Henri's security guards, a silent sentinel. Johnny wondered if he dared knock and see if Rachel was still mad at him. He wanted to tell her he had no choice, that she'd get her story, only not straight away. He looked at the security guard for inspiration, but he stared anonymously ahead, his thoughts unreadable from behind dark glasses. 'Bollocks,' said Johnny, marching through to the kitchen and grabbing a cold breakfast before heading to the cricket ground.

*

Vince walked up to Johnny as soon as he stepped onto the pitch. 'We've got a problem,' he said.

'Well, bugger me, that's a surprise. What's happened now?'

'Maxwell says he can't go on.'

'What? Why not? Is his voice okay?'

'It's his nerves.'

'He's got stage-fright? *Maxwell's* got stage-fright?'

'I'm kind of surprised myself, but there it is.'

Johnny approached the stage and saw the band sitting in the shade while the morning sun started to bake everything in its path. Circuits cajoled a squad of helpers into checking the cables,

Skipper's high-pitched voice could be heard swearing at his own crew, and Fletcher glared with increasing misery at the stage that, despite everything, at least looked like becoming complete. Andy, Mike and Joe looked expectantly at Johnny, while Maxwell's eyes were fixed forward like a solder's thousand-yard stare. In Johnny's experience, singers were never *too* scared to go on. Nervous before a big show, sure, he'd seen that plenty of times, even from Maxwell, but refusing to sing at all?

'Maxwell.' Johnny tried authority. 'What's this shit I hear about you not going on.'

Maxwell looked up at Johnny and then covered his face with his hands. 'There's no point,' he said. 'This whole thing is a pile of shit, and we've done nothing but stack one balls-up after another on everyone around here.'

Mike and Andy stared up at the blue sky. 'We've been hearing this all morning, man,' said Joe.

Johnny knelt down in front of Maxwell. 'It's not like you to be so negative.'

'Look around you, mate. It's not difficult.'

'I'm seeing a stage being built, and Circuits is doing a great job putting sound and light together.'

'Yeah, and we won't know until tonight. Christ, we'd have been better off if the Ancadians had bombed the whole place.'

'No, Maxwell. This is going to work. The Ancadians – if it *was* them – did their best to sabotage us, but they didn't make it. They didn't. The stage was rebuilt, and the lights and sound –'

'Are a leap of faith.'

'Sure they are. But look at what we've done from scratch. Look at what we've done *after* a fire just two days ago.' Johnny flung his arm in a random sweep. 'None of these lads are roadies. Dixie's a million miles away, but they're putting it together. You're telling me the sound and lighting might work; I'm, telling you, Maxwell, it *will* work.'

'Maybe it's our destiny to fail.'

'What do you mean?'

'We haven't got anything right since we came here. So we found the gold, then we were taken by the Ancadians and dragged St. Clements into our mess. We got our ship blown up and sunk, and as for the treasure, it's now even more lost than when we

277

found it. At least it was hidden on dry land before we rocked up, now it's at the bottom of the ocean somewhere. *No one* is going to find it now.'

'The treasure's the least of our worries.'

'And it's also the whole reason we came here in the first place.'

'Maybe it's a good thing that no one ended up with it.'

'What do you mean?'

'Let's face it, Maxwell. It didn't really *belong* to Blackbeard, did it? All that treasure we found was stolen. It was taken at sword and musket point and probably caused a lot of misery to a lot of people. I'd say the best place for all of it is the bottom of the sea where it won't do heartache to anyone else. It hasn't exactly made us happy, has it?'

'We went through a lot to get it.'

'It was never ours, Maxwell. We found it, we lost it. Maybe we should just leave it like that.'

'But what about St. Clements? Henri? *Us?* We set off this blockade by tangling with the Ancadians. It's our fault. They want Henri to quit, and then they'll come for us. We won't get away from them a second time, mate. This is all too much, way too much.'

'Everything you've said is right, Maxwell. The Ancadians are camped just offshore because of us, and if it goes tits-up tonight, we're fucked. But the only thing you've missed out is that it's *us* who decide that.'

'Us?'

'Well, you. Cold Steel. This concert is our last, our only chance to change things. Look, Maxwell, when I started managing you lot I'll be honest, I thought your time was up. You'd swallowed the star pill and you didn't give a shit. But you proved me wrong. And not just me, either. Quite a few people at Ozone were more than happy to cut you loose.'

'Really?'

'You know it' said Johnny. 'Too much fucking around, no goods onstage, bad press. They'd had enough, and you lot pulled your nuts out of the fire just in time to stop them getting roasted. You've managed it once, and that time you only had yourselves to look out for. Now you've got this whole island counting on you. Are you really going to let them down? They can't make this without our help; they need you, Maxwell. St. Clements *needs* Cold Steel.'

'*Needs* us?'

'You'd better believe it. And you know what, it's just as well it's you guys and not some other band sitting here with their knackers in a vice.'

'What do you mean?'

'Because Cold Steel are the *only* band that can turn this crap-storm into a heat-wave.'

'But we don't even know if the sound and lights are going to work.'

'He's got a point,' said Vince. 'We'd *all* feel a bit better if we knew we'd be heard beyond the front row.'

'You want a sound check?' asked Johnny. A chorus of approval greeted his words. 'I'll see what we can do.'

*

'I've only *just* wired the last speaker in,' said Circuits. 'We had an extra bank brought in this morning from the last ship. They were being used as ballast.'

'Ballast?' asked Johnny.

'Sure. Most people on cruise ships didn't like their music loud, know what I mean?'

'Couldn't have done the speakers much good, being down there.'

'And the others have been baking in the sun for three years. None of them are in good shape. I'm only even looking at them because I have to.'

'So is it ready?'

'As long as it works.'

'Can we test it out?'

'We can't take chance on the switches. Every time you power up and down, it puts a strain on the whole system. And everything here is just too fragile to keep switching it on and off. We can fire it up and everything could work fine, but if we shut it down then it might stay down for good.'

'Is it really that delicate?'

Circuits nodded. 'Most of this stuff has been either sitting in the sun or rotting aboard ship. The cables, speakers and lights have gone damp, been eaten by rats and had all manner of insects make home in them. The whole system has been put together from three incompatible ones. Jesus, Johnny, you should be amazed it's come together at all.'

'So if we switch it on and it stays on, we're good?'

'Hopefully. With a bit of luck I'll be able to see any strains in the workings and sort them before we have a major flip-out.'

'How about if we switched it on right now, and just left it on?'

'For how long?'

'For good. Don't switch it off till after the gig.'

Circuits rubbed his head. 'It's possible. I mean, it'll give us time to find any bugs before the concert.'

'That's great. The band need a sound check, and it'll make them feel loads better if they know the system works.'

'All about them, huh?'

'Welcome to my world,' said Johnny. 'We rush around like idiots, they get all the glory.'

'All right then, we'll go for it, but don't tell the band until we *know* it's working.'

*

A dozen workers surrounded Circuits. They nodded cautiously as he told them what to do, then sped off to different spots around the base of the stage. Circuits stood at what might loosely have been called a mixing desk between two sets of speakers. He wore a headlamp and a neck cord strung with different coloured lenses. 'A few less controls than you're used to, I guess?' he said to Johnny. 'Volume for the sound, on and off for the lights.'

'True, but also less to worry about, less to go wrong.'

'Say that at the end of the show.'

'Is it all ready?'

Circuits crossed his fingers. 'As far as I know.'

'So kick it in the guts, let's get this thing started.'

Circuits rested a finger on a large switch that had been gaffa-taped to the console and fed directly to the thick cable that ran out under the boarding and over to the stands. He flicked it and Johnny felt a solid thump from the current that shot along from the main junction box and flooded the improvised, cannibalised and repaired system. The large speakers hummed and Johnny could feel the diaphragms of varying age and size quiver with life. Seconds later, soundlessly, but as though a soul had been sucked away, he felt the power disappear.

'What's wrong?' he asked.

'I don't know.' Circuits flicked the switch back and forth. 'Oh, shit. Wait here.'

He scampered along the entire cable's length, quickly disappearing from view. Johnny sweated under the building heat, wondering if the concert would be decided by an inability to even turn on the sound. *The press will eat us alive. What the hell was I thinking about?* He looked at the empty stage, and then at the small army of workers still toiling away.

Lost in his pessimism, initially he didn't notice the gentle but insistent hand pushing him to one side. Only when it became firmer and accompanied by fingernails did he yelp in pain and turn around. It was Rachel.

'Jesus.' He rubbed his arm. 'Can't you just ask me to move?'

'I did,' she snapped. 'You didn't hear me. Now get out of the way. I can't photograph this excuse for a stage with you standing there. Christ, Johnny. Is that it?'

'What do you want?' He bridled. 'It's a bloody stage.'

'Months in the planning? Looks like it's all been thrown together at the last minute to me.'

'It might have been better if the bastards hadn't burned it down two days ago.'

'Who –?'

'The Ancadians, who do you think?'

'But why?'

'There you go, playing your damn game again.'

'It doesn't matter.' She jerked her head towards the security guard a few feet away from her. 'If he sees me even go near a laptop, phone, anything, I'll be dragged off to jail. I'm amazed they let me even use my camera.'

'Look, Rachel –'

'Forget it, you were just doing your job.'

'I wish I didn't have to.'

She smiled. 'You did what you had to, but don't think I've forgiven you. Yet. We'll talk about it later.'

'All fixed, Johnny.' Circuits ran back to the console and flicked the switch. Again a metal-plate thud stamped out from the speakers. 'Go get your boys.'

Chapter 47

'It's working perfectly?' asked Maxwell.

'Just as good as the Soundsphere stuff.' Johnny grinned a hangman smile and trembled inside.

'Bollocks, nothing was that good.'

'This is better. It's perfectly set up for the gear you've got right now.'

'What?' said Andy. 'You mean knackered and cobbled together?'

Johnny shrugged. 'Paint it any way you want, but it's where we are, and it's real simple. Either you get your arses onstage and show the world just what Cold Steel can do, or you give up without even trying. I never had you lot figured for quitters.'

Maxwell growled and stood up. 'I guess we're the ones who need to do the proving.'

He climbed onto the stage, followed by the rest of the band. Old, hastily modified guitars were passed up, and raw current sludged through the speakers and the band hooked up.

'Finally,' said Rachel. 'Something worth taking a picture of.'

'You didn't tell her anything, did you?' Maxwell's words boomed earthy and deep through the microphone.

'Do you see her smiling?' asked Johnny.

Maxwell's laughter shouted out a raw challenge. Vince and Andy riffed into Spider Woman, a dirtier, more blurred version than Johnny had ever heard, but it fitted the situation. The sound system warmed up, the diaphragms worked the music, and soon Johnny was tapping his feet and feeling the energy take him. There were no roadies or technicians to fine-tune the instruments, and Cold Steel went back to their roots and tweaked everything themselves. 'Make sure you're getting pictures,' Johnny told Rachel. 'How many other top flight bands can do that?'

'How many other bands *have* to?' she shot back.

The sound came together and Cold Steel dovetailed their instruments with the speakers' peculiarities. Sound check powered on through four, five and then six songs, before Fire in the Hold splintered to a sudden halt with a plectrum screech that set Johnny's teeth on edge.

'And *that's* how you do a sound check,' roared Maxwell. 'Cold Steel style.'

As he spoke, a flame-gout belched out of one of the speakers, toasting the boarded flooring black and creating a smoke signal that translated multi-lingual panic. Circuits picked up a black fire extinguisher and sprayed thick clouds over the flames. An angry humming buzzed from the other speakers.

'Shouldn't you shut it down?' asked Maxwell.

'No way.' Circuits coughed as the cloud of extinguisher gas blew over him. 'I can't promise it'll start again.'

'Well, what caused it?'

'What caused what?'

'The fire, for fuck's sake.'

Circuits pulled open an inspection hatch and ran nervous fingers along fragile wires. 'The speaker probably collected a lot of dust, debris, all sorts when it was ballast. Any number of hot wires could have set it off.'

'Oh, Jesus. So that means every single speaker's a potential fire risk.'

'It's alright. I've got it covered.'

'Really?'

'Sure, we've got plenty of extinguishers.'

'You'll need a few more if that pile of crap catches fire.' Johnny pointed to a haphazard heap of wooden spars and off-cuts in the centre of the stage.

'That's a special effect,' said Circuits.

'Bollocks.'

'You won't be thinking like that when it gets dark and the lights come on. It was an idea of Skipper's; we tried it last night and it works.'

Johnny's furrowed eyebrows spoke scepticism, but he forced a smile and turned to Maxwell. 'So, sound check done. Best you lads get out of sight.'

'Yeah, man,' said Joe. 'We wanted to talk to you about that. Do we *really* have to wade through shit to get to the stage?'

'Relax,' said Johnny. 'You won't be going barefoot.'

*

After a hurried meal, shower and change of clothing, Maxwell peered through the pavilion's shuttered windows. The ground's gates had been opened and a light dusting of fans were starting to sprinkle the pitch. He'd never felt so nervous before a gig. Johnny had only just talked him into going ahead, his nosey-arse girlfriend was *still* asking fucking awkward questions, and Johnny himself was nowhere to be seen.

The door creaked open and Johnny slipped through.

'Did you get lost?' asked Maxwell.

'Just having a chat with Captain Boots.'

'What about?'

'Pyrotechnics.'

'That's more like it,' said Maxwell. 'I bet the military have some amazing whizz-bangs.'

'You'd better believe it,' said Johnny. 'Now, there's a red line going around the edge of the stage. Don't go anywhere near it. We don't want a repeat of Tokyo, right?'

'Right.'

'Okay. So, it's show time. Are you ready for the way in?'

'Oh, man,' said Joe. 'Do we have to?'

'There's no other way, unless you want to walk through the crowd like a bunch of boxers.'

'How *are* you getting to the stage?' asked Rachel.

'You don't want to know,' said Johnny.

'No, I really *do* want to know.'

'Okay, follow me.' Johnny led her out the back of the pavilion and into a small courtyard cluttered with empty beer kegs and bottles awaiting collection. Whitewashed walls rose high on all sides, preventing anyone from looking in. He walked towards a circular manhole cover, connected a pair of metal rods lying next to it and prised it open. They were both hit with an immediate and overpowering stench of decaying human waste.

'Oh, Christ.' She went pale beneath her tan and gagged. 'What *is* that?'

'Sewer main.' Johnny slammed the lid shut once more. 'And it's how the band get to the stage.'

'And they're happy about walking through that?'

'Would you be?'

285

'Johnny, why are you guys doing *any* of this? It's not as though Cold Steel *have* to play last-minute gigs, and as for wading through, well, shit, to get to the stage – you must be in serious trouble.'

He grinned. 'After the concert we'll tell you everything.'

'What's wrong with now? I've got one of Henri's guards never more than ten feet away from me. Who am I going to tell?'

'*After* the concert.'

She looked at him and raised her eyebrows. 'Are you *really* sending the band down there?'

'I'm not sending them,' said Johnny. 'I'll be leading them.'

*

Twilight slowly settled over St. Clements like a silk sheet, and small lights came on along the seafront. Out to sea, roaming Ancadian gunboats threw up white bow waves that reflected the small amount of light from the stars. The spotlights around the stage took hold of the darkness within the cricket ground and kept it at bay. The stadium started to fill up, nervous expectation crackled around the stands, and people sought comfort through physical closeness.

A lone figure walked towards the stage, slight and unassuming. In one hand he held a guitar with easy familiarity. An all-areas pass labelled him as something to do with the concert, but few people in the crowd recognised him. He got nearer the stage, then past the ring of security and into the band-only area. Still barely noticed, he stepped onto the stage and plugged in his guitar.

Most people thought he was working for the band, tuning in one of their guitars, so the first few bars were missed, but after thirty seconds of note-perfect, ditchwater blues, everyone was listening.

Chuck stepped up to the microphone and sung in a voice that mixed bootleg whiskey with chewing tobacco. It matched his guitar playing perfectly, and a minute after he took the stage, twenty thousand spectators were clapping their hands and tapping their feet in time.

Spotlights flickered and winked out. The head torch that signalled Circuits' position constantly changed colours, which sent silent, shadow-like workers scurrying around the lighting rig, pulling out dead bulbs and ramming in replacements, then flicking their hands back before the instantly hot bulbs burned their fingers.

The sound system's deep, muddy growl mirrored the music, and it carried effortlessly to the pavilion.

'That guy's not bad,' said Maxwell.

'So get up there and tell him,' replied Johnny. 'He's not doing a full support slot.'

Maxwell grinned. 'Let him play just one more song, mate. Anything to get out of walking through that shit-tube.'

Johnny chucked waterproof orange overalls at Maxwell, then climbed into a set himself. 'Get changed, the lot of you.' He turned to Rachel. 'You sure you don't want to come with us? You'll get some great pictures.'

'No thanks,' she laughed. 'I'll go overland.'

Johnny zipped up his suit and laced a surgical mask over his face. The band stood before him, similarly dressed and anonymised, looking like an extreme facelift team.

'Do we really have to do this?' asked one of the band.

Johnny looked at five identically dressed musicians wearing masks, and wondered which one had spoken. It didn't matter. 'Yes, we really have to do this. But I'm not sending you. I'm going first and you're following me.'

He pulled on a pair of thin latex gloves and hoped they didn't rip against the first faecal obstacle he came across, then led the band out to the courtyard. Again he pulled up the cover and the battering ram impact of raw stench was no less sickening than before.

'Jesus,' choked a faceless band member from behind him. 'How far do we have to walk through this?'

'You can always crawl,' Johnny took a deep breath of what remained of the clean air, switched on his head torch and grabbed the metal handholds and descended into the darkness below.

Great waves of reeking human waste smell violated Johnny's senses as he stepped deeper into the shaft. He saw the head torches of the band following him, and heard their moans of disgust once they encountered the scent rising upwards. His booted foot found the bottom rung, then descended through putrefying liquid to step on the main's solid, tainted floor.

At what seemed like an infinite distance away, he made out a faint light further along the tunnel and he smiled grimly. Reach the light and they'd be under the stage. He started to wade through a river of polluted solids that emulsioned around his legs as the whole tide of effluent flowed slowly towards the treatment plant. The smell was like running into solid wall and he was only vaguely aware of the sloshing footsteps behind that told him the band were following.

Stepping through shit-filled purgatory, Johnny's phone rang. *Christ on a bike, can't anyone leave me alone?* He was thankful in a way, its persistent tone took at least part of his mind away from the trudge along the sewer. The caller eventually gave up, and Johnny's consciousness returned to the putrid march through an endless stream of excrement.

How long the eternal torment lasted, his senses didn't register. He kept his eyes fixed on the flickering glow-worm of light that signalled the end, and after what might have been minutes or years, it got brighter. It was definitely closer now. He could see the light fitting screwed to the sewer wall, stained and rusting, but the salvation offered by its benevolent light was almost intoxicating. He hurried the last few steps and stood under the light for a second before grabbing the steel rungs and climbing up to a wide concrete ledge. He looked up, his head torch sending a beam through the opened manhole cover, illuminating Fletcher's scowling face.

'You didn't get lost, then?'

'No.' The mask muffled Johnny's voice. 'Is the hose working?'

A sudden rush of collected sea and rain water torrented over Johnny, and it felt better than a temperature-controlled designer shower installed in a New York penthouse overlooking Central Park. The splattered collection of faecal matter, ranging from grey to white to brown and black slowly rinsed away from his protective clothing as though he'd been touched by the Messiah. The rest of the band arrived alongside him, and they too stood on the now crowded platform, awaiting the attention of the hose with almost erotic anticipation.

'Man,' gasped Maxwell. 'I *never* thought I'd walk through something like that.'

'I never thought you'd actually follow me,' replied Johnny.

Dripping clean water and feeling immortal because of it, he climbed the ladder and emerged beneath the half-lit hollow box of the stage. Above him, Chuck carried on playing, and it was surprisingly quiet inside the ring of speakers that faced outwards.

Johnny peeled off his overalls and mask and then his gloves. The band emerged alongside him and his phone rang once more.

'Hi, Randall, the band are just about to go on. Have you got a good luck message for them?'

'Are you shitting me? What's this I hear about Cold Steel spying on the goddam Ancadians? You'd better have one goddam shit-eating motherfucker of an excuse, because I'm two seconds away from pulling the rug out from Cold Steel for good.'

Chapter 48

'Randall, I –'

'Don't deny it, you limey bastard.'

'Randall, we weren't spying.'

'Oh, so now it's "we"? So it includes you as well?'

'I've been with the band ever since they left England, *as requested.* And if there's one thing they or I haven't done, it's spying.'

'Really? Well, the Ancadian government have been telling the American Ambassador a different story. He said you were on some bullshit cloak and dagger mission for St. Clements. So now the goddam US State Department has got *my* balls in a nutcracker and they're just about to bite a great big chunk out of *my* ass. And you say you haven't been spying?'

'No, we haven't. Look, Randall. We went looking for pirate treasure, the trail led us into Ancadian waters. We found some old artefacts, they got confiscated, we got locked up, escaped, and then had our ship blown out of the water by the Ancadians who left us to die.'

'That's not the story I've heard.'

'Well, my story's the truth.'

'And why should I believe you, asshole?'

'Because I've *never* lied to you.'

The pause lengthened and Johnny saw the band watching him. Free of their overalls and ready to go, they'd heard enough of the phone call to know it was about them.

'So what do I tell these hard asses from Uncle Sam?' asked Randall.

'Tell them to watch the concert on TV and they'll find out what really happened.'

'Jesus, Johnny. You're asking a lot.'

'You'll be getting a lot. There's plenty of interest in the gig, right?'

'Sure.'

'So Ozone will make a killing in royalties and album sales.'

'*If* Cold Steel do a good show.'

290

'You know they will. Even if you don't want to say it.'

'Aw, shit, Johnny. You'd better be telling me the truth, or the Ancadians will be the least of your worries.'

'Thanks, Randall. You won't regret it.'

'You hope not, you bastard.'

The line went dead, and Johnny turned to the band.

'What's going on?' asked Maxwell.

'The Ancadians have turned up the heat. They've accused us of spying and got the Americans involved on their side. Apparently some big US government hotshot is leaning on Ozone to get us unplugged, for good.'

'So what happens now?'

'What was always going to happen: you lads play the concert of your lives, and any time you like, tell the whole world what really happened to us.'

'You think we should?'

'Maxwell, this isn't the time to be questioning ourselves. We've got just one chance to give our side of the story. St. Clements has got just one chance to ask for help, and you guys have got to do the asking.'

Andy slapped Maxwell's back. 'Come on, Max. You're acting like a fashion designer at a rugby match. Where's your balls?'

'Likely to get chopped off if we screw this up.'

'So prove to the whole world that we're Cold Steel, and no one, *no one* plays metal like us.'

'Do it, Maxwell,' said Johnny. 'Be the singer I know you are. All of you, be the *band* I know you are.'

*

Chuck stopped singing and clapped his hands. He had the whole audience with him, and twenty thousand pairs of hands kept time with his movements, which were tiny in comparison.

'Do you want to see the band?'

Ragged cheers greeted his words.

'How about it, St. Clements, do you *all* want to see the band?'

This time a solid, living wave of noise washed over the stage from all directions. Chuck smiled, played a tick-tocking riff and looked to the small set of stairs he had climbed at the start of the concert. The spotlights shone white and lit up the stage. Suddenly, he wasn't the only one there.

291

The second set of cheers was the signal. Johnny nodded at the band. Maxwell took a deep breath and climbed the stairs. Johnny saw his hands tremble slightly. He felt a nudge from behind him and he turned around.

'When do I get my story?' asked Rachel.

'What? TV cameras and all the other reporters are back at the stands, and you're here. What more do you want?'

'What everyone else wants. The whole story.'

'By the end of the concert you'll have it. Listen to the band, they'll give you the story.'

'What do you mean? They've just gone onstage.'

'Listen to the band.'

'And what about the exclusive you promised to me?'

'You'll get that tomorrow. Tonight the band have to lay it on the line. Good and bad, right and wrong, nothing in between. Tomorrow, you, and *only* you, get to ask all those pissy, pain in the arse questions that *only* you like to ask. And this time, we'll give you the answers.'

'Promise?'

'Would I lie to you?' he smiled.

'You'd better bloody not, mister.'

Johnny stepped back and joined Circuits and Henri at the mixing desk. Circuits looked at him, smiled and gave the thumbs up. Rachel stood next to Johnny and readied her camera, but even her physical closeness couldn't keep him from looking at the stage. Chuck kept up his rapid-fire riff, the band came into view, and the cheers mushroomed. Maxwell looked uncertain and he gripped the microphone like it was a life jacket in a storm-sea. The lights dimmed and Johnny felt his heart double-tap inside his chest, willing Maxwell to sing, knowing, hoping, praying that once the first words came out, he'd settle and let his talent take over.

Chuck had set the tone: a blues start for the band. Maxwell looked down at Johnny, who nodded back at him. *Please, Maxwell,* he thought. *Please do this right.* Maxwell took hold of the microphone with both hands, the desperate grip of the tortured blues singer, and launched into Bad Girls and Dirty Women.

'Sometimes my girl gets out of line,

292

But that's okay, that's what I like.'

The lights went blue and Vince and Andy's guitars erupted into sound, matching Maxwell's singing with haunting lines. Chuck smiled and joined in, backing the band with slowhand blues. Maxwell's voice rose and fell, and the band delivered Bad Girls and Dirty Women in a way that had never been heard before. It was still Cold Steel, but deeper, more earthy, and dripped with hot blues fire that no one would have thought the band would or could have played.

Johnny was sucked into the music. He wasn't the manager, he wasn't holed up on St. Clements and wanted by the Ancadians, he was just a fan watching a good band become truly great. The song rose and fell, teased into tortuous continuity by the band, slowly building in intensity until its explosive climax. Lights fizzled and flickered, and Circuits' crew prowled in the shadows, changing bulbs, taping loose cables, and constantly checking speakers for signs of overheating.

Bad Girls and Dirty Women ended, and the crowd roared approval. Maxwell grinned and raised his hands in the air, fists clenched and defiant. Mike pounded the drum intro to Cold Steel's first number one single, In The Pipeline, and four jets of flame gouted from quarter points around the stage. There had been no time to even discuss Captain Boots' pyrotechnics, and Johnny had half-expected him to refuse. He wondered, not for the first time, how far everything was removed from normal safety parameters, but he couldn't deny their impact. The after-image burned onto his retina, Maxwell teased the crowd and the blues took a shadow-place to Cold Steel's driving metal, while Chuck met and matched their playing with added touches of his own. Johnny had always thought the band were peppered with genius, but now, as they filigreed their songs with layer upon fevered layer of hidden surprises, it became a constant, undeniable thing.

In The Pipeline was followed by No Love Lost, and the band stampeded onwards. Johnny counted five songs before they finally stopped to greet the ecstatic audience.

'This must be St. Clements!' Maxwell screamed. The crowd roared back their reply, and he flicked sweat-matted hair from his face. 'Then we're in the right place to play the best concert ever, right alongside one of your own.' Maxwell lifted up Chuck's arm, world champion boxer-style. Screams surf-rushed over the stage and it was a full minute before the cheers subsided and Maxwell's voice thudded back. 'But we didn't come here just to rock you. We've got news, important news, for you and everyone watching around the world. So don't go away. Here's a song about being on the outside. It's a song called No Nation.'

Just as they had at Rouen, the band slowed down the song and played with the soul and desolation of refugees. The sound's blurred distortion gave the song a more vintage feel, matching the imploring, desolate lyrics. Johnny, with his intimate knowledge of the band's back catalogue, recognised the songs, but they were all different to their recorded parents, giving the set an immediate appeal.

The band moved around the stage, making use of its central dynamic and playing the whole arena, not just one section. Mike's drum riser remained like an immovable raised island in the middle. Next to him, lying as though abandoned, sat a haphazard pile of wood. Johnny still wasn't sure what it was all about; then, next to him, Circuits put a red filter into his head torch and held a pen light over his head. Red lights flickered into life beneath the wood pile, then orange and yellow beams shot towards it from the rim of the stage, and suddenly the lighting angles showed up a sailing ship on its side, with the lights dancing off it as though it was on fire. A skull and crossbones flag sprouted from what seconds earlier looked like a random wooden pole, but was now the remains of a splintered topmast.

Twin guitars scraped down Johnny's spine and the band ground into Lined Up For Duty. Andy joined Maxwell on vocals, they blistered through the song's anti-war lyrics, then drove straight into Spider Woman.

Spider Woman screeched its ending and Mike pounded his drums. The audience clapped to the beat and Johnny's excitement built. The drumming continued, Joe's bass line gave depth and structure to the demonic noise, and with the spotlights still giving the ship's image a flaming halo, Andy and Vince slashed their plectrums through strings and they launched into Sinners Sanctuary.

294

The band didn't stop, went straight into Molon Labe, followed by Finger In The Pulse Of Passion. The final screeching note echoed back from the stands and Maxwell prowled around the stage.

'Well, all right, St. Clements!' he bellowed, and the crowd screamed back at him. 'How are you doing tonight?' More screams. 'We've got a message for the whole world to hear. And tonight, the whole world stands by while St. Clements goes under, or they do the decent thing and help out. But if they don't, things won't end here. Right here and right now, we've seen Ancadia's gunboats surround us. They're starving us out just because they want to, and it seems like the whole world's standing by and letting them do it.' Johnny heard the torrent of anguish. None of Maxwell's words came as any surprise to the audience, but to the watching world he hoped it was big news. 'They said we spied on them, that St. Clements helped us, and that's why they're surrounding us. Well, it's all lies.' Anger growled up from the audience. 'I'll tell you what we were when we got here,' said Maxwell. 'We were treasure hunters, and we found out real fast how many of those have been here before.' He grinned. 'We got lucky. We found our treasure, and sure, it was in Ancadian territory, but we weren't sent there by anyone, we went on our own, and we got it confiscated on our own. But that didn't stop the Ancadians locking us up, threatening to shoot us, then sinking our ship on the high seas and leaving us to drown. And they say we were spies, they say St. Clements helped us, and they're using that lie as an excuse to take over this island.' Maxwell clenched his fist and blazed a long-distance look to the stands, into the cameras' eyes, knowing their close-ups would tell the viewers the colour of his. 'Henri Chevalier's tried diplomacy, and it just ain't working. He's been talking to just about every world leader there is. But it's not on their doorsteps so there ain't a government on this planet that will help. Well, to hell with them. If they won't get off their arses, then it's up to the ordinary people to do it for them. Cold Steel's calling you, but more important than that, every person in St. Clements is calling you. Everywhere in the world, people watching now, take to the streets and march for us. Give your leaders our message, because we can't deliver it in person. You tell them you're sick of seeing them not help their fellow human

295

beings, and you pull their heads out of the sand. People of the world, do it for us.'

Smoke tendrilled upwards from the light-soaked ship and flares shot out and up from the stage rim. A Mexican wave of light circled the stage and Cold Steel launched into their first album's title track, They Don't Like It Up 'Em. Now that Maxwell had sent the message, Johnny knew they had to keep the concert going, keep piling on the awareness. And an hour after Maxwell's appeal, Johnny was tapping his feet and thoroughly enjoying the concert. Next to him, Rachel remained the consummate professional, photographing ceaselessly, while her equally digital memory soaked up every second of the show for subsequent reporting. On his other side, Henri nudged him and passed over a scribbled note. *Protests on our behalf have started in five cities. We have a chance.*

Lightning-hope burned through Johnny. It was working. At least, it was starting to work. The thought coalesced in his mind and the band charged on, firing off a louder, faster and much harsher version of Lock and Load. The southwest speaker coughed smoke and Johnny noticed the loss like a fistful of soap being punched into his left ear. Two workers ran over, pulled off the grille and disappeared into the casing. Less than a minute later, the full, thick sound returned.

The concert thudded onwards for another hour. The band were starting to slow in the tropical night and Johnny's emotions turmoiled inside him. They were running out of time. Soon the concert would *have* to stop. Purely in terms of time on stage, the band had played nearly two concerts. He turned to Henri, pointed to his watch, then jerked his head towards the band. Henri nodded and walked to the empty space below the stage.

Minutes later he reappeared. Broken Shaft crashed through its terminal drum cycle and Henri climbed the stage steps. Arms wide and with a nuclear-bright smile, the crowd exulted when they saw him. He embraced all band members, then picked up the solitary microphone.

'Tonight, my people,' he said, 'we have stood alone against Ancadia while the whole world stood by and watched. And were it not for Cold Steel, they would still be watching. Tonight though, thanks to the efforts of everyone here, the world has decided to help.' Cheers hosed over Henri, and he waited before speaking again.

'The words and appeals from our good friends, Cold Steel, have not gone unheard. To begin with, a few cities saw minor protests on our behalf.' More cheers. 'Some grew, some remained unheard. But Ancadia's greatest, most powerful friend and ally, the United States, has listened to the will of its people. We have learned that they have mobilised their own fleet and ordered the Ancadians back to harbour. We have their assurance that this dispute shall be solved by negotiation, and no other means.' Cheers drowned out Henri's words once more.

Johnny turned to Rachel. 'Good enough story for you?'

'I can't believe that just happened.' Her voice quivered. 'Christ, Johnny, you really took a chance on this working.'

'We didn't have a choice.'

'We thank Cold Steel,' Henri spoke to the crowd. 'And we thank you, for supporting them, and for supporting ourselves, which is the one thing we do best. Cold Steel have earned the rest of the night to themselves, and to all of you, I say celebrate this night in your own way.'

Elation competed with excited relief amongst both band and audience. Floodlights, normally reserved for sporting events, lit up the whole arena, which now slowly emptied. Sweat-soaked and exhausted, the band sat on the edge of the stage and passed around the remaining beer. Maxwell looked down at Johnny and smiled. 'How was the gig, mate?'

'The best. Any chance of an encore?'

Maxwell laughed. '*You* do the encore. We're taking a proper holiday after this shit.'

'It can start right now, *mes amis*,' said Henri. 'I invite you all, band and everyone who supported you, to a celebration at my residence. Allow me to thank you all personally on behalf of the nation. We are in your debt more than we can ever repay. We shall never forget what you have done for us this night.'

Johnny looked at Rachel and smiled. 'Can I get you a drink?'

'Sure.' She smiled back at him.

'So we're friends again?'

'That depends. You promised me an exclusive.'

*

It took an hour for the band to make the slow walk from the cricket ground to Henri's house. Weary satisfaction glazed the band members' faces. They edged through the audience, grinning and shaking hands, and Johnny saw more than the usual scripted, band-fan conversations. He sensed a real gratitude from the band, a feeling of a debt owed and properly repaid. Television crews floated among them like typhoon flotsam, zeroing in on anyone for an interview. Audience, band or Henri: all would have an angle, an opinion. Johnny grinned at his own anonymity.

'Don't think *you've* escaped all the attention.' Rachel nudged his ribs.

'A promise is a promise. I owe you a story.'

*

Johnny sipped a cold beer and collapsed into the sofa in Henri's large reception room. Relief rinsed through him and the tensions of the last week ebbed away, leaving him feeling drained and exhausted. Circuits, Skipper, Chuck and even Fletcher laughed together and relived the challenges and near misses of the past week.

'It nearly didn't happen,' growled Fletcher.

'But it fecking well did,' said Skipper, unawed by the location, looking as greasy as he always did and smoking his bamboo pipe. 'This fecking mediation thing that everyone's talking about will work, so stop bellyaching for once in your life and enjoy your beer.'

Johnny smiled and looked at the muted television screen, showing a repeat news story about St. Clements. Footage of an enormous aircraft carrier, fighters flying low over Ancadian gunboats, Alpinos' stuttering backtrack, Henri's announcement at the end of the show, and finally, shots of the band performing. Ragged cheers ran around the room as the concert footage played.

'When are we back in the studio, Johnny?' asked Maxwell.

'You really want to know?' He pulled out his phone.

'Maybe not.' Maxwell grinned. 'They'll get hold of us soon enough if we're late.'

'You'll *never* be late for anything as long as I'm manager.'

'And that's just what we like about you.'

Johnny's phone rang.

'Your boys pulled solid gold out of their asses tonight.'

298

'Hi Randall, I'm –'

'Two weeks.'

'What?'

'Two weeks and I want you in Twenty Studios, London. Cold Steel are getting internet hits all over, album downloads have ramped up after the news broke about your goddam adventures. We need to make the most of this publicity, and your boys are gonna play their part, *capiche?*'

'That was always the deal, Randall.'

'Just make sure that message gets across. We want compliance this time. This is the kind of good luck story we like. We can get some real mileage out of this.'

'How about embedded news coverage?'

'Embedded? Hey, you're not the goddam US Marines.'

'We'll get some great warts and all stories, we'll see the album develop and grow. If the band know they're being media watched they might behave a bit better as well.'

'You got anyone in mind?'

Johnny looked at Rachel and smiled.

THE END

We Are Cold Steel

Rick Brindle

A day after their historic concert on the Caribbean island of St Clements, heavy metal band Cold Steel are heroes. Now, all they have to do is stay out of trouble and enjoy a well-earned holiday until they start work on their next album.

Except that the owner of the recording studio hates all things Cold Steel.

Except that Cold Steel's record company has blackmailed the studio into accepting them.

Except that not all reporters are as friendly as band manager Johnny Faslane's girlfriend, Rachel Shaw.

With a tight deadline, Cold Steel have to get the next album out before their tour starts. They can't afford any delays, and Johnny has his work cut out keeping the band in line.

Feral former soldiers, reporters with an agenda, cake-obsessed studio execs and international criminals all work their way into the mix as the band hurtle from one improbable incident into another. They just want to meet their deadlines, but it seems that everyone else is out to stop it happening.

Can the band get the album recorded on time? Will it ever get released? And what will happen as their upcoming tour approaches? With friends and enemies in the most unlikely places, events unfold in a way that could only ever happen to Cold Steel.

We Are Cold Steel is the explosive sequel to Rick Brindle's acclaimed novel, Cold Steel on the Rocks.

Cold Steel and the Underground Boneyard

Rick Brindle

Cold Steel are back!

Their new album has just been released. Their previously cancelled Spanish tour dates have been rearranged, with the female trio and Spain's biggest metal band, Damas Infernales, supporting.

Cold Steel's biggest asset though, is Johnny Faslane, their brutally talented manager. But even Johnny can't fully eliminate Cold Steel's innate ability to spectacularly destroy their prospects, and even before their second concert ends, the tour is scrapped after an ill-advised trip back to the eighties, and the band are put into creative deep freeze by their record company.
Only an unprecedented event and a lot of money can possibly turn their fortunes around.

Like a five hundred year old treasure hoard that a long dead pirate once offered in return for his life, treasure that has never been found.

Cold Steel find a vital clue that gives them a head start in the search for the missing treasure and they seize on their one chance to prove that even spoilt rock stars can actually do something for themselves. At least, that's their plan, and it puts Johnny Faslane in a race against time to find Cold Steel before they engineer the mother of all musical disasters.

And it's not just the clock that Johnny has to fight. There are also two vengeful bands out for piece of Cold Steel, enraged mob family members and a reporter with a grudge.

It was never going to be easy, but now, is it even possible?

It's Not For Everyone

Rick Brindle

What do you do when your dream job turns into a nightmare.

Rick Brindle was a third generation military child. His father and grandfather served their whole lives in the Army, and all he wanted to do was be a soldier.

In 1989 he joined the RAF Regiment.

Life in the Regiment, though, quickly became toxic. Facing a culture of bullying, beatings, verbal abuse and sexual harassment, the community he wanted to be a part of became more like a prison. Most people around him went along with the abuse, some agreed with it, and some joined in, while the chain of command routinely looked the other way.

Set over thirty years ago, this is a story of surviving abuse that still resonates today. It's Not For Everyone is essential reading for anyone considering a military career. Sometimes funny, sometimes shocking, and sometimes sickening, it's one person's unprecedented true story of life in the RAF Regiment.

Printed in Great Britain
by Amazon

29893317R00172